Jenny grasped his sleeve. "Dinna look behind ye now," she said in a fierce whisper. "Forgive my rudeness, but it would be better if we weren't t'be seen speaking like this."

"Why not?" Latimer said. "You're afraid of something. Tell me what it is at once and I'll make it my business to take care of the problem. I won't have you upset."

She glanced at his arm and snatched her hand away. "It's not because I dinna want to talk wi' ye." Her voice was so light and breathy, he had to concentrate on every word. "Ye're a fine gentleman and blessed wi' charm. Oh, yes, charm indeed."

He knew better than to interrupt, but he would get to the bottom of this nonsense.

She looked at him once more. "Thank ye for taking time wi' the likes o'me. We'll no' meet again."

With that she ran, her skirts tossing, into an alley beside the millinery shop. As she pushed open a door, her bonnet fell back from her head and hung by its ribbons.

The girl had simply made her little announcement that he would not see her again and left him standing there. "Aha, Jenny McBride. Such words challenge a man like me. You only deepen my determination. The chase is on."

THE ORPHAN
STELLA CAMERON

MIRA®

ISBN 1-55166-883-1

THE ORPHAN

Copyright © 2002 by Stella Cameron.

All rights reserved. Except for use in any review, the reproduction or
utilization of this work in whole or in part in any form by any electronic,
mechanical or other means, now known or hereafter invented, including
xerography, photocopying and recording, or in any information storage or
retrieval system, is forbidden without the written permission of the publisher,
MIRA Books, 225 Duncan Mill Road, Don Mills, Ontario, Canada M3B 3K9.

All characters in this book have no existence outside the imagination of the
author and have no relation whatsoever to anyone bearing the same name
or names. They are not even distantly inspired by any individual known or
unknown to the author, and all incidents are pure invention.

MIRA and the Star Colophon are trademarks used under license and registered
in Australia, New Zealand, Philippines, United States Patent and Trademark
Office and in other countries.

Visit us at www.mirabooks.com

Printed in U.S.A.

For Patricia Smith

Prologue

7 Mayfair Square, London. 1823.

I want to orient you, to give you the clearest possible picture of your magnificent surroundings. And who better than this renowned ghost to accomplish the task, I ask you?

Allow me to introduce myself. I am the late Sir Septimus Spivey, noted architect knighted for his extraordinary designs, his innovative contributions to the face of this fair city, and his selfless pursuit of excellence for King and country. I am also the visionary artist behind the conception of 7 Mayfair Square.

This most beautiful house in England was built for my descendants, not, no, no, no, never…

Forgive me if I pause. Even when one has no blood to boil, extreme agitation can still rattle this or that.

It is absolutely not on for my great-granddaughter, Lady Hester Bingham, to continue taking paying guests (her so-called protegés) into my home.

I digress, but have not forgotten what I promised to do for you. It is difficult to remain focused when there is so much activity all about one. I must remember to tell you the latest about my would-be nemesis, Shakespeare. If you don't recall the name, don't bother to look him up. Not worth it. He's been here—you know, beyond—much longer than I have and I fear he is becoming buffle-headed in his extreme age. One tries to be generous, despite the fellow's taunts. I digress again. More of Shakespeare later.

My chosen resting place is in one of the magnificently carved newel posts at the foot of the stairs at Number 7, and on those occasions when I must travel elsewhere, I do not leave it gladly. Unfortunately, in addition to the inconvenience of dealing with the annoyances here, I am also required to continue training as a member of the Passed Over. Gliding, flying, entering without breaking— or opening—and so on. Attending Angel School is a particular trial to me, although I believe I have impressed some of my teachers. But, and most tedious, I cannot avoid mingling with certain others who fancy themselves worthy, or even superior acquaintances. So it is that Shakespeare wafts into my space from time to time. Do you know that he calls me "That ghost in a post?" Of all the unforgivable… Later.

Back to Number 7. Across an expanse of perfect black and white marble tiles in the foyer, I face the front door. All the better to see who comes and goes.

To my right (your left if you're entering the house— which you are unlikely to be invited to do) are the rooms known as 7A. This is where the current object of my undivided attention lives, one Latimer More, successful Importer of Rarities and Oddities. Which probably means he's nothing but a purveyor of cheap foreign rubbish. He is, in fact (and I shudder at the thought) the disinherited son of a Cornish China Clay Merchant. That's right—a tradesman's brat. No matter how much blunt he's managed to winkle out of unsuspecting clients with deep pockets and shallow brains, without extraordinary intervention

Latimer is not and never can be a Person of Importance. Regardless of his purported handsomeness and his pleasing presence that makes the ladies twitter, presently the ton is beyond his reach and what else matters, I ask you— what else?

I should mention that Latimer's sister, Finch, was the focus of one of my more successful missions. She used to live here with her brother but I managed to marry her off to a neighbor, Ross, Viscount Kilrood. Although they return from Scotland to Number 8 on occasion, and despite their free use of this house, there is no question of the Viscountess resuming residence at Number 7. Too bad the rest of that plan didn't work, the part in which Latimer would go to live with the Kilroods. Was that so much to ask?

I'll come back to Latimer More. To my left (your right if you're still in the same place) are rooms that were woefully neglected for years. Now they are expensively transformed but much too dull for my taste. Hester's nephew, Sir Hunter Lloyd, and his wife Sibyl—together with their squalling offspring—use these spaces when they are in residence. They have also commandeered most of the second floor, including a handsome library and a small but exquisite music room, although the quarters called 7B where Sibyl Smiles and her sister Meg lived before their marriages, remain much as they were.

How did I manage to mention 7B so calmly when I am about to embark on an exhausting mission to make sure it remains empty? Strength of character and will prevailed.

Hester occupies half of the third floor numbered—don't complain to me about confusion—Number 7. I must confess to a certain softening of my heart, the region that was my heart, that is, when I contemplate the lady. But after all, we share blood and she is, if moon-minded, a generous woman. The rest of the floor belongs—no, is used—by Hunter and Sibyl, and, may the saints preserve me, a foundling child of barely seven years, Birdie. Hester wants to adopt her, but I have other plans.

Note that, although Sibyl married just as I had decided she should and no longer lives at 7B, I did not succeed in removing her from the house.

My, my, I grow fatigued by my efforts to educate you—and to enlist your help. Please, dear friends, I fear there is an exasperating road ahead and I pray you will become my extra eyes and ears. I don't need your mouths unless I ask you to speak.

I forgot the servants' quarters over the back wing of the house. Easily done, given their lack of importance. Below stairs, the kitchens, pantry, dairy, and the rest of the essential facilities are well proportioned. Tucked into the L-shape behind the building is a garden that is both charming and productive. In mews beyond the back gate lie stables with coachmen's quarters above.

The entire household staff at Number 7 is a disgrace and should be let go at once. I'll say no more on that subject.

Now, to my problem. I have mentioned these "protegés" of Hester's. You now know that for several years I have struggled to get rid of them. My gentle heart would never allow me to do other than provide for their happiness at the same time, but I'm beginning to think that my softness works against me. I have had little fortune in getting rid of any of them permanently. They multiply rather than divide. Or they divide, then multiply and stay—or leave and come back—or waft in and out. Oh, fie, I am beside myself.

Might as well tell the truth of it: these intruders are lodgers and this is little more than a high-class boarding-

house. The shame would be the death of me, if one was able to manage that more than once.

Enough self-pity, even though I have every right to complain. Despite the thoughtless, selfish disregard for the dignity of my home, and despite repeatedly foiled attempts to correct the travesty, I am prepared to carry on until my will prevails. To this end I have another plan. As with my former efforts, there will be a marriage—possibly two— and with the inevitable success of my brilliant plan, this time I shall all but rid the premises of unwanted strangers. I have decided to tolerate Hunter and his family. After all, there is at least some distant relationship there.

First things first. When Meg Smiles married Count Etranger she also gained Princess Desirée, the count's insupportably forward young half sister. This impudent European royal has set her cap at, of all men, Adam Chillworth who lives in the attic at Number 7. I'm embarrassed to so much as mention that his address is 7C. Chillworth is a great, glowering north-countryman who fancies himself an artist. His being allowed to paint the princess— several times—by her careless brother has only encouraged the girl's tendre for Chillworth. That is a marriage I could never pull off. But, despite his common beginnings, Latimer More has the makings of a pseudo-gentleman, the manner and so forth. Seems to me that he could be groomed to at least appear polished. Etranger is bound to be overcome with relief to have his sister saved from the stained fingers, the big, stained fingers, of an uncultured dauber, especially if some of that intervention I mentioned is exerted with the ton.

Wonderful, you say? Get on with it, man, you say?

Well, don't order me about. What I haven't told you is that Latimer is besotted with one of Sibyl's stray friends, one Jenny McBride, a Scot (naturally) who is a milliner's assistant in a shop on Bond Street. You don't think that's so terrible? Well, the frightful possibilities make me feel faint.

Jenny McBride is a pauper and an orphan. She is shabby beyond belief. Shabby and scrawny, with impudent green eyes. And those eyes, their inviting expression, have Latimer going forth to Bond Street each day where he makes a cake of himself by pretending to encounter her by accident. And his sleeplessness, the set of his jaw, the determination with which he pursues her, are all too familiar. He intends to have her. And I know what his first step will likely be, only it's not going to happen.

Do you have any idea what a feat it is for a ghost to stamp his foot?

Jenny McBride will not be installed at Number 7. Or at least, not for long.

I have done some investigating of my own and discovered the pathetic conditions in which she lives. I regret this because she is a nice enough little baggage and deserves better. But charity begins at home and so it shall. If Latimer also tracks her to the hovel she inhabits, he will rush to Hester and play, unscrupulously, on her sympathies. I may not be able to work fast enough to stop him from embarking on this folly, but I have already located the perfect body—I mean, helper—to do for me what I cannot do myself. I know you will approve of Larch Lumpit, curate of very little brain and therefore eminently suitable for the purpose I have in mind.

All I have to do is make Jenny McBride decide that she will be most fortunate as the wife of a dimwitted country curate. That, and contrive to have Latimer turn Princess Desirée's head. Her brother will be so relieved by her new choice that he'll bless their marriage.

Jenny and Lumpit can take the child, Birdie, to live with

*them. Jenny will have a great deal in common with Birdie:
the pauper and orphan business. Bringing about a bond
between them should be simple.*

*See? Flawless plan, but then, would you expect less of
me?*

*I'm simply beyond telling you the tale of Shakespeare's
latest foolishness. It has everything to do with his morti-
fying piece of mangled tragedy,* A Midsummer Night's
Dream. *The man will insist on pretending he intended the
play as a comedy in the first place!*

Later.

1

"Good morning, Miss McBride."

"Good morning, Mr. More."

"And a very good morning it is indeed, don't you think, Miss McBride?"

"Aye, verra good, Mr. More."

Yesterday had also been good, as had the day before that, Latimer More recalled. In fact the weather had been much the same for at least two weeks and he'd appreciate a change so that he could remark on it to the lady. *Dashed nuisance, this drizzle.* How refreshing that would be. There were only so many ways to compliment a fine day and he believed he had used them all up and started repeating himself.

He had already doffed his hat. Jenny McBride, returning to Bond Street from her daily errand to buy fresh cakes for her employer, Madame Sophie of Madame Sophie's Millinery, raised her shoulders and her auburn eyebrows—and glanced about. She was such a self-conscious creature.

Latimer looked at the box in her hands. "Cakes for Madame Sophie?" He might have said, *as usual,* but didn't.

"Aye, for her clients wi' their tea this afternoon." She was breathless and bobbed on her toes.

He nodded and smiled, and she smiled back—with the inevitable result. Her very green eyes narrowed and shone and Latimer's heart found an extra beat. Her brown bonnet sported a jaunty silk rose the color of marmalade. The bonnet was of velvet to match her pelisse and both seemed too heavy for the weather. Latimer had been aware of this each time he'd seen her since summer had blossomed. Her outdoor garments varied little. Always the same pelisse, and one of three bonnets. The rose was new.

Yes, she must be hot. On this side of the street, buildings cast narrow shadows on the pavement. The sun beat directly on windows opposite and glittered on the elegant carriages of wealthy shoppers. Between their shafts, horses with bowed heads clopped along as if the smithy had shod them twice—and with lead.

"Excuse me, Mr. More, but are ye well?"

He watched her mouth form the words and only started when a swaggering dandy in striped trousers and a yellow coat bumped into him. "Never been better." He grinned at her. Never better except for the way his usually clear mind deteriorated whenever he was near her. "And you, Miss McBride, are you well?"

"Oh, yes, thank ye."

Her white skin reddened beneath a smattering of freckles the same color as her rich auburn hair. Little wonder she blushed, since he'd bent closer to examine her, the better to take note of every detail.

But she didn't step back.

Yes, Miss McBride held her ground under his scrutiny. Latimer straightened. "Did you know that our mutual friend, Lady Lloyd, is at 7 Mayfair Square?"

"Sibyl—Lady Lloyd, that is—she came to the shop and left a message for me." The girl looked over her shoulder and held the cake box so tightly the sides buckled. "Well, ye're kind to ask after my health, but I mustna keep ye."

"You aren't keeping me, I'm keeping you," he said in

what he hoped was a reassuring tone. Before Sibyl's marriage to Sir Hunter Lloyd, she and Jenny had been part of an unlikely little club, the purpose of which remained unclear to Latimer. In truth, and at his own urging, Sibyl had left her message a week since. Soon, after a brief visit with her sister Meg and her husband in Windsor, she was to rejoin Hunter at Minver, the Lloyds' Cornish estate. "I'm glad you've heard from Sibyl. No doubt she invited you to Number 7?"

She looked at the toes of her dusty black boots and murmured, "Aye," but Sibyl hadn't received a response.

Very well. Enough of this. He might know little about courting an inexperienced female who was without guile, but there were no longer any excuses to continue these farcical morning meetings. He had to take some masterful steps toward his goal.

Men had goals. Men pursued and accomplished their goals. They did not mince about exchanging niceties, in business or in matters of the heart—and body.

Jenny McBride was Latimer's goal.

Gad, but his shirt was damp against his back. Warm it might be, but surely not warm enough to make a man sweat while he stood still.

Jenny, Miss McBride, looked miserable, but not from excessive warmth he thought. *He* disturbed her. She was unsure if she should stay or go, speak or not speak.

She needed him. She needed his protection and care, and she should have it. He was man enough to admit that his hesitation had slowed the hunt. That was over. He'd catch the girl he'd decided was going to share his home and bed—and soon.

Marrying her might be challenging at first. Some of his friends would make his life a misery for it, but he'd marry her nevertheless. He would make her forget the hours of toil, for which she was paid a pittance no doubt. He would teach her to appreciate the finer things, to look to him for whatever she required. He would provide everything she needed, and a great deal she did not need but over which she would bubble with happiness when he surprised her with gifts. A bauble here, a new gown there...many new gowns. And pretty slippers to replace the practical black boots. Women—with the exception of his sister Finch, Sibyl and possibly Sibyl's sister, Meg—did not have the strength of mind possessed by men. They must be pampered. Allowances should be made for them.

Jenny McBride would become his wife, his lover, his unquestioning supporter in every decision, every endeavor.

That he had been dubbed, and was still thought of in some circles, as The Most Daring Lover in England bored him. He'd come to loathe the title. With Jenny McBride he would temper the skills, the inventiveness for which he'd been renowned. Her sensibilities would be far too delicate for such exhausting exercise. Yes, he would be her gentle, restrained bedmate and take his satisfaction from her tender adoration.

Today was the day and he would seize it.

"You are quiet, my dear."

She rose to her toes again. "Forgive me. Ye seemed involved in your own thoughts."

So he probably had. "What do you do in your spare time these days—since you no longer meet with Sibyl's group?"

"Nothing."

"You don't do *anything* in your leisure hours?" He inclined his head and waited until she looked at him. "You do have leisure hours, don't you?"

"No. That is, I have a verra busy life."

"But you do nothing when you are not working." He

saw his probable *faux pas.* "Oh, my dear girl, are you telling me that when you finish work there is barely enough time for sleep before you must return here?" He was becoming lavish in his forms of address to her, but, after all, he was once more a man of action and must sweep her off her feet. "Dear, dear, Miss McBride, do be honest with me. I am concerned for your welfare."

"Yes. Verra nice, I'm sure. Um...yes, well now."

Latimer frowned. She wasn't even looking in his direction, and she'd begun to sidestep in the oddest manner. "Jenny? I mean, Miss McBride. What's troubling you?"

"Not a thing, thank ye, sir."

Not a thing? He frowned. She'd become unnaturally still. Not a trace of pink remained in her face and fright shadowed her eyes. Her attention had fixed on something past his shoulder and he began to turn around.

She grasped his sleeve and told him, "Dinna," in a fierce whisper. "Forgive my rudeness, but it would be better if we weren't t'be seen speaking like this."

"Why not? You don't look or sound yourself. And you're afraid of something. Tell me what it is at once and I'll make it my business to take care of the problem. I won't have you upset like this."

She glanced at his arm and snatched her hand away. "It's not because I dinna want to talk wi' ye." Her voice was so light and breathy, he had to concentrate on every word. "Ye're a fine gentleman and blessed wi' charm. Oh, yes, charm indeed."

He knew better than to interrupt, but he would get to the bottom of this nonsense.

She looked at him once more. "Thank ye for taking time wi' the likes o' me. We'll no' meet again."

With that she ran, her skirts tossing, into an alley beside the millinery shop. As she pushed open a door, her bonnet fell back from her head and hung by its ribbons. She disappeared and he heard the door slam behind her.

The girl had simply made her little announcement that he would not see her again and left him standing there. "Aha, Jenny McBride. Such words challenge a man like me. You only deepen my determination. The chase is on."

Jenny sucked the tip of the middle finger on her left hand. She never pricked herself—or hadn't pricked herself for years. She leaned over the white lace cornette she had sewn inside the crown of a bonnet and was awash with gratitude when she found no stain. Not a speck of blood would be missed by Madame, who used a large glass to examine every inch of her famous hats.

She was trapped, Jenny thought.

At exactly the time, the only time, when she had ever felt a soaring joy, her dreadful landlord had managed what he'd attempted to do since she rented a room from him almost two years earlier. Morley Bucket had her in his power and there was no way out. Mr. Latimer More, the best, the most exciting, the most handsome of men had done something amazing; he'd *noticed* her and was inclined to be friendly. But everything in her life had gone so wrong that she dare not enjoy their exchanges—unimportant as they doubtless were to Mr. More—even one more time. She didn't know exactly what his business was but it must bring him to Bond Street each day at about the same time. In future she'd have to go to the baker a little later.

Her finger stopped bleeding. She found a long enough piece of discarded white linen in the scrap bag and made a dressing to protect her work.

Bucket had been on Bond Street that morning, watching her with Latimer More. He had made sure she saw him

sneering at her with his long, thin nosed raised in the air.
An evil wart of a man, that's what he was, and he sneered
rather than frowned because he was completely sure he
owned Jenny. Not a day went by when he didn't slink into
her sight, just to make sure she never forgot who could
take away her freedom if she didn't follow his orders.

Jenny rested her chin on her chest. He was more rodent
than man and he was nibbling at her determination to remain independent. Because of unforeseen circumstances
she owed him more in back rent than she earned in a year
and he knew it. Bucket was certain she had no hope of
paying him back within the six weeks he'd begrudgingly
given her. Unless a miracle occurred, he was right. The
hours and days would pass while Jenny would become
ever more familiar with the feeling that she was in a box
which grew steadily smaller.

Could she ask her employer to help her? She didn't
think so. Madame had confided that her family had fled
France with almost nothing and she had been able to open
a shop only through the generosity of a friend. The lady
watched every farthing, even though she was long past
needing to.

"Jenny, Jenny, Jenny, you are dreaming when you
should be working."

Madame Sophie's heavily powdered round face pro-
truded through the blue draperies that separated the workroom from a tiny hall leading to the shop.

Fortunately Jenny had seated herself again and was
holding her needle and the lace cornette. "Aye, Madame,
I'm a wee bit o' a dreamer, but perhaps when my mind
goes on little trips, it gathers inspiring notions about a new
stitch, or a way to make a precious feather do the work o'
two."

Humming, her daffodil yellow dress rustling, Madame

stepped down into the workroom and crossed her plump arms. A well-covered lady with almost black hair and bright blue eyes, her height was such that in poor light she could pass for a child. She said, "If two feathers are required, two feathers are required. Perhaps you have left your mind behind on one of its *little trips*."

Jenny said, "I'm sorry." The lady was kind, but it would be impossible to ask her for money.

"La, la, sorry is silly from you, my girl. You are my little treasure. A master-milliner in the making." She gestured expansively and a smile crinkled her pretty face. Madame was not young, but neither did she seem old—her age was a mystery to any who dared discuss the subject. "One day you will have your own establishment and all of London's most elevated ladies will clamor for your creations."

"They'll no' clamor for mine if they can have hats by Madame Sophie. Not that I'll ever have such a place o' my own." Self-pity sounded ugly and Jenny would not tolerate such things in herself. "I have no plans t'own a place, anyway. I'd as soon keep learnin' from ye."

"You flatter me. How do they say it? Butter me."

The suggestion annoyed Jenny. "I do no such thing, Madame Sophie. When ye employed me I could sew quite well, it's true. But I knew nothing about millinery. Ye need not have taken me, but ye did, or I'd still know nothing about makin' a hat."

Madame Sophie clapped her small, well-shaped hands. And she chuckled. "You have spirit, Jenny. I saw it then, when you came and I could hardly understand a word you said. Not that the Scottish brogue isn't pretty. You had such audacity. You told me how good you would become at your work."

Jenny used a hand to cover her smile. Madame's English

was perfect, her accent very attractive. "I was really verra frightened ye'd no' offer me the job. And I wanted it so badly."

"And I am fortunate—most of the time—that I saw your potential. Now, the promenade bonnet for Lady Beckwith."

Jenny touched the piece in front of her. "The cornette is almost done."

"Yes," Madame said, turning down her small mouth. "A message just arrived to say we are to line the bonnet with the pink satin after all."

"Aye," Jenny said, and began to remove the fine stitches she used to attach the circlet of lace. "It will be pretty." Ladies changed their minds daily. She expected to make alterations.

Madame Sophie unhooked her large glass, with its silver and mother-of-pearl frame and handle from her waist and scrutinized Jenny's work. "Mmm," she said, and "Mmm-mmm." She turned the bonnet this way and that, interjecting noises of approval into a tune she hummed frequently.

When she looked at Jenny again, it was through the glass she'd forgotten to lower and Jenny struggled not to laugh at the spectacle of a huge blue eye, the lashes batting slowly.

Madame remembered herself and put the glass back at her waist.

"Where is the scrap bag?"

A rush of warmth accompanied Jenny's discomfort. "It's...I'll get it for ye." She jumped up and hurried to retrieve it from the cutting bench where she'd left it open with pieces scattered.

Jenny turned around to find Madame examining her brown bonnet. "The rose makes all the difference," she said. "You are a clever girl. You have a good eye. I put these pieces of silk in the scrap bag myself."

"I should have asked if I could use some of them like that," Jenny said, looking at the floor.

"I give all that is discarded to you, remember?" Madame said. "You asked if you might have these things for the birds' nests. If you choose to save some for yourself, why should I mind? La, la, la, they are of no importance to me so I am glad for you to use them." She took a piece of pale green gros de Naples from a pocket, and a length of deeper green ribbon and tucked them into the bag Jenny held. "Perhaps you will find a purpose for those."

Jenny bobbed a thank you and sat to continue removing the cornette from Lady Beckwith's bonnet.

Madame stood at her shoulder—humming.

Uncomfortable with such close scrutiny of her work, Jenny was especially careful as she snipped stitches apart.

Madame didn't leave.

Jenny set down the bonnet and scissors and turned to her employer. "Was there something else, Madame?"

"No, no. That is, perhaps—perhaps, yes, a little something." She patted Jenny's arm lightly and sighed. The shop bell rang. "It is nothing. Just a thought I can't remember anymore. Ah, there is the bell. I must see who is our visitor. The sunshine makes the ladies think of pretty new hats."

She went, hands fluttering, and Jenny was grateful to see the curtains fall shut behind her.

Immediately she returned to her scissors, but faint disquiet interfered with her concentration. Several times in the past few days, Madame had hovered in the workroom, almost invariably standing close to Jenny and watching her. And on each occasion she'd started to say there was something she wished to discuss, only to insist she'd changed her mind.

What if Madame was thinking of dismissing her?

Jenny's eyes stung a little and she squeezed them shut. Without her position, there would be no hope at all of warding off Morley Bucket.

The shop did exceedingly well, and because Jenny was a fast, accomplished needlewoman, when the elderly woman who used to work with her retired, Madame had suggested there might be no need to replace her. Jenny had agreed and received a small increase in her wages. She prayed her position was safe.

A single tap on the door to the alley startled her and she made to get up. It would be a delivery.

Before she was fully out of her chair, the door opened and Mr. Latimer More stepped inside, hat in hand, his dark hair ruffled and his almost black eyes glittering as he sought her out. Not the smallest of smiles softened his, well, his interesting mouth.

Jenny plopped down on her chair once more and glanced toward the blue curtains over the entrance to the hallway and shop.

Mr. More closed the door behind him and came to stand, all ominous watchfulness, on the other side of her table.

When she recovered somewhat she said quietly, "Mr. More, this is where I'm employed."

"So I see," he replied, his voice also low. "And a cramped place it is. Not at all healthy, I should think."

Jenny clapped her hands to her cheeks and shushed him. "Madame mustna' hear ye say such things. She would be hurt. Perhaps angry—wi' me. Anyway, since I am the only one who works in this room, it's perfectly healthy and large enough. And nice. In winter there is a fire to keep me warm and in summer the walls are thick enough to keep me cool.''

He turned his face away to study the room more closely and even as she struggled with annoyance at his rash remarks, she found pleasure in observing him without being observed. His hair was curly, more so since the breeze had played with it. A very nice nose, he had, and a mouth that was wide, the lower lip fuller than the upper and both clearly defined. Men often did not have particularly appealing mouths, but Mr. More...

He was looking directly at her.

Jenny gave a quick smile and wrinkled her nose.

''Good,'' he said.

She frowned her puzzlement.

''Good, you've forgiven me for saying things you didn't like,'' he told her. ''Where do you live?''

''In rented rooms,'' she said and closed her mouth firmly. She would not tell him anything she preferred to keep to herself. After all, as long as he didn't know where her rooms were, or anything else about her situation, she could maintain some dignity.

''I am concerned for you. Since you ran in here this morning, I've been considering what I should do to help. Will you please tell me what frightened you when we were talking?''

Jenny returned to the cornette. ''I was in a hurry t'get back. Madame Sophie's verra kind t'me but she'd no' understand if she discovered I was dawdling about my errands.'' There, now that sounded true enough.

''I should be happy to have you call me by my given name.''

She almost cut not only thread, but lace at the same time.

"If you're not comfortable doing so in front of others, could you bring yourself to do so when we're alone?"

"But we're no'..." He wanted her to use his given name? She couldn't rebuff him by refusing—even if they were never likely to be anywhere alone. "Aye, and thank ye for the honor."

"These things are usual, not an honor, among friends, Jenny. It is satisfactory for me to call you Jenny?"

Well, Jenny McBride might have no family she remembered, and she might feel unworthy of attention from a fine person she'd been told was well fixed—Latimer—but she was no fool. She couldn't be sure of his reasons, but he was taking an interest in her.

"Jenny?" Standing behind her now, so close she imagined she could feel him, he still spoke softly, but he sounded different. She didn't know the reason she thought this.

"Oh. Aye, o'course ye can call me Jenny."

"Thank you." He touched the back of her neck lightly. "You have a button unfastened here. Allow me to deal with it."

Jenny straightened her shoulders and held her breath. His fingertips were cool yet the skin they brushed burned. He leaned past her to set his hat on the table and she felt his warmth, smelled the plain soap he must use. She couldn't help but glance up at him and, withdrawing his hand from the hat, he paused and returned her gaze. Up close she could see a small white scar beneath his left eye, and note dimples at the corners of his mouth, and faint vertical lines beneath his cheekbones. His eyebrows arched clearly and swept away a little at the very ends. And when his lips parted, he showed square teeth that looked very strong.

Oh, my goodness. She put her hands in her lap and studied them.

"Now I can do this properly," Latimer said and, when he had fastened one button, he ran his fingers downward, checking each one.

Jenny closed her eyes and breathed through her mouth. His hands grew still on her shoulders. He didn't say a word, just stood there with his thumbs and fingers spread in a manner that was too intimate, yet not really intimate at all. Why would he attempt to be intimate with her?

He stepped away and the loss of him was like a blow. With measured steps he walked to stand beside her again and this time she realized that he studied her with his brows drawn down and his mouth shut tightly enough to form a white line about its firm edges.

If only she could hide from that assessing stare, for she looked down at her dress and turned cold. He was seeing how shabby she was. When she went out, the velvet pelisse—heavy though it was at this time of year—hid whatever threadbare garments she wore. In the workroom she donned an apron that covered a good deal. Madame Sophie paid all of her attention to the hats, not to Jenny's worn frocks, but Latimer More looked straight at a darned cuff where a piece of lace she'd used to cover the frayed edge didn't quite disguise the mending.

His eyes narrowed. He was appalled to discover that what appeared pleasant enough at a distance, or, better yet, covered up, was in fact a well-made, clean, but cheap garment.

When she met his eyes, he looked away. He felt sorry for her. No one need feel sorry for Jenny McBride. She'd been alone in the world for a long time and had managed to fend for herself. It wasn't through carelessness that she was in such a pickle now, either.

Pity could be saved for someone who needed it. "Was there something ye wanted to see here at Madame Sophie's?" she asked. He would no longer want to say he'd come on her account. "Of course not. What can I be thinking of. No doubt ye took a wrong turn. Nothin' else would bring ye into a milliner's shop."

"I came to see you, as you know well."

She stood up. "If ye turn left from the door and walk out of the alley, ye'll be on Bond Street."

"I am here because you need me and I have no intention of allowing you to cut me, young lady."

Jenny heard the approach of Madame Sophie and quaked. How would it look when she saw Jenny and a man alone here?

Madame presented herself in one of her usual manners. She swept the curtains aside and hopped down the step.

And she drew back at once. "What," she said, staring at Latimer, "is this man doing here? Inappropriate, Jenny. Most inappropriate."

"I'm sorry."

"No need to be," Latimer said, bowing to Madame Sophie. "Afraid I came in by the wrong door. Don't know much about these things and I'm a bit out of my depth. Forgive me, dear lady. I had looked for this young woman without success but was finally fortunate when I saw her enter here earlier. I came as soon as I had a while to spare."

Jenny was not given to swooning but that might create the diversion she longed for.

To her horror, he took Madame by the elbow and steered her in the direction of the shop. "I should have come in by the front entrance and spoken with you. Forgive a fellow who didn't think, will you?"

And Madame Sophie smiled up at him and said, "But of course."

"Could the young lady accompany us, do you suppose?"

"Er. Jenny, come along if you please."

Dragging her feet, bemused as to what might come next, Jenny followed.

When they stood in the blue and gold showroom, among the displays of Madame Sophie's marvelous creations, Latimer surveyed his surroundings, lingered a bit long over cherubs that formed the gilt legs of chairs and tables and cavorted around the ceiling, and said, "Amazing. I've never seen anything like it."

Jenny smiled and busied herself moving hat stands around.

"You see," Latimer said to Madame, "it was the rose that caught my eye. The color of marmalade it was, and I knew I had to have one."

Jenny gaped.

"I see," Madame said quietly. "You want this for someone in particular, of course."

"It's for me."

Murmuring to herself, Jenny cast her eyes heavenward.

"You desire a brown velvet bonnet with a silk rose the color of, er, marmalade?"

"Just the rose," Latimer said and Jenny could hear laughter in his voice. "I am tired of the inconvenience and expense of buying a fresh rose for my buttonhole each day. It's a waste of all those flowers, also. Much better in someone's garden. I've decided to start a trend. Silk roses for gentlemen's buttonholes. I'd like several in the marmalade color please, and make them as barely opening buds. Will they be ready tomorrow?"

Jenny faced the window and couldn't look away from Morley Bucket. He stood outside, staring at her.

"We will have them for you in the afternoon, Mr....?"

"More. Latimer More. Thank you. I'd like them delivered to the address on my card. Good day to you."

Latimer passed much too close to Jenny, in fact he bumped into her and placed a hand around her waist as if to steady her. He said, "Please excuse me. That was clumsy," before walking out into the street.

Still transfixed by Morley Bucket's insolent, hooded-eyed regard, Jenny noticed a heaviness in the pocket of her apron and felt inside. She turned her back on Bucket, made sure Madame wasn't watching her, and looked at what Latimer had given her. She had no doubt he had given it to her when he'd been "clumsy."

The gold sovereign in her hand brought tears to her eyes. Tears of gratitude for a good-hearted kindness. Tears of shame that she had been handed charity.

"Finish Lady Beckwith's bonnet before you leave this evening," Madame Sophie said. "Make the gentleman's rosebuds in the morning. He doesn't live so far away. You can take them to him tomorrow."

2

"The worst thing a man can do—unless he wants to lose the upper hand with a woman—is to let her think he's chasing her," Adam Chillworth told Latimer. Adam lived at 7C Mayfair Square, the attic, whereas Latimer was on the ground floor at 7A.

Latimer crossed his arms and paced his booklined sitting room—which also served as his office—and barely stopped himself from telling Adam what he could do with his opinions. The north-countryman's pragmatic approach could be dashed infuriating.

"Y'do see my point?"

"No," Latimer said, "I don't because I *am* chasing her, and I *am* going to have her. She needs me."

Adam's bark of laughter only sharpened Latimer's annoyance. "Enjoying my sherry, are you?" he asked the big, and far-too-handsome-for-his-own-good buffoon.

"Aye, it's good enough. I did thank you, I think."

Of course he had, but Latimer didn't feel contrite. "Comfortable in my best chair, are you?"

Adam slid his rump forward, stretched out his legs, rested his elbows on the arms of the green-cushioned gilt chair, and adjusted his body several times. "Aye, comfortable enough."

"Then I'd appreciate an explanation for your laughter, sir."

More often than not Adam was silent. He used to keep entirely to himself, but since Sibyl's marriage to Hunter the previous year, when the four of them had grown closer, he'd taken to seeking out Latimer's company. He still rationed his smiles and was renowned for his dour countenance—although he positively grinned at the moment.

"Why did you laugh at me?" Latimer persisted.

Adam's unfashionably long black hair curled over his collar. Showing his white teeth in that grin, he looked like a devilish pirate. He cleared his throat and waved a large, well-shaped hand. "I laughed at you?" he said, and chuckled again. "I suppose I did at that. You're chasing the little redhead because you want her and you intend to have her. And *she needs you?* Perhaps I was wrong to laugh, but if I had to decide what drove you to make an idiot of yourself over a girl, I wouldn't settle for *her* need as the answer. You don't know what or who she needs. It's you who want her, pure and simple. She's quickened your essentials and they won't rest until you've bedded her."

The temptation to call Adam out passed mercifully fast. Latimer went to the window and resumed his watch for the delivery of his damnable silk rosebuds—and Jenny.

"You've no guarantee it'll be the girl who'll come with the flowers for your hat," Adam said and broke into guffaws. "Fetching idea, that," he managed to choke out.

Latimer couldn't help smiling, although he wouldn't let the wretch see he found him amusing. "You bounder. She does all of her employer's errands," he said and promptly lost the battle with his own laughter.

Adam joined him at the window and slapped his back. "Of course she does," he said and offered Latimer his glass of sherry. "Drink some of this. You're going to need it. Are you sure you don't want to call off your little plot? You do know the whole household's...well, I was going to say they were laughing at you but it's worse than that. Sibyl had tears in her eyes when she spoke of you and Jenny McBride, and she wasn't crying because she thought you were funny. She's worried about you being *lonely* and—'' He met Latimer's gaze and shrugged. He didn't finish his report.

''Why did I share a confidence with you, Chillworth? Your brain is pickled in linseed oil. You shouldn't be allowed out of that attic of yours. Why don't you go back there. Lock the door and paint. Don't worry, you'll feel better soon enough.''

Adam wasn't listening. He'd moved to give himself a better view of the square. Precisely, he was watching a figure hurry through the central gardens. Princess Desirée, the half-sister of Count Etranger, who was married to Sibyl's sister, Meg, all but ran along a flower-lined path. Under one arm she carried her huge cat, Halibut, who was as at home at Number 7 as he was at the Count's London home at Number 17. The princess seemed to find frequent excuses to be in residence at Number 17 and was not at all content at Riverside, the Etranger home in Windsor.

''I'll take the sherry after all,'' Latimer said, removing Adam's glass from his fingers and taking a deep swallow. Unlike his fellow, he wouldn't sink to making jokes about a man's affections. Not that he'd get any reaction out of Adam, who insisted Desirée was too young for him *even if he were interested.* A child, he called her although she'd be twenty on her next birthday.

''I don't think Jean-Marc should allow a lovely girl—a princess—to run around alone like that,'' Adam said. ''It's not safe when there's so many as might recognize her. She could come to harm. Wouldn't be any different if she weren't a princess. Looking the way she does... Not a good idea.''

Pity wouldn't be something Adam would appreciate, but Latimer did pity him. He'd known Princess Desirée since she was a gangly seventeen-year-old with big gray eyes and a cross disposition, and he'd liked her then. Adam might protest, but Latimer had watched him while Desirée had developed an attachment to him, and he had seen how Adam had turned his back on a growing affection of his own. If Latimer were to mention that tendre now, Adam would call him a fool, remind him of the difference between Desirée's station and his own, and become a hermit in the attic for days, if not weeks.

The princess had arrived at the steps to Number 7 and slowed down as she carried her oversize gray-and-white feline to the door. She was indeed a lovely girl, and all the more so since what had once given the impression of short temper had matured into a lively intelligence and charming, if sometimes slightly naughty, wit.

"Look at that," Adam said. "She's not strong enough to carry a great, ungrateful animal around. Where's Old Coot? The man takes too long to get to the door. Why won't he let Evans, or whoever the new under-butler is, do these things now? She shouldn't have to wait outside like that."

A slam shook the house, voices murmured in the foyer and grew louder as Desirée passed 7A whilst still calling to the butler. She laughed as she pounded up the stairs to find Sibyl and her baby boy.

"Phase one complete," Latimer said, looking through lace curtains and craning his neck to the right. "Desirée safely in the house and not a moment too soon. I think...*yes*, I see Jenny McBride."

"If you're quick, man, there's still time to change your directions to Old Coot."

"And disappoint Sibyl and the princess?"

"You're sure the invitation Sibyl left at the hat shop was for today?" Adam stationed himself to see Jenny the moment she drew closer.

The empty glass slipped in Latimer's hand. He put it down and rubbed his palms together. A mature man of the world shouldn't look at any woman and feel like a callow youth confronted by the first female who awakened his manhood. "I know exactly what I'm about," he said. "You can let me take care of my own business. And you can stop leaning on me for a view of Jenny. You've seen her before."

"Not since Sibyl and Hunter's marriage."

"She hasn't changed. Help yourself to the sherry." There she was and the shortness of breath and hammering of the heart took over as they did each time he set eyes on her.

"She may balk, y'know. She may say she can't stop to see Sibyl's baby, or whatever scheme you two concocted to keep her longer. You'll never get her alone anyway, so there'll be no chance to do a thing about what you've got on your mind."

"Don't speculate further about what's on my mind." Staying close to the railings that protected passersby from taking a tumble into the deep below-stairs entryway, Jenny walked slowly past the house. She glanced up occasionally, only to hide her face beneath the brim of her brown bonnet again.

"She's a winsome enough creature," Adam said. "What d'you know about her people, though? Who is she really? I don't mean those things ought to matter. You know better of me than that. But I'm pointing out that you don't know a thing about her. You're infatuated, that's all, and—"

"Shut—up," Latimer said. "Get yourself—and me—a drink, sit down and try supporting a friend."

Jenny reached the steps but instead of going up to the front door, she backed to the edge of the pavement and allowed the heels of her boots to overhang while she raised her chin to study each floor of Number 7. If anything, she was paler today than yesterday. He thought of the deplorably worn stuff of her dress, the way her bones were far too easily felt… He thought of how it felt to feel her.

"Sherry, or something stronger?" Adam said.

When he'd put his hand on her neck she'd bowed her head as if unconsciously submitting to him. What in Adam's faint and pleasant northern brogue had become Latimer's *essentials* reacted to the recollection and stood to be noticed. They demanded to be noticed. "Er, something stronger, please." To touch her skin, to explore the length of her spine through the thin dress, and to take his hands away had been torture.

"What d'you want?"

"Not to take my hands away."

"That's rubbish, More. Will you have a brandy?"

Latimer grimaced and said, "Brandy, yes."

Holding a small hatbox, Jenny climbed the steps until he could no longer see her and he strode to press his ear to the door. She used the knocker and this time Old Coot—no doubt hovering nearby—let her in at once. Unlike Princess Desirée, Jenny kept her voice soft. He heard her whisperings and Old Coot's cracked rumble, and the two went on for so long that Latimer became convinced his plan would fail and she'd go away again.

"Jenny? Is that…it is Jenny?" Sibyl called from the second floor. "Come up at once. I'm so glad I learned how Latimer had run into you." Sibyl sounded delighted to see her friend. "Come on, or Sean will be asleep again."

Whatever Jenny responded was still incomprehensible, but from the sounds that followed, Latimer could tell she had done as Sibyl asked. *"Excellent."* He pounded a fist into the opposite palm and swung back toward the room.

Adam held two glasses of brandy. "You'd better sit down before you succumb to apoplexy," he said. "If you do that you'll be no good to a girl in need."

3

Sibyl took Jenny's hat and pelisse, plopped her on a plump, russet-colored ottoman and went to take a wiggling armload from Princess Desirée of Mont Nuages. Jenny was grateful to have made her curtsy while still wearing her outer clothes. She'd decided to put on her best dress today, just in case Latimer were to make another appearance at the shop while she was working, but it wasn't in very good condition.

"You will *adore* him," the princess said, chattering like any ordinary girl. "He is the most beautiful baby in the world and if Sibyl and Hunter do not watch over him very closely, I shall make off with him."

"You'll do no such thing," Sibyl said, and carried her offspring to Jenny. "Here. Meet Sean Lloyd who is six months old and a most charming fellow. Unless he's hungry or wants his linens changed—he isn't at all charming then."

Jenny held out her arms and took the little boy on her lap. "Och, he's a bonnie bairn." She kissed a rosy cheek and nuzzled her face into a fragile, sweet-smelling neck. "Hello, Baby Sean. I want t'cuddle ye tight for ye make my heart so big. He's lovely, Sibyl, and I think he's got Hunter's—I mean, Sir Hunter's—nose and mouth, and your blue eyes and blond hair. Ooh, it's so soft and curly." She hugged him close and shut her eyes.

"I've been longing to ask you something, Jenny," Princess Desirée said. "No, don't try to get up, silly thing. I was at some of the club meetings with you and Sibyl last year, remember. We have shared a good deal."

Jenny nodded. She remembered too well.

"So I shall ask you a question. Who did you intend to be the father of a child for you?"

"*Desirée,*" Sibyl said. "We should never speak of that again."

Their daring club had been formed to examine how females who did not expect to marry might still enjoy the pleasure of having a child of their own. Or such had been the excuse for their delvings into matters that some—almost all—would find unsuitable for unmarried ladies. The princess had supplied a particularly useful tome on paintings and statuary which had been closely, very closely, studied. Jenny blushed at the thought.

"I don't see why the subject of our former investigations should now be considered wrong. If you don't want to answer, Jenny, then of course you shouldn't."

"I'll be truthful," Jenny said, jouncing Sean on her knee. "I had met Phyllis Smart—ye will remember Phyllis well—at the shop and she was pleased wi' my work. She took t'visitin' and chattin' wi' me and then she invited me t'join her group. That's how I was lucky enough t'meet Sibyl." She smiled at Sibyl, whom she thought even more beautiful than ever. "And you, of course, Your Highness. But I really only wanted the fun of being with interesting people—and a lovely place t'come and be with them. I'd no notion to have a wee one o' my own. How could I when I'd not enough for, well, not enough to care for a baby as well. So I never even thought about a man for the job."

Princess Desirée and Sibyl laughed together and Jenny

blushed. They had no need to discuss her unfortunate phrasing.

"I wish I could stay awhile," she said, and meant it with all her heart. "I have t'go back though or Madame Sophie will be upset with me."

"Didn't the message arrive before you left?" Sibyl asked. "We sent Foster, one of the new maids, with a note for your employer."

"I see." Jenny's tummy tightened. She must not risk losing her employment. "I walked here very directly. What does Foster look like?"

"Nice, and she's got lots of initiative... Oh, she went by carriage. She probably got to Bond Street after you'd left. It'll be perfect, though. I told Madame Sophie you must have forgotten I'd invited you for tea today, but that I intended to make you stay once you were here. I said I'd appreciate having you for the rest of the afternoon, so you'd be back tomorrow."

She had forgotten the invitation was for today and felt small for not having had the courage to write and deliver a response. "Forgive me for not getting in touch wi' ye, but I canna do that to Madame," Jenny said, rocking Sean who gurgled and patted her face, apparently very pleased with himself. "I've a lot t'do before I go home this evening."

"Well," Sibyl said comfortably, "I suppose we should wait for Foster to report back anyway. If you have to leave, you shall go by carriage and be there quickly. But until Foster returns, why not enjoy ourselves? I'll ring for tea."

A tap sounded at the door and Sibyl said, "Come in."

The maid who entered wasn't young, but carried herself well and had a pleasing air. "Madame Sophie sent a note back, m'lady," she said to Sibyl. "And she told me to tell you she'd look forward to seeing you before you leave for Cornwall. When you go in to order some new hats."

Foster bobbed, tipped her head to show off smooth brown hair worn in a chignon at her nape, and reached for the door handle.

"Thank you, Foster," Sibyl said. "Please tell cook we'd like tea and a mix of her delicious little cakes. Perhaps some paté and cress sandwiches. And egg, too. Egg sandwiches."

Jenny's mouth watered, but she didn't look away from Madame's note. As soon as the maid had left, Sibyl opened the envelope, read quickly, and handed the sheet of paper to Jenny. "See?" she said, smiling. "Your Madame Sophie *insists* you take the rest of the day off and says you should have asked her for permission to come here when I first sent the invitation. She's glad Latimer told me he'd seen you."

Dear Sibyl, by using a little bribery, she'd secured Jenny's freedom for a few hours. Jenny read Madame's words. They were exactly as Sibyl reported them. In addition, Madame Sophie wrote a reminder for Jenny to deliver the rosebuds safely to Mr. Latimer More. Well, she would most certainly do that before she left Number 7. She'd not be strong enough to leave the box without trying to set eyes on Latimer.

What a pickle she was in. In some ways a lovely pickle. She touched a stray curl at her nape and could actually feel Latimer's fingers there. A delicious shiver traveled the length of her spine. Such careful, brushing fingertips, but they didn't disguise his strength.

But no matter how strong Latimer was, he would have had no experience with the likes of Jenny's landlord, Morley Bucket. She would not put Latimer into the path of such a dangerous, violent man. For his sake, but certainly not for her own, she would discourage him from seeking her out again. Jenny found it hard to swallow and blinked to clear her tearing eyes.

She probably only imagined that Latimer liked her a little. He was a gentleman in the finest sense and as such, courtliness came naturally. She was such a widgeon. Beautiful, accomplished women surrounded him, while she was nothing more than an impoverished would-be hat-maker who had no family, no history. Latimer might be able to overlook some shortcomings, but surely not that she'd been an abandoned child brought up in an orphanage and turned out onto the street at thirteen with one spare dress and hardly any money.

Morley Bucket didn't know the details of her life, but his thin nose could sniff the air and sense when someone was vulnerable. He only preyed on those he considered helpless. Another day had passed. How pleased he must be to mark it off because it brought him closer to getting his wish, or so he thought. Jenny McBride would not easily give in to a man who owned one of those houses where men paid for certain services and who was said to have great wealth from all sorts of despicable schemes.

She rocked Sean while he sucked a thumb and settled contentedly on her shoulder. The room was quiet and when she looked up she found Sibyl and Princess Desirée watching her with gentle smiles on their faces. She smiled back and cradled the baby's head. "He's so sweet," she whispered. "So innocent."

As if she'd pinched him, Sean jerked upright and howled. He opened his mouth wide, displaying two perfect teeth at the front of his lower gums, and yowled. Tears squeezed from his eyes and took a circular route around his pudgy cheeks.

Sibyl lifted the babe from Jenny's arms. "He's eaten

and been changed. Now he's tired. I'll have nurse take him
to his cradle and sing him a lullaby. He tries to help her
and then he falls asleep.''

By the time the nurse had come and taken Sean away,
tea was delivered and Jenny sat on her hands, afraid she
would disgrace herself by showing how hungry she was.
Sibyl piled pretty little cakes, and a heap of sandwiches
cut into the shapes of stars onto a plate and gave it to
Jenny who set the delicacies on her lap. She bit her lip
and willed herself to wait. To her relief, Sibyl put just as
much food on two other plates, served tea and started eating hungrily, as did the princess.

Jenny ate a lemon tart, schooling herself to be slow, to
make several bites out of it. Then she sipped tea and
paused in case her stomach should rebel against the surprise of rich food.

"I wanted to write to you," Sibyl said. "There is no
reason for two good friends who live near each other to
lose touch, but I don't know where you live."

Promptly Jenny put a tender bread star into her mouth
and chewed. Egg! Wonderful, fresh egg mashed with butter was layered thick between the slices of bread. She pretended she hadn't heard Sibyl's question and took another
sandwich and another, keeping her eyes downcast while
she ate and drank her tea to the bottom of the cup.

Sibyl filled it. She did not ask about Jenny's lodgings
again.

"We shouldna lose touch," Jenny said hurriedly. "Let's
make sure we don't. The shop's verra convenient to Mayfair Square."

"That's wonderful," Sibyl said.

"Wonderful," Princess Desirée echoed.

"So." Sibyl put more sandwiches on Jenny's plate.
"Are you still pleased with your place of work?"

"I love it," Jenny said promptly.

The princess sat on the very edge of a burgundy velvet couch. "When Sibyl goes to order hats, I shall go as well. I am long overdue for some fresh creations. I particularly need evening headdresses. Have you seen any of the new French turbans?"

"Aye," Jenny said, feeling excited. "I've just made one of purple crepe lisse. It had a single peacock feather secured by a diamond pin—the lady's diamond pin. She was so pleased with it."

Princess Desirée pushed her lips out in a pout and frowned. "That's exactly what I was thinking of having."

"And it will suit ye," Jenny said. "We'll want to make a few adjustments so it doesn't look like the other lady's. That'll be easy enough. Gold piping perhaps, and a lovely piece of amber to hold the feather in place. I could trim an ostrich plume to thin it out, and paint a little gold throughout."

The princess's smile was filled with delight and Sibyl raised her brows at Jenny. "You may have to make two of those," she said. "But I can't wear purple. We'll talk about it."

"Meanwhile, I have the most serious issue to resolve," Princess Desirée announced. "I am to be painted by Adam."

"*Again?*" Sibyl said with evident disbelief. "He's painted you twice already."

"So this will be his third portrait of me," Desirée responded calmly. "This time I shall commission the piece myself because it is to be a gift from me to someone I admire."

"Who?" Sibyl and Jenny asked in unison.

Princess Desirée shook her head. "I can't tell you.

Please don't ask again. When the time is appropriate, I'll take you into my confidence.''

Jenny bounced in her chair. "That's no' fair. Ye're teasing us.''

"Let her have her fun," Sibyl said. "We'll probably lose interest soon enough.''

"Pah. You won't goad me into telling you a thing with such obvious taunts. Now to my dilemma. The *pose*.''

"Adam will arrange you," Sibyl said. "I doubt if he'd be amused by your interference.''

"Adam is the finest painter in the world and he is my friend. But I have a definite purpose in mind for this commission and the choice will be mine.''

Jenny, who had never as much as seen someone being painted, couldn't imagine why Princess Desirée was so agitated. "Ye'll sit in a chair, or on a stool, I suppose. P'raps in a beautiful dress—or some lovely fabric draped about ye. And with a flower in your hand. If ye like, I'll do your hair for ye. I'm told I'm good at that. Ye'll want t'wear jewels around your neck, I'm thinking, and you might want one or two in your hair.''

"Or I may decide to wear my new opera hat—with the draping you suggest. A lavender chiffon, I think. Very Greek and dramatic.''

"Lavender chiffon?" Sibyl sounded horrified. "Not unless it's made into a gown, my girl. Jean-Marc and Meg will never stand for your being painted in a chiffon *drape*.''

"La," was all she got in response. "Now, help me perfect a sensual pose.''

Jenny scrambled to steady her teacup.

Sibyl covered her eyes with the back of a hand and murmured, "Sensual?''

"Sensual but natural. I don't want to look awkward, as if I am uncomfortable. I shall pose on a beautiful bed."

Rhythmically eating cakes and sandwiches, Jenny looked from the princess to Sibyl and back again.

"I refuse to allow you to upset me," Sibyl said and got up to replenish Jenny's food and tea. "Sometimes you are beyond all."

"Jenny will help me. Pretend that chaise over there is a bed. I may even use a chaise if I can achieve the effect I want." She stood and shook out the skirts of her peach silk day dress with its lace-trimmed underskirt of lemon-yellow. Once seated on the chaise, she removed her slippers and reached beneath her dress to strip off embroidered stockings.

Fascinated, Jenny watched every move.

"Skin is sensual," Princess Desirée said in a deliberately husky voice. "Bare female toes may drive a man mad."

"And where did ye learn such things," Jenny said. "Or have ye found another o' your useful books? The ones from the count's library that ye're no supposed t'read?"

"I read only romantical stories now," the girl said. "I find them adventurous and brave. The men are haughty, a bit overbearing—just as they are—and the women are shown with honesty, as intelligent, daring, passionate creatures of great honor. Triumphant books. They teach me a good deal about the world. But you're almost right because it's from these books that I gather helpful information on matters of love and attraction."

Jenny glanced at Sibyl and said, "I like those books a great deal, too."

"So do I," said Sibyl.

"I intend to become a writer of romantical books myself," Princess Desirée told them. "If you are good and kind to me, I shall let you read them first—but that will take some time. Tell me what you think about this?''

She reclined on the chaise, with her head at its foot, and scooted until her neck rested at the edge and her face was viewed upside down. One slender arm she threw back so that the hand stuck out in mid-air, the other hand she rested on her tummy. Both bare feet were planted where her head should have been and her dress slid to her calves.

Jenny clamped both hands over her mouth but her giggles could still be heard. Sibyl didn't attempt to stifle her own mirth.

"What's wrong?" Princess Desirée asked and sounded as if her voice had to squeeze past the awkward angle of her throat. "Not enough skin?"

"You look ridiculous," Sibyl said, "as if you are in pain."

"Time spent with you, Sibyl, could make any sane and sensible person feel pain."

"In that case," Sibyl said, "you obviously could not possibly feel any pain at all." She turned to Jenny in appeal. "Do you see what she does to me? She makes me appear as much a badly behaved child as she is."

Desirée scrambled back to a sitting position. "You're no fun at all anymore, Sibyl. Not a bit. You're a boring old matron who enjoys ruining the enthusiasm of others."

Sibyl studied her nails. Jenny saw her bring her teeth together and straighten her back. "You're partly right. I am boring and will do something about that—although it is not kind of you to talk about it."

At once, the princess rushed to throw her arms around Sibyl's neck. "You don't have to change anything. You're perfect as you are and I'm a shrew to suggest otherwise. It's just that I have been making these plans for some time and when you criticize what I intend to do, I doubt myself.

And I mustn't, I must have faith in my decisions. You don't know what it's like to pretend you're happy all the time when inside you are the saddest of people.'' She shook her head at Sibyl. ''Please, do not try to make me explain why I am sad. I just am, but in time I intend to become most contented.''

Princess Desirée's cat slunk from behind the chaise. Jenny remembered Halibut from previous visits. His tummy swayed from side to side and he looked at her with unblinking, deeply golden eyes. He jumped heavily onto Jenny's lap, flopped down and began to wash himself. His pink tongue made loud, wet noises.

''Even my cat is given more consideration than I am,'' Princess Desirée said.

''Oh, Desirée.'' Sibyl got up. ''I believe you really are unhappy. I certainly would never deliberately make fun of you when you are seriously asking for help. Tell us why you are so downcast.''

''She's a lot on her mind,'' Jenny said, seeing something familiar in the princess's manner. ''For now, ye're serious about the posing, aren't ye?''

''Yes, I am.''

''Then we'll help ye, won't we, Sibyl?'' She didn't wait for an answer. ''The pose ye tried was no' attractive. Ye look stiff, awkward. But ye're no' accustomed t'such things. Surely between us we can learn what would look best?'' She looked at Sibyl.

''Of course we can,'' Sibyl agreed, but made no move to actually *do* anything.

Pushing Halibut carefully to the floor and trying to ignore the hiss she got for her pains, Jenny went to Princess Desirée and urged her to sit against the chaise pillows. ''Now, put your legs on the seat. Bend your knees so ye seem comfortable and relaxed. Just so.'' She arranged the wonderful dress to fall in folds that outlined her limbs but did not appear unsuitable. "I like your bare feet. Tuck one back under the other ankle, so only the toes show."

"The madman-making toes," Sibyl said, and laughed.

Jenny ignored her. "Here, hold this wee book. It'll make ye seem scholarly. And put your head on the pillows. What d'ye think, Sibyl?"

"Um. Very nice. Restrained but soft. Most appropriate."

"Most dull," Princess Desirée snapped. Then she bowed her head and said, "Forgive me, Jenny. I sound ungrateful when I'm not. Sibyl, let me pose you. Then I can see for myself what these things look like."

"I am a married woman and a mother," Sibyl said, although the corners of her mouth twitched. "It would be most unsuitable for me to cavort about in such a manner."

The princess tossed her head and said, "Fie. You are becoming stodgy. Unsuitable indeed." She turned to Jenny, her eyes pleading. "Will you have the courage to help me?"

Courage? Oh, yes, Jenny thought, she had courage. Without it she'd be in the clutches of something dreadful by now...or she'd be dead. "I'll help ye," she said, peering past the princess to see through the window. "But I mustna' be late leavin' or it'll be dark. I don't like to walk home in the dark."

"We'll send you by carriage, of course."

Jenny shook her head at Sibyl. "I won't hear of it. If my coming here is to put you out, then I'll no' come."

"I won't mention it again. I must trust you to be sensible and ask if you need to be driven. Now, these poses."

The princess set about arranging Jenny, first in the pose she had struck herself, with her head lolling from the end of the chaise. Jenny refused to take off her boots. "Ye

must use your imagination. I'm no' so fond o' lacin' me
boots as t'do it often.'' In the feet of her stockings, there
were holes that could no longer be mended. "Ow." A firm
sideways twist of her neck hurt.

"Sorry," Princess Desirée said. "But you look far too
awkward. Not relaxed at all.''

"I am awkward, and I'm no' relaxed a'tall."

Sibyl came and supported Jenny's head. "Wiggle
around before you break your neck," she said but she
didn't sound one bit serious.

"I want to see something else," the princess said. "May
I try again, Jenny?''

Jenny sighed and said, "O'course."

"Climb on the chaise facing the back."

Jenny rolled her eyes and didn't move.

"Well, I mean *sit* on it, lie on your side facing the back,
then cross your ankles high on the arm."

Clutching her skirts to maintain modesty, Jenny resolved
to be a good sport and follow directions. When she was
curled around with her ankles atop the single arm—as high
as she could get them—she held very still. "So ye think
it's your back ye want painted."

"Oooh," Princess Desirée said, sounding exasperated.
"No, I do not want my back painted. Don't move. Let me
do everything." She went behind the chaise and grasped
Jenny's ankles. These she hauled high until Jenny's knees
bent over the back of the chaise and her feet dangled behind.

Princess Desirée clapped her hands. "We're getting it
right."

Her exuberance was drowned out by Sibyl's laughter
and the laughter grew louder and wilder.

"I'm going to ignore her," the princess said into
Jenny's ear.

Jenny giggled. "If ye do this, he'll still be painting your back."

"No, no, no. You do not think. Turn your head so that you look toward the artist."

This contortion was excruciating but Jenny did as she was told, and giggled some more.

"Allow your left arm to drape to the carpet. Yes! Just so, Jenny. Oh, bravo. Don't you agree, Sibyl."

Evidently Sibyl was too moved for words.

"But," Jenny sputtered, "ye would have to stay like this for some time, I believe. Ye wouldna be able to do it."

The Princess sighed hugely. "One must suffer for art. That has always been known." Braced on her elbows, she lay on her tummy beside Jenny and looked down into her face. "Oh, no, don't look like that. It is not at all sensual. Push your lips out. Say *purple prune* and let your mouth remain in a soft pout. Like this." She demonstrated. "Allow your eyes to go out of focus so that you appear to look into a mysterious distance."

"I didn't know prunes were purple," Sibyl remarked. "Do be careful not to *cross* your eyes, Jenny."

Jenny ignored the reference to her eyes and said, *"Purple prune,"* but didn't feel as if she looked any different.

"Say it again, and turn your face a little more toward the room." Princess Desirée helped Jenny with this. "Now, *purple prune.*"

The princess's latest efforts forced Jenny's shoulder from the seat of the chaise and she felt insecure, as if she might fall on her head, but she dutifully said, *"Purple prune."*

"Lick your lips to make them shine."

"Why am I doing this?" Jenny said, finding Sibyl.

"Because you are far too nice," Sibyl said and her delighted expression didn't please Jenny. "Actually you do look quite sensual. Or perhaps wanton would be better."

"I could never look wanton—"

"Say purple prune," Princess Desirée insisted.

The noise Sibyl made could only be described as cackling and Jenny also heard what sounded like her hands slapping her thighs.

"All right," she said loudly. "Let's finish this." She licked her lips, said, *"Purple prune,"* and her shoulders slid completely over the edge of the seat cushions.

Sibyl's mirth rose to hysterical levels.

"Purple prune," Princess Desirée demanded, then, "Oh, please, one more time. I think this is going to be ideal once we perfect it."

Jenny said, "Purple prune," through her teeth, the instant before the top of her head met the beautiful, multigreen carpet. She said, "Ouch. Now it's your turn."

"What'll you be up to next, Princess?" a booming male voice asked. "This has your agile mind written on it."

"Oh, fie," Princess Desirée moaned. "Why must I always bosh these things. Why are you here? I didn't hear you knock."

"I think you mean botch," said another man. "We knocked several times but little wonder you didn't hear. You were making a racket." *Latimer.* Jenny squeezed her eyes tightly shut and desperately tried to consider some way out of her predicament that might retain, well, *any* dignity at all.

"Damn it all, Adam. Get out of my way. Jenny will do herself an injury before long."

Something thumped loudly and Jenny opened her eyes to see that the princess was sitting on the floor where she had evidently landed after some mishap.

In front of her own face were a pair of immaculate top

boots and above them, buff breeches fitted to muscular thighs. Jenny looked all the way up and into Latimer's upside-down face.

She slumped, simply gave up holding herself tense to remain in the position that pleased the princess, and let herself go limp. Her head ached. She felt weak and sick. She slithered from the chaise and prepared to will her own death.

Powerful arms scooped her from the carpet before she'd completely tumbled to into a heap. She closed her eyes again, but not before she saw Latimer gazing down, with great concern, into her face.

Her hair escaped its pins and loose, heavy braids fell free.

That was the end. She would never recover from such horrible embarrassment.

"Now that," Princess Desirée said, "is *absolutely* sensual. Don't you all think she looks like Romeo's Juliet. Beautiful and dead—only without the tomb."

4

Latimer had enjoyed the spectacle of Desirée leaning over Jenny and managing to persuade her to say *purple prune,* but now he wished he and Adam had arrived after the experiment.

He agreed with Desirée that Jenny looked sensual lying in his arms with her face turned away and her eyes closed while her mouth still glistened from the licking she'd been ordered to give it. Seeing her hair fall from the braided coronet she'd worn amazed him. He'd never seen quite such thick, long, or exceedingly auburn hair before.

But she wasn't closing her eyes to look sensual, and she wasn't in a swoon. He knew enough of her nature to presume that she was humiliated.

"You've had a shock, Jenny," he told her quietly. "I shall set you on the couch and you will rest."

Her eyes opened at once. "Thank ye, but I canna stay any longer. Kindly set me down."

Latimer did as she asked at once but regretted that he had to let her go at all. On the other hand, he'd held her too long and mortified her yet again.

Holding her unraveling braids in one hand, her attention was on the carpet. "Please excuse me for causing such a display," she said. "I'll leave at once."

"Don't punish me, Jenny," Desirée said. "I was a monster to make you do my bidding."

"No such thing," Jenny told her. "If I hadna been willing I would have refused. It's just time for me t'be away home."

Sibyl didn't look at all comfortable. She met Latimer's eyes and sucked in one corner of her mouth. He smiled at her. She wasn't responsible for Desirée's antics, or Jenny's willingness to participate in the game.

"Evening is coming," he told Jenny. "I will accompany you home."

She dropped to her knees and picked up a hairpin, then another. Desirée joined her, followed by Sibyl. He hesitated and avoided looking at Adam before joining the search.

The pins were long and strong but blended with the carpet. Of course she would need a goodly number of them to secure those heavy braids. He sighted the glint of metal and reached for a pin, only to have it snatched away by Adam, who had also joined the hunt.

They didn't speak and the only sounds were of rustling dresses and thumping knees—and Halibut's outraged demands to be noticed as he went from one to the other and received no attention.

Jenny bumped heads with Desirée, who yelped, and Jenny mumbled an apology. Then she sat on her heels and surveyed the scene. "Stop," she said in a good, strong voice. "I've enough of them for now. Kindly save any ye should find later."

The rest of the group continued to cast about, running their fingers this way and that.

"We are ridiculous," Jenny announced. "I dread t'imagine what a newcomer would make of us."

"I was thinking about a painting," Adam said. "For a fee—a very nominal fee—d'you suppose I could persuade you all to do this for a few hours a day. For a few weeks."

Desirée giggled. "You would be the one to think of such a thing."

"That might be because he's a painter," Jenny remarked, and Latimer saw how hard it was for her to squelch a laugh. She had pulled one braid forward over her shoulder and was rapidly tightening and straightening the hair.

Sibyl had paused and she watched the group with a smile on her face. "You were always the one with the quickest wit," she told Jenny. "What do you think Adam might call his painting?"

Jenny said, "You go first."

"Close Encounters," Sibyl said promptly, and when nobody showed enthusiasm she added, "Well, we are all close, aren't we? And we are encountering each other." She sounded aggrieved.

"I shall put it on the list," Adam told her. "Next?"

Desirée sat on the carpet and hugged her knees. "Rainy Day Revels. Subtitled—Picking up Pins."

Sibyl groaned.

Jenny said, "It's no' rainin'."

"Who cares?" Desirée said with obvious displeasure because her suggestion had not been met with enthusiasm.

"It does have possibilities," Latimer said. "Remember that one, Adam."

Adam agreed and added, "And you, Latimer?"

Latimer looked around the group and said, "Tea at the Asylum."

"*Latimer.*" Sibyl looked and sounded incensed. "Why can you not be lighthearted like the rest of us? Make a game of it?"

He wrinkled his nose. "Rather thought I was. You've got to admit it's all a bit mad."

"Three Women and Two Men Searching for Fallen

Hairpins,'' Adam said, with an air of having found the most brilliant title.

The company sent up a great groan and Latimer said, ''Boring, Adam.''

''What other response could I expect from a man who has decided to give up anything with a spark of life in it?'' Adam remarked. ''A boring man doesn't respond to something that's brilliant in its simplicity.''

Adam's comments annoyed Jenny. ''Latimer's no' boring,'' she said, snapping her brows together. ''He's the most interesting of men.''

In the silence that followed, she exchanged her frown for a blush. There wasn't any way to pretend that she hadn't called him by his first name in front of others, and made it absolutely clear that she admired him.

''Thank you, Jenny,'' Latimer said. His smile was in his eyes. ''I'm glad you recognize my sterling qualities.''

Jenny feared anything she might say could well get her into deeper trouble, and looked away.

''Latimer's title is on the list,'' Sibyl said, grimly, Jenny thought.

Adam grunted.

Jenny sensed Latimer watching her and felt helpless. There was no hope of more between them yet she ached for the want of his touch.

''Jenny,'' Desirée said. ''It's your turn now.'' The princess continued to pick about in the carpet, as did Sibyl.

Absolutely nothing came to mind. Miserable, she wanted to leave them, but at the same time, could hardly bear knowing that once she did she'd think of nothing but Latimer.

''Jenny?'' he said quietly. ''What do you think Adam should call his painting.''

"Carpet Cleaners," she said and closed her mouth firmly while she got to her feet.

Adam was the first to chuckle, but the rest followed suit before the communal clearing of throats started.

Latimer said, "That's wonderful. It's what we are. Carpet Cleaners. Picking out...pins."

When she was satisfied her hair wouldn't easily collapse again, Jenny pulled on her pelisse before either Adam or Latimer could get to their feet to assist her. She put on her bonnet and tied the ribbons firmly, picked up the oversize reticule she carried for work, and gave the little hatbox containing silk rosebuds to Latimer.

"Thank ye verra much for the lovely tea," she said. "Sibyl, I love Sean. And I'll look forward to seeing ye and the princess at Madame Sophie's. We'll make ye some beautiful hats. I'll look for something just right for the evening headdresses. Good day t'ye all. I'll find my own way out." She had no business being here like this and should never have stayed in the first place. With a wave, she opened the door and hurried downstairs.

She heard Sibyl call, "I'll see you in the next few days,"

"Wait." Latimer caught up with her in the foyer. "Let me take you home."

"I couldna'," she said, but wished it were otherwise. "It's no' a long way and I like my solitude."

"Do you?" He stepped closer, pushed back one side of his coat and put his hand in the pocket of his breeches. "Look at me, Jenny."

Courage, she told herself. Courage had brought her this far and she would never let it go. She raised her chin and looked into his face. How difficult it was to see his eyes so clearly, and his questioning expression.

"What do you see in me?" he asked. "Nothing at all?"

Jenny swallowed. "I see a good deal. I see a man of honor and kindness."

"Honor and kindness?" His mouth tightened. "Do you *feel* anything about me? Anything at all. No doubt you consider that an unfair question, an inappropriate question given that we haven't known one another very long—that is, not to converse, or on a personal level. But I would still like to know if you *like* me. What you know of me, that is."

What would he say if she told him how he filled her thoughts and dreams? "I do like ye," she told him. "Ye've warmed my heart wi' your greetings when ye see me." She must stop or she'd be pouring out the longings of her heart and afterward she'd be left with an even deeper sense of loss.

"I'm glad," he told her. "Any day when I don't see you is less satisfying."

Jenny spun away and walked rapidly to the front door. Her chest was tight, and her throat.

"The rosebuds are lovely," he said. "I shall definitely set that trend I spoke of. Perhaps you would put one in my buttonhole. I'm clumsy with things like that."

He had opened the box. "I'd be glad to." And then she'd be glad to get away before he discovered another reason to detain her.

She took one of the rosebuds she'd made for him, rose to her toes and threaded the stem through his lapel. "This is a good color. And most will think it's real. Oh, dear, now I sound over pleased wi' mysel'."

When he didn't answer or move, she paused, still standing on her toes, with one hand resting on his chest behind the lapel. "Will it do?" she asked. Beneath her fingers, his body didn't yield at all. He felt warm and solid, and so very much a man.

"Jenny," he said softly.

She let her heels meet the ground.

He sighed. "What am I going to do with you?"

She shook her head slowly. "I dinna know."

"What's this?" Before her face he held the sovereign she'd returned at the bottom of the small hatbox. "You must have dropped it here by mistake."

"No, no," she said. "Please dinna make me cry and I will if ye try to gi' it t'me again. I'd cry because ye've a generosity such as I've never encountered before. And I'd cry because I'm no' in need o' charity and ye'd shame me. But I am touched that ye thought to help me."

"Oh, my dear girl." He caught the hand that rested on his chest. "I wouldn't shame you for the world. I beg you to forgive my persistence, but you are not well fixed, I think. I didn't give you this out of pity, but out of concern."

"Thank you," she said, and could scarce blink hard enough to keep her eyes clear. "Good night."

She slipped from the house, closing the door behind her without glancing at Latimer where he stood in the foyer.

The evening was still light enough and she sped through the streets, heading east. She thought longingly of the comfort and warmth at Number 7, and even wished she might return to the workshop on Bond Street. She could not relish the place to which she must return.

For some distance she checked behind her to make sure Latimer wasn't in pursuit, then felt absurd for entertaining the idea that he would leave his home to trail through the streets after her at such a time of evening. Men didn't like to be thwarted. They considered their attentions precious and to be taken seriously—they did not persist without encouragement.

A costermonger who carried a tray of pickled fish

shoved his wares in front of her. "Nice jellied eels, my pretty. A special price to you."

"No, thank you." Her stomach rolled and she turned her head away. A special price for food not fit to eat. The stench was overwhelming.

Going by way of alleys and narrow, mean streets she knew well, she covered ground fast. Just as well, since the light had turned to gray-mauve and the edges of all she saw were becoming blurred.

"At last, Jenny McBride." Morley Bucket rolled into sight, his back against a crumbling stone pillar at the entrance to a once fine house. The establishment was now a rooming house fallen into disrepair. Wails and shouts came from open windows where dim light shone yellow through dirty curtains. "What a good thing I know you come this way. Makes it easier t'find you. Looking at me 'ouse, are you? Oh, I've got lots of fine properties. You'd be surprised. I'm a rich man."

She made to walk on, but he stepped in front of her. "I need to go home," she said.

"To whose 'ome, dearie? You live where you do at my pleasure. You're a debtor, you are. One step from the work'ouse. If I wasn't such a good 'earted man, you'd be there already."

"I've told you I'll get the money to pay you."

"Nah, you won't. But I'll play your game till the time runs out. It might be a good idea for you to stay away from the fancy gent. He means you no good, I can tell you. Probably wants to get for nothing what I'm prepared to make sure you get paid well for."

"Stop it," Jenny said, breathing with the very tops of her lungs. "Get out of my way."

"By all means, your ladyship," Bucket said, and moved to one side. "But don't forget what I've said. The clock's tickin' and you're pinnin' your 'opes on a gent what wouldn't look at you if 'e didn't fancy you in 'is bed.''

She glared at him. ''Ye think everyone's as horrid as ye are.''

''Hah.'' He opened his mouth in a wide guffaw, showing off a fine complement of gold teeth. ''I know what men are, missy. They've 'elped make me wealthy and they are all the same. What they want is what's under yer skirts. They want ruttin' rights between a pair of soft, white thighs for as long as they're interested. And they pay well for the privilege. But you know I've got something really special for you. P'raps you ought to snap it up before you ain't got the chance no more.''

''Excuse me,'' she said and moved as quickly as her wobbly legs would go.

Bucket laughed and the sound chilled her. ''There's the little'un, ain't there? He'll be waitin' for you and gettin' worried if you're too late. He'll be on the street the same as you, Jenny. Unless you do what you know you ought to do.''

''I'll pay, I tell you.''

''Nah, you won't pay. You can't. Give in. You're already spoken for and that doesn't 'appen to the likes of you very often. Give in and let that certain gentleman buy you from me—clear your debts.''

''Stop it.''

He could keep up with her without as much as walking fast. ''I'll stop it when you sees sense. This gent will keep you in nice gowns and all that other stuff women want. A widower 'e is, and lonely.''

''Leave me alone.''

''Can't do that. The gent's gettin' anxious. Wants you to be his companion and 'e's not so old that 'e won't be wantin' to teach you some tricks. He knows plenty, or so I've been told by some of my girls.''

His *girls*. The women whose services men paid for. Bucket wanted to sell her as a rich man's plaything.

Jenny ran as fast as she could and Bucket shouted after her one last time. ''Good old Bucket could 'elp get you ready for the rich geezer. He'd never know I'd taken a bit of the shine off the merchandise. I might even decide to give you a shillin' or two. Just so you'll 'ave something of your own in your pocket, and you'll be primed, like, to please your protector.''

5

The streets grew even narrower, but Latimer knew where he was, and now he knew why Jenny had guarded her address so carefully and refused to have him see her home. She believed he'd be horrified that she lived in the slums of Whitechapel. She'd judged him a shallow snob who would see her poverty, be unable to separate the girl from her misfortunes, and turn away. He was furious, and even more so at the thought of her being in this place, walking through these lowly and dangerous streets.

He's seen that fellow stop her and had been about to beat him on the spot—until he watched Jenny for a few moments. She knew the man and was afraid of him. Best find out the exact lay of the land before attending to Mr. Morley Bucket. On any other occasion, Latimer would wish he didn't know who the man was, but now the acquaintance would prove most useful.

The girl dodged in and out of alleys so quickly that Latimer had to keep his wits sharp. He didn't want her to discover him before he found out exactly where she lived, but he couldn't afford to get too far behind or he'd lose her.

A hunched and aged woman, dressed in black from head to foot, shuffled along with a basket containing bunches of wildflowers. The day was old and the flowers must be growing old, too, but Jenny stopped and spoke close to the woman's ear. Latimer heard chuckles and Jenny took a bunch of flowers and found a coin to press into the woman's hand. Carrying her flowers, she scurried on her way, breaking into a run from time to time.

By the time Latimer reached the flower lady, he'd found a coin of his own and he gave it to her. Her wrinkled face fell lax with amazement at her windfall and she tried to give him all the flowers she had. He said, "Three will do nicely, madam," and took what she gave him.

He went on his way with the sound of her, "Bless you, kind sir," coming to him repeatedly.

Latimer didn't have to take note of street names. Even if he weren't gifted with an unerring memory for direction, his own warehouses were in Whitechapel, had been for years, and he could have navigated the place in total darkness. He'd done so more than a time or two.

He turned another corner and sent up thanks for his good fortune. Barely in time, he'd seen Jenny enter a brick building blackened by soot. Looking up, he saw that he was in Lardy Lane. Jenny's building had no number, but that didn't matter. Of far more concern was his dilemma in discovering which of the rooms crowded inside was hers. Dim lights showed at grimy windows on each of five floors. If his guess was right, the people of no-number Lardy Lane were lucky if they had a single room to call their own.

A boy came from the door Jenny had used and slouched against a wall with one foot tucked up behind him, against the brick. He held something edible in one hand and seemed intent on pushing as much of it as possible into his mouth at one time.

Latimer sauntered across the lane and approached the boy from the side. "'Evening," he said as he drew close. "Think it'll stay fine?"

"Nah." The child considered a strip of purplish sky between buildings on either side of the dirt way. "Reckon it'll rain before mornin'. But it won't get cold, so it won't be so bad."

"This where you live?" Latimer asked, indicating the front door that stood open and hoping he sounded only mildly interested. "I've got a place not far away."

The boy set his second foot on the ground and looked Latimer over. "Bit fine for these parts, ain't you?"

"My warehouse isn't half a mile from here. More & More, Importers. Perhaps you've seen it?"

"Can't say as I 'ave."

That line of conversation seemed to be closed. "I'm looking for a friend of mine. I brought her these flowers, but I've lost her address. I know it's on Lardy Lane, and I think this is her house, but I'm not sure. If I can't find her, she'll think I didn't come at all."

"You sure you've got the right lane?" Once more Latimer was scrutinized. "The people 'ere is poor. You don't look like you'd know any poor people."

What did he say to that? Something that was bound to be taken as a platitude? "I wish I could find Jenny McBride."

Choking on the final piece of a bread he'd put in his mouth, the boy, who looked to be around ten, reached back and tried to thump his own back. Latimer helped with a firm swat between the shoulder blades, and another, before he was confronted by watery eyes in a thin face overhung with spiky, tow-colored hair.

"Can you breathe?" Latimer asked.

"'Course I can."

"You don't happen to know Jenny McBride, do you? What's your name, by the way?"

"I'm Toby." And Toby was very suspicious of a

stranger who asked him about Jenny McBride, whom Latimer had little doubt was known to the boy.

"I'm Latimer," he said.

"Latimer?"

"Latimer."

"You sure?"

Latimer took out one of his cards and handed it to the boy before he cursed himself for his own stupidity. The child wouldn't be able to read and would think he was being ridiculed, or duped into pretending he could read the name he'd been given.

Frowning, concentrating intently, Toby sounded out, "La-ti-mer M-ore."

Latimer stopped himself from marveling that the young fellow could read. "That's right. And Jenny's a friend of mine. And here's a shilling for your trouble."

The child looked at the coin and his eyes opened wide. He rubbed it with a sleeve and murmured something to himself. But gradually his shoulders fell and he held the money out to Latimer. "Jenny wouldn't like it," he said.

Toby had given himself away. "The money is for you," Latimer pointed out. "But you should make sure Jenny doesn't mind, of course." Inspiration came. "See the rosebud in my buttonhole?"

"Yeah. Right dandified it looks."

This wasn't the moment to put the little boy in his place. "Jenny made it for me. It's the same silk as the roses on her hat."

The rosebud received attention to its look and feel before Toby, still holding the shilling, ran inside the building without another word to Latimer.

Dressed as he was, loitering in this area wasn't a good idea. At the very least he might attract the notice of someone Jenny might wish to avoid. He stepped inside the front door Toby and Jenny had used and moved into the gloom at the bottom of some stairs. Somewhere an infant cried, but it was sounds of fright and anger that disturbed Latimer. Women pleading. Men shouting. And the place smelled rancid.

Jenny lived here? He wondered what had brought her to such a pass.

Well, it would not do. Her pride, her determined spirit might fight him, but she would have to allow him to protect her. She would leave this building at once.

Down the stairs came Toby, clomping as if he were a small horse. When Latimer said, "I'm here, Toby," the boy jumped and stumbled down the last few steps.

Latimer said, "Sorry to frighten you."

"You didn't frighten me. Nobody frightens Toby. I slipped a bit is all."

"Of course. Did you give Jenny my card?"

Toby straightened his back and said, "I didn't say I knew any Jenny."

"You did really. And you do. And you gave her my card. Could you take me to her?"

Without warning, Toby sat on the bottom step of the stairs and hunched over.

"What's the matter, boy?" Latimer said, bending and putting a hand on his shoulder. "I'm a good man. I think Jenny would tell you that. Let me help here."

Toby shook his hanging head.

"Did she say she didn't want to see me?"

"Yes."

Latimer blew out a long breath. "Did she say why?"

"I'm not supposed to talk about it. Only say she thinks you're ever so good, but it would be better for you to go away." A small hand, palm up, offered the shilling. "I mustn't 'ave it."

Latimer closed Toby's fingers around the coin. "You can accept a gift, my boy, and with my blessings—let's hear no more about it." His temper began to rise. "So Jenny presumed to send a message telling me what would be good for me. Look, young Toby, she's a friend of yours, isn't she?"

"Best friend I ever 'ad. Only one what cares enough to look out for me. And I looks out for 'er."

"Is Jenny in some sort of trouble?"

"Well—nah, I looks after 'er so she's all right."

Latimer didn't miss the small hesitation. He sat beside the boy. "Does Jenny's family keep in touch with her?"

Toby held his head in his hands.

"Do they?"

"I don't talk about other people's business. Specially not Jenny's."

Latimer had an idea. "Would you please go back and ask her to see me? Tell her I won't interfere with her business in any way as long as I can see she's safe. Then I'll leave." Might he be forgiven for bending the truth.

"She ain't daft," Toby said tersely. He looked about him. "'Ow could she be safe in a place like this? You're just trying to trick 'er into seeing you."

"So you think I should go away, too."

Toby was quiet for a long, tense time. Then he said, "I'm frightened for 'er," and Latimer's stomach flipped over. "It's the landlord, see. 'E wants 'er for somethin' she don't want to do. It's on account of 'er owin' back rent—she got behind because she 'elped Ruby when she 'ad a baby and it was sickly. It costs to 'ave a sawbones, but the baby would 'ave died else. Then there was the medicine. And Ruby got ill, and the sawbones 'ad to come again. And with Ruby not workin' there wasn't no money for food. Old Bucket reckoned it was all right for Jenny to owe for a bit, then 'e said 'e never said no such thing. Now 'e sniffs around all the time.''

Latimer already knew who "Bucket" was but nevertheless asked, "Is Bucket the landlord?"

"Yes. All the time 'e watches Jenny. Makes her 'ead bad, it does. And mine."

The thought of Morley Bucket being anywhere near Jenny—and this child—made Latimer's head hurt, too. The man was involved in every possible kind of low, often illegal, undertaking. The implications were shocking.

Morley Bucket was known to Latimer from the days when he'd frequented gambling hells of poor reputation. There he'd felt less likely to encounter anyone he knew. Bucket had been somewhat of a celebrity in the gambling houses, tossing money about, drinking excessively, laughing loudly and always accompanied by hangers-on, both male and female, who fawned upon him.

"Jenny's in danger," Latimer said, surprising himself. He hadn't planned to blurt out something to terrify the boy. "She could be, that is. That's why I'd be letting her down if I didn't try to help."

Toby looked at him through the gloomy shadows on the stairs. He said, "She thinks she can manage all on 'er own, but she can't, can she?"

Relief flowed through Latimer. A chink had appeared in Toby's resolve. "I'm not sure," he said carefully, "but I doubt it. If this Bucket man is determined to trap her, she doesn't have the defenses to fight him and win. Not on her own."

"But you reckon you could help her?"

Triumph was premature, but Latimer felt triumphant anyway. "I believe I can make sure she's safe."

"She won't like it," Toby said.

"If you take me to her, you mean?"

"Yes. She'll be cross with me."

Latimer thought about that. "You could go up to her room and let me see which door is hers. Then I could say I followed you on my own."

"I'd know it was a whopper," Toby said, frowning hugely. "You got to learn not to lie. I used to 'ave a lot of trouble with that till Jenny came along."

"Is she expecting you back at once?" Latimer wasn't about to give up.

Toby stood up. He put the shilling in his pocket and said, "Thank you, sir. Now come with me. I'll take you to Jenny and say me prayers I'm doin' the right thing."

It was impossible not to be impressed by a ragged boy whose sunken cheeks testified to lack of food, but who spoke reasonably well and with intelligence, and who displayed a sense of honor.

They climbed to the top floor where ceilings were so low that Latimer had to bow his head. Toby went ahead, rapped once on a door, and opened it when a voice from inside told him to come in.

"I've something for ye," Jenny said clearly. "I forgot to gi' it to ye when I got inside. Look."

"Jenny, I've brought someone t'see you."

Latimer admired the boy's straightforward courage and followed him. Jenny, having obviously risen with haste, stood in front of a wooden chair with pieces of material and sewing supplies scattered on bare, dried out boards at her feet. She held her open reticule in one hand, and several pastries in the other.

"Is it all right?" Toby asked anxiously. You said he was good and I think he is."

Jenny looked at Toby and smiled. "Ye did what ye thought was best. Would ye go outside a wee while—take these wi' ye. They were left over at the shop and Madame gave them t'me.''

"I've 'ad me bit of bread already. You 'ave 'em.''

"You need more to eat than a piece of bread,'' Jenny said. She glanced at Latimer and her eyes were too bright. "Here, Toby. Take them t'please me.''

With an unhappy expression, Toby took the cakes and left at once.

Latimer made a move to pick up the items Jenny had dropped.

"No.'' Something in her voice brooked no argument.

He tried not to be too obvious, but glanced around the room. That she was poor hadn't been in doubt, but the level of that poverty reduced him to bemused fury at whoever or whatever had caused her to fall on such hard times.

A single candle, on an upside-down basket was the only light. A cushion she'd obviously made from scraps brightened the seat of her scratched and chipped chair. Against one wall stood a narrow metal bed covered with a gray blanket. A pillow had a crocheted cover made of brown wool. In a crate turned on end with its open side exposed, slats of wood had been forced across the width and secured in spaces on either side. On these makeshift shelves stood several cups and plates, knives and forks, and two saucepans. A metal basin and jug was stored on top of the crate. Latimer found no evidence of food and the only other things in the room were pushed into a space beside the chimney breast. A pallet on the floor with several items of worn-out boys' clothing spread on top, and several books piled at one end. Jenny's clothes hung on a bar between hooks screwed into the wall.

He couldn't meet her eyes.

Small splashes of bright color caught his attention. Ranged along the bed and propped against the wall stood a number of tiny dolls. Each one had a cloth face and hands and was dressed in meticulously crafted clothing. One doll with hair fashioned from red-brown thread, wore a green ball dress decorated with gold lace. Her headdress was gold and so were her fan and the slippers that poked from beneath the skirts.

"Is that one you?" Latimer asked, thinking to break the awkwardness. He picked up the doll and looked at Jenny over his shoulder.

"Hardly," she said. "The poor don't go to balls."

He pretended he was still interested in the doll. "Any little child would love something so perfect and miniature."

"Perhaps I should sell them in the streets," she said.

"You will sell nothing in the streets."

The silence that followed increased the tension between them.

"Should you like the doll?" she asked. "Mayhap ye've a small relative who would enjoy her."

She wanted to give him something and this was all she had. It was the truth, he felt it and tucked the doll into his pocket. "The child Lady Hester Bingham has taken in— you'll remember Lady Hester at Number 7—the child's name is Birdie and she'd be excited to have this. Thank you."

He remembered the flowers and offered them to her. Jenny blushed, and blinked rapidly. She said, "Thank ye. You're so kind," and set the stems inside a tin. There was no sign of the bunch she'd bought herself, and he'd wager they were to be found in another room in this hovel—given as a gift from a girl who had nothing, to someone whose life she sought to brighten.

"Are ye satisfied?" she asked suddenly, leaving her lips parted to breathe. "Ye wanted to see just how the poor live? Well, ye're welcome in my castle. Here—'' she felt about in her reticule and produced another pastry ''—take this. I've not fetched water yet or I'd offer ye some.''

''Thank you.'' Latimer took the dry pastry he was certain she'd intended for her own evening meal, ate it and said, ''Very good. I didn't know I was hungry.''

''Good. Now, if ye'll excuse me, I've a good deal t'do before bed and that's the only candle I have until I can get more.''

She was brave, but she was also incensed.

''Latimer.'' She pressed her hands into her skirts. ''Ye'll be wantin' to get on wi' other things yoursel'. Thank you for making sure I got home safely. Forgive my rudeness. I doubt ye understand my feelings.''

''You're ashamed and angry,'' he said. ''I might as well be blunt. How could I not understand your feelings when you've tried so hard to keep your private life a secret. That's where Toby sleeps, isn't it?'' He pointed to the pallet.

''It is. He was a chimney boy, but whenever they forced him up, he couldna bear the stone all around him so tight, and the dark. He'd scream so loudly the fine people would get upset in case their own children were disturbed. In the end the man who owned him left him on the streets. He's a fine, intelligent boy. He likes me to give him lessons and learns fast. Somehow I'll be sure he makes his way in the world.''

Latimer almost groaned. The picture became more and more complicated, not that it would have to if Jenny would only stop trying to be so strong and let him help her.

''Good night t'ye, then,'' Jenny said.

''I could ask Lady Hester to rent you a flat at Number 7''

"I like it here," Jenny said, and the corners of her mouth turned down. "I've friends here."

"Don't be ridiculous. Come with me at once."

She stood firm. "I know ye mean well, but ye're rude wi' it, and overbearin' and I'm no in need o' a rude, overbearin' man—or any man at all."

By now he should have learned more about communicating with females. They were such an emotional lot. "I am *not* overbearing. No one says I am. And I'm certainly not rude. Gather up your things and come along."

"I will not."

"Oh, yes, you most certainly will." With that he put an arm around her waist, the other beneath her knees, and hauled her off her feet. "And I've changed my mind. You must be fed and made comfortable at once. One of the servants from Number 7 will return for your things tomorrow. Tonight Sibyl will see to it that you have what you need."

She was insubstantial and her feet, kicking up and down, made no impression on Latimer, other than to annoy him yet again.

"You can't make decisions for other people," she told him. "Put me down or I'll…"

"You'll what?"

"I'll—I'll hit you."

Funny as the idea was, he managed not to laugh. With a completely serious face he said, "Please don't do that. You might hurt me."

Her mouth trembled. "I shouldna like t'do that, but ye'd ha' driven me to it." Next she wriggled.

Latimer kissed her. He couldn't help himself. At first her mouth was rigid beneath his and she felt as if her body had turned to stone. But then she placed her fingers on his jaw and responded, as if experimenting, he thought. Latimer moved slowly, gently. Her inexperience was obvious, but her lips softened and she pressed them urgently to his. Even as his mind told him to stop, to pause and then kiss her again, his will didn't get the message and he parted her lips to run his tongue along the sharp edges of her teeth. He opened her mouth wide and when he thrust his tongue against hers, she made excited little sounds, twisted in his arms, and copied every move. Their faces rocked together. They changed angles to deepen the kiss until Latimer's legs no longer felt so strong. For a heated moment he thought of the meager bed and longed to feel the gray blanket beneath their naked bodies.

A howl, Toby's howl, stopped them and the door slammed open.

Toby, holding an ear, shot into the room and lost his footing. He fell against the iron fireplace.

On the threshold stood Morley Bucket.

6

Jenny realized that she was clinging to Latimer and quickly relaxed her fingers. "Put me down," she whispered.

He obliged, but set her firmly behind him and confronted Bucket. "Are you hurt, boy," he said to Toby, and when the child got up and shook his head, added, "Good fellow. Takes more than a bully's blow to hurt a man of honor."

She made to go to Toby but Latimer shot out an arm and said, "Soon enough, Jenny. Kindly stay where you are."

Men could be so overbearing. However, an overbearing man standing between her and Morley Bucket pleased her at the moment.

"Now, now, now," Bucket said, advancing a step or two. His tall, narrow body seemed even more stooped than usual. "What's this? Entertainin' gents in my 'ouse, are you, Jenny girl? You know that's not allowed. I run decent lodgings for decent people."

"Have a care," Latimer said, and the hand he still held in front of Jenny became a fist.

"Dinna let there be violence," she told him, shuddering inside her thin clothes, but not because she was cold.

"All high and mighty miss perfect," Bucket said, leering at Jenny. "Good job I came by, even if it was only to see if you needed anything. I'm a generous man, Jenny McBride, but I'll not stand by and allow a sneaky one who's no better than she ought to be to bring down the reputation of my property—or to make a fool of me. Don't forget you've an outstanding debt to me and I've been a patient man—so far."

"Get out," Latimer said, itching to pound a fist into the man's jaw. "Leave now and never come near Miss McBride again."

The lifestyle he enjoyed had taken its toll, but Morley Bucket was still in the prime of his life. He showed no fear, although he must know physical confrontation was possible. "Well now, if you aren't full of yourself for a gent what's been caught red-'anded like," he said. The candlelight shone on his greased-back colorless hair. His eyebrows were so light they were hard to see at all, and the rims of his eyes were pink between sparse white lashes. "What was you about to do when I came in 'ere all un-suspectin'? Play tiddlywinks? I saw what I saw and *Miss McBride* isn't free to shop her wares around. But we won't go into that. Take off, sir, and we'll forget you was ever in this 'ouse."

Until he recalled how drunk Bucket had always been, Latimer wondered that the man didn't recognize him. "I won't be leaving," he said.

"Look," Bucket said, all reasonable. "I understands the needs of men's flesh. Oh, yes, I understand very well. So, instead of interferin' in a personal matter between Jenny and me, why not visit me elsewhere." He slipped a card from his pocket. "You come to me at this address. You'll get whatever you want in the 'ighest class 'ouse in England."

Jenny fumed and trembled at the same time. Bucket accused her of being a woman of few morals and advertised that nasty house of his in the same breath. She looked at Latimer's long, straight back, his broad shoulders and the way he braced his strong legs apart. She didn't regret the kiss. The memory could never be taken from her. But a man like him didn't willingly become involved with low riffraff. He'd be gone soon enough and there wouldn't be any more pleasantries exchanged on Bond Street.

"Didn't I ask you to go?" Latimer said.

"'E did," Toby chimed in. He walked boldly up to Bucket, placed his fists on skinny hips and said. "Leave us alone."

"You whore's bastard," Bucket roared, and landed a cuff on the side of Toby's head. "I'm sick of you 'anging about. I'm goin' to finish you once and for all. D'you think I don't know who warns 'er when I'm coming?" He grabbed Toby by the collar and lifted him from the ground. "How often do you sit guard outside while she 'as 'er fancy fellows in 'ere?"

Toby got two good fistfuls of Bucket's hair and pulled while he kicked the man's slack belly as if it were a feather bed for jumping on.

That was all Toby got to do. "Stay where you are, Jenny," Latimer said, his voice strange and low. He hauled the boy away from Bucket. Red-faced and ready to go back for more, Toby breathed hard and held his fists up like a miniature pugilist, but stayed out of Latimer's way.

Jenny closed her eyes, but couldn't keep them closed because she was afraid for Latimer.

"Sure you don't want t'think about this?" Bucket said. "You soft ones fall the 'ardest."

Latimer's first cut caught Bucket beneath the chin and raised him from the ground. One of Bucket's flailing arms pounded Latimer across the throat and he choked, but didn't lose focus on the other man.

A blow to Bucket's stomach forced a whining howl from him. He bent over, clutching his middle, and Latimer brought a fist down on the back of his neck.

Slowly Bucket rolled forward and landed on his knees with his forehead on the floorboards. He wheezed and moaned and muttered warnings about the penalties for murder.

"Had enough?" Latimer asked.

"Dirty fighter," Bucket said. "You fight dirty."

"I asked if you'd had enough."

"The law will take care of you," Bucket said, coughing.

"The *law,*" Latimer sputtered, disbelieving his own ears. "Surely you jest."

Bucket staggered to his feet, weaving and holding his jaw. "We'll see who *jests,* Mr. Clever. There's more than one kind of law."

"You're leaving," Latimer told him. "And you will never threaten Miss McBride again."

"You don't know what's between 'er and me." Bucket fixed his light blue stare on Jenny. His eyelids half-covered his eyes as if he were weary...or considering what she would look like disrobed. "There's a score to be settled and it's no business of yours, is it Jenny girl? Tell 'im to 'op it."

Taking Latimer by surprise, Jenny ducked forward and stood, toe to toe, with Bucket. Arms akimbo, she looked up into his face. "Ye," she said, "are an evil wart o' a man."

Latimer swallowed a laugh and stood ready to go to the rescue.

Jenny shook a finger in Bucket's face. "Ye weren't born. Ye were drooled out o' a pig's mouth. Your insides are riverbed sludge. Your brain's a...it's a...well, it just is and it's an awful thing. I've a good mind t'smack your skinny nose flat. Then you'd have t'find something else to peer down when ye're sneering.''

"Finished?'' Bucket said.

"Ye've no color a'tall. Something nasty must ha' sucked it all out of ye. Ye're the image o' a white rat. A white rat wi' warts, flashin' teeth, and a bad smell. Ye smell like whatever the pig was eatin' before she drooled you out.''

Toby examined his shoes and his back shook.

Latimer longed to laugh but couldn't risk allowing his attention to wander.

"We'll continue this conversation later, my girl,'' Bucket said, fixing Jenny with a malevolent stare that dripped threat. "We have urgent matters to discuss. Some opportunities won't wait forever. I think you know what I mean.''

He turned the handle and threw the door open before marching out and thumping down the stairs. A cat yowled and Latimer had no doubt the man had kicked the animal in passing.

"I'll be back.'' Bucket's voice wound its way upward through the stairwell. "Make sure you're ready for me.''

Jenny whirled toward Toby and put her arms around him. "Where d'ye hurt. That pig hit you hard.''

"Son of a pig,'' Toby said with a grin.

"Aye, that, too.'' Jenny turned the boy's head to one side and examined his ear. "Imagine a man hitting a boy. Only cowards hurt creatures smaller than themselves.''

"I thought you might be about to hurt Bucket,'' Latimer said mildly.

Jenny turned on him. "Dinna ye make fun o' me when I've suffered such a shock. If he'd stayed another second I'd ha' blacked his eyes and thickened his mouth and knocked his ugly nose off his face. And that would only have been the start."

Latimer said, "I believe you."

"She's afraid to squash a beetle," Toby said and completely gave in to mirth.

Jenny wasn't laughing. Her face was filled with uncertainty and anxiousness. "Thank you for coming to our aid. If you hadn't been here, Bucket might have done much worse to Toby. And to me, perhaps."

"Bucket won't be doing anything to you again," Latimer said. "You don't live here anymore. I'm taking you to Mayfair Square where you'll be very comfortable. I will pay whatever you owe that man so he has no excuse to follow you."

"Ye will not." Jenny could really frown and turn the corners of her pretty mouth down. "Ye canna decide what others will do, and ye canna expect a body t'accept charity without shame. I thank ye, but no, I'll deal wi' my own troubles."

Latimer looked at his pocket watch and had the strangest notion. He wished his sister Finch were here. Finch knew how to say the right thing at the right time, whereas he could be a bombastic blunderer. But Jenny *should* do as he told her, damn it. He knew what was best and had only her interests at heart.

Well, perhaps there might be an interest or two of his own involved as well.

"Ye're lookin' at your watch. Ye're obviously late for somethin'. Good night t'ye. Gi' my best to Sibyl and the princess if ye please."

"I certainly will. When next I see them. I looked at my watch because I know you work early and must need your sleep. If you insist upon remaining here, you'd best get to bed."

"I'll do that," she said and offered him her hand as if she intended to shake his.

Latimer raised her fingers to his lips and kissed them for a long, long time. The lady didn't attempt to take her hand away and when Latimer opened his eyes—with his mouth still on her skin—Jenny's eyes were closed and she wore an expression of soft bliss. Unfortunately he couldn't revel in the small victory with Toby standing by to observe everything that happened.

Jenny looked at him finally and did remove her hand. "Good night."

"Good night, indeed." He sat down with his back against the door and turned up his collar. "Since I can't leave you alone, I'll have to sleep here. If either of you need to go and relieve yourselves, kindly wake me up and I'll accompany you." Crossing his arms, he rested his head and closed his eyes. "Otherwise I'd appreciate some silence."

What was she supposed to do? Jenny thought. She couldn't throw him out bodily—even if she wanted to. A new sound startled her. Latimer snored softly. She couldn't believe it. What person could go to sleep so easily in the midst of a disagreement? And in a room that didn't belong to him.

She glanced at Toby who sat on his pallet and looked glum. The room didn't belong to her, either, and Toby had nowhere else to go.

"Do you like Bucket?" Latimer's question startled her. His eyes were open again.

"No, ye know I don't like the horrid creature. But I don't fear him, either."

"You should. He has no conscience. People like him are the most dangerous of all. Jenny, be reasonable, please. I'll try not to order you to do things, but let me help you when you need help. You need it now. There's room for you in Mayfair Square."

When she found her voice she said, "I thank ye for offerin', but I canna go." She no longer felt so sure of herself.

"Please," Latimer said and his pleading eyes and voice further weakened her resolve. "Let me take you there. 7B is comfortable and feminine. Meg and Sibyl made it so and it's not being used."

She shook her head. "I've t'stay wi' Toby, but I'm grateful for your kindness."

"Yer don't 'ave to worry about me," Toby said in a loud and unconvincing voice. "It's time for me to make me own way. I've only stayed in case yer needed me, Jenny. I can look after meself."

"No," Jenny said, devastated at the idea of letting him go. "You belong wi' me."

"I don't. I don't belong t'anyone anymore. I'm free to do what I want. I was trying to find a way to tell you I wanted to leave. It's for the best." He rose from his pallet, selected an ancient coat from the pile of clothes, and went to the door.

Latimer looked from the boy to Jenny. She shook her head.

"You shouldn't go out there tonight," Latimer said.

"It ain't none of your business. Or yours, Jenny. I've already spent too much time here with yer. I'm a lad and I want t'be with lads. I've friends who want me with them. Let me go, sir."

Uncertain what he should do, Latimer got up.

Promptly, Toby opened the door. He said, "I'll never forget you, Jenny. Maybe we'll see each other again one day." With that he went out of the room.

Jenny listened to the sounds of him leaving. Her throat closed and hurt so much she couldn't swallow.

"He's a brave lad," Latimer said.

"I can't bear to think o' him trying t'make his way. What will he do? Fall in wi' thieves and learn t'pick pockets? He may have to if he's starving."

"Will you come away with me now?" Latimer asked. "Lady Hester stays up later than she likes any of us to know. I'll speak to her and I know she'll agree to what I suggest."

Jenny rubbed her face. She had nowhere to turn—except to this man she hardly knew but already cared about. There was no sensible choice but to do what he suggested. "Aye, then. Thank ye. I'll come wi' ye, but I'll only stay the night—if Lady Hester agrees—and I'll be gone early in the mornin'." She'd go to work as usual, but what would happen when work was finished for the day she couldn't guess.

Latimer took her pelisse from the rod and held it out while she slipped it on and fastened the front. When she raised her head, he held her bonnet. This he put over her head himself. Then he tied the ribbons and stole her breath yet again.

"That's all you need," he said.

But it wasn't. She turned her back on him and gathered all the dolls into her reticule. Leaving them behind, even for a night, would upset her. Next she pulled her nightgown from beneath the pillow and rolled it tightly around a few other items she'd need immediately. She had no intention of borrowing from Lady Sibyl Lloyd.

Jenny and Latimer said little while they left the building and crossed Lardy Lane. She did ask, "How do you know your way so well?"

"I have business in this area," he told her. "Have for years."

Jenny wondered just what that business might be, but she wouldn't probe. She searched darkened doorways for Toby, but he was nowhere in sight. They turned a corner, and another, and another, and reached the archway at the entrance to the small, cobbled square where the coster-mongers plied their wares by day.

"Once we're on a suitable street, I'll hail a hackney," Latimer said. He'd pulled her hand beneath his elbow and covered it on his forearm with a gloved hand. "You've done far too much walking for one day."

He held her so close she couldn't help touching him while they walked. He felt so solid and safe to be with. She straightened her shoulders and reminded herself that she was an independent woman, not a fluttering violet of a thing in need of protection.

She pulled him to a stop and disentangled her arm from his. "I can't do it," she told him.

Latimer held her shoulders and planted her squarely in front of him. "And we can't go through this again. It's too late, and this isn't a place for you to be at such an hour."

She shook her head. "But I can't do it. I can't leave Toby. Please let me go. I've got to find him."

Not half a dozen steps had she run before Latimer caught hold of her arm again. "Very well," he said and didn't even sound annoyed. "I expected this. But I'm coming with you to look for him."

They didn't look far. The instant they reentered Lardy Lane, a shadow separated from the houses on the other side and flew toward them. When he arrived, Toby was panting, but he gulped several times and said, "Did yer

7

Oh, no. No, no, no. Don't even think about it because it will not happen.

I've been prepared for Jenny McBride to worm her way into Number 7. I've already got a plan for that. She won't stay long because the curate I mentioned will sweep her off her feet and take her far away from here. But that tattered boy shall *not* enter my home—not even step through the front door. He is a street urchin.

Give me patience! Shakespeare approaches. Am I not suffering enough without that pompous, self-important oaf coming to torment me?

"What do you say, sir? Well, I do declare, you've been eavesdropping again. You might want to think about avoiding that, old man. In that frightful tragedy of yours— eh?—you know the one. A Midsummer Night's Dream *or some such foolishness. What? Of course it's meant to be a tragedy. You messed it up and you can't wriggle out of that now."*

Dash it all, he's not going away.

"Look, Will—isn't that what your cronies called you, Will? Well, Will—I'll get rid of him soon enough—I met an interesting chap at school the other day. Angel School, you dolt. What other school might I attend? Too bad you're above learning anything from anybody. You're going to get bored with being important among the newcom-

forget something, Jenny? Tell me what it is and I'll get it for yer. You can wait 'ere with 'im.''

Latimer caught Toby by the shoulder and said, "She came back because of something she *can't* forget. She'll be all right now she's got you again."

*ers but this is where you'll stay until you grovel, and beg
for the Higher Ones to take you into the program after all.*

"I was about to speak of John Fletcher.

*"You don't want to? Why ever not? Wasn't he that won-
derful, generous man who helped you write* Henry VIII
and The Two Noble Kinsmen? *No, you blinking well
didn't write* Henry VIII *on your own and keep your voice
down or we'll have him dragging himself and parts of...I
mean he'll bring his wives around to irritate us.*

*"Do you know how ruinous it was to have two desperate
lovers whispering at each other through a wall?*

*"I'll talk about whatever I want to talk about. Pah on
your comedy, sir. Piffle. We both know the truth.*

*"Let's return to Mr. John Fletcher. Oh, really? You
have to go now? What a pity. I shall miss you."*

There he goes, nose in the air.

*There he goes, arse over head, nose into a passing me-
teor. He's making no progress at all with his flying.*

But I told you I'd get rid of him.

*Now, I have two dilemmas. How do I make absolutely
sure that ragamuffin, Toby, doesn't enter Number 7? And
what excuse shall I use to introduce Mr. Larch Lumpit to
Jenny McBride—and keep him around until he's snapped
her up?*

*The boy is the final blow. What cruel fate. I wonder, no,
you don't suppose the Reverend Smiles pulled a few
strings, do you? Did I tell you about Reverend Smiles?
Late father of Meg, who was Meg Smiles, and Sibyl, who
was Sibyl Smiles. He's a member of the In Group up here.
Positively flew through Angel School and already has his
wings. Fully grown and matured wings, mind you. He was
angry with me when he thought I might have had something to do with his daughters' less than admirable behavior but he's put all that behind him and actually cham-*

pions me. Keeps telling me I'm doing well in school and he expects my wing buds any day. Then I suppose I'll be called a ducky boy. Ex-people with budding wings are called ducky boys because, well, imagine a duckling's wings and you'll know.

There I go again, wandering away from the center of the problem. I got involved with the notion that the Reverend Smiles might gain pleasure from complicating my already complicated task by adding this Toby, but it's nobody's fault other than that Latimer...and the pauper, Jenny McBride. Did you see that room she was living in? Spare me. We won't think about it.

And yes, I saw the kiss. A connection with carnal implications if ever I saw one. There is no time to waste or I'll have more than kisses to worry about.

But wait. Oh, my goodness. Oh, my word. The means of introducing my willing accomplice into the picture is perfectly clear now.

Time to mobilize Larch Lumpit.

8

Toby stood on the pavement, watching the hackney coach pull away and listening to the horses set up a clatter in the dark.

"He's never been in a carriage before," Jenny whispered to Latimer. "He's still excited."

"So I gathered," Latimer said. "But it's getting late and we've things left to do. I say, Toby, time to go in and get warm."

Reluctantly Toby turned toward the house and slowly began to climb the steps.

"We're too much trouble, Latimer. Why not gi' this up and let us be on our way? We'll find a place and no' put anyone out."

"You've found a place where you won't put anyone out. Number 7 Mayfair Square. Good, kind people live here. They'll become as fond of you as... We will all want what's best for you." A damnably foolish slip. He couldn't imagine what had made him so careless.

"Ouch," Toby said and squealed.

Latimer swung around, but Jenny was already kneeling beside Toby—who sat on a step—and tried to look at his knees in the gloom. "Did ye trip?" she asked him.

"No, I didn't. I don't know what 'appened."

Latimer hadn't forgotten Toby's enthusiasm in the cab. No doubt the boy wasn't concentrating and, regardless of what he said, he had tripped. "We'll take a look at that knee inside," he said and used his key. "In we go."

The sight of Old Coot shuffling toward him at such an hour concerned Latimer. "Is all well, Coot?"

Head and neck thrust forward, the old man approached and tapped Latimer's arm, indicating he wanted to speak quietly. He glanced about and said, "Whole house is in an upheaval, Mr. More. Lady Hester's decided there must be a sitting room for everyone who lives here. Where they'll *gather*. I ask you, why would they want a sitting room when they've each got one of their own? On your floor, too, Mr. More. One of the done-over rooms. Piano brought in. Cards and the like. It's beyond me."

Most things were beyond Old Coot. "Ah, yes, well, this will be interesting, but I have company to attend to." He opened the door wide and beckoned to Jenny and Toby who stood now but hadn't made upward progress.

"A Mr. Lumpit is already lolling on a couch in there. Doesn't see me except when he wants something more to eat. He's a curate from somewhere or other. I haven't been told why he's here." Old Coot hmphed and peered outside. "More company, I see. Oh, it's you, Miss Jenny."

Latimer grew agitated. He feared Jenny might leave, but hesitated to pressure her into the house. And he wasn't interested in household intrigues at the moment. "We'll need to see Lady Hester. Please tell her I want to bring Miss Jenny McBride to her." He wouldn't mention Toby in advance.

"Now?" Old Coot said, his creased face pinched in umbrage. "You want me to climb up all those stairs *now?"*

"Of course not," Latimer said, waving Jenny and Toby forward. "Slip of the tongue. Send Evans. I understand that's why Sir Edmund Winthrop recommended him to Lady Hester and he was hired, to do all the running around for you." Evans was the new under-butler. Sir Edmund had become Lady Hester's frequent companion in the past few months—to the consternation of all at Number 7.

Old Coot hitched his shoulders. "Her ladyship wouldn't like it if Evans were to go up there. She wants the people she's used to around her. I'll go." He set off and climbed the stairs more smartly than was his habit.

Jenny advanced to the top step. She held Toby by the elbow.

"Come *in* out of the cold," Latimer urged.

The boy's eyes were fearful. He looked about inside the foyer and shook his head.

"It's all right, Toby," Jenny said. "Latimer wouldna take ye here if it wasna safe.

Toby caught a foot on the threshold but, amazingly, fell backward rather than forward and smacked hard on the top step. Latimer lifted the boy up, took no notice of the resistance he felt in his slim body, and deposited him in the foyer. Jenny entered without a word and positioned herself in the shadow of a large, rather ugly bronze plinth with one of Lady Hester's collection of old urns on top. Made of wood, the urn was carved into the shape of a swan. Jenny looked up into glassy black eyes on either side of a yellow lacquered beak that served as a spout. She jumped and took a step away.

"What's goin' to 'appen?" Toby asked. "'Ere, watch out for that ugly great swan thing, Jenny. If it fell, it'd flatten yer."

Jenny said, "I'm perfectly safe here, thank ye. Don't keep askin' Latimer questions. He'll tell us what's t'be soon enough."

Voices came from the second door on the right, a room that had been redecorated during Lady Hester's spiffing up period. She had spiffed up just about everything she saw.

The door was only open a little, but Latimer heard Sibyl's voice, and Adam's, and that of a man he couldn't identify. Much as he'd like to see Sibyl, whom he expected to need, he was not interested in making new acquaintances this evening.

Adam slipped from that room and closed the door quietly. He wore his dour and suspicious expression. He nodded at Jenny and beckoned to Latimer.

"What is it, man?" Latimer asked.

Adam turned his head aside and spoke low. "Can't go into it now for obvious reasons." With the slightest inclination of his head, he indicated Jenny. "When you do whatever you intend to do about Jenny, come to Lady H's new inmate sitting room. There's a fellow there who's looking for Jenny. Don't like much about him and neither will you. I don't think he's likely to give up, but let's make sure he doesn't get to see her tonight. We need time to make plans."

Latimer made no attempt to stifle a groan. Could be Bucket calling himself by another name. "Is he tall and very thin. A pale chap with a lot of gold teeth?"

"Short and round. Shiny-faced and balding."

"Well that's not... We may have some complicated days ahead. Keep your visitor where he is and I'll get there as soon as I can."

"Aye." Adam went back into the sitting room.

Toby stood beside one of the heavily carved newel posts and kept his hands tightly clasped before him.

"Why don't we wait in my rooms?" Latimer said. After all, Toby would count as a chaperon for Jenny. "You can both sit down in there."

"Ow." Toby slid down the post and his bottom—where there was little meat, met stone tile with a thunk.

"How did ye do that?" Jenny asked. "I think ye're tryin' t'be vexin' and ye're succeedin'."

"*Trying?* Talk to whoever puts the polish on wiv' a knife around 'ere. Barely leaned against this 'ere fancy post and me feet went out from under."

Latimer offered him a hand which Toby accepted. On his feet again, he surreptitiously rubbed his derriere.

"I hadn't noticed you were clumsy before," Latimer said. He was almost sure the lad was drawing attention to himself because he wanted to be asked to leave. Clearly his surroundings disturbed him.

"I'm not clumsy." Toby looked annoyed at the suggestion.

Jenny said, "Not at all, although you could be nervous, Toby."

"I'm not nervous about anythin'," Toby said, sounding belligerent. "But we got to go somewhere else. We don't belong 'ere."

"Back to Lardy Lane, perhaps?" Latimer asked and instantly regretted the words. "Let's not wrangle. Once you meet Lady Hester, you'll know this is a good place to be."

"Mr. More," Old Coot said from above. "If you'd make your way up here, Lady Hester will see you now."

"Poor man," Jenny said quietly. "He's too old to climb up and down like that."

Latimer agreed but didn't say so. Old Coot's biggest fear was that he'd lose his place at Number 7. It didn't seem to matter that he'd been told he would always have a home there, he guarded his position as an active member of the staff.

"Go ahead of me, Toby," Latimer said. "Jenny, would you take my arm, please?"

She did so gladly. As closely as she had watched for

signs of his growing bored or annoyed with the task he'd undertaken, she'd seen none.

The house was quite familiar from the times she'd been there to meet with Sibyl's club. What fun that had been. A little naughty, it was true, but a wonderful diversion for a girl who had few chances to be with other young women.

Toby missed the next two stairs and started to slither down. Latimer saved him once more and didn't say a word about the incident. He did look at Jenny with raised brows.

From each flight they climbed, a new vista opened to reveal plaster-worked ceilings, tall pillars, chinoiserie screens and more bronze plinths supporting fanciful wooden urns that depicted animals and birds.

Old Coot awaited them outside Lady Hester Bingham's rooms. Unlike those of the tenants, these doors bore no numbers although Jenny knew they were thought of as simply Number 7.

The old man knocked, waited to hear his mistress's demand to "Come," and opened the door to the boudoir where she preferred to receive visitors. "Mr. Latimer More. Miss Jenny McBride, and—" He flapped a hand toward Toby.

"Toby," Latimer said.

Her ladyship sat in her favorite receiving spot on a daybed that had once been black lacquer but was now painted a deep shade of purple and inlaid with gold leaf. Black velvet draperies at the narrow windows had been exchanged for purple. After years of mourning for her late husband, she had come into the light again. Blond, blue-eyed and pretty—although her age remained a mystery—she reclined against piles of luxurious pillows. A mauve evening dress flattered her statuesque figure.

Behind Lady Hester, and far less pleasing to Latimer, stood Sir Edmund Winthrop of Number 23 Mayfair

Square. The man was affable enough but was a widower of barely six months and Latimer found his recent and ardent attachment to Lady Hester distasteful.

That lady used a tortoiseshell lorgnette to examine her latest visitors, one by one. "Latimer, you're pleased about something. Good humor suits you."

"Thank you, Lady Hester." It was true that he was exhilarated by his increasing acquaintance with Jenny but he didn't want to discuss the reason for calling on Lady Hester in front of Sir Edmund.

She leaned forward to see Jenny more closely. "I remember you. Friend of Sibyl's, am I right?"

"Yes, m'lady."

"Yes, well." Lady Hester took in every inch of Jenny, and Latimer had no doubt she was assessing the condition of her clothes. "What am I thinking of? Sir Edmund, this is Latimer More, one of my protegés. He lives on the ground floor."

Latimer said, "We've met, I believe, Sir Edmund," but shook the man's hand anyway. "This is a friend, Miss Jenny McBride, and her young friend Toby."

Sir Edmund's gaze passed over Toby, but he smiled at Jenny and bowed over her hand courteously. "Pleased to meet you." A fleshy man, nevertheless he had enough height and breadth to give the impression of being substantial and vigorous. He wore his straight brown hair cut short and had a square, ruddy face. A luxurious mustache gave him a jovial air.

"I didn't know you had company," Latimer said to Lady Hester. "Forgive me for intruding. I'll return tomorrow perhaps?" If necessary he could ask for Sibyl's blessings on Jenny sleeping at 7B. He'd find a spot for Toby in his own rooms.

Sir Edmund bent over Lady Hester and kissed her brow.

"I was about to leave, wasn't I, my dear? Looks as if Mr. More is in need of your wisdom."

Latimer smiled to himself. He was actually feeling possessive of Lady Hester. Ridiculous. Sir Edmund was an upstanding man and if he and Lady H could find some happiness together, why not?

"Good night, Sir Edmund," Lady Hester said. "Don't forget to give Myrtle my regards."

As soon as the man had left, Lady Hester said, "Myrtle is Sir Edmund's late wife's niece. She keeps an eye on him. Poor man, he's devastated by his loss, but who better to understand that than I? Now, you had something you wished to talk to me about?"

"Yes," Latimer said, beginning to wish he'd spared Jenny and Toby from witnessing this interview.

"Sit down then, Jenny, dear. That nice little French chair is comfortable. That's right. And you, master...?" She ducked her head toward Toby.

"Toby, er, lady."

"Toby? A good name. Toby what, may I ask?"

The boy leaned sideways and his leg banged into a low, oval table. A porcelain figurine fell sideways and one graceful hand holding a bunch of grapes broke off.

Toby gasped and flattened his palms to his sides. Latimer glanced at Jenny whose eyes were huge and horrified. "I shall search for a replacement," he said.

"I'll pay for it," Jenny said. "Toby, apologize and wait outside, if ye please."

"I can deal wiv me own troubles," Toby said, managing to sound quite rude. "I'm ten and I knows what's what. I don't need anyone to do stuff for me."

"Bosh," Lady H said with feeling. "Grown-ups do overreact sometimes, Toby, but there's no call to snap just because they embarrass you. Their offers were made in good heart. Come and sit beside me right here.'' She patted the space by her on the daybed.

Toby didn't move. "I'm sorry about your pretty thing, lady. I reckon I can find one like it at a market.''

Latimer put a fist to his mouth. He smiled at Jenny who looked aghast.

"Right now, young man,'' Lady H said as if Toby hadn't just suggested he could replace her piece of Dresden from a market stall. "These may be quite strange surroundings for you. It's more than likely you're so stiff you aren't aware of what parts of your person you do or don't move. Come along. Have you had your supper?''

"Um.'' Words deserted Toby and he crept past the table, lifting each foot with enormous care.

Once he was close enough, Lady H (perish that she ever hear one of them call her that) took hold of his hand and guided him to sit atop the plush purple and gold cushions on the daybed. She looked at him through her lorgnette.

"Your Ladyship,'' Latimer said. It would be best to settle matters and be gone before there could be another disaster. "As I think you know, Jenny is a milliner's assistant and works in the Bond Street shop of—''

"Madame Sophie,'' Lady Hester finished for him. "Sophie remarked on that. I've bought many a hat from Madame Sophie. Wonderful, wonderful.''

"Hmm, well, Jenny is in somewhat difficult circumstances having found herself, quite suddenly, without a home.''

The lorgnette was turned on Jenny. "How can that be?''

Jenny returned her hostess's stare, but when she opened her mouth, no sound emerged.

"Her landlord is a most unpleasant fellow,'' Latimer said quickly. "He—ahem—seemed to think that he had the right to walk into Jenny's flat whenever he chose." He raised his eyebrows significantly at Lady Hester.

"There's no need to worry about me," Jenny said. "I can—"

"Silence," Lady Hester said. She employed an ivory fan to shield her shocked expression from Jenny, and said to Latimer, "You don't say. That won't do at all. Not at all."

"I'm a very capable person," Jenny said.

Latimer considered tying a scarf around her mouth to silence her.

"I'm sure you are," Lady Hester said. "And your young friend here? Is he also in difficult circumstances?"

"Toby has been living in my flat," Jenny said, pleasing Latimer with her straightforwardness.

"So you have championed him?"

"In a way, my lady. Toby has been a great comfort t'me also."

"I don't need no champion," Toby said. His throat jerked. "I'm my own champion, I am."

"Poor boy," Her Ladyship murmured. "What of your family, girl? Why aren't they making sure all's well with you?"

Jenny breathed very deeply. "They're no in a position t'help me, so I dinna worry them wi' my problems. Rightly so. I'm too old to run for help if I'm in a wee bit o' trouble."

Lady Hester turned to Toby. "And you? What of your people."

He frowned as if confused.

"Your mother and father," Lady Hester said. "Your family."

Bright color slashed along Toby's prominent cheekbones. "Ain't got none. Never did."

Her ladyship chose, mercifully, not to point out that
Toby wasn't exactly right in his response. "Imagine,"
Lady Hester said to Latimer. "Two such young creatures
all alone in the world. I declare, it's a sin that these things
can happen."

Toby jerked forward and slid to the floor as if thrown
by an invisible force. He stayed where he was, his eyes
fixed on the carpet.

"Will you look at that," Lady Hester said with tears in
her eyes. "Too weak to hold himself in one place. When
was the last time you had a really good meal, child?"

"I 'ad a piece of bread and some pastries Jenny brought
'ome," he said. "Very good they was, too."

Lady Hester rose majestically from the daybed and bent
over Toby. She helped him up and walked with him to a
chaise covered in mauve and lavender striped silk. "Climb
into that," she said. "Go along. All the way. Now turn
around and sit against the cushions. Summon Barstow,
please, Latimer."

He used the cord that connected to the room of Lady
Hester's companion and housekeeper. Dressed in her customary gray and with keys clinking from a chain at her
waist, Mrs. Barstow arrived in minutes, listened to her employer's instructions to bring a special tray for Toby, and
other food for Jenny and Latimer, and left. Barstow's heels
hit the floor like hammers—making her displeasure known
as she left the room.

"I don't suppose you've had time to eat properly," her
ladyship said to Latimer. "Been too busy, I should think."

"'E's good, 'e is," Toby announced without raising his
face.

"I'm sure. But it's hard to *remain* good on an empty
stomach."

"My lady," Latimer said, putting his hands behind his

back. "You are the one who is good. You are always ready to come to the aid of those less fortunate than yourself."

"Most people are," she said, subsiding onto the daybed again. "One does what one can, but I can't take care of the whole world."

"No," Latimer agreed. "But you have managed to touch a remarkable number of lives. I know you wouldn't wish me to enlarge on that, but—"

"Absolutely not. I've only done what any God-fearing woman would do. Get to the point, my boy. What is it you came to ask me?"

Latimer cleared his throat. From the corner of his eye he could see Jenny gesturing to him. He didn't look at her since he expected her to try to stop him from doing what he intended to do. "7B remains unoccupied," he said. "Would you consider having Jenny as a tenant?"

"Och, no," Jenny said hurriedly. "What Latimer meant t'say is that I'd be awfu' grateful to spend the night there. Tomorrow I'll look for a permanent place."

"And what would be wrong with a permanent place at Number 7B Mayfair Square, miss? If it were available?"

"She can't afford it," Toby piped up.

Jenny half-rose from her chair, but sat down again. "Ye shouldna interfere, Toby. Ye don't know what my reasons are. This is a beautiful house, my lady."

If it would be other than completely unsuitable, Latimer would take Jenny in his arms. In fact, he'd like to do so regardless, only she'd be furious with him. When he looked at her the strangest sensations overtook him. On the one hand he wanted to cradle her, to convince her she would always be safe with him. On the other hand, the thought of holding her at all brought a shudder and an urge to hug her so tight she'd scarce be able to breath.

Lady Hester had become quiet. After a single tap, Barstow entered with the maid, Foster, at her heels. Barstow balanced a tray in one arm and whipped a large napkin over Toby's chest and stomach. She tucked a corner of the linen beneath his collar then put the tray on his lap.

"Cor," Toby said with reverence. A bowl of soup in which vegetables and pieces of beef were visible sent up fragrant steam. Bread rolls split in half and buttered added to the mouthwatering aroma. A pink syllabub topped with cream and cherries wobbled in a footed glass dish. And there was a large cup of hot chocolate.

"Eat up," Lady Hester said, beaming. "Thank you, Barstow. Foster. Barstow, I'll have to ask you to remain up. I shall need you again before long."

Foster had left a second tray on the oval table. This bore what smelled like hot meat pasties, and there was cheese, fruit, and bread, a glass of beer, and a glass of lemonade.

Toby had curled himself over his soup bowl and was making his way rapidly through the contents.

Latimer sat on a chair that matched the one Jenny used. He'd best back up her request to spend the night. Later he'd speak to Lady Hester alone and see if she would even consider having a new tenant on a permanent basis. "Will it be acceptable for Miss McBride to sleep at 7B tonight?" he asked.

"Do you owe money to your former landlord, Jenny?"

He looked to Jenny who addressed Lady Hester. "Yes, my lady."

"How did such a thing occur and why have you not repaid your debt?"

"I say," Latimer interrupted. "I hardly think—"

"Something happened," Jenny said. "I had no plan for it. Nothing put aside."

"She 'elped someone," Toby said. He'd finished his

soup and was chomping his way through the rolls and butter. "She only 'ad enough ter pay 'er own way, but—"

"Lady Hester doesna' want so many details. I've about four weeks t'find the money to pay what I owe. I intend to manage very nicely."

"And if you can't pay?" Her ladyship offered Jenny the cheese and fruit. "You say you want to stay here for one night and tomorrow you'll find somewhere else. I assume you mean somewhere cheaper. And you'll do this before tomorrow evening. What if you don't find a place? Will you return to wherever you've come from? Tell me, Toby, will it be safer for Jenny to be in that place tomorrow than it is today?"

"If she tries to go back, someone should tie 'er up first," Toby said. His eyes had taken on a sleepy droop, but he was managing to spoon up the syllabub very nicely.

"I wouldna go back there if I could help it." Jenny had accepted a wedge of cheese and a piece of bread. She held a small plate in one hand but didn't attempt to eat anything. "Ye're verra kind, but if I can just sleep the night ye'll no have t'worry about me further."

"Ring for Barstow, please, Latimer," Lady Hester said and he obliged.

When she arrived, Barstow had wiped away all expression and stood with her nose elevated and her hands clasped at her waist.

"Is the bedding in 7B aired?" Lady Hester asked.

"It's kept aired because that's your wish, My Lady."

"Good. Give the key to Miss McBride, if you please."

Barstow's nose came down and she blinked, but she removed a key from her chatelaine. Rather than give it to Jenny, she put it on the table.

"Thank you," Lady Hester said, although she didn't appear pleased. "Have you finished your supper, Toby?"

He nodded and Barstow took the tray away. Then, despite his attempt to turn his face away, she wiped a ring of chocolate from around his mouth.

Latimer said, "I'll find a place for him in my rooms."

"He's had places in other people's rooms," Lady Hester informed him. "Your offer is very nice, but he's to have a place of his own. The first room inside the second-floor entrance to the servants' quarters, Barstow. That nice, cheerful little one. Make sure there's a fire and see what clothes you can find for him. He'll be wanting a bath before he sleeps, too."

Barstow's rounded eyes and open mouth made it difficult for Latimer to remain serious.

"You two aren't related?" Her ladyship's question took in Jenny and Toby.

Toby shook his head.

"As I thought. Very well, you may stay here with us until you make alternate arrangements. Off you go with Barstow now."

Toby got to his feet at once and said, "Jenny?"

"Do as her ladyship tells ye. Ye're among friends."

Barstow waved him ahead of her and Latimer was almost certain she muttered, "Orphanage now," as she followed the boy from the room.

Latimer said, "You are very kind, my lady. Should we ask another of the servants to show Jenny into 7B?"

"I don't want to be a bother," Jenny said. She put the plate aside and stood up. "I'll pay for my bed, of course, but I dinna think I can immediately."

Her lips trembled and she pressed them together, but she stood straight, with her shoulders back and Latimer wished he could wipe these times from her mind. What he dare not do was say in front of her that he would be paying for her room.

"Don't worry your head about it," Lady Hester said. "You'll pay me in time. You show her to 7B, please, Latimer. I'm sure Jenny is capable of getting herself settled in. Some of Sibyl's things are in the wardrobe and drawers. I know she'll be happy for you to use them. The fire is laid. Set a taper to it. Latimer, make sure the candles light. We'll discuss what is to happen when you finish work tomorrow, Jenny. I'll expect you."

"But I'll have t'be lookin' for—"

"There will be no time for you to search for other lodgings tomorrow. I shall confer with others about suitable places you might try. Now, off to bed with you, gel."

This was not a dismissal that invited tarrying. Jenny curtsied and hurried toward the door. Latimer picked up the key she'd forgotten, and followed her.

At the door he paused and smiled at Lady Hester. She winked hugely and waved him away with her fan.

9

Spivey here:

Now see here. Would you have done any better keeping that boy out of the house? I'm supposed to be able to do such things but you're not, you say? As usual, you are willfully misunderstanding the question. My gentle tossing about of Toby was masterful. It was the addlepated responses from those who should know better than to make excuses for him that ruined my efforts—as they would have yours!

He tripped because he was still excited from the hackney ride? He fell because the grandeur of the house overwhelmed him? He slipped because he was frightened and hoped he'd be told to leave? Poppycock.

He should have been told to leave.

Yes, yes, yes. That is what should have happened. They were not supposed to make excuses for the urchin. Trying to stop him from entering the house was impossible, but they were supposed to see how unsuitable he is at Number 7 and throw him out.

If I could, I'd sweat.

He thinks he can replace Hester's Dresden in a street market? And Hester rewards him with a room that's quite comfy, thank you?

Then there's Lumpit who can't follow instructions.

Give me strength.

I told him to arrive at seven tomorrow morning, just in case the girl managed to spend the night, and to ask to see her then. So the overzealous rattle comes at seven this evening, announces that he's looking for Jenny, and doesn't realize that rather than being entertained by Sibyl and Adam, he's being kept out of the way until Latimer can assess and deal with him. Pshaw!

Jenny will spend the night. The boy may well stay forever. I am no closer to arousing Latimer's interest in Princess Desirée—or hers in him. Hester's little Birdie hasn't even met Jenny, and...

Oh, good night.

10

Everything was a jumble, Jenny thought. What was she doing in this great house and about to sleep in a fine bed that had been Sibyl's? And being shown the way by Latimer More, a gentleman women probably swooned over—a single *man* any well-born girl's mother would want to snare for her darling?

"You know the way, of course, Jenny," Latimer said from behind her on the stairs. "You've spent many an hour at 7B so you'll be at home."

"Aye. Thank ye for your… Kindness isna enough t'say. Ye're a generous man." She walked across the balcony to 7B and remembered the key on Lady Hester's table. "Oh, dear. I forgot the key."

Latimer leaned around her and unlocked the door. He paused, holding the handle and looking into her eyes. "But I didn't." His face was close to hers and she glanced at his mouth. She thought of the kiss and her own lips parted.

Lightly, he placed a hand at her waist while he opened the door. "Let's go in, shall we?"

Jenny stepped inside the sitting room.

She might be poor and an orphan, but it wasn't seemly for her to be alone with a man like this, any more than that kiss had been seemly. Although it had been wonderful. It hadn't been mentioned again. After all, she could never refer to such a thing. And Latimer must only have done it because everything had been so strange. But being at Number 7 was strange, too, and she must be strong enough to discourage any further impulsiveness.

Latimer left the door wide-open and lit a candle. This he offered to Jenny. The wavering flame cast light and shadow over his face and turned his dark eyes to near black. She settled her fingers on the candleholder, but he didn't release it to her until they had stood there for too long.

"I'll light another in the bedroom, shall I?" he asked, and when she nodded, finally turned away.

Jenny's heart beat hard, almost painfully. She drew a deep breath and realized it was the first in many seconds. *Impulsiveness is dangerous.*

"Let's get a fire going," Latimer said. "Bring the light."

In the bedroom, he took off his coat and tossed it on the bottom of the bed before kneeling to set kindling afire. Jenny stood behind him, holding the candle aloft, watching his capable hands, seeing how his dark hair curled at the nape, stirred by the sight of white linen straining across his big shoulders. She had never seen a gentleman without his coat before, or been alone with one anywhere—least of all in a bedroom.

He might laugh at her thoughts, but she felt vulnerable and liked it, felt an intimacy and liked that, too. But impulsiveness must be avoided.

"There. You will soon be nicely warm."

She was already warm. "Thank ye. I dinna know what I should say t'ye." But she must not behave as if she wasn't worthy of consideration. "Most wouldna care what happened t'someone they'd no responsibility for. Ye're different, Latimer More. Ye've such a goodness of heart. One day I hope I can do something for ye in return."

Latimer turned his face up to hers. "I'm not here because I expect you to repay what little I've done. You owe me nothing."

What did she feel in him? Anger? Or some even more intense emotion? He stood and she felt overwhelmed by him. There had been too many new experiences, too many new sensations, and in too short a time to allow her to get used to any of them.

She smiled at him but he looked away.

"I'll have hot water sent up for you," he told her. "I don't think Sibyl has retired, so I'll tell her you're here and be sure she knows you'll be using some of her things."

"I will not," Jenny said at once. "I've got what I need and tomorrow I'll go home for the rest and take it elsewhere."

"That place is *not* your home," he told her. His mouth set in a straight line and the corners turned down. "You will never return there. Do you understand me?"

"I understand that ye're tryin' t'help, but ye canna make yoursel' responsible for me."

He planted his fists on his hips. "I think I already have."

She would never have imagined that matters between men and woman could be so difficult. "But I haven't given ye the right to tell me what I must do."

"Can you find your way out of this muddle yourself?" How sharp he sounded.

Men. It was always the same. Even when they seemed grown and made you want to hug them for their strength and goodness, they managed to spoil everything by turning into sulky boys. "Latimer," she said, resisting the temptation to use a sharp forefinger on his chest, "when ye talk like that, ye sound overbearin'. Findin' my way out, as ye put it, may be awfu' hard, but I'll do it, just as I've done everything for myself for as long as I remember.''

"You're upsetting yourself." He caught her by the shoulders and backed her into a chair. "Be calm. I know it's the way with women that they're given to these attacks of hysterics, but they can't be good for you."

Jenny bobbed up again. "Hysterics? Who's having hysterics?" When threatened by logic, men needed to save face. She sat once more. "I admit to being greatly tried by my circumstances, but I am no' crying or shrieking. I am no' prostrate or havin' fits. And I'll find my own way out o' my problems because I must. What kind o' human being expects another t'smooth their way?

"In the mornin' I'll away early to Bond Street. In the wee shop where they print books and the like, Skinner and Flynt, they've a board where ye can read of places for rent.''

"I cannot be angry with you. I cannot." Latimer roamed the room. "You may say I have no right to take any responsibility for you, or to tell you what I think you should do, but you're wrong. If I were an overbearing sort of fellow, I'd point out that it's unseemly for a woman to be alone and that in the absence of a male relative—as far as I can tell—I must do what my conscience tells me to do and take care of you. And, miss—'' he braced his weight on the arms of her chair and stared down at her ''—if you remember, in Whitechapel I became involved with that wretch Morley Bucket, whom I consider very dangerous. I saw his treatment of you and the way in which he behaved as if you were his property. My interference with his plan makes me involved in your affairs. Think about it, and you'll agree.

"Evans is a strapping fellow. And he's got a good head on his shoulders. In the morning I shall instruct him to go with Toby and clear your possessions from that place. Since there will be nowhere else to take them, they'll come here, to Number 7, until you are settled.''

''Oooh,'' Jenny threw her arms wide, closed her eyes and let her head fall against the back of her chair. ''Ye are *so* reasonable. Why canna ye make it all easier by tellin' me ye've your own business to attend to and ye don't have more time t'spare for me? Tell me I'm t'go away. Tell me I'm a nuisance. *Get rid of me.* Why canna ye put me out o' my misery and just *do* it?''

''Because I've never been fond of liars and I'm a dashed poor liar myself. I do have my own business to attend to, but I've also got time for you. I want to have time for you.''

He remained where he was, leaning over her, inclining his head to look at her closely.

Jenny shook her head. How did a person argue with the likes of Latimer More? ''I'm sure I'll find a new place easily enough,'' she said. ''And as soon as I can, I'll go to visit whatever looks suitable.''

Latimer sank to his haunches. His neckcloth had slipped undone and in the shadow of evening, his jaw was darkened by his growing beard. He was marvelous. He was the most handsome, charming, and desirable man she'd ever met. Jenny felt unnaturally chilled but at the same time her breasts swelled, or so they felt, and she ached between her legs and into her thighs. It was too bad there'd been no chance for Sibyl's club to take their investigations further. They'd been studying sexual things and there was no doubt but that what Jenny felt now was sexual and caused by Latimer's presence. It could also be that her own willful, worldly mind and body played more of a part that she cared to admit.

Latimer tucked a knuckle beneath her chin and raised

her face—and looked at her mouth again. The sensation inside her became as if the parts that tingled and ached were all joined by a white hot thread.

"Promise me you won't return to Lardy Lane."

"I promise." Her voice sounded far away and she was almost certain Latimer had hypnotized her into submission.

"Promise me you will not run away to be rid of me."

"I don't want t'be rid o' ye." And snappish she sounded…and her tongue was unruly. "I mean, I love my work and I wouldna leave it, and there's Toby to consider, and I will not give up on being my own woman—not for any man."

"So that's why you won't run away? Because of Toby and your work."

"Yes." She began to imagine the feel of his mouth on hers. "And because I'd be sad not t'see ye again." *Impulsive again.*

When he smiled, his eyelids lowered a little. He looked sleepy, the kind of sleepy that made Jenny want to cradle him in her arms and smooth his face—and his body. She shivered. Sibyl had once told her that she'd imagined what Latimer would look like without clothes. That was before she married Sir Hunter, of course. A blush suffused Jenny and she spread a hand over the skin above the neck of her dress. Sibyl had said that Latimer's… That *the* Part was never completely at peace. It was, in fact, always what Sibyl referred to as almost ready.

Jenny was steadfast in ignoring an urge to check Latimer's Part.

"Is there anything else you'd like to share with me, Jenny?"

She'd like to share a great deal but she doubted that what she had in mind counted as an answer to the question. "I've everything, thank ye."

"I wouldn't put it past Lady H to offer to keep young Toby. She'd probably have some supposed duties for him at Number 7, but he'd be comfortable and never want for anything. What would you say to that?"

"I'd say it was wonderful."

"Good, good, I'll know how to answer if she asks me how I think you'd respond to the idea. Are you sure I can't get you anything other than hot water?"

"Quite sure, thank ye."

He cleared his throat. "You didn't eat anything at Lady Hester's."

"Neither did ye."

"No." His mouth remained slightly pushed forward. "But I intend to remedy that now. I could bring food here and we'd share it."

Learning to refuse what you longed to accept was a great trial. "I'm no' hungry, but thank ye." If he'd asked her if she was lonely and might like company, she'd have been even more hard-pressed to refuse.

"If your bed isn't comfortable, or you aren't warm enough, come straight downstairs to me and I'll take care of it."

Jenny looked hard at him and said, "Aye, I'll remember ye said so."

11

Creeping through the house on his way back from the kitchens, Latimer thought over his parting remarks to Jenny several more times, and winced several more times. He'd been able to tell from her expression that she was worldly enough to wonder exactly what he'd meant by telling her to come to him if she needed anything.

He'd eaten cold lamb in the kitchen and intended to get to bed. He wanted to start dealing with his own business first thing in the morning and be in Bond Street watching for Madame Sophie to close her doors for the day. Jenny never left until an hour or more after the shop shut, but he must be certain he didn't miss her.

Voices still came from the guests' sitting room and Latimer grimaced. Of course, some dratted visitor had arrived and said he was...looking for Jenny? Adam had told him, two hours ago, that he and Sibyl would keep the man entertained until Latimer could get there. What could this man possibly want with Jenny? She didn't know anyone— or so she said.

Dragging his feet, he went to the door and listened, attempting to find tolerance and understanding for whoever the poor brute was. Best to begin by thinking the best of a fellow.

"Middle Wallop has long been known as a parish from which great men sprout," a hoarse voice announced.

"That's why I was so enthusiastic about becoming assistant to Vicar Crawly. That was some ten years ago and although one wouldn't wish ill on a soul, particularly so Godly a soul as the vicar, who could have expected him to carry on so vigorously when he was, even then, one-and-ninety?

"I have to do *everything*. Visit all the sick—and, since the ladies of the parish make delectable baskets for me to deliver to each one, there are always many who are sick. And most of them don't offer me so much as a cup of tea. I lead the Parish Council and those who teach Sunday School—to say nothing of actually patrolling the classrooms and trying to remember what doesn't sound quite right. Can't have the little ones getting their parables mixed up, or starting to enjoy Sundays, can we? People who wish personal enlightenment come to me. I try to use those occasions to teach them how one should be hospitable to visitors. Every one of them gets a glass of sherry. Oh, it's not the good plonk. No, no, I give 'em a thimble of the communion pish. They wouldn't know decent sherry if I gave it to them."

Latimer opened the door and went in, overwhelmed with guilt at the thought that his friends had entertained this boor for hours, and only out of consideration for him because they knew he was concerned—more than concerned—for Jenny's fate.

"Good Lord," he murmured with feeling. At first it was impossible to seek out the room's occupants because everywhere he turned his eyes, they were assaulted by red. Brilliant red with a slightly orange tinge. After all, as a man who dealt in art of various kinds, he was astute in matters of color. Red papered walls—a sort of silken red background with scrolls of even deeper red velvet all over it. A vast sideboard of the darkest of mahogany, encrusted

with carvings of fruit, must presumably be intended to hold
an entire buffet if the inmates decided to put on some
revels. Twin mahogany étagères fronted with diamond-
shaped glass and filled with crystal and china flanked the
windows. Where could it all have been before this? Packed
away somewhere, no doubt. Three couches made a square
with the fireplace. Red brocade couches, with mahogany
enhancements, arms, legs, and the like. And the carpet...
Latimer turned his eyes to the ceiling. The carpet was certainly not anything he would import from his impeccable
eastern sources. Whatever her ladyship had paid for this
overthick purplish thing of indistinct pattern had been far
too much! And while he thought about it, who in their
right mind would paint a perfectly marvelous molded ceiling red—and pick out the intertwined circles of fleurs-de-
lis in ashes of roses?

"Good evening to you, sir," the fellow with the husky
voice said.

Latimer turned his head slowly from an upright mahogany piano with a red and tasseled antimacassar draped
along its top. It would have been far more at home in Mr.
Morley Bucket's "finest 'ouse in London."

"You don't look too well, if you don't mind my saying
so," the gab-blower said, so earnestly that Latimer felt
obliged to nod courteously at the corpulent cleric, who
occupied the couch immediately facing the fire.

"I was *right*, man. I usually am. You're ill. Sit down,
sit down at once."

Latimer recollected the glass of hock he still held and
drank a hefty draft. "Ill? Not ill at all, sir. You took me
by surprise is all. But thank you for your concern."

"Name's Lumpit," he was told. "Mr. Larch Lumpit,
curate to the Reverend Crawly at St. Philomena's in Mid-

dle Wallop—'' he waved a hand airily ''—a ways north of London. And you are?''

''Latimer More, importer.'' The soft sound of breathing that reached him from the nearest couch came from Sibyl, who had slipped sideways to a most uncomfortable-looking position, and was asleep. ''I'm originally from Cornwall. My sister Finch and I came here several years ago. Finch is an expert on ancient glass.'' *Stop it. You're catching whatever verbal disease Lumpit has.*

''Most interesting,'' Lumpit said, but already his eyes had drifted from Latimer and settled on some vision of his own.

On the third couch, and most visible to Latimer, sat Adam. Give the man his due, sleeping he might be but he'd managed to remain upright even if his chin was on his chest. Latimer wove a path through the obstacle course of furniture and lowered himself—with a thud—beside his friend. The snuffling and mumbling that followed meant Adam was waking up, and Latimer felt some remorse.

''So, Mr. Lumpit, what brings you to Number 7 at such an hour?''

''I didn't just come, my dear man. I've been here a very long time, hours in fact. Came at seven as I was told…'' Lumpit's round brown eyes shone damply, and showed some confusion. He blinked and said, ''I've come in hopes of meeting a Miss Jenny McBride. Is she known to you?''

Latimer took another swallow of hock. He'd never been much of a drinker, but he needed time to think. ''I know Jenny McBride. I'm sure Lady Lloyd explained to you that Jenny is a friend of hers.''

''No, she didn't.'' Lumpit frowned at Sibyl, then at Adam, and said, ''That man isn't her husband, is he?''

''Ah, no. He's Adam Chillworth. He's an artist. Lady Lloyd is married to Sir Hunter Lloyd, barrister.''

"Then what is she doing keeping such late hours with a man who isn't her husband?" Beneath his cassock, he planted what Toby would probably call, great plates-of-meat, wider apart—a feat Latimer would have thought impossible if he hadn't seen it done. The cassock strained over the man's knees. He coughed, obviously to gain Latimer's attention, and said, "I'm a man of God and above reproach, but still I shouldn't care to be accused of aiding an unsuitable liaison."

"Coot mentioned you were here earlier," Latimer said. "He also said that Lady Lloyd, and Adam, were being so kind as to entertain you while you waited. They are also old friends. We have all been well acquainted for a goodly time."

"Well acquainted?" Lumpit frowned. "But the lady's husband isn't here to chaperon her and you gentlemen think it perfectly suitable to keep company with her— alone?"

There was no point continuing this absurdity, Latimer decided. "Tell me, Your Grace, how do you know Jenny?"

Lumpit's full, shiny face turned puce. He smiled and waved a hand before him in a self-deprecating manner. "Not *Your Grace* of course, Mr....?"

"More."

"Yes, of course. Mr. More. I understand that my manner and deportment could give the impression that I am already a member of the church elite, but alas, that is not yet so. And if my vicar, Reverend Crawly, who is now one hundred and one, continues as he is today, I fear it may be a long time before I become a vicar myself. One can't show self-importance, you know, or vanity. Wouldn't do—even if one was shallow enough to suffer from such sinful tendencies. One must wait until one is called to higher things. At the moment, the highest of callings for me must be looking after Reverend Crawly, lightening his burdens, following his—"

"Quite so," Latimer said with haste. "But Jenny McBride, sir?"

Lumpit leaned ponderously forward and refilled his glass from a decanter of Madeira. This done, he rolled back again and took his time savoring what was certainly not his first taste.

"What brings you to Number 7, Mr. Lumpit?" Latimer grew impatient. He was already disquieted by the arrival of this man in the first place.

"I already told you. Several times. I am given to think that Jenny McBride may spend the night here. If she ever comes, that is. And I wish to make her acquaintance."

How did Lumpit know Jenny might be here, Latimer wondered. "So you know her?"

"Never met her," Lumpit said, and chortled. "But I will. It was Miss Ivy Willow who sent me here. She's a friend of Mrs. Phyllis Smart and her small son—I've never met them—but Mrs. Smart told Miss Willow that Jenny McBride was in these parts and could well turn up here tonight since she doubted she'd be able to stay where she was living. Lady Lloyd was evidently well-acquainted with all three ladies when they gathered here for prayer meetings." Lumpit stopped to blow his nose before continuing. "The Lord moves in mysterious ways, doesn't he, Mr. More? Miss Willow had recently had news of poor Miss McBride's misfortunes from Mrs. Smart, and Miss Willow knew I was in need of a wife!"

Latimer couldn't think of a thing to say and didn't bother until Adam elbowed him. The black spy continued to feign drowsiness. "I'm sure I misunderstand you," Latimer said to Mr. Lumpit, and landed a return poke to the devil at his side. "You can't mean that you intend to ask a young lady, a stranger to you, to become your wife just because she may be between living arrangements, and you *need a wife?*"

"Generosity may become a fault, I know," Lumpit said, checking the light brown hair combed carefully forward over his pink scalp. "But I like to think I make a virtue of it. You are absolutely right in your assessment. I shall take Miss McBride as my wife, to love, honor and obey me, and in return I shall provide her with my championship. She will never again have to worry about where she is to sleep."

Latimer swallowed.

Adam elbowed him again.

"It's possible that Miss McBride could spend the night here," Latimer said, and got another sharp dig in the side for his efforts. "After all, she's a friend of Lady Hester Bingham—who owns this house. But I wouldn't know about these things. You'll be wanting to get to your lodgings, sir. Let me see if I can hail you a hackney."

"But there's the rub." Lumpit squirmed on his couch. "I find myself in an unenviable position, for I've been robbed, you see. No money about me. Not a penny, dear sir. Of course I shall send word to my vicar and he will make sure I get the assistance I need to return home, but that doesn't help me now, does it?" His chins jutted.

Adam ahemed and slapped Latimer's back. "He's got a point there, my friend. There is the rub. Why did you not tell me, *hours* ago, of your plight, sir. I'd have found a bit of blunt to get you by till your own funds arrive."

"I'm not given to borrowing," Lumpit said. He rotated to look behind him at the sideboard and Latimer couldn't help but wonder if he looked for food, or the chamber pot hidden in its cubbyhole. Lumpit scooted around again, bouncing to accomplish the task. "No, Lumpit makes his own way, thank you."

"You just said you can't take a hackney to your lodgings because you don't have any money," Adam sputtered. "What was that if not a request for the fare?"

"It had nothing to do with the fare," Lumpit said. "I was robbed before I could acquire lodgings and pay for them. What's the point of a hackney if you've nowhere to go?"

"Finch would know exactly what to do," Sibyl said, as brightly as if she'd been wide-awake all the time. She winked at Latimer and he almost chuckled aloud. "Finnie leaves a key to Number 8 with you, doesn't she, Latimer?"

He saw the direction of her reasoning and could have kissed her for finding a means to at least buy time before Lumpit could confront poor, dear little Jenny. Once more, she was the blameless victim of a man who would use her. One was a brothel-keeper, one was a curate. Very little difference between the two in this case. They both wanted to use her for their own ends.

"You do have a key to Number 8, Latimer?" Sibyl repeated.

"Er, yes, of course. I look in from time to time. Jennings takes good care of things and there's always a small staff on the premises to keep things up."

"Quite so," Sibyl said. "So, since there is no room for Mr. Lumpit here, he could use a room next door, couldn't he? You don't think Finnie and Ross would object?"

"No. Finnie would take anybody in, you know that." He narrowed his eyes and thought about what he'd said. "Any person of merit, that is."

"Nicely done," Adam said, louder than he should have. "Very well, up with you, Lumpit. Latimer, you get the key. Sibyl, take yourself off to bed before you fall over where you are. Good night to you.''

She stumbled upright and beamed. ''Good night to you, Adam. And good night to you, Latimer.'' She trotted to the door, opened it, and left. But only seconds passed before her head appeared again and she added, ''And good night to you, Your Grace. If Jenny should come here, we'll let you know. But we'll make sure you get home safely to Middle Wallop.''

12

If he did anything to frighten Jenny, she would run away. And he would forever berate himself for a fool. But he was about to take a dangerous gamble. He'd take it because he'd convinced himself of his own restraint.

Now he would find out just how badly he'd deluded himself.

As he'd expected, she hadn't locked 7B. He turned the handle smoothly and slid the door open just enough to allow him to slip inside and close it again.

He stood in the darkness allowing his eyes to adjust.

All he needed to quiet his troubled mind—and heart—was to look at her and be certain she wasn't distressed, that she slept, warm and comfortable, in a bed that was her due.

Hovering, he decided what he would do. A candle must be lit. If luck were on his side, he'd be able to accomplish his desire without waking her, but if she should open her eyes, he could not consider shocking her as a deeper shadow moving among all the others.

A sudden squalling of cats in the kitchen garden stiffened his spine. They moaned and shrieked by turns and he was sure Jenny must wake up at any moment.

He lighted a candle anyway but didn't look around at the pretty blue sitting room that had been Sibyl's. The cats' cries died away to an eerie grumble and faded altogether.

Not a sound came from the bedroom.

With soft tread he approached, holding the candle before him. When he entered the room he smelled at once the soap she must have used to wash, a scent of lilies. Ever more slowly he drew close to the bed and held his breath while he looked at Jenny.

He hadn't thought to ask her age, or even thought of it at all, but in sleep she appeared very young. Yes, she was sleeping deeply, her face relaxed and her hands resting on the white sheet over her breasts.

Relaxed, comfortable and warm, safe. She was all of these and so he could leave.

He put the candle on a chest beside the bed and took great care in carrying a chair to set beside her. How simple it was to know what should be done, but how difficult it could be to obey reason when so much more of a man was involved.

He sat, crossed a calf over the opposite thigh, and jiggled his foot. To be silent and observe when one wanted to move, to feel, to entice a response, was penance enough for any sin he might be committing.

In sleep she was exceedingly pale and her freckles showed plainly. He was most attached to those freckles. Her hair was down but in two thick, shiny braids that rested precisely over her shoulders. She made him smile. She made his intense longings all but unbearable.

She had brought her own things. Ah, yes. Her spirit would not allow her to borrow from Sibyl. Agreeing to spend even one night through charity would haunt her. She wore a childish yellow gown with sleeves that must once have reached her wrists but which now barely covered her elbows. The neck had been freshly bound with yellow satin ribbon that contrived to show off how old and worn the gown was. The same ribbon circled the ends of the sleeves.

He would like to replace her hands with his own.

Latimer closed his eyes and willed all carnal thought away. And failed. He would, if he didn't control himself, try to take her in his arms and make love to her until dawn broke.

"*Latimer!*"

He opened his eyes and saw hers. Sitting up very straight in the bed, Jenny's eyes were wide and frightened. He had done that, he had frightened her, dog that he was. "It's all right, Jenny. Forgive me. I couldn't stay away because I had to know if you were settled and asleep. Now look what I've done, I've awakened you."

She pressed her hands to her cheeks and the covers settled about her hips. The gown had a yoke and was gathered over her breasts, small breasts perhaps, but round and firm and more than enough to fill his hands. A small tear over her heart showed more pure white skin, and a suggestion of a pink nipple.

Latimer shifted in his chair and crossed his legs entirely. She must not see what she could do to him. Like her age, her experience was a mystery to him, but despite the hard life she'd led, he didn't feel anything worldly in her.

He tilted his head and asked, "Have I stolen your tongue? If so, I am very sorry."

"Soon enough ye may wish ye had taken it," she said, but her voice wasn't as strong as her words. "Ye frightened me so badly, my heart's jumpin'."

"I'm sorry, Jenny. I did the wrong thing in coming and now you're angry with me."

"Och, dinna sound so sorry for yoursel'. I'm the one wi' the right to trounce the life out of ye for the badly behaved one ye are. I'd a good mind to wallop ye right now." She threw back the covers and swung slender legs and feet over the side of the mattress. The nightrail didn't reach her calves, a fact she'd evidently forgotten as she planted her hands on her hips and treated him to a fierce glower. "Did ye no' think I'd already been frightened enough for one day? Why did ye come? Sittin' there by the candlelight and lookin' all strange wi' your eyes closed." A choke scraped in her throat. "I thought ye were dead beside me," she said and started to sob quietly.

Aghast, Latimer got to his feet and said, "Jenny, please don't cry. Oh, please, no. What can I do to make you stop? Tell me. I'll do anything."

Her crying only increased and her thin shoulders shook. He glanced at her ankles and feet, then at the rest of her body. Lingering on her flat belly and the outline of a rounded bottom that showed through the gown didn't do a thing to help his increasing arousal. He wanted to comfort her and make love to her at the same time. He was a predator. Only predators considered soothing a desirable creature before leaping upon it to do their will.

He was also more intrigued by her than he'd been by any other woman he'd met. She had courage and a spry mind.

"Jenny." He took her by the shoulders. "Listen to me. I want you back in that bed and calm again. Then you can listen to me for a change."

Mutiny shone through the tears. "What ye want is t'make sure I dinna disgrace ye. Or keep on making ye feel helpless. Men dinna know what t'do when there's tears. Well, I'm no the cryin' sort, so ye can stop worryin' yoursel'."

"Are you going to do as I ask and listen to me? Please?"

"I dinna think I will. No." She sniffed several times and Latimer took out his handkerchief for her. "Thank ye.

I'm just stoppin' my cryin' and I have t'sniff and gather mysel'. There. Ye're safe again.''

The little madam. "My concern is not for my safety. And I assure you I'm a hard man to embarrass. I should like to sit down. I can't if you don't.''

She sat on the side of the bed and swung her feet.

"It's late, Jenny. You should be asleep.''

"Hah!'' She pointed at him. "Ye dare t'rant at me for no' sleepin'? I was until ye decided to sit by me like a corpse at somebody else's wake. Ye know ye had no right t'come in here wi' me in bed like that.''

"I told you I was merely making sure all was well with you.''

She sniffed again and used his handkerchief. Bright moisture still clung along her bottom lids.

He got up, raised the bedcovers, and waited until she slipped her legs inside. Jenny slid down and quickly pulled the covers up to her chin. "I'm rude when I've no right t'be,'' she said. "I am grateful for all ye've done but I think I'm unsettled. There's been so much t'deal with. And there's so much more t'come. I'm comfortable, thank ye. Away t'your bed. Ye need your sleep.''

"I wouldn't get any if I went there.'' Now there was a well-considered remark. "But I'll go, of course.''

He got up but faltered when he started for the door. Looking back at her, he said, "Good night, then, Jenny.''

The sheet covered her mouth now and her "I am verra worried,'' was muffled.

Latimer swung back to her and returned to the bed. "Of course you are. No innocent young lady, no lovely, innocent young lady—all alone in the world—could be expected to feel otherwise than worried. A bounder is on your heels demanding money. You didn't say how much money, did you?''

"No."

When he'd accepted that she didn't intend to tell him the amount, he continued, "He has threatened you. You've told me you have limited time to discharge the debt and I know there is something he wants from you in exchange for canceling the thing. What does he want you to do in exchange?"

Her face crumpled but she didn't make a sound. She turned away from him and wriggled to the other side of the bed.

Now, what had he said wrong?

"I'm making a hash of this. I'd better just go, but we will have to discuss how your affairs are to be handled."

"I'll pay Lady Hester for havin' me tonight. I told her so and she said she didna mind waitin'. I'd be obliged if ye'd remain here the while."

He shifted from foot to foot and caught sight of her little dolls. She'd brought them with her and they stood in a row on the dressing table. He swallowed at the sight of them. Dash it all, he was becoming soft. Dolls, made by a girl who had little of her own, and treasured enough to be taken with her in place of something more practical, actually saddened him. The doll she'd given him, which he was to give to Lady Hester's Birdie, was still in his room.

"Mr. More?"

"Latimer. The next time you call me *Mr. More* I won't be able to answer you. What is it, Jenny?"

"Nothin'. Ye must be verra tired."

Women were not naturally subtle. He smiled. "I'm not tired. I've always been a man who enjoyed the night." Yet another well-considered remark, he thought. "I mean that I think well at night when it's quiet." *The perfect recovery.*

"Sometimes I do, too, only I'm often so tired I can't stay awake."

He could see her reflection in the glass. She held one braid and stared straight ahead at the wall. No particular insight was needed to deduce that Jenny didn't want to be alone. She also didn't want to admit to the slightest weakness.

What to do? He knew what he wanted to do, but that wasn't an option. There were other possibilities that would cheer him, he supposed. Jenny was unlikely to agree to any of those, either.

"Latimer?"

"Yes, Jenny."

"If ye're not about t'go t'bed, could ye sit wi' me again? Just until I go t'sleep? It won't take long."

"My pleasure." *Indeed, very much his pleasure.* Once more he took his place on the chair beside the bed, the far side of the bed from where she now curled on her side with her back to him.

The room became silent.

Latimer attempted to be sent into a trance by candlelight flickering over the walls. Never had been much for trances. There was no sound at all of Jenny's breathing which suggested that she was probably still awake.

That nightrail was too small, and not only in length. Between her shoulder blades, the tapes barely made knots and her back was visible where the opening gaped.

She sighed.

Saint Latimer had a certain ring to it. But he didn't care for the title himself. If he had the chance, how long could he content himself with stroking her through the gown? Fine material between skin and skin could be a powerful stimulus. Thin stuff might be almost like no barrier at all. To caress her from head to toe—and he wouldn't want to miss an inch of her—would be—*torture.* No, no, it would be a rousing incentive to keep his original plan in sight.

There were more obstacles than even he had anticipated, but none he couldn't overcome.

"Latimer?"

"Yes, Jenny?"

"Would ye mind if I talked a wee bit?"

"I'd enjoying listening to you, my dear."

"I doubt it. I've nothing but questions ye can't answer for me, but maybe I'd feel better if I heard them aloud mysel'."

"You probably would. If I can help, I'll tell you."

She sighed again and he thought she sniffed. Why did women have to cry at such moments? So much better to get angry and shout about the injustice of it all.

"I am in a muddle, aren't I?"

Since he had nothing constructive to add to that, he said, "Hmm."

"Well, I am, and although I've the harsh tongue of an old crone, I've not so many years on my shoes that my boldness matches my words."

What a surprise. "I would never call you bold. I would say that you are determined and that is a good thing."

"Thank ye," she said quietly. "I don't even feel determined enough tonight. If ye remind me I said that, I'll deny it."

"Of course you will, so I'll forget you did." He chuckled and resolved not to forget it at all. "This is a most uncomfortable chair." And he was a conniving bastard.

"Oh, it's too bad o' me t'have kept ye in it. Go t'your bed and bless ye for tryin' t'help me."

So far he'd done nothing to help either of them. "I can't possibly leave you. You'd never admit it, but you need me here—or someone who will reassure you that you are not alone. I do suffer with my back from time to time. An old riding injury." At twenty, he'd fallen from a donkey at his father's China Clay mines in Cornwall and pulled something or other in his back which still liked to remind him of the ignominious event.

Jenny tutted. "Ye should be lyin' down when it's givin' ye the fits."

"It's not so bad."

"Ye know I'm right. Men have t'be so strong, even when they're hurtin'."

The fire burned well but he rose and bent over to add coals. And he placed a hand in the middle of his back and uttered a hushed, "Ouch."

"Latimer? Stop with that fire now. Straighten up while ye still can. It's wonderful warm in here."

Taking his time, he did straighten and turn toward her. She'd stayed on the opposite side of the bed, but faced him and gifted him with a dark frown.

"I just can't leave you on a night like this," he told her, then raised his eyebrows and said, "By jove I think I've got it. If you'll think the idea has merit."

Some confusion made that frown even deeper.

"Have you heard of bundling?"

Her mouth fell open.

"I thought you might have because it's certainly in common usage in many parts. Or so I'm told."

"Aye," she said slowly. "I know about bundling. I've never had the need since I've never... Well, I've not been betrothed to a man who'd a need t'share my bed but bridle his passions."

He threaded his hands beneath the tails of his coat, nodded and beamed. "You do know. We have no board to put between us, but with you inside the covers, and me outside the covers, the same decorum will be observed. Don't you agree? I can stretch out. We can talk. And the entire arrangement will be most satisfactory to both of us."

Jenny wrinkled her nose and narrowed her eyes. She raised her chin to look down at the place where he'd indicated he would "stretch out," and secured the covers more tightly about her neck for all the world as if she hadn't been angry enough to stand before him in her revealing nightrail. "I don't think that would be suitable."

We'll make it suitable. "I shall leave as soon as our conversation is over. Trust me, Jenny, I think you will be much more settled if you talk through those matters that are on your mind."

"You do?" she asked.

"I most certainly do."

"And you're sure this is acceptable. I would die if someone here got angry wi' me or thought ill o' me."

"It's acceptable, but there is no way my presence here will ever be known. There are developments I must talk over with you, too." One in particular whose name was Larch Lumpit.

"Verra well, then."

"It would be wise to lock the door, however," he told her, and made haste to do so.

"Are you hungry or thirsty," he asked as he returned.

"I'm not, thank ye all the same."

Latimer sat on the chair to pull off his boots.

"What are ye doin'?"

He jumped and looked up at her. "Taking off my boots. I can hardly put them on a delicate lace coverlet."

"I suppose not," Jenny said.

Next he took off his coat, then undid the buttons on his waistcoat.

"What are ye doin' now?"

There was panic in that question. "Getting comfortable, my dear. Nothing more." And he removed his neckcloth before laying down on his side with his back to her.

"Are ye comfortable now?"

He wasn't. "Perfectly, thank you. Aah." Arching his back slightly, he stretched.

"Where does it pain ye? Here?" A light hand settled on his spine—between his shoulders. "Should I rub it for ye? I used to do that for a lady I knew in Scotland."

"Rubbing would be a great help. The pain is here." With two fingers, he indicated a spot several inches below his waist where he truly did experience pain on occasion—usually when he'd been wrestling with packing crates at the warehouse, although it had happened on certain other occasions.

Jenny was expelling a deep breath. The tips of her fingers settled next to his on his spine. "Here?"

"Exactly. You have the perfect touch, I can tell." What insignificant moments could become salve to a needy man.

Gingerly, she pressed her fingers in to feel the bone. "Does it hurt to do this?"

"Oh, no, it feels...useful."

"Good. Tell me if there's any pain." She alternately marched her fingers upward and pressed deep, and used her knuckles to rub downward again. Her patience and strength amazed him. His erection didn't.

But his body was unruly. His heart beat faster at the thought that hers were the fingers that touched him quite intimately and tried to make him more comfortable. He arched his neck and let his eyes drift shut.

"There could be much t'be said for this bundling," Jenny told him. "It's an innocent way for a man and a women who are only friends—if I may call ye my friend—to be alone together without fear of impropriety."

She was a soft baby creature in the talons of an eagle. "I must point out, Jenny, that what you say of us is absolutely true. It might not be true if you were with some other man. Not that I wish to make you nervous.''

"Och, ye never could. Ye're too honorable. And what ye say is right, I know. How does this feel?''

His buttocks ached and he needed to undo his trousers, but he wouldn't change a thing about the way he felt. ''It feels remarkable. Is there any part of you that might benefit from some attention?''

"Och, no, thank ye. I'm strong and well.''

He thought she had a sturdy constitution, but he didn't know how well she was. There had been too many opportunities to observe the results of too little food for too long.

A most unusual sensation settled on him. Even though Jenny had trouble, he felt at peace with her. And he felt optimistic. Illogical. But perhaps not. He thought of how she looked in the nightrail. As appealing as if she had been dressed in satin and lace—perhaps more so. Innocent, outspoken—in the extreme—and sensual because she was naturally so. Sensual and wholesome. Hah, what a mixture. She was unforgettable.

He'd have to be sure he never had to forget her.

She continued to massage his spine. To gain better leverage, she dug her fingers into his rear and used her thumb to work the tissue.

"Talk to me, Jenny," he said at last. "Let me listen to what concerns you."

"What concerns me? I'm so comfortable, I wish I could pretend this was the way my life is all the time."

If he had his way, it would become so—minus the bundling thing.

"I canna hide from what's bound t'be. Mr. Bucket will want what I owe and as ye reminded me, the days are passin' till he'll tell me my time's run out and I must pay at once.''

Latimer sent up a prayer and said, ''I will pay him for you. And—''

''No.''

''Please let me finish. I will pay him now. And later, when you are able, you may pay me back if you wish. I would prefer that you accept my help as a gift because it would give me so much pleasure.''

''No,'' she repeated. ''Never. I'm indebted to one man. Would it be better for me to be indebted to another instead? I canna accept.''

''And the person you helped, the one who caused you to be in debt. Is there hope that—''

''Ruby barely lives. There's hope her husband will find better employment somewhere up north and send for her and the wee bairn. If that happens, I think she'll try to send me something. I've told her she's no t'worry hersel' about it. It's only thinking of the healthy face on her sweet babe, and her own smiles, that help me to keep the fear away most of the time.''

Very carefully, Latimer turned toward her. He nodded with the seriousness he felt. ''I understand. But I don't understand why you won't let me help you.''

''Because it wouldna be seemly,'' she said. Her face was inches from his and her earnest green eyes shone. ''Just knowin' ye care means so much t'me.''

''Jenny, knowing you at all means so much to me. But I will never stand by and allow Bucket to make you his victim. He has offered to cancel the debt if you do as he asks.''

Her lashes lowered. ''Toby should never ha' talked about that.''

"But you won't do Bucket's bidding. Can't say I blame you. Nasty idea he has."

Not too long passed before she treated him to a wicked grin. "Ye're no' a good spy, Latimer More. Ye're fishin' because Toby doesn't know what Mr. Bucket suggested and neither do you. And I'm not tellin' because it embarrasses me."

Latimer held very still. He'd assumed Bucket had come up with something distasteful but feared it might be more unthinkable than anything he'd dreamed up. "Tell me at once."

"There ye go again. Bein' overbearin'. I'll not tell ye because ye've no need to know."

"Jenny—"

"I promise I'll come t'ye if there's more trouble than I can handle."

She'd said nothing to calm him. "What if there's more trouble and I'm not where you can reach me quickly?"

"Dinna borrow problems, Latimer. First things first. A place to live, and by tomorrow—today now, I suppose."

So matter-of-fact. He had a vision as if he looked down on the two of them from above. There were more than a few fellows who would laugh themselves sick at the idea of Latimer More using bed covers to keep his distance from a desirable female.

"Ye had something to tell me." Jenny said.

Somehow they had moved closer. Brushing curls away from her face took no effort at all. "You've had a difficult time of it, haven't you? For a long time?"

She closed her eyes and he continued to run the backs of his fingers over her hair and the contours of her face.

There was pleasure in just touching her. He felt strong and able to do whatever she might need of him. He felt

protective and possessive—and unsettled by both of those
feelings.

When he smoothed her ear, she didn't show anything
but pleasure, and his fingers, curling against the side of
her neck, made her smile. Tonight he would prove to himself that he was the strong man he thought he was. He
would resist temptation.

"I think ye're tryin' t'put me t'sleep," she said. "I'm
not sure ye'll manage, but I'll enjoy the effort. Now, what
was it ye needed to talk t'me about."

Latimer propped his head on a hand, the better to study
her face, and the fine-boned hand that kept the sheet in
place. "Mr. Larch Lumpit," he said.

"Who?"

"Mr. Larch Lumpit. Curate. Assistant to Reverend
Crawly, Vicar of St. Philomena's in Middle Wallop."

Jenny stared at him. "I dinna know what ye're talkin'
about."

"He's an acquaintance of Ivy Willow. You do remember Ivy?"

"O'course. She was a colorful one. I didna see her after
Sibyl and Sir Hunter's weddin'."

"And you know Phyllis Smart, too."

"Aye. I've seen her only once or twice since Sibyl's
group stopped meetin' but I like her well enough."

Latimer abandoned some caution and rested a palm on
her cheek. His fingers he spread over her hair. "Seems
Phyllis Smart was aware of your difficulties and told Ivy
Willow. Ivy told Mr. Lumpit, who happens to be in need
of a wife."

Jenny put her hand on top of his, but didn't try to remove it from her face. "Latimer, ye're no' makin a lot o'
sense. I may ha' said somethin' t'let Phyllis know my circumstances. And I suppose she could ha' told Ivy. But I

dinna see what any o' that would be to a curate I don't
know. A man who is in some place I've never heard of.''

"Larch Lumpit was told by Ivy that you are in great
need of assistance. Lumpit decided the generous thing to
do would be to invite you away from London and your
troubles, and take you as his wife. He would make sure
you had nothing to worry about but him.'' He almost de-
plored the pleasure he took in painting Lumpit's proposal
for exactly what it was.

Jenny said, ''That's daft. If he writes, I'll no' answer.''
And with that, she ducked her face beneath the covers and
burrowed closer to Latimer. ''Middle Wallop,'' she grumbled indistinctly.

The pressure, even if not very substantial, of her body
wriggling close to his, all but undid Latimer. He put an
arm over her and pulled her as near as was possible in
their current situation. And Jenny nestled and snuggled,
and adjusted herself. Finally she rolled over again and
blithely settled her bottom into his lap.

Latimer parted his lips and stopped breathing. He would
happily stay exactly where he was indefinitely—no, grate-
fully but *unhappily* where he was indefinitely. Since he
still rested his arm across her, Jenny threw away all caution
and laced the fingers of one hand with his. She actually
settled her cheek on top of his fingers. ''Nothing will come
of such silliness,'' she told him. ''What a foolish name,
Larch Lumpit. Makes me think of a shiny, blow-bellied
fellow with a small, red mouth.''

Points would definitely be awarded because he wouldn't
tell her she'd made a fair description of Lumpit.

"He can stay in Under Wallop, or wherever and keep
his *generosity*. Y'know he only wants a maid he need no'
pay.''

"You're probably right," Latimer agreed. "Only he's not in Middle Wallop. He's here in London to look for you. Right now he's asleep next door at Finnie and Ross's house. Number 8 Mayfair Square."

13

Morley Bucket wanted respect from the woman he kept.
Respect, understanding, and sympathy when he needed it,
that's what he had a right to. He could rely on Persimmon
Jolly to get her work done—so to speak—but there were
times when her hoity-toity, get-off-me-eyelash-I-want-to-
wink attitude drove him to the end of his patience.

"Look 'ere, Persimmon, I'm not in the mood for any
of your airs or your games. I'm a man what's oppressed
and I expect consideration from those I've been good to."

"And who would they be, Mr. Bucket?" Persimmon
said. "Give me their names and I'll pass your expectations
along at once."

"Ungrateful 'ussy." The nonsense he put up with from
the woman. "Don't forget who it was what took you when
your fine gentleman was ready to add you to a wager."
Lush, she might be. Desirable, she might be, and clever,
and, well, different. But she was a haughty one, who behaved as if she was doing him a favor whenever she came
to him. She was haughty even while she did things he
doubted many a lady would have dreamed of. And she
was a grasping, spiteful baggage if ever he'd met one, and
the damned rub was that he'd have to play along with her
until he'd finished making the deal for Jenny McBride.
Persimmon was his eyes and ears in a certain camp and it
was time to put her to real work.

She wrinkled her nose, as she usually did, at his big, cozy rooms on the top floor of the house he operated not far from St. Pauls. And a very fine house it was, too. Large and well proportioned, built of white stone, it fitted in with the surrounding grand houses so well that nobody in the neighborhood ever complained—least of all the gentlemen who could slip away from the constraints of connubial bliss, enjoy a bit of real fun, and be home again in no time.

"All this red is so gauche, Mr. Bucket. Not tastefully done at all. The couches. The transparent chiffon screens. All those pillows on the floor as if you planned an orgy. Grapes in red glass, and pink sweetmeats. And *too* many tassels and tufted things. Bad enough to walk through so much crude design on the lower floors—one expects it there—but it quite puts me off up here."

Morley frowned and assessed the room. "It's comfortable," he said defensively. "I 'ad it done for you because you look so good on a bit of red."

Persimmon grew red herself and opened her fan. "I do not look good on a bit of red. Too gaudy. Too obvious. Pale skin like mine needs softer tones. Perhaps the lightest of pinks would be flattering."

The thought of Persimmon's charms spread naked on pale pink did have possibilities. But he had more important things to think about than her big bubbies and rounded thighs.

"I don't like it when we meet here, Mr. Bucket."

"Well, I can't do anything about it tonight, can I? And I've asked you for two years to call me Morley. You're the only woman what I've ever granted the honor to. I'd appreciate it if you'd do me the favor of tryin' to please me."

She smiled broadly, showing off small, perfect white

teeth. "I was hoping we might please each other this evening, Mr. Bucket."

He got the expected little thrill, the wiggle down there. "There isn't anything you say without thinking about it first. You think about how much you can annoy me and it's too bad."

Persimmon raised a hand to smooth her perfectly arranged coiffure. Her dark hair was always beautifully dressed, as she was herself, and her whole toilette was impeccable. Not tall, nevertheless she carried herself so well that she appeared taller than she was. Just the right amount of paint was applied to a smooth face with a small bowed mouth, a pert nose, and eyes the color of violets. Her brows arched just so and her lashes were thick. And then there was her body. Oh my, yes, that body. Persimmon dressed discreetly. Tonight she wore an evening dress of deep blue crepe with stiff satin scrolls around the hem. The gown was high at the neck and showed little skin, but disguising the voluptuous body beneath the tasteful outfit was impossible.

She watched while he examined her, lingering here and lingering there. He wasn't sure how pleased she looked, which was unusual since she invariably preened—with reserve, of course—if a man undressed her with his eyes.

"We've got decisions to make," he told her. "Big ones."

Persimmon put her hands behind her back and moved her hips from side to side, setting the stiff hem of her skirt to swaying in circles.

"This is serious," he told her.

"Excuse me, Mr. Bucket, but didn't you hear me tell you I assumed we'd be pleasing each other this evening?"

"Um. Perhaps I was thinking about other things."

She shook her head and shavings of polished silver sparkled in her hair. "I think you know by now that I don't concentrate well if I have unfulfilled needs."

"Well." He puffed up his cheeks. "Neither do I. I just thought we'd deal with business first."

"Quite so, dear Mr. Bucket. But business comes in various forms. Take off your clothes and get on your hands and knees."

His gut squeezed instantly. She could excite him with a word or a touch, and whatever she had in mind would make him forget he had a care in the world.

"Get on with it," she said, pointing at one of the screens. "I'll go back there and get ready."

Morley shed his coat but didn't take his eyes off her when she went behind the screen. Her gown was the first item of her clothing to appear over the top.

He took off his waistcoat, neckcloth and shirt, sat on a couch and began pulling off his boots.

A white satin petticoat joined the gown, and another. Through the almost sheer red panels in the screen he could see her moving, adjusting some black item.

Being caught with his trousers on could have consequences even he could scarcely withstand. He dropped them to his ankles and stepped out, then took off his hose.

When he'd first met Persimmon, she had been mistress to a gent who, upon losing heavily at the tables, added her to the pot. She had emptied the man's brandy over his head and gone to wrap her arms around Morley's waist. Pressed so close that when he looked down at her he saw her breasts layered against him and all but free of her gown, Persimmon had turned her violet eyes up to his and whispered: "Protect me, sir. I'll be ever so useful to you." And she'd been useful to him ever since. Persimmon had become a prize who satisfied his most demanding and wealthy clients.

He stood warming his bare behind before the fire.

Persimmon strutted from behind the screen, looking at him sideways from time to time but not coming near him. She had on one of those Frenchified corsets, black, and tight enough at the waist to make sure a man could put his hands around it. Her drawers were probably French, too. Made of black silk, they divided in half between her legs from the front to the back of her waist. When she walked he saw glimpses of her white belly, and other things.

Back and forth in front of him she strode. She'd kept on boots with little heels and laces to the middle of her calves. Her black silk hose were held in place with silver garters and embroidered silver roses ran in a straight line up the back of each leg.

"I thought I told you to be on your hands and knees, Mr. Bucket." The camisole she wore beneath the corset spilled over in a frill that left her breasts naked.

Morley swallowed. "That you did, Miss Jolly, that you did. But I think I feel like finding out your punishment for disobedience." Her body was an eyeful, more than an eyeful, and he'd made a pretty penny out of it. But sometimes a man got bored with games that titillated other people.

Persimmon yawned. She dropped to her back on the pile of cushions she'd criticized and propped one booted ankle on the opposite knee—with predictable results. Morely got a box seat view inside those drawers. She wagged her foot up and down and put her hands behind her head.

"C'mon then," he said, and added a chuckle. "Punish me."

"I don't have the energy, Mr. Bucket. Or the inclination."

"Is that so?" He left the fire—unwillingly—and went to stand beside her. "I don't expect lip from you, my girl."

She smiled and stretched her arms over her head. "What do you expect from me, Mr. Bucket? That's what I'd like to know. Loyalty? Hard work? Putting up with having your rich pigeons between my legs?"

He seethed. "You're mine and you know it. I'm very choosy who else gets between your legs. It's only them what need extra incentive to remember Bucket favorable."

"And I work very well for you, don't I? You've never had a dissatisfied customer, have you?"

He stared down at her breasts. They were big ones, especially on so little a woman, but they stood up, firm and round, the nipples a gold color and erect. "Oh, no, love, not a one. And if you don't have no *inclination*, my pet, you'd better get the message to those." He pointed at her breasts.

Persimmon smiled the way she often did, wicked like and only with her eyes. And pinched herself, rolled her teats between the fingers of each hand. "They've got the message, I assure you," she said. "They know what I like, and what I want."

What Morley wanted was to make sure neither of them missed one tiny step of what had to be done while he got Jenny McBride into the hands of her admirer—after Morley had coached her a bit first. There was enough money in the offing there to set a man up for a long time.

"Persimmon," he said softly. He had to be careful because she'd already questioned him about Jenny and seemed suspicious that he had too much personal interest in the girl. "You ought to let me do that for you. I know exactly how."

Her expression became conniving. "Maybe I ought, maybe I ought not. What will I get if I decide I ought?"

She'd get a doing that would leave her begging for more, that's what she'd get. And with his cock up her alley, but not getting her there too fast, she'd be all ears and ready to give him what *he* wanted.

Persimmon was pouting.

"I just 'appen to 'ave something special for you. Came by it real recent."

"What is it?" She moistened her lips and grew still.

"You'll just 'ave to trust me. Never let you down, 'ave I?"

She pushed out her mouth and thought before saying, "No. But with what you've got hanging down there at the moment, Mr. Bucket, this may be the first time."

He almost laughed. She was convinced that one look at her and any man would forget what was on his mind while his pride and joy jumped to attention. If it didn't, she decided it meant he didn't have what it took. Well, she was wrong there because he had what it took all right—whenever he wanted to. "Better see what you can do about it," he told her. After all, there was time to get around to whatever business needed to come up.

"Give me my box," she told him and when he brought it from a table inside the door, she rose onto one elbow and opened the lid. From inside she selected a collection of small items, then waved the box aside.

Morley took advantage of her preoccupation in putting on tight-fitting silk gloves to pull her legs apart and kneel between them. Her furious slapping at him was easily quelled and her wrists trapped against the pillows. He bent over her, but she turned her head aside. "You know I don't do that," she said. "Not with any man."

She wouldn't kiss or be kissed, although he'd been tempted to force her often enough. "Just once," he said, wheedling. "Come on my little bird, don't tell me you wouldn't enjoy my tongue in your mouth."

Persimmon's answer was to struggle against his grip on

her wrists and buck up and down beneath him. He snickered and looked at his privates. The way she was going, there wouldn't be anything *hanging* for some time.

She looked, too, and said, "Let's have a good time, shall we? Unless there's nothing more you'll want from me after I leave here tonight."

Threats were a regular part of her tricks, but he wouldn't push her. He let go of her wrists and she threw a second pair of gloves at him.

Without a word, she took a bag, pulled it over his cock and tied it a bit too tight around the top. He knew what he was to do next and unlaced the corset slowly. He drew laces from their holes and she took him in her gloved hands. A minute and Morley couldn't keep his arse from bobbing about. He got hot and began to sweat. She pulled on him and he jerked after her fingers.

The corset parted at last but he didn't bother to pull it from beneath her. She paused to pull off the chemise, but left the drawers, stockings and boots where they were.

On her belly she piled pieces of the sheerest lace. Two of these she placed over her nipples. "Here you go, then. Make the most of them."

If he could have helped himself, he would have, but he wanted her in his mouth. She chose the lace because she got the most feeling out of it. He pulled with his teeth and barely heard her whimpers. As long as he had the gloves on, he would lift her heavy breasts and push them against his face.

Persimmon giggled and arched her back. He buried his nose in her flesh and nipped her through the lace. The giggle became a thrilled shriek.

Morley opened the lid on her box again and said, "There's something I want to borrow."

She bared her teeth and nodded, and caught hold of his ballocks.

"'Ere," he said, panting, "not so fast or you'll miss something you'll like." He could scarcely believe she was allowing him to lead the proceedings. She liked to hurt him, to make him crawl about and beg. He couldn't think what had got into her.

He found one of her favorite toys, a short-handled whip with four cropped tails, each tied in a knot at the end. It was, she said on the occasions when she used it, all in the wrist. She'd flip the wicked little device back and forth, making the knots pound in quick succession on whatever part of him she chose.

"Look, my lovie." He held the whip aloft. "We both know you like this."

Alarm stifled her giggles. "I'm not made for that. You'd bruise me."

"Not to worry, pet. The bruises won't show." He took a pot of grease from the box, unscrewed the top, and coated his hand and the whip.

She grew still. Then she smiled and shook her head. "You wouldn't."

"Wouldn't I?" Planting one hand on her stomach, he wedged her legs apart with his knees and put the business end of the whip against her. "It's only fair I give you as much pleasure as you give me."

"No!" She wiggled and tried to thrash her legs.

Slowly, never taking his eyes from hers, he turned the whip handle this way and that, working it inside her, the little tails disappearing alongside.

"Oh, oh, oh," she panted. "Oh, oh, yes, Mr. Bucket, yes, yes."

The heightened color in her face excited him, and the way her flushed breasts bounced when she tried to make him work faster. Morley only slowed down to enjoy her every shout, her tossing head and writhing hips.

At last the knots slid into her and when he could go no higher, he rotated the handle. She lifted her legs straight into the air and bumped her bottom on the pillows. He'd already emptied himself once but his rod was already poking at the end of the silk bag again.

"Mr. Bucket," she shouted. "Oh, Mr. Bucket."

She didn't even notice when one of her pieces of lace slid away and he wrapped his tongue around her bared nipple. Persimmon Jolly hated her precious skin touched by the naked hand—or tongue—or anything else.

Sobbing, ecstatic, she gasped for each breath and he marveled at her ability to hold back against her body's reactions.

"Making it last, are we?" he asked her, but knew she didn't hear.

Quite without warning, he stopped twisting the whip inside her.

Persimmon continued to thrash for seconds before she opened her eyes and blinked at him.

"That little red-haired piece is tryin' to double-cross me," he said thoughtfully. "She's got some gent with deep pockets wrapped around her little finger. What d'you make of that?"

"Mr. Bucket?"

"Oh, I know. A right shock it was to me, too. We're goin' to 'ave to take special measures, I can tell you. You'll 'ave to make sure our client don't get wind of it. That'll mean you keep 'im nice and busy and don't let on there's anything that might not be going according to plan. Can you do that?"

Persimmon slapped his face. "Bastard," she said. "You ask me for what you want while I'm like this?"

"Oh, dearie me." He gave the whip some rapid twists and pumped it up and down. "What got into me? Distracted by worry, I suppose. My client already paid an 'andsome advance against getting Jenny McBride. I never expected 'er to find a way out of Lardy Lane till I *rescued* 'er and 'anded 'er over. Can you be sure our customer don't get edgy on account of having to wait longer than expected to get 'er?"

"Yes," she said. "Yes, yes. Don't stop."

This time he didn't. "We've got to get rid of this gent what's got it in mind to 'ave Jenny McBride himself."

With her mouth lolling open, Persimmon heaved her entire body up and down, then gasped when she allowed herself a release. Morley made to withdraw the whip but her hand closed like iron on his. "I'll be ready again in a minute."

Selfish bitch. "Anything you want, darlin'. I've got a plan. Are you listening to me?"

"To every word, you clever man."

"Good." He hooked her legs over his shoulders and contemplated how he would extract his own pleasure when the time came. "You've followed instructions so far? Not a soul knows who our client is?"

"Not a soul. I'm ready again now."

"If anyone finds out and it gets back to 'im, he's got the power to close us down."

"I know. I'm ready."

Morley used the tips of his fingers to spin the whip all the way around. This brought howls of delight from Persimmon and one of her hands to help him do the best possible job.

"I've got a plan. This is what 'as to be done. You hear me?"

Another spasm racked her and she fell lax. "I hear

you." Rivulets of sweat had ruined the perfect paint on
her face. Her body shone wet all over, and Morley thought
she looked more desirable than he'd ever seen her.

He withdrew the whip and she all but purred her satisfaction with his efforts.

"You'll do it again, won't you, Mr. Bucket?"

"Of course I will. Although I'm sure you won't be-
grudge me a turn first."

She peeped up at him from beneath lowered lashes.
"That's what I want, too, you know that."

He didn't know any such thing, but he'd accept what
she said. "You're going to have to steal something valuable."

Persimmon looked at him sharply. "I'm no thief."

"No, of course you aren't," he said and began to enter
her. "But this won't be difficult and it absolutely has to
be done."

"Put your thing all the way in," she told him. "We've
got the whole night ahead of us to have fun with—and to
talk about the other business."

"Yes. Anyway, when I tell you to, you'll take something from our client and we'll use it to get rid of Jenny
McBride's suitor."

"How?"

Restraint was too hard now. Morley threw himself into
the job at hand and Persimmon actually clung to him. She
was different and he wondered why. It couldn't be that she
finally felt something for him? Nah. But she might.

"How, Mr. Bucket?"

"We'll put the item where it'll be found at just the appropriate moment. Then we'll 'have this interferin' bloke
out of the way. They'll throw 'im in jail and I'll get the
rest of the money for Jenny."

His chest and her breasts jostled together. He slid in and

out of Persimmon like a fatty sausage that didn't want to stay in its skin, then didn't want to stay out of its skin.

"Who is this man?" she asked, her voice growing higher once more. "The one who's getting in the way. Don't stop, Mr. Bucket. Harder. Yes, that's it. Harder."

He obliged her to oblige himself.

"Who is he?"

Couldn't hurt for her to know. "Name's Latimer More. Found out he's some sort of importer with plenty of blunt and connections in high—"

"*Latimer More?*"

She didn't just grow still, she pulled away from him and scurried backward on her knees. "Did you say, *Latimer More?*"

"What of it?"

She crossed her hands on her left breast as if to calm her heart, closed her eyes, and shook her head. "You don't know, do you?"

Morley swallowed and held on ruefully to his still-throbbing rod. "What is it I don't know?"

"In some parts Latimer More is a legend. There's never been a woman who denied him."

"You've got the wrong gent." He frowned at her. "Pull yourself together."

"You pull yourself together and start thinking harder. You've got a bigger problem on your hands than you think. That scrawny Jenny McBride must have more to her than the eye can see. And if Latimer More's decided he wants her, she won't be turning away from him, not for anything."

Exhausted and more than a little tetchy, Morley flopped onto his side. "She won't 'ave a choice if he's locked up."

She became thoughtful. "I don't know. I just don't know. There are women who would line up to swear he's as honest as the day is long. Some of them are very important. It wouldn't surprise me if one of them took the blame for him just to gain his favor.''

"Women," Morley said. He was drained and didn't want to listen to Persimmon's dramas.

"Yes, women," she said, and stood up. "They love him. They fight over him. They pay each other to stay away from him. Latimer More is known as The Most Daring Lover in England.''

14

Something was wrong.

Instead of following her usual routine of locking the shop and then leaving the premises from Jenny's workroom, Madame Sophie had come through the Bond Street door and was locking it from the outside.

Latimer dodged between waiting carriages and approached the lady before she could gather up the bag at her feet. She was also going home very early.

"Good afternoon, Madame," he said, and doffed his hat when she saw him. "I don't know if you remember me. Latimer—"

"Of course I remember you, Mr. More." Her raised left brow and the sparkle in her blue eyes suggested that Madame had both a sense of humor and a healthy delight in men.

His own smile was automatic. "Thank you." He should go on his way and return to find Jenny. But what if the workroom had also closed early and she was gone? "Forgive me, but I had hoped to deliver a message from Lady Lloyd to Miss McBride. I don't suppose it would be appropriate since you won't be on the premises."

"It would not be." She had slipped the handles of the bag over her arm. "But Jenny left, ooh, perhaps fifteen minutes ago."

The usual throng traveled the pavements of Bond Street.

Latimer scanned one direction and then the other. Surely Jenny wouldn't have returned to Lardy Lane. By God, anything might have happened to her. He slapped his gloves into one palm and looked over his shoulder at the opposite side of the road. He had to do something...as soon as he decided what it should be.

"Skinner and Flynt is a book bindery, I believe. Do you know it?"

He gave Madame Sophie his whole attention. "I've heard of it." Bless the woman for her insight and delicacy. Jenny had spoken of the place. "Which way would one go to visit the establishment?"

"That way." She gestured to the right and when he started to thank her said, "Of course you're grateful. Don't waste time here," and walked past him to a shining black phaeton, one of the low-slung variety, that any highborn lady would be proud to own.

Casting any thought of dignity aside, he took off his hat and ran in the direction Madame Sophie had indicated. He wove in and out of strolling female shoppers and garish dandies, barely missed upending a costermonger selling lemon water, and almost overshot the very small premises of Skinner and Flynt.

The shop was dingy inside. Latimer went in and heard the steady slide and thump of some equipment barely visible behind high counters. Not a soul came forward to ask what he wanted.

There was no sign of Jenny.

The board she had mentioned was easy enough to spot. Notices, mostly small and handwritten, were scattered there. He didn't have time to read them.

In the street once more, utterly frustrated—and afraid for Jenny—he cast about, knowing that every second counted and that he must have a plan of action. Perhaps the most sensible decision would be to go to Lardy Lane. And if she wasn't there, he'd wait in case she went there after viewing some lodgings.

This was a nightmare. He had no right to insist she do anything, but he should have insisted she accept his protection anyway.

Several boys, respectably dressed but making enough noise to let it be known they were up to no good, raced in circles around a bench. Latimer had to go that way, but he stopped in mid-stride and stepped close to the windows of a gentlemen's tailoring establishment.

The boys were chanting and what he made out was, "Faded clothes, Faded rose, Holes in her shoes, Nothing to lose." Over and over they repeated the silly ditty before he got a plain view of Jenny McBride sitting there, head bowed and twisting a handkerchief in her fingers. A *brave* lad pulled her hat over her eyes, then all the way off. Latimer stepped quickly toward them but the band rushed away before he could do more than land a cuff to the biggest bully's ear as he ran past.

As much as Latimer craved to go to Jenny and take her away from here, she must need a moment to compose herself.

With a turning of his heart, he noticed that the handkerchief she held was the one he had given her. He could see the *L.M.* his sister, Finch, had embroidered on it.

Jenny's bonnet was on the dusty ground. She picked it up and held it in her lap. Not once did she raise her eyes. People walked in front of her and gave curious stares.

Everything had come to this, Jenny thought. She felt like a bird with a broken wing being picked on by the strong ones. The children could treat her the way they had because she was nobody—to anyone but herself. And at this moment she wasn't sure how much spirit she had left.

Dust had turned her brown bonnet gray. Her rose—and how dare they call it faded—had been crushed, but she knew how to make it fresh-looking again. For now, though, she had bigger problems.

A long shadow fell across her and she didn't have to check to make sure it was Latimer standing beside her.

"May I sit with you, Jenny?"

She stood up at once, making much of brushing off her bonnet and replacing it. With a smile, she said, "Latimer, how lovely t'see ye. It's a nice offer ye make but I was only taking a wee rest. I've to go look at some lodgings. There are lots of suitable places."

"Where are they?" Latimer asked. "These *suitable* places—what areas are they in?"

She tilted her face up to his and her stomach made a flip. He held his hat under his arm and his dark hair was ruffled. He was such a man, so full of life. And only that morning she'd awakened with a sense of unreality, just in time to hear the outer door close at Number 7B. She had spent the night with Latimer sleeping beside her on the bed—with the covers between them, of course.

"Jenny, I asked you a question."

Gone were the smiles. He was angry with her.

"Jenny?"

"Oh, several places. I'm sorry, I wasna thinkin' too clearly."

He curled his lips. "I saw the boys. Drat the little wretches' hides. If I hadn't needed to see you more, I'd have rounded them up and taught them a lesson."

Latimer had seen her shamed. She kept her feet close together to hide her shoes beneath her skirts. "Children have high spirits. Sometimes they're no' well directed."

"That's as may be. I'll accompany you to these suitable places you intend to visit."

No, he mustna persist. "Thank ye very much but I'd best go alone." She started walking fast.

Latimer kept pace without as much as lengthening his stride. "And why, miss, should it be best for you to go alone?"

She crossed the road. The sun had brought out flies that pestered patiently waiting horses. Groups of young men with nothing to do but annoy others, took pleasure in planting their walking sticks on the skirt hems of any unfortunate young woman who was alone and got too close. There was movement and sound everywhere. Laughter vied with the shouts of costermongers, and voices raised in argument.

By the time Jenny was on the opposite pavement, Latimer was with her again. "I won't allow you to go alone," he said, his tone annoyingly even.

"Ye canna stop me," she told him, and planted her feet. "Verra well, I'll have t'be completely honest. I dinna want ye wi' me. I prefer to attend to my business on my own. I'm no a wee child."

"I never said you were. I know you're eight-and-twenty."

"Three-and-twenty," Jenny said and shook her head. "That was a mean way to ask a lady's age, not that ye ever should do such a thing. I've a good mind to ask how old ye are." She didn't care.

"Very old," he said, and brushed something from her bonnet. "Ancient, in fact. I won't see thirty again. And I'm a dangerous fellow. Ask anyone and they'll tell you. My reputation is appalling."

He had a bit of the rogue about him and his expression showed how much he liked funning. "Aye, I've no doubt.

Now, I've got t'be on my way. I'm glad of your concern, but please don't detain me longer or I'll be wi'out a place for the night." She almost smacked a hand over her mouth. She was a foolish lass sometimes.

"Promise me something and I'll let you go," Latimer said. "Promise me you will not go to Lardy Lane, that if you should see Morley Bucket you will refuse to speak to him, and that whether or not you find a place today, you will return to Mayfair Square to let me know. After all, you have possessions there."

That she did. "Ye asked three promises, but I'm feelin' generous toward ye so I'll say yes to all o'them. Goodbye, Latimer."

He bowed and she sped away, trying to lose herself in the crowd. At the first corner she looked over her shoulder. At first she didn't see Latimer and felt relieved and sad at the same time. But there he was after all. His hair and the top of his face were visible over those around him. He was coming her way and she had no doubt but that he was following her—even if he was attempting a nonchalant saunter.

Jenny wasn't so tall but she ducked down as low as she could and scurried on until she reached an abrupt left turn into a lane. Regret it she might, but she made the turn and rushed on, lifting her skirts and running. To her right were the backs of houses that looked decent enough. To her left a curving, gray stone wall stretched a long way. There wasn't as much as a cubbyhole to hide a body.

She came to a row of windows in the stone wall, tall, arched windows with grimy colored glass in them. Next there were two long steps into a church vestibule. Jenny took the steps and stood before a heavy black door studded with brass. A signboard on the left wall of the vestibule announced: St. Cedric in the Lane, and listed times of masses. She expected the door to be locked, but when she put her whole weight into pulling on the handle, it creaked open and she tiptoed inside.

This would be a Catholic Church. The orphanage in Edinburgh had been run by good women, but there'd been no time to nurture the children's spirits so Jenny's experience of churches was nearly nonexistent.

Staying on her toes she made her way down one of three aisles. The place was smaller than she would have expected, but she liked the altar, which was raised at one end and faced the rows of wooden benches. Candles flickered there, and in sconces on walls and pillars. A big cross with Jesus on it hung on the wall behind the altar.

It all made her sad, but she did like it there. Her thin-soled shoes made sounds that whispered upward like the scratchings of mouse feet on the flagstones.

Something she'd never smelled before wrinkled her nose, but she decided it was a holy smell. There wasn't another soul there and, despite the candles, it was quite dark.

The outer door opened and closed. Jenny heard a man's clattering footsteps but couldn't see who had come in. If Latimer found her here he'd know she'd lied when she spoke of having places to visit.

She could hide under a bench, but if he spied her, she'd die of shame. Beside her stood a tiny wooden shed. Well, it couldn't be a shed but it had two doors. Probably places for people to go inside and pray alone.

Jenny opened the nearest door and peered in. She'd been right. The space was big enough for one large person at the most and had a seat built along one wall with a lower piece of wood for kneeling on the opposite wall.

In she went and sat in absolute darkness on the hard seat. The footsteps had stopped. Jenny clasped her hands before her and closed her eyes. It shouldn't be possible for a woman to irritate herself yet she did. First she had cast about for a hiding place because she didn't want Latimer to find her. Now it seemed he'd left the church and she felt like crying for the loss of him.

She would pray. She could do that well enough. Sincere words sent to Jesus were heard. The ladies of the orphanage had told her so and she'd trusted them because they were as kind as they had time to be.

Please, she prayed inside her head, *help me find lodgings where I'll be happy. I promise I'll repay Mr. Bucket his money as I can.*

There now, that was well enough put. But she should thank Jesus for something, she thought. *Thank ye for letting me know Latimer, even if only for a wee while. Please keep him safe.*

Now those, she decided, were good prayers.

A noise came from the church. It sounded like a pile of books toppling over. She listened carefully but didn't hear anything being picked up. A footstep came, then another, and another, and another. The clip, clip of a man's heels. Her heart thundered and she pressed a fist to her breast.

Latimer wanted only the best for her. She should be honest with him. Honest, but firm. She ought to say, no, she hadn't any places to look at yet, but she'd find some and intended to set off at once. And she might assure him that, yes, she'd keep her promise and report back to Number 7. He hadn't thought to specify a time when she must be there, so if it wasn't until tomorrow or the next day, she'd still not have told a fib. Meanwhile she knew what she would do. Until darkness fell, she would hunt for places to rent. If she had no luck by then, she'd use her key to enter her workroom at Madame Sophie's. She could sleep there and be up very early in the morning to freshen herself in good time for work.

Latimer's heels clacked against the stones several more times.

If she'd asked Madame for permission to sleep in Bond Street, she would probably have given it. Deceit was the same as lying and Madame deserved better than that.

Perhaps just one more night at Number 7?

She bobbed up and opened the door. "Latimer. I'm here and I beg your forgiveness for bein' such a widgeon."

Out of the shadows, he came, and put a hand over her mouth while he pushed her back into the little room. "No need to apologize, Jenny. I'd forgive you anything."

Not Latimer, but Mr. Morley Bucket squeezed in with her and sat holding her tightly on his lap. "I never expected this little windfall," he whispered into her ear. "I'm keeping my 'and where it is. Your beloved Latimer was at the end of the lane, but 'e was looking the wrong way when I slipped by the back of 'im. If you was out of sight by the time 'e turned back—if 'e turned back—my back would be all 'e saw and 'e don't know me well enough to recognize me. That's the way it all goes if my fate's smilin'. If it isn't, 'e could be around these parts. If you don't want 'im to come to a sticky end, keep quiet."

Jenny tried to speak but Mr. Bucket ground her lips against her teeth. "Do what I told you and you could make things ever so much easier. You might say you could save someone what's dear to you a lot of trouble. And after the coast's clear, you and me will go somewhere nice and private where we can 'ave a cozy discussion."

Psst. Spivey here.

I don't know about you, but that nasty shock may have taken years off my afterlife. And I swear (my hand is up-

*raised and don't forget I'm in Angel School) I had nothing
to do with that dreadful man creeping up on Miss McBride
like that.*

*What a dilemma. Latimer may not come here at all, in
fact it doesn't appear that he will. I don't want the girl at
Number 7, and that slack-bellied Bucket person could easily be the answer to my...no, no, I will not use the word
here and in this context. The beastly Bucket could take
Jenny McBride away and make sure she's never seen in
Mayfair Square again.*

*But can I allow such a thing to happen to one so pa-
thetically disadvantaged? What would Meg and Sibyl
Smiles' dear departed father do in my position? Foolish
question. The Reverend Smiles would bring about some
showy rescue complete with trumpets for the good one,
and opening the flame-spitting doors to—you know what—
for the other. I must consider this carefully.*

To do or not to do? that is the question.

*Gad, that was an inspired comment if I do say so myself.
I may offer it to Shakespeare. He could use some new lines.*

15

A woman, even a diminutive woman, couldn't simply disappear. Yet one moment Jenny had been there, scurrying along, making a poor job of trying to outdistance him, and the next moment—poof—gone.

Latimer had raced all the way to Piccadilly and now retraced his steps along Bond Street. Damn it all, how could he have let her get away? The crowd had thinned. The shops were all closing and the workers going home. He leaned against a wall at the opening to a lane and breathed into a fist. He didn't believe Jenny had promising lodgings she was off to see. If so, why had she sat on that bench looking so desolate?

A piece of silk the color of marmalade fluttered to the pavement beside his feet. He stooped to pick it up, then ran it between his fingers. His breath caught in his chest. What cruel fortune. This could only be from the rose on Jenny's bonnet and must have fallen as she ran because the bullies had damaged the flower with their tricks.

He put the petal in his pocket, and saw another floating like a feather in the light of a glowing sunset, twirling, rocking and coming to rest at last in exactly the same spot where the first had landed. Once more he caught it up, but this time he had seen where it came from and he strode into the lane, searching ahead as he went. The rose petals had come from this lane, which meant that, at the very least, Jenny had passed this way.

The backs of houses lined one side of the lane. A high stone wall curved gradually away on the other side. He wasn't sure what might lie behind the wall. Now he remembered looking in this direction before. There'd been someone in the passageway—a man, not Jenny.

This was a fool's errand if ever there'd been one. A desperate man reading pieces of silk as ladies might read tea leaves at the bottoms of their cups.

With a sinking heart, he turned back—and saw another petal caught in a honeysuckle bush by the back gate of one of the houses.

He was losing his mind. Snatching the latest petal, he turned around again and marched along the lane. There was nothing to be lost by searching it to the end. After all, he had no idea where else to look for Jenny.

Following the curve of the wall he saw what hadn't been evident before, a row of windows with stained glass almost obscured by grime. The windows of a church built between the establishments on Bond Street and whatever lined the street at the opposite end of the lane. He came to steps leading into a deep vestibule where a painted board stated that he was on the threshold of St. Cedric in the Lane.

Jenny would have no reason to spend time in a church when she was racing against the waning day to find a new home. Even the thought made him desperate—and furious. She belonged with him. As yet she didn't know exactly the nature of her future because it wouldn't be seemly to rush at a woman and inform her she was to be his wife— not without some courting first. In the meantime her place was in the midst of friends at Number 7 and enjoying the comfort of 7B in particular.

He was not a boor. Miss Jenny McBride would be appropriately courted and won. She liked him. He'd seen it in her eyes—and felt it in her kisses. There was still the matter of tempering his ardor, which was not suitable for a tender creature who had not been exposed to carnal matters.

Why, just to think of her meek sanction of him on her bed the previous evening might be a laughing matter, if it were not so dear—and reassuring. It would fall to him to initiate her into the ways of the world and he'd do it with pleasure. Perhaps she might even prove more passionate than he assumed her to be…but he must not hope for that. Her sweetness in his arms, her acceptance of him into her body, her willingness to bear his children, those were the treasures he sought.

But for now he had nothing of her and could not be sure when he would catch up with her. Catch up with her he would, though.

A heavy, studded door barred the way to the church. Locked, no doubt.

He took the two steps and went closer. A scrap of orange silk had caught between the door and its jamb.

This was amazing, almost as if she had left a paper trail.

Very well, he would explore further. The door creaked and squealed as he pulled it open. Inside, candles glowed on an altar and around the church, but there was still too little light to see clearly.

Slowly he walked the length of the first aisle, all the way to the front of the church where pristine white linen cloaked the altar. To the left, draperies hung over two doors in the back wall and Latimer explored each one. Both were locked. On one door was a discreet sign to inform visitors that they had found the rectory where Father Aflak lived. There was a bell, but Latimer had no intention of ringing it.

He toured the other two aisles, stopping to replace a heap of fallen books in a pile at the end of a pew. Thread-bare needlepoint kneelers and pathetically worn hymnals spoke to the poverty of the parish.

There was no doubt that the pieces of silk had come from Jenny's rose, but Latimer didn't believe she'd actually entered this church. In despair, he took the center aisle once more, then the side aisle that led to the door.

When he reached the back of the pews, he knelt for a moment and prayed, "Keep your child safe and bring her back to me. Amen." Resting his brow on his laced fingers, he contemplated an image of Jenny behind his closed eyelids.

Against the side wall, not more than a few feet from him, was a confessional. This surprised him since he understood there were so few in use as yet. There must be some very forward thinking parishioners at St. Cedric's. He got up. The polished wood of the confessional creaked and the noise stopped Latimer. He stared hard at it, but discarded any thought that Jenny would hide inside. She'd be terrified in there.

Perhaps his first instinct was right and he should wait in Lardy Lane. Of course, he ought to believe the promises Jenny had made and expect her in Mayfair Square to report on her efforts.

He raised his head, straightened his shoulders and walked toward the door.

A smooth, soft thing blew against his right eye. He knew what it was before he peeled the petal away. If he believed in such nonsense, he'd say something otherworldly was trying to get a message to him and the message was that Jenny was very close. And he was being begged not to give up and leave.

One hesitant step after another, he walked a short distance along the same aisle again. Someone or something squealed. He stared at the confessional again and would have sworn it rocked the slightest amount. Narrowing his eyes, he approached until he was immediately outside the doors. Not a sound was to be heard. No matter, he would check inside anyway.

Latimer threw open the left door.

He just made out Bucket sitting with Jenny on his lap. The man had a hand clamped over her mouth and was forcing her head against his shoulder. Her eyes pleaded with Latimer.

"Interfere, and she'll suffer," Bucket set. "Take off, you interferin' blighter."

Latimer made his answer short and to the point. He grabbed Bucket's nose and twisted. The man moaned and released Jenny in favor of grappling with Latimer's hold on him.

"Move aside, Jenny," Latimer said. "Our friend will be leaving. Kindly sit in here until I come for you." He didn't want her wandering around, or observing whatever transpired between himself and Morley Bucket.

He hauled the man out by his nose and an ear, spun him around and jerked his arms behind his back. The fellow seemed disposed to complain so Latimer forced his arms higher and said, "All you've got to do is behave yourself, follow orders to the letter, and perhaps things will go easier for you. Cross me again and the story will be different."

"Fool," Bucket said. "Just because you've a reputation with the ladies doesn't make you so important you're outside the law."

Either Bucket had remembered seeing him before, or he'd made enquiries. "What does the law have to do with it?" Latimer asked. "Are you suggesting I should turn you in for molesting a young woman?"

"You may 'ave the upper 'and tonight," Bucket said. "But you'll get what's comin' to you and I'll be there enjoyin' every minute of·your misery."

"Oh, really. Well, we shall just have to see about that." He marched him on, deliberately stepping on his heels until Bucket howled with pain. "I'm offering you a chance to escape into this great Town. Relief is within your grasp. All you have to do is give me your word that you'll stay away from Jenny. She hasn't done anything to you."

"That's what you think," Bucket said and struggled fiercely. "She knows I got plans for 'er. She agreed they was fair on account of she owes me money."

"Ah, yes. She owes you money because she helped a friend in deep trouble."

"I'm a businessman," Bucket whined. "If I listen to every bleedin' heart story what comes my way, I'll be on the street in no time."

"And you have plans for Jenny." Latimer shoved Bucket to his knees and pressed his head down until his forehead met cold stone. "What plans?"

"Wouldn't you like t'know? Well it's business. *My* business. And I'm not tellin' you anything about it."

Latimer tired of this pointless prattle. He hauled Bucket to his feet again and pushed him to the door. "Stay away. You understand?"

"I understand what you want for yourself, More. Wouldn't 'ave thought she was your type."

"So you don't want to go free? You want me to make sure you end up somewhere you won't like, where your every move will be watched? And all because you want to own Jenny. You are a lecher, sir, a lecher without a conscience. You mean to steal away her innocence, then use her for some devious plan."

Bucket tried to straighten his rounded shoulders.

"P'raps I 'ave been a bit hasty. You've got to remember 'ow often I gets taken for granted, and cheated. I'm just a poor man tryin' to make an honest livin'. But for you, I'll try to put what 'appened with Jenny behind me. She's a disappointment, I can tell you, but I'm goin' to let bygones be bygones."

And, Latimer thought, *he* would shortly be crowned King of England. "Very well," he said, opening the door and dragging the man down the steps to the lane. "Lose yourself. If I see your face again, I shall do my duty and make it look different."

A shove, and Morley Bucket stumbled to the ground. "Are you going to bother us again?" Latimer asked.

"Oh, no, sir. Not me. It never was my intention y'know. Things got out of 'and. I'll be on my way now, and good luck to you."

Bucket employed a rapid, limping gate to go toward whatever lay at the far end of the lane from Bond Street. He actually turned back once to sweep off his hat and offer an exaggerated bow.

Latimer re-entered the church.

The petals disquieted him. They had been a sign that led him to Jenny. Without them, he would not have come here. Their appearance had not been by any usual means.

He hastened to open the door to the confessional. Inside, Jenny sat scrunched at one end of the seat. When she looked at him he could tell she'd been afraid that something would go wrong and Bucket would be the one to come for her.

"Hush," he said at the sight of her tearful eyes and shaking body. "It's all right. He's gone and you're with me now."

She began to cry softly.

Latimer leaned in and kissed her forehead.

Jenny moved so fast he had no time to prepare himself for the onslaught. One of her arms shot around his neck and she pulled his face down to hers. She kissed him, actually took the initiative to press her lips to his while she uttered little sobbing moans.

With a strength that amazed him, Jenny pulled him all the way into the confessional. He overbalanced and fell to sit on the bench. Squeezed tight beside him, Jenny held his arm with both hands and buried her face in his shoulder. Her fear overwhelmed and angered him. She didn't deserve such callous treatment. In fact, every one she met should want to make her way peaceful and happy.

He ran the backs of his fingers across her cheek and ear. "Dear Jenny, you aren't yourself. Please let me take you back to Number 7. Lady Hester already told me she hopes you will return tonight. You should go to bed at once."

"Only if ye'll come wi' me."

This one needed to be saved from herself. "I'm sure you don't mean that. Not exactly."

"I *do* mean it." She touched his face. "It's a close fit in here, but I don't want to go out there yet."

There were times when sacrifices must be made. "Should you like to sit on my lap? It would make more room."

Promptly Jenny accepted his suggestion. "Thank ye," she said, getting settled. "I know I shouldna mention it or ask ye t'do it again, but I've never slept so well, or felt so safe as I did wi' ye last night."

"Hmm." He hadn't slept well at all. Even with the covers separating them, Jenny had curled close enough to keep him aroused and staring at the ceiling—and hot enough to wish he could strip. It had been said of him that he was always partly aroused. He'd listened women whisper about it in places he preferred to relegate to his past. They were partly right.

He groaned at the thought and she put her face close to his. "Did he hurt ye out there?" she asked. "Your poor back? Are ye sufferin'?"

"No." *Yes.* "I was just thinking about last night."

"Ye would be," she told him. "I'm a thoughtless one. Ye must have been cold but tonight ye'll be the one t'wear your nightshirt and get between the sheets."

Laughing would be a poor idea. "And you will be outside the covers. Am I right?"

She ran her fingertips over his face as if she were memorizing it. "Aye, ye're right."

"We'll make sure you're very comfortable." But he wouldn't be with her because he'd already tested his restraint to its limits. "We ought to go now."

"I dinna think I can yet," she said and sighed. "I've had a bad turn and I'm gatherin' my strength again."

If she wanted to remain in an out-of-the-way church, in a confessional, on his lap and pressed to him, how could he refuse? He patted her back.

"It's so peaceful here, Latimer. And so...well, *cozy* for want o' a better word. There's none who know we're here."

Except Morley Bucket. "You have nothing to fear with me," he told her.

She settled her bottom more comfortably, but didn't increase his own comfort one whit. "There's a lot said about men—among women, I mean. Ye wouldna believe some o' the nonsense. It has t'be forgiven because there's many who are ignorant o' the truth. Oh, there are the Mr. Buckets of the world, but it'd be wrong to judge all men by him. A woman had only t'meet ye t'know how pure a man can be. Ye've a pure heart and soul and not a wicked thought in ye.''

This was a cruel joke. On him. If he valued his sanity, he'd best find a way to shed the wings she'd awarded him, slowly of course. "I'm sure my heart is gray beside your white one.'' Softly he placed his hand on her left breast. "I can only imagine what goodness beats there.'' Her coat lessened the intimacy of his action, but not the audacity under the circumstances.

She didn't say a word, but neither did she remove his hand. Probably because she was too shocked to move.

He squeezed a little. "I feel the beating.'' And he felt a firm breast he'd rather touch without clothing in the way.

Jenny still didn't speak, but she nestled her face into his neck and sighed.

Latimer rubbed a little. "You didn't really have prospective lodgings to visit, did you, Jenny?''

She brushed her lips across his neck!

What had he done? How would he negotiate this courtship he intended to have without unsettling the delicate balance it required? And without driving himself to *madness?* "Answer my question, please.''

"No,'' she said. "Nothing sounded right and they all cost so much.''

"As I thought. You are in need of a suitable home where you can take your time finding a new place—if you insist on moving again.''

Undoing the buttons on her pelisse was inevitable. He slipped his hand inside and replaced it on top of her dress. Made of muslin, the bodice he encountered was tight and buttoned down the front, and cut low enough to expose a soft swell of flesh above the neckline. Latimer seriously worried she might feel his reaction beneath her. He would take comfort in the probability that she wouldn't take particular notice, or understand what had happened if she did.

When she spoke again, her voice was breathy. "I think perhaps I should go to a friend for a few days."

"Who would that friend be?" He was going too fast with her and causing her to retreat from him. Reluctantly he removed his hand.

Jenny caught his wrist and replaced his fingers where they had been with enough enthusiasm to strain the neck of her dress and ensure that what he held was barely covered. "Jenny," he whispered into her ear, and kissed her neck. "Perhaps we should undo these buttons to make sure they don't break off." And while her chest rose and fell with each short breath, Latimer touched his lips to her bosom while he slipped buttons from their holes.

Either she would be too shocked to say or do anything, or her outrage would drive her to berate him and speak of her honor—or she might not realize there was anything untoward in an experience that could bring her pleasure without danger. Without immediate danger.

"Jenny, who is this friend you might go to?" He cupped her naked breast and fought for his own breath then.

"Oh, Latimer." Her back arched.

Latimer responded to what he felt was a request and eased her sleeves down, drawing the bodice with them. The lightest brush of his palms over her nipples hardened them. He bowed his head, but thought better of taking one of them into his mouth.

"Oh, *Latimer.*" She leaned so far back he had to support her with one arm. Fortunately she was small enough to make it easy to wrap that arm all the way around her and beneath her arm. One wouldn't want to neglect anything.

In the near darkness, he saw the arch of her neck, the

way she kept her arms tightly at her sides—and the thrust of her high, round breasts. She might need fattening up a bit, but he found every aspect of her desirable, irresistible in fact.

Despite his best efforts…all right, so he hadn't made determined efforts to avoid intimacy. How extraordinary her smooth skin felt. In his hands, her breasts had weight and resiliency—and touching her like this wasn't enough.

He opened his mouth over a nipple and played his tongue across the tip. Her cry wasn't one of dismay. For a moment he lifted his mouth and drew diminishing circles with his fingers, made them smaller and smaller and, finally, took the bud between his teeth to nip.

She pressed herself harder against his face, and caught at his hair. His rod ached with need. His goal must be to make certain she suffered no remorse for this. Remorse would only lead to her drawing away from him. Jenny brought her other breast to his lips, and she felt her way inside his coat and under the bottom of his waistcoat. He managed to undo the latter with one hand. Jenny followed quickly by unbuttoning his shirt and drawing it open. She stroked his skin and reached up to plant her own kisses there. Then she managed to astound him by pressing her bared breasts to his chest. If she'd been a cat, she would have purred her pleasure. As it was, the sound she made wasn't so different.

Heaven and potential hell, rolled together. Only heaven where their skin rolled together. Forget everything else, he willed himself. "Jenny," he murmured. "You are so lovely."

"So are ye."

He grinned. "You have perfect breasts."

"Shh. Ye mustna speak such things aloud."

She made him feel very young. He reached down to

capture one trim ankle. "No one hears us here. You have such nice ankles—and calves. Smooth skin. And I like your knees, and the feel of your flesh on the inside here." His hand was between her thighs. "Ah, yes, this is particularly delectable."

"*Latimer.*"

He supposed that was a protest, but not one to be taken seriously, not unless she demanded that he stop.

"You are finely made, Jenny McBride." To demonstrate his meaning, he cupped her bottom. "Beautiful. Desirable. And you are the sweetest one, my dear. You deserve to have someone to enjoy, someone who also enjoys you."

"I feel so much. I feel everythin' and some o' it tingles, or aches. I'm confused by it all, Latimer. I've no' experienced anythin' like it. I like touching you, too." She raised up enough to kiss his chest again.

Every move she made played more havoc with his most unruly part, not that he wasn't enjoying the sensation.

"A good ache, I think," he told her and returned to stroking the insides of her thighs. Inch by inch he stroked higher until he encountered hair and found it damp. He grimaced in triumph. At least she didn't find the whole business of sex unspeakable, not if her body were to be believed.

He entered the hair with a knuckle and parted her very slightly.

Jenny started and held on to him by his shirt. "That's— well, it's most stimulatin'." She parted her legs herself, no doubt to give him more room. "D'ye know how this feels?"

"How does it feel?" One lesson at a time. He wasn't prepared to talk about his own responses at such times.

"It feels better than anything."

Latimer massaged her, gently, slowly. Haste was a mistake made by too many. He nuzzled her breasts, pulled her skirts above her knees and held them apart with one of his legs.

When he touched the center of her swollen parts she threw her arms over her head and her hips bounced. He was ready for the frustration that awaited him, but he would do this anyway because he wanted to enjoy her pleasure. If it was meant to be, his own would come later.

Jenny's release shuddered through her and she continued to shift her hips back and forth with the waning waves of her climax. She mumbled incoherently. His hand she kept clamped between her legs which she squeezed tight together.

He let her grow calmer before he lifted her to sit again and wrapped her in an embrace that might be too tight. He needed to hold her like that while he tried to compose himself.

"Was that so verra wrong t'do?" she asked him.

"Not really. Men and women find ways to pleasure each other without stepping over the line." Most would question if his actions fell on the appropriate side of that line. "It's natural."

"Why did ye do it?"

How like a woman not to know when to leave well enough alone. "I wanted you to feel close to me. And to feel close to you myself. A kind of close bonding to prove we are drawn to each other."

"Well," she said. "We proved that, anyway. But I feel so strange. Won't it be difficult not to think o' this every time I see ye?"

He did hope so. "Why difficult? Pleasant things are good to think about." Need tightened his belly. He could scarcely stop himself from driving his hips upward beneath hers. "Now, will you answer my question at last? Who is the friend you think to go to?"

She turned her face away and Latimer kissed her breasts again.

"If it would please ye," she said, "I'd let ye repeat what ye did before."

"Thank you, my dear but I couldn't force myself on you again, not so soon. Who is your *friend*, Jenny?"

"There isna one. There, does it please ye to have me admit I don't have even one good friend I can go to?"

"It does not. But then, it's not true. You have me and I am an excellent friend who will most certainly give you a home. So there you have it. Things are not so glum."

She sat upright and began scrambling with her clothes. "Oh dear," she said. "It canna be good t'do such things in a church."

Latimer thought about that and felt uncomfortable himself. "Why do you think that?"

"You *know*. It was sexual. I'm not so green I dinna know that. Awfu' nice, but sexual. D'ye think God's angry wi' us?"

"Only if our hearts are impure," he said, wishing he'd had the foresight to save her from such worries. "Your heart could never be impure, and neither was mine." In fact, he was right, by jove. "However, just in case a touch of impurity should ever spring between us, we'll choose where we're together more carefully in future."

"Oh, Latimer," she whispered. "Do you think we'll do those things again?"

"I suppose we might… Shh." Someone was walking through the church.

Jenny clutched him, but quickly let go and buttoned her bodice.

Latimer dealt with his own clothes more slowly, all the while concentrating on what he was hearing.

"It canna be Mr. Bucket, can it?"

Holding her close with one arm, he finished fastening his shirt and waistcoat.

"Well, can it, Latimer?"

"I don't know." He'd never had an opportunity to take particular note of how Bucket's boots sounded. "Be still and quiet."

The steps grew closer and whoever came cleared his throat, then coughed.

"It's no' him," Jenny said. She patted his cheek reassuringly. "Dinna fear."

Latimer caught her hand and kissed the palm, never shifting the center of his concentration from what was happening in the church itself.

He could have sworn the fellow picked up a book and leafed through pages. He'd have to be blessed with extraordinary eyesight to read in that gloom.

Then, and there was no question about it, the door to the adjoining cubicle opened and closed.

"It's someone come t'pray," Jenny murmured.

Latimer's knowledge of the Catholic Church and its practices was sketchy. In fact he knew almost nothing about it. "Then we shall go at once and not disturb him."

With a swishing sound, a lattice-covered opening was revealed above their heads, in the wall separating them from the second small room. A curtain had been drawn back and faint light shone in there, a faint light that showed the shadow of a man's sharp-nosed profile.

The throat was cleared again and a low, clear voice said, "Stop whispering to yourself, my child. Speak up. How long has it been since your last confession?"

16

There couldn't be a soul who didn't suffer difficulties from time to time. She didn't want the folk in Mayfair Square to feel sorry for her, but she would lift up her head and be grateful for their help. Jenny entered the foyer at Number 7, walking in front of Latimer who held the door open and made sure his smile was for her alone. That smile was a wee bit gentle, but a lot more wicked.

She ought to be worried about what they'd done together, what it meant, and if she was in danger of becoming a fallen woman, shunned by all. Yes, well, she was in danger true enough, but she refused to worry about it—much.

"You look well," Latimer told her. "Very well. Glowing, in fact. Exercise must agree with you."

"We came by carriage," she reminded him.

He managed to kiss her neck, and he said, "I was referring to our earlier exercise."

Jenny pretended to frown at Latimer—and saw Mr. Adam Chillworth standing a few feet behind him. His arms were crossed and she could not imagine what that narrow-eyed stare meant.

"Good evening to you, Latimer and Jenny," Mr. Chillworth said. "Welcome to bedlam, formerly our quiet home."

Latimer turned to him. "What now?"

Adam Chillworth indicated the staircase. A wispy girl of no more than six or so, sat astride the bannister in a very unladylike manner. Her legs, clad in white stockings, stuck out on either side of her, and the toes of her pretty pink slippers pointed exactly at the ceiling. She held on tight and slid down, inch by inch, using her bony arms and thin hands to stop herself again and again. Her dress was a cloud of ruffled pink sarcenet and pink roses trimmed her pantalettes.

"For God's sake, Adam. Who put her up to that and why haven't you taken her down. Lady Hester will never forgive us if she hurts herself. *Birdie,* hold on and I'll lift you down."

Birdie shook her skimpy brown ringlets. Many hours had probably passed since someone had used an iron and some rags on her hair, and the curls had grown long and narrow with straight tufts at the ends.

"She'll be all right," Jenny said. "Wee girls have to spread their wings, the same as boys."

"That's ridiculous," Latimer told her. He strode toward the child. "Why are you doing this?"

"I'll not tell you, Latimer. I'll admit it was a friend of mine who gave me the idea, but I won't get him into trouble. He didn't tell me to do it and I can manage very well, thank you."

Jenny was aware that Birdie had come into the household as an orphan rescued by Sibyl and Hunter, and that Lady Hester had taken to the child at once and insisted on providing a home for her. "How old is she, Mr. Chillworth?" she asked.

He stood beside her, watching Latimer stand with his hands on his hips trying to decide what to do next. "Older than you think. Eight, I believe. Pleasant enough for a child, but too often bored."

"Oh, sir, was it Toby who was her example?"

"You would please me by calling me Adam. After all, I believe you are to live here."

"For a night or two at the most," she informed him. "Was it Toby?"

"I have no idea. I heard Barstow shrieking before she rushed away. Then Coot grumbled at Birdie and people have been coming and going ever since, telling her what she must do, and ruing any attempt to get close to her because she kicks them. Can't say I blame her. She's not hurting anyone there."

Toby arrived. He ran to gather speed, then slid across the beautiful stone tiles. "Look at 'em," he said, pointing to his feet. Rather than his dusty old boots with cracked tops and holes in the bottoms, he wore smart ones polished to a bright sheen. "Lady Hester said I must 'ave new boots. And Evans—'e's the under-butler—Evans 'as a brother at 'ome what grew out of these." He spread his arms and looked down at a serviceable coat and trousers. His shirt was newly acquired, too, and someone had cut his hair.

"Ye look handsome," Jenny said, but felt she and Toby were like rescued puppies. A curiosity for now. Petted and pampered, and looked upon with pity by people with good intentions. Their welcome would wear out soon enough and then there would be embarrassment for everyone.

"I've a job," Toby said. "Lots of jobs. Coot gives 'em to me and I've been busy the whole day. I like it 'ere."

"I'm going to hold your waist now, young Birdie," Latimer said. "Don't wiggle or you'll fall."

Jenny bent over Toby. "Did you teach her to do that?"

"I did not, Jenny. I wouldn't. She's a *girl*." He looked sideways at Jenny. "But I did do it meself and she did see me."

"And copied you. And now she's protecting you from blame."

Toby turned pink. "I don't need no protection from a girl."

"You'd do well t'be gracious—and more careful of your behavior in future."

"I will be," he said at once. "I want to stay 'ere forever. I've 'ad pie and cake and all manner of good things. And for supper I 'ad a piece of real beef with potatoes and Yorkshire pudding and gravy. I've me own room and a palace wouldn't 'ave one better. Coot says I'm a good worker and he'll put in a word for me if I need it." He stopped talking to look at her more closely. "You're not sayin' nuthin', Jenny. Don't you want me stayin' 'ere? I'll go if that's the way of it."

She ruffled his hair and grinned. "I want ye t'be as happy forever as ye are today, ye silly laddie. Now away to wherever ye're supposed t'be and make me proud o' ye."

"Got you," Latimer said with satisfaction, finally managing to catch Birdie about the waist. "Down you come now."

"I'm off," Toby said, and retreated to the steps that led below stairs.

"Enough," Latimer roared suddenly. "There'll be no more kicking, young lady."

"Then let me get to the bottom," Birdie said. "I finish what I start and I'm not a weakling who has to be watched like a baby."

Latimer started to lift her anyway.

"Stop that," Sibyl said, running downstairs, her skirts rustling. "Latimer, take your hands off that child or I shall…well, I shall, that's all. The overbearing arrogance of men. Away, away." She flapped a hand at Latimer and put a sheltering arm around Birdie's waist until she'd bumped into the newel post at the bottom.

Birdie then craned around to Latimer and said, "You may take me down now," which he did.

The child was pleasing to look at. Not a beauty but elfin and with bright brown eyes that shone.

"I take it the crisis is now over," Latimer said.

Adam shifted his weight and crossed his arms in the other direction. "No such luck. We could go in there—" he nodded to the guests' sitting room "—only we have a visitor asleep on a couch. The one you were kind enough to quarter in Ross and Finch's house. He's waiting, he says, or said. Couldn't say it now, could he? Not since he's snoring."

"Can't we talk right here?" Latimer asked.

"No," Sibyl said promptly. "What if that man wakes up and comes out? Come upstairs."

"And risk waking up your Sean?" Adam said. "Then listening to Lady H's opinion of us. I don't think so, thank you."

"Good grief." Latimer marched to the door of 7A. "What am I thinking. In here we go."

Sibyl went, with Birdie and Adam. Feeling out of place, Jenny hung back and it was Adam who appeared in the foyer again to hold her arm and usher her into Latimer's rooms. "We all want you with us, don't we, Latimer?"

Latimer scowled at Adam and said, "Thank you for stating the obvious."

Sibyl sat on a couch that was a beautiful shape, but the material on it was brownish and worn, although Jenny could see gold threads here and there. She decided it was faded.

"Sit beside me," Sibyl told Jenny. "And you two men

sit, too. You make me nervous with all that pacing and posturing.''

"Posturing?" Adam said.

Latimer opened his mouth to add a complaint, Jenny could see it forming, but Sibyl said, ''Yes, posturing. Now let's deal with whatever nonsense is going on here. Birdie, don't sit too close to the fire.''

Birdie sat on a footstool and stared into the flames Latimer had stirred to life.

''You tell it, Sibyl,'' Latimer said.

''It's not so very bad, just rather a lot happening all at once.'' Sibyl smelled very nice to Jenny. Much like the lovely soap she'd used the previous night and that morning. ''I told Lady Hester that Hunter and I would like to have Birdie with us for the rest of the summer. She needs a place to run around and be with other children. Minver is perfect. There are the vicar's daughters and some other nice children in the area. And the vicar's wife has offered to give Birdie lessons with her own girls.''

''Och,'' Jenny said. ''It sounds verra nice.'' She closed her mouth and felt foolish for having spoken out of turn.

''Jenny's right,'' Latimer said. ''What an excellent idea, Sibyl. What do you think, Birdie?''

''I want to go,'' Birdie said. ''But I don't want Lady Hester to be sad.''

So that was the big trouble they spoke of, Jenny thought. Lady Hester was upset at the thought of Birdie going away.

''And was she?'' Latimer said. ''Upset at the idea, was she?''

''She's been shut away in her rooms ever since I spoke to her of it,'' Sibyl said. ''She asked Birdie if she'd like to go and when the child said she would, Lady Hester said, *''Go then,''* and shuffled into her bedroom as if she'd grown exceedingly old in only a few moments. Then there's Sir Edmund Winthrop.''

Jenny remembered the pleasant gentleman from the previous evening.

"Apparently," Adam said, "Lady H was too upset to have Sibyl or Birdie stay, but she sent for Sir Edmund at once and he came. They're up there together."

Latimer made a horrible face and went to a trolley with sparkling glass bottles on it. "I think we would enjoy a little fortification," he said.

"I thought Sir Edmund was gentlemanly," Jenny said. "Hasna her ladyship been a widow for a long time?"

"Years," Adam said.

"Then perhaps it's a good thing she may ha' met another gentleman who pleases her—just t'keep her company, o'course."

Three pairs of eyes sought her out. Sibyl and Adam looked curious. Latimer's glance was knowing and she felt hot.

"The man is obviously lost without a wife," Sibyl said. "Our concern is that they are becoming close too quickly. Hunter agrees that Sir Edmund and Lady Hester don't seem well matched. If he were to ask her to marry him, it could be because he wants her to ease his life as his wife did."

Latimer carried two small glasses with delicate stems and gave one to Sibyl and one to Jenny. "Sherry to warm your hearts, ladies."

Jenny looked into the golden drink, sniffed it, and found the fruity aroma pleasing. She took a sip and swallowed, and felt a warmth travel through her. She'd never tasted strong drink before but decided this was nice.

The glass Latimer gave to Adam, like the one he had

himself, contained something of a paler gold. Possibly it was stronger and appropriate for men.

"All we can do about Lady Hester and whatsisface is keep our eyes and ears open. If she wants to marry him and there's no impediment, then we can't stop her. But we'll be watching, right?"

A chorus of, *"Right,"* went up.

"So now we can enjoy our drinks and speak of more cheerful things. Don't worry young Birdie. Lady Hester is very fond of you and will miss you, but she wants what's best for you and going to Sibyl and Hunter for a few weeks is best."

"'Fraid we can't tie everything up with a bow yet, Latimer," Adam said. Each time he drank from his glass his nostrils flared and he took his time before swallowing. "There's the matter of Mr. Larch Lumpit of Middle Wallop."

"Och," Jenny said before she could think. The day had been a tumult and she'd forgotten the man Latimer had mentioned. "Excuse me."

"No need," Adam said. "My sentiments exactly."

"Mine, too," Sibyl assured her.

"He's in the guests' sitting room, snoring," Birdie said without turning around. "He wobbles all over. And he makes a lot of noise when he eats—which is all the time. He's all pink and shiny, and—"

"Thank you, Birdie," Sibyl said. "If you can't be seen and not heard, you'll have to go to your room."

Birdie hunched her shoulders, but she giggled.

"Why isn't the fellow at Number 8?" Latimer said. "Or gone altogether? Drat him. I was good enough to let him stay at Ross and Finch's—although I'm not comfortable with that. Jennings said he'd keep a close watch on him, though. He jolly well should have waited to be invited back here.''

"But the man's anxious," Adam said. Jenny thought his smile peculiar. "I'm sure you can understand that, Latimer? He's made up his mind about something and intends to follow through."

Sibyl said, *"Adam,"* and gave him a cross look. "I don't believe in all this banter when people's happiness is at stake. Jenny, do you know this Mr. Lumpit?''

"I do not. Latimer was kind enough to tell me about him. I was shocked, I can tell ye. I've no interest in seein' him at all. In fact, I'd be much obliged if he could be sent away."

"So he shall be then," Latimer told her.

Sibyl sighed. "Jenny, this is an acquaintance of Phyllis Smart and a friend of Ivy Willow. They are our friends, remember. We learned a great deal together." She drew in her cheeks as if suppressing a smile. "Mr. Lumpit is here at their suggestion. It's a fright, I know, but wouldn't it be kind to be hospitable to the man and gently let him know you appreciate his generous thoughts, but you don't wish to marry him?''

Jenny groaned. She couldn't help it, and she took a larger sip from her glass. The lovely warmth had made its way to her legs which were pleasantly heavy. She studied Latimer, who stood with a hand on the mantel, and wished there were just the two of them there. He was all she wanted to look at and no wonder, he would steal any woman's breath—even before they knew him.

"Sibyl's probably right, Jenny," he said. When his lips came together, she imagined his teeth closing carefully on her…she couldn't bring herself to as much as form the word in her mind. But she felt that feeling again and squeezed her legs tight together. That didn't stop the sensations she had.

"Jenny?" he said.

"You're right," she said. "It would only be kind."

"That's settled, then. Why don't I ring for some refreshments?"

"Because we might as well wait for Desirée to arrive," Sibyl said. She twirled her glass on her knee and appeared interested in what she saw through the window—which had to be very little.

Adam set his glass down with a slap. "I think I'd best go back to my painting. Perhaps I'll see you tomorrow."

"You'll remain where you are," Sibyl told him. "Desirée's message said she wanted to talk to all of us because she has something important to tell us."

"Perhaps she's getting married," Birdie said, and bounced on her stool. "Wouldn't that be exciting?"

Jenny didn't understand why the other three became so silent. "Weddings are always excitin'," she said to the little girl. "I saw a bride goin' into a church once. She looked so lovely."

"I think it's time for you to get ready for bed, Birdie," Sibyl said. "Barstow will be looking for you and getting upset all over again if she thinks you're missing."

Birdie pouted, but she got up quietly and said, "Good night," politely, before she left.

"When are you going to join Hunter?" Latimer asked Sibyl after the door closed.

She glowed and Jenny recalled how happy Hunter and Sibyl were together. "Tomorrow morning Desirée and I go to see about hats at Madame Sophie's. Then I'll finish overseeing the packing and we'll leave early the following day. In fact, I'd best see how things are progressing in that department now. I'll tell Coot to send Desirée here to you. After all, she can tell me her news in the morning.''

As she opened the door, she turned to Adam and said, "Don't forget you've got something for Latimer. Goodbye all.''

"And then there were three," Latimer said. He had eyes only for Jenny. "Got something for me, have you, Adam?''

"Came by special delivery," Adam said. "Rider from Windsor. Seems Finch is at Riverside with Meg and Jean-Marc. She intended to surprise you in a few days but now she's on her way here, or will be in the morning. Which means you'll see her before the day is out."

Latimer held out his hand and took the envelope Adam produced from a pocket. "Nice of you to read my personal correspondence so you could report it to me."

"I didn't, or I didn't open it. Actually, the envelope wasn't sealed. Coot took the thing to Lady H who thought it was for her and read the letter.''

"And told the rest of you what it said? Oh, never mind. I shall be glad to see Finch, I always am."

"She's coming in a rush because one of the servants took some things down to Riverside for Lady H and the *goings on* here were reported. Finch thinks you need looking after, old man."

Latimer rubbed his face. "This is enough to drive a man to leave his home.''

"They told her about me," Jenny said quietly. "And she thinks I'm a bother t'ye. Probably fears I'm keepin' ye from your work. That's what it means. I'll away now.''

"You won't go anywhere, do you understand?" Latimer raised his voice. "You will remain where you are, where you belong. The rest of your possessions have been retrieved and put in 7B where you will be comfortable and beyond the reach of any who would do you harm. Finch will love you."

This time it was Adam who covered his face.

"Dinna shout at me, sir," Jenny said, getting to her feet. "It's a sad thing when bullyin' spoils a kindness."

"I give up," Latimer said, throwing up his hands.

Adam hummed a little, then said, "I don't think you do, you know. You're not the type. Best calm yourself and avoid bullying the lady."

"I *never* bully."

"You just did," Jenny told him. "And it wasna pretty."

Latimer pointed at her, waved a finger at her, but kept his lips tightly together while he shook his head.

"Smart chap." Adam collected glasses and began clinking the lovely bottles as he poured fresh drinks. "Always did say you're smart, Latimer. You know when to be quiet."

A tap, and the door opened to admit Evans, the under-butler. A brisk, square-faced man with a capable air, he was as straight-backed as poor Coot was bent and had a full head of thick blond hair. Jenny had seen him for the first time that morning and appreciated his cheerful smile. She wanted to thank him for his kindness to Toby, but this wasn't the moment. "Princess Desirée of Mont Nuages," he said gravely, and bowed.

Evans backed away, leaving Desirée, complete with her lovely gray-and-white cat, standing near Adam. She handed him the cat and took off her gloves, bonnet and cloak, reminding Jenny that she hadn't taken off her own bonnet, or her pelisse.

The men greeted Desirée, happily on Latimer's part, somberly on Adam's.

Desirée went directly to Jenny and pulled her down on

the couch with her. "Yesterday was fun," she said. "I'm so glad to see you again."

"Thank ye, but perhaps I should leave now."

"*Dammit.*"

Latimer gained everyone's attention.

"What did I just tell you?" He closed his eyes and moved his head from side to side as if his neck hurt. "Forgive me. That was an appalling outburst and I have no right to behave as I am. Desirée and Adam, will you join me in assuring Jenny that we would like her to remain with us?"

The two of them gave enthusiastic assent.

Jenny wished her cheeks didn't throb. She took off her bonnet and set it aside while she smoothed her hair. What a fright she must look. Her dress was a poor affair, but she had grown too warm and if these people really wanted her here, they must tolerate her clothes. She started to remove the pelisse and Latimer hurried to help her.

She tried not to compare the cheap cotton chintz of her own skirts, with the peach-colored silk the princess wore.

"There," Desirée said. "That's much better. I do have something to tell you. I'd thought Sibyl would be here."

"Packing," Latimer said. "Said she'll see you in the morning."

Desirée nodded and said, "You must wonder why I spend so much time at Number 17—on my own except for dear Halibut, and the servants of course."

Adam had hooked one elbow over the back of his green and gilt chair and half turned away from Desirée. He didn't comment on what she'd said.

"I thought it was because you loved *us* so much," Latimer said. His voice was light, but he looked at Adam with no sign of a smile.

"That's part of it," Desirée said. "At Riverside with

Jean-Marc and my dear Meg, I am like a silly ghost present at every meal and in the drawing room in the evening. I don't want to intrude on them. They are so much in love and need to be alone with Serena, and the new baby on the way.

"Jean-Marc concerns himself because I show no interest in another season and I don't encourage the advances of men who try to court me. He's convinced I'm on the shelf. So I prefer not to be where he looks at me and worries all the time."

"On the shelf?" Adam said, apparently to the wall. "Not yet twenty, but on the shelf?"

The princess looked at him and Jenny swallowed hard. There were tears in Desirée's eyes. "And I do enjoy my friends here in Mayfair Square, but I've come to tell you that I'm off to Mont Nuages to visit my father."

Latimer caught up the bottle from which he'd filled Adam's glass, and his own, and refilled his friend's.

There was sadness in this room, pain. Jenny clenched a hand and looked from one man to the other, and at Desirée, whose mouth trembled.

"This is a terrible imposition, but I hoped someone here might like to take Halibut in," she said.

When the silence had stretched too long, Latimer said, "How long would that be for?"

"I may return one day," Desirée said and tilted her face up as if trying to make her tears flow backward.

"Surely you don't mean you might not come back?" Latimer asked his question of Desirée, but watched Adam whose face was cold and stiff—and white.

"I thought ye were havin' your picture—"

"That was a joke," the princess told Jenny quickly. "I wish you well, Jenny. You are dear and deserve good fortune."

Jenny wanted to cry herself. "I'll be happy t'take Halibut. He'll be well cared for, I promise ye."

Adam rose and turned to Desirée. "When will you be leaving?" he asked.

"Tomorrow I travel to the coast," she said. "I know this is sudden, but Monsieur Verbeux—he was with Jean-Marc here in England for some time before returning to my father—Verbeux has been doing some business for papa in Scotland and sails for France again within two days. He will accompany me on my journey."

"Aye," Adam said. "Convenient for you. I hope your father has learned to like you better."

"For God's sake," Latimer said, but didn't continue after Adam shook his head.

Adam swept up Halibut. "We two shall do well together. Neither of us *needs* anyone."

He went out of the room, shutting the door behind him with exaggerated care.

17

*S*pivey here:

You may take those frightful grins off your faces at once. I know what you think, but it's not true. I had nothing to do with those petals floating around in front of Latimer— and you certainly can't prove otherwise.

I am NOT getting weak. If I were, after these latest debacles I should certainly make sure to become my former pitiless self.

A child actually sliding down my bannister and thumping, mind you, crashing into my newel post! Rattled my brains, I tell you. The only bright spot in all of this is that she is to leave for some weeks, and with luck she'll have so much fun (have you noticed how everyone is always so determined to have fun) that she remains with Hunter and Sibyl forever. And we mustn't forget the departure of Sibyl and the darling little Sean. Another triumph for peace. But mark my words, this Jenny will be here, taking up space and meddling. Latimer shall not have her—and no, he did not have her already. You should have more self-respect than to spy on such tawdry events as took place today, but it was nothing. Such dalliances are not enough for Latimer More, and the girl would be no match for him in…well, in areas where I understand he excels. She would quickly bore him.

But the princess. I am desolate at this latest turn of

events. Mind you, I am terribly insulted by her rude comments about ghosts. Ignorance invariably makes a person appear as stupid as they are. But I am desolate that she's leaving. How can she when I planned to marry her off to Latimer? You heard how anxious her brother is to get rid of her. He likes More and would have accepted him for her. Foiled again by these self-centered people.

Then there is that foul animal. I have encountered him on a number of occasions, you know. The wretch detests me and takes great pleasure in letting me know how well he sees me. Victimizes me unmercifully. He ruined my pleasure in walking through doors successfully by waiting for me on the other side and making a terrible fuss. But I must be generous there. Sir Thomas said so. That's Sir Thomas More—he's headmaster of the Angel School. Did you notice my wing buds are growing larger, by the way? No, I suppose you wouldn't have.

Larch Lumpit, vapid twit that he is, is my only hope of salvation at Number 7. I've given him a good talking to. All this making a nuisance of himself. Really. But I mustn't forget I chose him as my borrowed body because he is empty. There is almost nothing going on in that head other than a petulant desire to have everything he wants, and to be admired.

I digress. Often do. Comes of being extremely intelligent. As I said, Lumpit's had a talking to. He knows he'd better get the job done with Jenny. After all, although I believe Latimer would discover her too prissy for him, I can't take chances—more chances. I've told Lumpit that if he fails with this simple task of impressing Jenny and making her see how fortunate she will be when he gives her his hand— well, if he fails, his vicar will find out Lumpit wants his job.

I shouldn't need to tell you that I wouldn't employ fibs to get what I want. No, no, not now that I'm a changed ghost. Anyway, Lumpit does want his vicar's job.

18

"Miss Jenny?" Coot stood in the open doorway to Latimer's rooms. "There is a Mr. Larch Lumpit in the guests' sitting room. He's complaining—I mean, he's remarking on the amount of coming and going from the house. Apparently he was awakened by Mr. Latimer leaving to take the princess home."

Jenny had watched Latimer and Desirée until they became enveloped by complete darkness in the gardens at the center of the square. Desirée's announcement, and Adam's reaction, had left her very sad. She turned from the window. "I'm sure Mr. More would be sorry t'hear he'd disturbed Mr. Lumpit, but I canna do anythin' about it."

"No," Coot said. He sniffed into the back of a hand, rotated his forward thrust neck, and rolled perilously far forward. "Mr. Lumpit is enquiring for you, Miss Jenny. Apparently he thinks you've already been told he's here to see you."

"I have." She went closer to Coot and dropped her voice. "I dinna want t'see the man. I don't know him and I don't think I want to."

"Don't blame you, miss." Coot looked past her as if talking to no one in particular. "Thought I'd better carry the message, though. He does seem determined to remain in the house until you talk to him."

The thought of being even more of a nuisance here was too much for Jenny. "Then I will see him. I'll away t'him right now."

"Can hardly have you with him unescorted, miss."

"Och, he's a clergyman, isn't he? My honor's no in danger wi' such a person. Please, when Mr. More returns, would ye kindly tell him I'll deal better wi' Mr. Lumpit on my own." She couldn't bear to consider Latimer coming to chaperon her, and possibly losing his temper with this stranger. "I'll ha' no difficulty speakin' wi' the man and gettin' him to leave."

Coot looked dubious, but nodded and led her to the appropriate door. He walked in and announced, "Miss Jenny McBride to see you, Mr. Lumpit."

Jenny walked past the old man, who retreated with obvious reluctance.

A large gentleman in a long black robe buttoned from neck to hem—and gapping between every one of those buttons—rose, making humming sounds in his throat. He wasn't very tall, which exaggerated his girth.

"Good evening to ye," Jenny said. She would take a confident approach.

The humming continued before the man swallowed several times, and she noted the wedge of cheese he held at his side. His mouth was too full to allow him to speak.

"Yes, well, I was told ye wished t'see me because ye thought ye had business wi' me. That's no' possible since I dinna know ye. I'm sorry for your trouble. Good night."

"Stay," he said around his cheese. "Sit down, if you please."

Ooh, she shouldn't have come after all.

He finished swallowing, reached for a glass of something, took a big mouthful, and then gathered himself. He smiled, a disconcerting sight. "At last we meet, Miss

McBride. Mr. Larch Lumpit, curate at St. Philomena's in Middle Wallop, at your service—'' he shot out a hand but when Jenny made to shake it, he lifted hers to pouting red lips and kissed it "—very much at your service, my dear."

"I dinna need anyone's service," she told him, snatching her hand away. "But thank ye."

"No, no, no. You are *not* to thank me. It will give me pleasure to allow you to please me."

Jenny gaped at the man.

"Sit down at once," he said and when he approached her as if to make sure she followed his orders, Jenny did sit.

A rumble rose through his chest and he put a hand over his mouth. "Pardon," he said. "I'd hoped to see you last evening, but wasn't so fortunate. I came around several times today, with no more luck. I'm staying at Number 8 until I can find more superior lodgings."

"I see." Jenny knew very well that Number 8 belonged to Latimer's sister and her husband and must be very grand. "But I dinna suppose ye'll be stayin' now ye realize I'm no' the person ye're looking for."

He frowned and thick brows seemed out of place over his large, almost childish blue eyes. "I've already said you *are* the woman I'm here to find. And you're going to be very happy about it." He lowered himself back onto a couch and planted his enormous feet far apart. "One of my—er, our parishioners is Miss Ivy Willow. Delightful woman, if a gossip. She has a friend named Phyllis Smart. I believe they're both known to you."

Jenny didn't want to hear the story Latimer had already told her. "Yes, and it was suggested that you should come to see me for some reason. I wish I had more time to spend thanking you for your thoughtfulness."

"You are every bit as humble as I was led to believe."

Mr. Lumpit's eyes became luminous and his shiny face and chins trembled with emotion. "Most suitable. Miss McBride, I know all about your appalling life. The degradation to which you've been subjected, the squalor of the slums in which you've lived, the deplorable characters with whom you have consorted—terrible, but in the past. And we must learn that self-pity is invariably a tool to gain attention—and unworthy of a woman who knows her place."

Jenny's temper boiled. She decided she would let the horrid man have his say until he had no further reason to remain. Then she would be rid of him forever.

"You probably wonder why a man such as myself would consider a person of such dubious background."

"No, I wasna wonderin' that."

"Of course you were. The answer is that I have an infinite capacity for pity. I pity you, Miss McBride, and believe I was sent to you by a higher power."

"I didna know Ivy Willow was a higher power."

Lumpit's face reddened and so did his scalp, visible between the strands of hair he'd combed forward over an almost bald head. "I see I am to be thoroughly tried. But I shall prove myself worthy of my task. We won't overtax you tonight. You must already be overwhelmed by so much attention. In due course, as soon as the formalities are dealt with, you, my dear, shall become *Mrs. Larch Lumpit*. No, no, don't thank me. Calm yourself, please. I am not accustomed to hysterical outbursts. You may celebrate your good fortune quietly—savor it and give thanks for it."

"How kind ye are, but—"

"Middle Wallop is a delight. You will find great satisfaction in visiting the sick and listening to the ladies tell their troubles to you. Of course, in the case of those who require more superior wisdom than you can give, you will send them to me, but not, I repeat, *not* unless it is absolutely necessary.''

''Mr. Lumpit—''

''Your first duty will be to look after me. Naturally.'' He reached for a small fruit tart and put the whole thing into his mouth at once. ''Are you a good cook?'' he mumbled.

''I canna cook a'tall.'' If Ivy and Phyllis were here now, they'd get a piece of Jenny's mind.

Lumpit paused with his mouth open and Jenny looked away.

''Well,'' he said, making smacking sounds with his lips, ''I must say I'm shocked. That will have to be corrected in short order. I wasn't told you were defective.''

Defective?

''Would ye kindly leave now, Mr. Lumpit?''

''I shall call you Jenny until we are married. Afterward, of course, you will be Mrs. Lumpit at all times. And a very nice ring that has, too.''

Jenny seethed. She got up and stood behind her sofa. ''This is the most outrageous conversation I've ever had, not that ye've allowed me t'say much.''

''It isn't a woman's place to talk when her husband's talking, Jenny, and—''

''I'm no' your wife and never will be.''

A deep breath raised his tummy and pulled harder on his buttons. ''I was prepared for this and I am not at all disturbed. It may take a day or two for you to believe your good fortune, but I am a patient man. I'll be here for you, dear Jenny. My needs are your needs and never the twain shall part—again. Go to your bed at once. You need a great deal of rest to prepare for what lies ahead. Tomorrow we shall discuss formalities. Good night.''

* * *

Spivey here:

If you're considering laughing at me again—don't. If you had any decency, you'd be moved by my crushing burdens.

Think of all that's at stake. The very endurance of Number 7 and all it stands for. I will get rid of the orphans and paupers. And I do confess to a certain new hope. Sir Edmund Winthrop is a fine, upstanding man who, despite the opinions of the interlopers here, is very fond of Hester (not that I understand why) and I should not at all mind if he were to—well, if something were to transpire between the two of them. I'm sure he'd rule this house with a firm hand.

What? What do you say? He might prefer his own home and want to sell her holding in this one? You are spiteful and I know where you get your cruel ideas. My advice to you is to avoid the so-called wisdom of scribblers. A pox on any who think women should be allowed to write. This one, who insults me and meddles in my affairs regularly, is not to be trusted.

I'm off to deal with Lumpit. Wait till you see the change in him. You'll have new respect for my powers when you are confronted with the new and charming Lumpit.

Oh, joy, perhaps my work will not be so difficult. I see he has left her a gift. That's the ticket, Lumpit, old man. Sweep her off her feet with little tokens of your esteem.

Later, people.

"All I did was leave you while I saw Desirée home. How could you see that man in my absence, and leave *instructions* for me not to interrupt you?" Latimer sounded furious.

The moment Coot had seen Lumpit out of the house,

Jenny had seated herself on a red couch once more. And she had closed her eyes in hope of finding peace and sanity again. "Thank ye for lettin' me deal wi' him," she said. Latimer More might have to learn that some women weren't bowled over by high-handedness.

Latimer shut the sitting room door and sat facing her. "I hardly *let* you, Jenny. You made the decision yourself."

"And ye understood that t'be the appropriate thing," she said. "It's a wise man ye are not to impose your will where ye've no right."

He rested his head on the back of the couch. Jenny noted that his hair was grown long enough to touch his collar—and that he had a growth of dark beard on his face. He looked raffish and she thrilled to the thought of Mr. Latimer More having a wild side. Not that he really did, but the possibility was exhilarating to consider.

"Finch is a special woman," he said. "You remind me of her—in some ways. She thinks she's as good as any man and is forever seeing how far she can push poor Ross."

"And how far is that—usually," she asked innocently.

"*Usually,* it's a deal too far. That's what happens when a strong man allows his judgment to be addled by infatuation."

Jenny half-reclined in the corner of her couch. "So that's all ye think it could be wi' him? Infatuation."

Latimer let out a long sigh. "Women and word games. A dangerous combination. My brother-in-law adores my sister. He'd better if he knows what's good for him."

Laughing, and clapping her hands, Jenny said, "Listen t'ye. Overbearin' again. Ye're to decide what's best for the whole world and make sure it happens."

"I love my sister," he said coolly. "I take responsibility for those I love."

There was no suitable response. They both fell silent,

but Jenny's heart beat faster and faster. She wasn't a fool. She knew full well that for some strange reason, Latimer was attracted to her. His intentions were not at all clear; after all, she wasn't suitable for him as other than... She wasn't suitable as other than a plaything for Latimer More and, although she was sure she loved him, she would not throw away her life for an affair—even if it did transport her. She would not be his mistress until he grew tired of the novelty of being with a poor woman and moved on.

Latimer looked up and moved to sit at the end of the couch closest to her. He rested an elbow on the arm and his chin on a fist—and stared.

At first Jenny attempted to look anywhere but at him, but she gave up and returned his stare.

"You have spirit," he told her.

"I think I like ye saying that."

"When you go to bed, one of the maids will come and sleep in the little bedroom that used to belong to Meg."

Her stomach tightened, but she didn't look away. "That won't be necessary." So he'd decided he didn't want to spend the night in her room, even if she did give him the inside of the bed.

"Is that yours?" he said, indicating a small package on the table before them. Wrapped in brown paper, it had been tied with a thin, black ribbon.

She shook her head. "Why should it be mine?"

Latimer leaned forward and read aloud, "For Miss Jenny McBride from Mr. Larch Lumpit, curate of St. Philomena's at—"

"Middle Wallop," she finished for him. "Silly, pompous man. Whatever it is, I don't want it."

"Shall I open it for you?"

"Curiosity can be a bad thing, Latimer."

"Who's curious? Let the thing stay where it is. I only thought to help."

Jenny wriggled against a cushion. "That's a fib, but please do open it. I can hardly wait to see what lovely trinket Mr. Lumpit brought for me."

Once ribbon and paper were discarded, a thin, leather-bound volume was revealed and Latimer commenced to riffle through the pages. Jenny jerked a foot up and down with impatience.

"Well, this will be most useful to you," Latimer told her. "It is entitled, *A Wife's Duties Toward Her Husband* and it's written by Dr. Horatio Bottom."

"It wouldna' be written by a woman, would it?" Jenny said. "After all, we need men to tell us what t'do at all times."

"Of course," Latimer said and put the book on the table. "Although I'm a forward-thinking man who believes women have only to be given the opportunity to be able to take the lead in almost anything. And I, for one, should be intrigued to be led. By the appropriate woman, of course."

The fire had burned low and Latimer got up to pile on some fresh coals. "Nothing like a good fire," he said. "Something intimate about sitting by the fire with one who is better company than a man ever hoped to have."

How was she supposed to respond to such a compliment? She smiled at him and this time, rather than sit on the couch next to Jenny's, he sat on hers and lifted her feet onto the seat. He'd have had to be blind not to notice how she tried to pull her boots beneath her skirts. He frowned, a little thoughtfully, she thought, and looked away. Only inches separated them but it felt much larger.

"Jenny, do you understand why I decided not to accept your tantalizing invitation to spend another night with you?'' He waved a hand. "How devilish exciting that sounds. Brings things to mind that you haven't even guessed at.''

"I understand," she said, but he was right in thinking she didn't have any idea what thoughts might be in his mind.

"Do you?''

She looked at him sharply. "Do I understand why ye prefer not to spend the night wi' me? O' course I do. Ye've your own comfortable bed and ye dinna ha' t'share it wi' anyone. Out o' kindness, ye made a big enough sacrifice last night.''

His expression was different from any she'd seen before. She thought he was trying to show nothing at all, but anger flashed in his eyes—and they were quite black at the moment.

"So you think it was a sacrifice, hmm?" He put an elbow on the back of the couch and laced his fingers together. With his thumbs, he made circles. "Interesting how lack of experience can hide the truth.''

Jenny considered what he said. "Ye mean it wasna a sacrifice?''

"That's what I mean.''

"Then... Well, thank ye. Ye're gracious, even if ye do fib now and again.''

Before she guessed his intent, Latimer took hold of one of her boots and pulled it from beneath her skirts. Showing no emotion, he undid the laces and slipped it off—and set it down carefully. He repeated the process with the other boot while Jenny tried and failed not to blush. If her stockings were plain white cotton, at least they were clean and without holes.

"You'll be more comfortable without those," he said, indicating the boots. "Particularly when you've walked so much today. You almost asked why, if it wouldn't be a sacrifice, I've chosen not to be with you tonight?''

She would not waffle about and tell part-truths. "That's what I was about to say, yes. But it's no' my business."

"Can't imagine anyone else whose business it might be but yours and mine. It's because it wasn't a sacrifice that I can't do it again—not until things are changed between us."

When there wasn't a good answer, it was best to be quiet.

"Do you understand what I'm trying to tell you?"

She shook her head.

With one finger, he stroked the bones on the top of her feet. "Do you remember this afternoon when I held your ankle."

Jenny swallowed. "Aye."

He got up, removed his coat and waistcoat, and sat again.

Jenny couldn't stop her eyes from growing wide. She supposed gentlemen felt free to remove their coats—and perhaps their jackets—in a sitting room if they were alone, or with a very close friend, even a female friend.

Were they familiar enough for such things? She immediately knew the answer to her own question. They had been all but naked together—to the waist anyway.

"You seem uncomfortable," he said and loosened his neckcloth and undid several buttons on his shirt. "I've never been a man who thrived on the constrictions of clothing. In fact, the more often I can do away with it altogether, the better."

"I canna blame ye," she said, but rued her empty words. "I mean, I'm sure it would be comfortable for those comfortable in their own bodies, as comfortable as ye are."

"As comfortable as I just told you I am," he pointed out. "I've never been entirely naked with you, have I?"

Taking a breath at all was difficult. "Ye know ye have not." Jenny put her hands in her lap and tapped her fingertips together.

"You might find you enjoy nakedness yourself. True, it isn't as exciting when one is alone, but with someone you want to touch, and to have touch you, it is, I assure you, the most stimulating thing in the world."

"I do believe ye're teasin' me, Latimer. Goadin' me, even. It's a poor business when a man such as yoursel' has t'gain his pleasure by makin' someone like me feel foolish."

"Foolish?" His marvelous smile was there again. "Be absolutely certain I have no interest in having you feel foolish. If I could have my wish, you would never feel foolish again, or suffer any discomfort of any kind. It is my most ardent desire in life to bring you pleasure, Jenny. I intend to do whatever I must to be in the position to please you often, every day, many times a day."

She shuddered a little, but with excitement. "I dinna know what ye expect me t'say. And I dinna know for sure what ye mean which is probably as well. Is that gold-colored stuff ye drank wi' Adam verra strong?"

Latimer dropped back his head and laughed, showing his strong white teeth and making deep dimples beside his mouth. "I'm not in my cups, if that's what you mean, miss. In fact I am completely sober—and completely focused on what has become most important in my life. But enough of that. You have already been overtaxed. Do you remember how I slipped my fingers around your ankle today?"

Not owning a real fan, Jenny flapped a hand in front of her face.

Latimer laughed again. "If you could see how utterly charming you look you would understand why I cannot go through another night watching you sleep."

"You slept, surely," she said.

"Very little. There is much you don't know, such as what happens to a man's body when a woman who attracts him presses herself against him."

"Oh!" Jenny said. She couldn't help herself. "Why did ye no' tell me. I'd ha' moved away."

"Because I didn't want you to move away," he said and looked as if he was enjoying himself. "I should tell you that the house has retired. I sent Coot off before coming to you."

So, she thought, she was to understand that they would not be disturbed. He suggested that the thought of being alone with her was dangerous, yet sent the household to bed and made himself comfortable with her in this sitting room—alone.

Lightly, he touched the top of her foot again, and he moved close enough to put both of her feet in his lap.

How could something so wonderful not be right? It was. They were simply being companionable.

His long fingers played about her feet and ankles. He moved her skirts a scant inch or so to study the latter. "Finely made," he said, "like the rest of you."

He leaned against the back of the couch and his shirt fell open. She might have touched him there before, but only in darkness. Smooth, black hair flared, then became a thin line that ran down the center of him and disappeared inside his clothes. He had flat, brown nipples and muscles that stood out hard. Not a fingernail of extra flesh showed anywhere.

"I liked it when you put your hands on me," he said. "You surprised me."

"Y'mean I was forward. I dinna know what came over me."

"Instinct came over you. Men and woman are meant to enjoy each other, and instinct led you to do something that came naturally. You have lovely limbs. They're narrow where they should be, and they curve where they should. I can see them now."

He was, Jenny realized with a jolt, looking at the outline of her legs inside her skirts and imagining them without a thing on them. She wanted to move, to pull her limbs up underneath her or put her feet firmly on the floor, but she would not be a ninny.

Latimer's gaze settled on her knees and he smiled.

There was nothing to be done but hold still and pretend she hadn't begun to tingle all over.

The smile disappeared when he reached her thighs. The muscles beside his mouth tightened and his breathing grew more shallow.

Jenny pressed her legs tight together. He used the pads of his fingers on her feet, and the pressure was hard.

His chest expanded and he shifted on the couch, rested a boot on the opposite knee, but kept Jenny's feet where they were. She wasn't such a know-nothing that she didn't understand what she was feeling. She remembered Sibyl's comments about Latimer's unmentionable parts being unusually responsive—Jenny felt a good deal happening there now.

She glanced at Latimer's face again and the stark intensity was as thrilling as it was terrifying. Men were so complicated. She never would have said such a thing of them before Latimer, before today. He stared at her hands where they rested in her lap and she snatched them up, then felt scalding heat rush up her neck and over her face, and replaced them where they had been. Oh, fie, as if her hands made any difference to what he was imagining now.

Undressing her with his eyes, touching her with his eyes, he reminded her of how it was to feel his hands upon her skin. She grew moist and could hardly stop herself from leaping up. But if she did, she wasn't at all sure it wouldn't be to throw herself into his arms.

Moist and deeply aching, her time with him earlier had awakened her, now he stole away every shred of belief that she was in control of her body. All he would ever have to do to make her lose herself, was look at her. She put a hand to her throat. The truth shook her.

Latimer inclined his head and allowed his eyes to half-close. His lips parted. He had switched his attention to the hand at her throat and while his eyes settled there, he splayed one of his hands over his bared chest. Such a long-fingered, broad-palmed hand. He leaned a little closer to her.

Jenny touched a button on her bodice, turned it around and around. She felt him watch her, then found him waiting when she raised her eyes to his. He ran the tip of his tongue along the edges of his teeth and regarded her fingers and the button again.

She was not a child, to misunderstand the silent messages of a man who had already let her know he wanted her. Slowly she slipped undone the top button, then the first one between her breasts, and another, and another. Jenny loosened her bodice all the way to the high waistline of her dress. She checked Latimer's face but he had rested his temple on the back of the couch and was contemplating her chest unwaveringly.

She had made broad promises to herself not to risk throwing herself away on a dalliance with Latimer that would only leave her wounded and alone—and unwanted by any other.

There was such longing in his face.

She did not have to debase herself for any man's longing. But Latimer was not *any* man, and if looking upon her would bring him pleasure, then she would please him. He would not hurt her, not really, of that she was convinced.

Calming the butterflies that must be flying in swarms through her insides, Jenny spread the sides of her bodice and smoothed her camisole down. She wore no corset to uplift and make more of her breasts but she stroked them with her own hands and settled her fingers beneath—and felt as if she would give this man anything.

Without warning, he removed her feet from his lap and bent her knees so that he could sit closer to her.

Neither of them seemed capable of speaking. Careful to hold nothing but a wrist, Latimer took one of her hands to his mouth and repeatedly kissed the palm. One by one he took each finger into his mouth and sucked deeply as he drew it out again. His eyes had closed and something near pain passed over his features.

When he was done, Jenny pulled his hand to her and copied each move he'd made and, while his eyes remained closed, pressed his palm and fingers over her breast. He bowed over her knees and filled each of his hands with her tender flesh. Stroking, lifting, pressing together, pinching her nipples between his fingers, he shook his head from side to side and sweat beaded on his brow and on his chest.

"I must look after you," he said in a voice that sounded long unused. "You are exactly what I thought you were, and I will not be guilty of spoiling that."

He might as well have spoken in a language she didn't understand. "Thank ye for your carin'. That's what ye're sayin? That ye want t'protect me from somethin' that would hurt me?''

Latimer withdrew from her, he pulled her legs down, pulled her flat on the couch and settled a pillow beneath her head. ''Don't ask me how I'm to do it, but I will, even if I am destroyed by the effort.'' He dragged off his shirt, threw it on the floor and lay atop her.

His kisses were deep and near mad in their ardor. Jenny put her arms around his body and stroked his broad, damp back. He opened his mouth over one of her breasts and she barely held back a little shriek of pleasure.

''Help,'' he said resting his face where he could pass his tongue over the tip of a nipple while he fondled the other. ''Help me, please, to guide us through this damnable expected period of polite courtship.''

''Courtship,'' she repeated, ''but that's what—''

''People who are to be married go through. Yes, I know. And I know it would be unseemly to proceed with undue haste.''

Had she not been quite speechless at what he was suggesting, she would have told him that he hadn't mentioned anything so serious to her before, which wasn't surprising given the brief period of their...well, whatever it was they'd been doing together.

His back rose and fell as if he were suffering. She should definitely have learned more in Sibyl's group. She should have insisted the rest of them continue with their exploration. There must be a way to ease Latimer's discomfort. He held her hip, then stroked and squeezed her bottom. And a hot brand flowered within her.

''Ye're a lovely man,'' she told him. ''I'm no' adept at the right words for such occasions, but I'm just followin' what my heart tells me t'say.''

''Whatever you say destroys me in the most satisfying

way, dear Jenny. What beautiful breasts you have. I said that before, but it should be said often. Beautiful.''

She had a thought and said, ''Thank ye,'' while she bent sideways and managed to reach the part they called a penis. She wasn't sure she cared for the word, but it was what it was. She cupped it with her hand, or tried to. His trousers got in the way terribly, and anyway, there was too much of him for one of her not very large hands.

Latimer lifted his head and panted. He shifted against her fingers, then helped her take an even more intimate hold on him.

''There you are, Latimer.'' A woman's voice sounded excited as the door was thrown wide-open. ''What have you come to, sleeping in this ghastly sitting room? I took the mailcoach from Windsor with one of Jean-Marc's men to watch over me. The whole thing was less than comfortable, but I had the feeling I must get to you as soon as possible.''

Jenny was disposed to cry but held back the tears and was grateful that Latimer gathered her in his arms and lay entirely on top of her, shielding her from prying eyes.

He cleared his throat. ''Lovely to see you, Finnie, old girl. Scotland keeps you and the family farther away than I would wish. But you didn't have to break all records getting here. Tomorrow would have been lovely.''

''Well, that's a nice welcome. You'll freeze, lying there like...'' Her voice didn't fade, it just stopped.

''Mind waiting in my rooms, would you, dear sister?'' Latimer asked.

''No. No, no, not at all. Um, I'll do that at once.'' Finch's voice trilled upward and disappeared in a squeak.

Latimer was terribly heavy, but Jenny would have had him remain there forever. She never wanted to show her face again.

The door clicked shut quietly.

"And so the power shifts," Latimer said, settling his face briefly in Jenny's neck. "Prepare yourself for an inquest and the most furious courtship ever visited upon a woman."

He sat up and Jenny went to work on her buttons while he dressed. When her clothes were straightened, her hair returned to some semblance of order, and her boots back on her feet—by which time he wore his shirt, waistcoat, neckcloth and coat, Latimer offered her his hand formally and helped her up.

"Thank ye," she said. "I'd best away t'my bed—Sibyl's bed that is."

"Your bed now—at least for a while. But first you'll meet Finch." He opened the door for her and said. "I haven't had practice with much pretty talk that was sincere, but I love you."

19

"Can I no' away t'bed, please?"

"I understand your instincts," Latimer said. "But this is no time to slink off and hide. You are guilty of nothing. If you don't meet my sister now, she'll assume you think there's something to hide."

"Your sister came t'see ye. She doesna even know I exist."

How wrong Jenny was. She would have to learn how quickly news traveled in some circles. "We can't stand in the foyer whispering. Finch will come out and see us—and we'll look suspicious. I think she does know about you. I'll explain why later." He was painfully aware that Jenny hadn't responded to his declaration of love.

"I don't see why I canna meet her tomorrow, or on some other day?"

"Because—" He wasn't a man who raised his voice, dammit. "Please, Jenny, I understand these things. Do it for me, my love."

Her green eyes shone. He thought she might be close to tears, but there was a more complex emotion than simply not wanting to meet Finch.

"What is it?" he asked her. "You look sad."

"I'm no' sad. I'm overwhelmed. Surely ye see how that could be. I've no settled place t'be. I'm at the mercy of others." She paused and reached out to touch his mouth.

"And ye said ye loved me, Latimer—but I don't know what t'say t'ye back."

Bloody wonderful. "Well, even if you don't love me, my feelings aren't going to change. I love you and I want you to be my wife. For one thing, there's only so much frustration I can stand. I have a man's needs and—" He broke off, appalled at himself. "Oh, Jenny, forgive me."

"Ye want t'marry me? Why? I'm no' suitable for ye."

He took her by the shoulders and barely managed not to shake her. "How dare you have less than the best opinion of yourself? You are a wonderful girl. How many people could hold up as you have under such circumstances? You *are* suitable. And I will have you. Subject closed."

"I've a good opinion of mysel', thank ye. I'm also sensible. Ye're already important and gettin' more so. I overheard them talkin' about ye here. How ye're considered an authority on the things ye import and people come t'ye from all around—even out of England—wi' requests for things they want. Ye'll need a wife ye can be proud of, not one ye ha' t'hide away, or one ye've to tell to keep mum wi' others so as not to embarrass ye. Anyway, ye've no' asked me, so it's no a problem."

Latimer looked at the door to 7A. It was blessedly closed. "I told you I *love* you. I told you I want you to be my wife. You haven't as much as returned one of my sentiments, but I do believe you feel something for me."

She was close to tears and he didn't know what to do about it.

"I feel a great deal for ye. I've never felt as much for a soul in my whole life, and dinna expect to feel like this again. If we love someone, we aren't selfish enough to let them do something that would harm them. I'll no' harm ye, Latimer."

Now here, he thought, was progress. "You're concerned
for me because you love me?"

She nodded her head and said, "Yes," in a small voice.
Tears began to roll down her cheeks.

"And that makes you unhappy?" She'd made him
elated.

"It makes me feel helpless."

"There's no need." Where should he start, *how* should
he start to make her comfortable with the things she
thought she couldn't do? "Should you like to visit my
warehouses? I'd like you to see them. And if you'd care
to learn more about the things I deal in, I'll teach you."

He knew when he saw longing in another. Jenny said,
"Perhaps."

"Jenny—" he tucked a curl into the braid she wore
looped at the back of her head "—you're going to be the
best wife a man ever had. You're the only wife for me."

"I canna say more now, Latimer."

"Come." He took her by the hand and led her to 7A
where he opened the door with as broad a smile on his
face as he could muster. "There you are, Finnie." He
wanted only to be with Jenny.

"Here I am," Finnie said, "exactly where you knew I'd
be. You sent me here." She looked not at him, but at
Jenny.

"So I did. I'd like you to meet Jenny McBride, the
dearest of girls. Jenny, my sister Finch, Viscountess Kilrood."

Jenny bowed her head and curtsied, and when she stood
upright again, she still didn't lift her face.

"Hello, Jenny," Finch said. "I'm pleased to meet someone my brother thinks of so highly."

"Aye," Jenny said and added, "and I'm pleased t'meet
Latimer's sister."

An awkward silence followed with Finch, her light brown eyes filled with dismay, staring at Jenny while Jenny averted her face. The slump of her shoulders radiated misery.

He had made a mistake. Forcing Jenny to meet Finch late at night after she'd been through so much—including their encounter this evening, which had left *him* shaken—was foolhardy. Jenny had begged him not to do it, but he, hardheaded scoundrel that he was, had not been able to wait to show her to Finch and to have Finch be happy that at last he'd found the one woman who could complete his life.

"Good job you came today, actually Finnie," Latimer said in a rush. "Sibyl's off to Cornwall again tomorrow. You'd have missed her—and Sean. He's a strapping little fellow."

"Then it's a good job for two reasons," Finch said and smiled valiantly. "I couldn't bear to miss Sibyl and Sean, and I'm meeting Jenny for the first time."

Jenny turned up the corners of her mouth.

Latimer slapped a thigh. "And you don't know the other news, do you? Desirée is going to see her father in Mont Nuages and says she *may* come back. Can you imagine? She *may* come back."

"Oh, no, no," Finch said. "I've been afraid of something like this. Jean-Marc's been tetchy and Meg isn't herself. When does Desirée go?"

"Soon. Tomorrow, I think. She's to meet Verbeux, the man who used to be Jean-Marc's assistant, on the coast and sail for France directly."

"Oh, that silly, silly man." Finch blinked and touched the corner of each eye. "There's still time for him to act. Just some small sign. Something to give her hope."

"He doesn't know how," Latimer said, but he felt as

angry as Finch did. "And he's filled himself with reasons why he shouldn't anyway."

"And he's miserable," Finch said.

"Absolutely. And mark my words, he's gone to ground and I'll have to watch over him to make sure he doesn't starve himself to death."

"Surely Desirée won't stay away forever," Finch said.

"I know little or nothing about the workings of the female mind, but I assume this was supposed to force his hand."

"Apparently ye know nothing o' the workings o' the female mind," Jenny said in a cool, clear voice that played a scale on Latimer's spine. "If ye did, ye'd no' talk away as if I wasna here."

If he could have spoken, he would. As it was, the joy that filled him also dumbfounded him. There she stood, shoulders straight, in one of the worn-out dresses he'd have to do something about, her auburn hair shining as beautifully as did Finch's more definitely red coiffure, and she wore an expression haughty enough to put any lady of the *ton* to shame.

He did love her. He *really* loved her.

"Men can be unfeeling creatures," Finch said, adding her scowl to Jenny's. "And you're right—they don't know a thing about the way we think. I don't know why we put up with them."

His sister had always been a quick-witted thing, but she didn't usually pretend she was innocent of the crime under investigation. However, in the interest of encouraging a bond between Finch and Jenny, he wouldn't point out that Finnie had been as guilty of forgetting Jenny's presence as he had.

"Ye mean Adam, don't ye?" Jenny said and now Finch was the sole recipient of her attention. "I was here when the princess said she was leavin'. A sadder person I never saw, but Adam's all locked up inside his silly head. He'll let her go. See if I'm no' right. And then he'll pretend t'be happy wi'out her when he's dyin' inside.''

Finch shook her head and Latimer realized he was about to deal with the second crying female of the evening. ''You are right, Jenny. Silly man. I've watched him suffer about things before. He used to be painfully shy. Then he gradually came out of that because of the rest of us. If Desirée really goes, we'll all have to work hard to make sure he doesn't retreat again.''

''Och.'' Jenny snapped her fingers. ''She asked for someone to look after Halibut for her. I offered, but Adam picked him up and made off wi' him. He said they'd suit well together because they didn't need anyone. The ninny.''

''Ninny indeed,'' Finch said.

''But the cat will give a reason for visitors, won't he? I'll ha' to visit him.''

''You won't visit the attic on your own,'' Latimer said. He wouldn't have Jenny spending time with handsome Adam who might be looking for solace.

He became aware of two pairs of eyes regarding him in that oddly expressionless way women had when they were sending a message that a man had just said the wrong thing.

''I mean, Adam can be daunting when he's in a bad mood and you have a gentle heart. I won't have it hurt.''

''Thank ye,'' Jenny said, putting plenty of sarcasm into her tone. ''Anyway, perhaps some distance is what's needed to prove if there's anythin' there for the two o' them. In fact, I think distance is a good thing before men and women take steps that change them forever.''

Oh, no, Latimer thought, she wasn't going to get away

with trying to force any distance between the two of them.
"How are Ross and the children, Finnie?" He quickly
added, "Ross is Viscount Kilrood, Finch's husband. They
have two children," for Jenny's benefit.

"They are more than well," Finch said. "When there's
a suitable moment I want to ask you about a trip to Cornwall."

"Sibyl and Hunter will be happy to have you," Latimer
told her.

"It wasn't Sibyl and Hunter I was thinking of visiting."

"The old man?" Latimer whistled a breath out on a
single note. "Funny, I hadn't thought about him in ages."

"We're talking about our father," Finch said to Jenny.
"Our mother is dead. Papa cut us off—apart from a small
allowance—when Latimer decided to set up business in
London and I came with him because I love the antiques
business. And, of course, I love Latimer."

"Thank you, Finnie," Latimer said, and meant it most
sincerely.

"I'm sad for your trouble wi' your father. Seems so sad
to have a father and no' see him."

Latimer noted the wistfulness in her voice, and saw
Finch's sharp look. When Finch didn't ask any questions
about Jenny's family he could have hugged her. He *should*
hug her, dammit.

"You haven't given your old brother a hug or a kiss,"
he said lightly and went to pull her into his arms. "You
only grow more beautiful and charming."

Close to his ear she whispered, "What on earth are you
doing with this girl?"

He pulled back. "We're all tired. In a moment I'll see
Jenny up to 7B, then I'll take you next door. Oh, hell, I
should talk to you about Lumpit, but it's late."

"Tomorrow will do," Finch said. "I have a rough idea

of who the man is, although I can't imagine why he's staying in my house when he appears to have no business here.''

"No," Latimer said. "As you say, though, tomorrow will do. Finnie, I don't want to part from you without giving you our news." He held a hand toward Jenny and she took it reluctantly, and with alarm in her eyes. "I've finally found the woman I thought didn't exist. Jenny McBride. We are to be married."

Jenny made a choking sound. He felt her stiffen.

Finch's mouth opened slightly. She looked at Latimer, then at Jenny. "Married?"

"Yes. For the first time ever, I know what happiness is." And if Jenny would say something similar he'd feel a whole lot happier still.

"I see," Finch said. "That's...wonderful."

Jenny held his hand tightly.

"We think so," Latimer said. He didn't like the way he felt.

Finch, pretty in green taffeta, avoided his eyes and said, "Where did you meet?"

He was to be interrogated by his sister who, no doubt, considered it her duty in the absence of their father. "We met here," he said. "At Number 7. Jenny is an old friend of Sibyl's and knows Desirée, too."

Missing the glance Finnie directed at Jenny's clothes was impossible. "Ah, yes," she said. "The group that used to meet here. I heard about it."

At that Jenny blushed.

"And that was more than a year ago," Latimer said, anticipating the next question and bending what was real just a little.

"Why didn't you introduce me to Jenny before?" Finch

asked. She gave Latimer a hard stare. "Is there something else you'd like to tell me?"

Damn it all, she was asking him if he'd got Jenny with child. "Nothing really, except I hope the two of you will become great friends."

"Ye dinna meet me because although Latimer tells the truth when he says we met when I was fortunate enough to be included in Sibyl's circle, we hadna seen each other for months, not until we started seeing each other along the way on Bond Street. I work on Bond Street in a millinery shop. I'm the milliner's assistant. Then Latimer found out I was in a wee bit o' trouble and he wouldna let me deal wi' it alone."

Latimer seethed at listening to Jenny defend herself to Finch. "You couldn't deal with it alone, although you have certainly tried."

"So," Finch said, "you've actually *known* each other, how long?"

He wouldn't distress Jenny further, but later he'd have a few things to say to Finch who meant well, but could be too sharp on occasion.

"I suppose—"

"I'll deal with this, Jenny. Finch, Jenny and I are betrothed. This is my decision to make, and not your decision to question. If you came to interfere with my—"

"*Don't,*" Jenny said, cutting him off. "Families should always care for one another. Your sister wants what's best for ye. Leave it be, now. Please."

This was perfect, now the woman he loved was coming to his sister's defense.

"You're right," Finch said and went to Jenny's other side. She slipped a hand under Jenny's arm. "My brother has always had the best taste—in all things."

If only she knew. Now that was a horrible thought.

"He has the best o' sisters or I'm much mistaken," Jenny said.

Latimer sighed. He would keep quiet and allow them to compliment each other.

"We're about the same height and build," Finch said, looking sideways at Jenny. She put out a foot on which she wore a stylish green half-boot. "Lift your skirts and let's make a test."

Prickling raised the hair on the back of Latimer's neck.

With disturbing reluctance, Jenny lifted her skirts the smallest amount, to reveal her clean but badly worn boots and, after a hesitation, Finch put her foot beside Jenny's. "Hah," she said and he'd have to admit she managed to sound merry. "Just as I thought. Our feet are about the same size. How perfect."

Jenny looked at him, but Latimer couldn't think of a thing to say.

"Latimer," Finch said. "You wouldn't believe how badly I need to make room in my wardrobes at Number 8. Living between two homes is quite complicated, you know, Jenny." She clapped her hands. "We shall have such fun. Spend the day with me tomorrow and you shall try everything on. I rather think the waists on my gowns will have to be made smaller, but I'll send for a modiste and that shall be accomplished in no time. And slippers and boots? My, there are so many of them I'll never wear again and they are yours."

Latimer found he couldn't look at either Jenny or Finch.

"And lots of *personal* items. They're all beautiful, but I can't wear several sets at a time. The nightrails and robes. Oh, this is marvelous. Do say you'll come."

"I ha' t'go t'work," Jenny said. Her voice didn't wobble and for that Latimer was grateful.

"Oh, *work*," Finch said. "Why should you be sewing

hats for other people when you're going to marry Latimer? He won't allow you to do such things again.''

''I make hats because it's my job. It's what I'm paid to do and I need the money. I'm no' a kept woman—by anyone. It's true that Latimer has persuaded Lady Hester, bless her, to take me in but when I can, I'll pay her for the room. I've debts, y'see, and I pay my own debts. And I dinna take charity.''

The most horrible silence fell. It couldn't have been more suffocating if a heavy blanket had been thrown over them. He knew how good Finch's heart was and that her offers had been made out of kindness, but he also knew how proud his Jenny was, how determined to keep her head up even when she was threatened by a worm like Bucket.

''Toby is a wee boy who stayed wi' me in Lardy Lane. That's in—''

''Whitechapel,'' Finch finished for her. ''I know the lane and I know Whitechapel. When Latimer and I came to London, and until my marriage, we worked together there. Not a good place for a young woman alone.''

Jenny nodded. ''But Toby is a grand boy. And he's no' had any advantages. When Latimer brought me here, he brought Toby, too, and Lady Hester likes him. She's given him a room he thinks belongs in a palace and jobs t'do to help pay for his keep. He's no skills and he's but a wee lad—twelve and still recoverin' from going up the chimneys—and he canna do for himsel'. I do have skills and I like them. I do well carin' for mysel'—or I can if I'm no' bein' oppressed by an evil man.''

''I've offended you,'' Finch said. She sat down in one of Latimer's green chairs. ''And I'm ashamed of myself. I get carried away. I always did. Ask Latimer. I only thought how lovely you'd look in some of my things. I have too many and that's foolish. Anyway, anything I have, anything at all that you'd like to use, is yours.''

Latimer almost groaned. Finch gushed like a pump beneath the hand of an overzealous scullery maid.

''Thank ye,'' Jenny said. He felt her hand tremble again and thought she might have swayed a little.

''When Latimer and I were young, our father was always parsimonious. He had worked for everything he had and thought we should do the same. So we did. He always reminded us that one day he'd be dead and we'd be rich because he'd been careful to guard his money.

''Then, when we said we were coming to London, it was terrible until we got away. He didn't shout, just didn't speak at all except when we were taking our trunks to the carriage. Then he told us we were to be cut out of his will. We knew how it was to be very worried about how we should manage, I can tell you. The business took some time to become successful and by that time all the money my father had grudgingly given me to live on until I was married was gone. Latimer had gone through his savings, too. There were times when we went hungry.''

Latimer cleared his throat, pulled Jenny close so that he could put an arm around her and said, ''So there you have it, Jenny. Finnie and I have, on occasion, had to make a loaf last two days.'' Such mockery didn't become him but he had to stop Finch from burying herself any deeper with her effort to rescue the moment. ''Jenny will want for nothing. She wants for nothing now. She's had such a long day. I'll just see her upstairs before I take you next door.''

''Yes, yes, I see,'' Finch said. She wrung her hands. ''I apologize for being so foolish.''

''Ye weren't foolish. Ye were kind. I'm just no' polished enough to express mysel' properly. I'll bid ye good night.''

Finch went into action. She all but leaped from her chair and took fast, short steps to plant herself in front of Latimer and Jenny. "Where are my manners? You must come with me, of course, Jenny. Latimer can see us both to Number 8. There is a beautiful room next to mine and it shall be yours. You need rest. You need to be made a fuss of."

She thinks you need to be protected from me. Latimer held Jenny tighter.

Jenny looked up at him with terrible alarm and said, *"Lumpit."*

He looked to the ceiling and repeated, "Lumpit."

"The clergyman?" Finch said. "The one staying at Number 8?"

"Yes," he told her. "The one staying at Number 8 who is determined to persuade Jenny to marry him. He refuses to accept that she doesn't want to be his slave and thank him daily for rescuing her from a squalid, pitiable existence. His words, not mine, right Jenny?"

"Yes," she said. "If it's all the same to ye, I'll sleep in 7B."

"Oh, how awfully bizarre." Finch bobbed on her toes and rolled to her heels and back. "Yes, well, I suppose you might prefer it at Number 7. But perhaps I should stay here, too."

She bloody well wanted to chaperon Jenny. "You have your own home," Latimer said. "There isn't a comfortable spot for you here."

"Oh." Finch bobbed some more. "Of course, you're right. I'll have breakfast here in the morning."

"Jenny leaves early, and you know I have to be at the warehouse almost before the cocks crow."

"Yes, yes, so that won't do. But you shall both come to me for dinner tomorrow. No, don't even attempt to de-

cline or I shall never forgive you for not loving me enough
to spend time with me when I've come all this way to be
with you, Latimer.''

"Thank ye," Jenny said. "I'll be glad t'come. Good
night."

Finnie had been sweet when he took her home. She'd
told him she found Jenny delightful, her simplicity refreshing. Also, Finch had noted, Jenny McBride had a good
mind and might very well make him a suitable match.

In his own rooms again, Latimer spun his hat across the
room to land, as was his intention, on top of his coat stand.
The evening was still warm. The scent of flowers had been
heavy outside. He put a hand in his coat pocket and his
spine prickled. His fingers had closed on the silk rose petals. They had come loose as she ran from him. There was
no more mystery than that to their appearance.

He was tired, but his eyelids didn't as much as droop.
This vigilance that had become part of him was unlikely
to relax until Jenny was his wife and she was no longer
in any danger.

When he'd escorted her to 7B, she had left him at the
top of the stairs, gone into her quarters and shut the door
without as much as offering him a smile.

He poured himself a brandy, but set it down untouched.
It wouldn't do to breathe spirits on Jenny, and if he drank
now he might well do that when he went to beg a good-
night kiss.

One tap on her door and, if she didn't answer quickly,
he'd leave at once. But how much better he would sleep
after just one of her sweet kisses.

He left 7A quietly and went up the stairs on the balls
of his feet. Light shone under the door of 7B. In other
words, she wasn't in the bedroom yet.

Latimer tapped on the door.

An immediate rustling made him frown. Jenny's simple dresses didn't rustle.

She didn't come to let him in.

A man could change his mind about how persistent he'd be. He tapped again, more resolutely, and said, "Jenny?" with his mouth close to a panel.

The rustling continued.

Damn it all, what was she about? *"Jenny,"* he said more loudly, tossing caution away. "Open the door or I'm coming in."

Rapid footsteps crossed the sitting room and she opened the door—but only an inch or two, allowing him a view of her eyes peering out at him. "Away to your bed, Latimer. We agreed t'speak tomorrow."

"That was before I discovered I wouldn't be able to sleep without just one kiss."

She didn't smile. "I'm closing the door now."

Now *that* wasn't the Jenny he knew talking. He took hold of the edge of the door and pushed it wide enough to admit him. Jenny staggered backward and sat on the blue-and-silver couch with a thud.

"Now," he said, and shut the door behind him. "What is all this about? Why are you behaving strangely?"

"I'm not. I'm tired and gettin' ready for bed."

"Since I left, you've had more than enough time to be in bed and very possibly asleep. You were in this room when I came up here. Why?"

"I'll not be questioned by ye. It's a price ye're putting on your friendship and ye disappoint me."

That stopped him. But only for long enough to regroup and change strategy. "Poor sweetheart, so it must seem. I only ask the questions because I care. Don't close me out when something's worrying you."

She tweaked a silk throw over several pillows made of gathered circles of taffeta. The taffeta rustled beneath the sliding silk.

"Jenny?" He made sure he didn't stare at the throw, or the pillows. "Tell me what it is, please."

She inclined her head and blinked rapidly. Her lips drew back from her teeth, and she shook her head slowly.

"What?" He was rapidly going mad. "Don't do this to me. There's something wrong and you are to tell me about it at once."

Jenny only shook her head again.

"Very well," Latimer said and strode to the couch. He whipped aside the throw.

"No!" Jenny tried to tug the silk away from him.

She was no match for him and he tossed the thing on a chair. then he picked up a pillow. Jenny threw herself on top of the pile and spread her arms as if to protect them.

Startled, Latimer did the first thing that came into his head; he hauled her up by the waist and slung her, kicking, over his shoulder. Then he scooped the cushions onto the floor.

An envelope had been stuffed hastily behind the seat cushion, leaving only one end visible. Trapping Jenny with an arm across the back of her thighs, he retrieved her treasure and pulled out a piece of paper folded in two.

"Dinna, dinna. Please Latimer. Let me down and gi' me what's mine."

He considered and did set her feet on the floor once more. She made a grab for her precious letter but he held her off easily.

"Ye're no' t'read that. It's personal. Gi' it t'me, please."

"Soon enough," he told her. The slow, heavy thump of

his heart sickened him. "Please sit down and control yourself."

She started to speak, but closed her mouth again and stood by the fireplace. She crossed her arms on the mantel and buried her face.

Latimer unfolded the paper and read:

You can't hide. Sooner or later you'll be alone and I'll have you, Jenny McBride. All I need is a few moments when your bodyguard gets careless. I want to teach you the things that please me. Your being with More doesn't please me at all and you shall pay for that. I know how to deal with people who cross me. Perhaps I can't hurt you too badly after I've made such plans for the two of us, but I shall enjoy watching the other one die.

20

"**S**ir?"

Latimer spared only a glance for the woman who had appeared at his side. For an hour he'd watched Sibyl and Desirée inside Madame Sophie's shop with Madame and Jenny waiting upon them and in deep discussion. When they weren't laughing.

Except for Jenny. Jenny didn't laugh.

"Sir?"

"On your way," he said. "I'm a busy man." He was also a very worried man. The previous night he'd finally persuaded Jenny to tell him she'd found the letter when she turned down the covers on the bed. Bucket, or someone in his employ, had been able to get into 7B and leave the house without being seen at all.

That morning, before Sibyl and Desirée arrived, he'd managed to tell Madame Sophie that Jenny should not leave the shop until he returned for her, and the lady had been deeply worried but had agreed.

He would have to go to Whitechapel but could scarcely stand to let Jenny out of his sight.

"I've put myself in grave danger by coming here," the woman persisted. "If I'm seen, I'll likely be done for."

Latimer looked at her fully for the first time. A short woman. In a dark gray pelisse and bonnet, with gloves on her hands and a heavy veil over her face, she made a nondescript impression—except for a notable bosom, a narrow waist, and charmingly flared hips. He gave his attention to her veiled face but could see only the glitter of her eyes in the shadows.

"I'll tell you what I've got to say quickly," she said. "Then I won't bother you again. I'm not here because it's an easy thing to do, but my conscience would never have rested if I hadn't tried to warn you."

"Let's dispense with the mystery, shall we? Such intrigues gain no admiration from me."

"I'm here to do you a favor. I didn't have to come, but I don't like to see good people treated badly just so someone else can get a fat prize. You're in a lot of danger, Mr. More."

Her use of his name shook him. "Very well. I'm listening. But first, what do you gain from this?"

"I have a ministry," she said. "I'm trying to make up for past sins by doing good works. There's nothing more you need to know. But if you'd rather I leave, then I will."

She had his attention. "Say your piece," he told her.

"This is a hard one," she said. "Send the little Scot away, far away, and make sure she never returns to London. Do this for her good and for your own. She isn't what she seems to be. Follow her blindly and you'll rue the day you met her."

Latimer held up a hand. "Don't you think I can tell when you're parroting what you've been told to say? Go back to your friends and tell them to leave us alone. If they do us no harm, I'll do them no harm. If they persist in this behavior, I'll have them up before the law."

"I don't have any friends," she said. "And you're the one who'll be taken before the magistrates if certain people have their way. You're a nuisance to them."

Latimer's mouth was dry. He wasn't disposed to believe

a word she said, but what could it hurt to let her finish? "Go on."

"She doesn't have any love for you. And she knows secrets she'll never tell you. Don't believe what she says to you. She was sent to suck you in, that's all. Suck you into a scheme so big that your life is expendable if you get in the way. You're already in their way. Get rid of her."

"Get away from me," Latimer said, turning on the woman. "What lies are these? And why are you trying to injure Jenny? What has she done to you? Go, or I'll detain you for mischief."

She moved backward, then turned and began walking away. A few yards distant, she looked at him again and called out, "I'll give you something to think about. How many girls have you known who lived in slums and worked for a pittance but who could read any book you put in front of them?"

"I very much doubt Jenny reads well."

"Try her, sir. Be nonchalant, but I'd be surprised if she had to ask you for any help. My advice is to put her out of that house and out of London."

Latimer wished the wretched female weren't shouting at him loud enough to turn heads. "Good day to you," he said.

"And good day to you, Mr. More. I wonder if she can write. You know, write things like threatening *notes*. What do you really know about Jenny McBride?"

21

The moment Latimer opened the front door, Jenny said, "Don't worry. I'll be ready in plenty of time," and she'd hurried away to 7B, desperate to be alone and try to understand his behavior after he'd picked her up in a carriage at Madame Sophie's. He'd been silent and frowning, and several times she'd caught him staring at her strangely.

"Jenny, dear. There you are." With Sir Edmund a solicitous step in front of her—and holding her hand—Lady Hester reached the landing outside 7B. Over her arm she carried a heap of dresses in a variety of lovely hues. "That wicked Desirée has left for Mont Nuage. *Mont Nuage* where her father—the Crown Prince—will care no more about her arrival than he did about her last departure. We all know a man like that doesn't change. Really, these young people are so aggravating."

Jenny bobbed and smiled sympathetically at Lady Hester—and thought that had she ever known a mother, she'd have been more than happy for her to have been a lady who cared as much for others as did Lady Hester Bingham.

"Did she leave that beautiful Halibut over at Number 17 with nothing but servants to care for him?" Lady Hester asked. "That darling animal is a person, or close to a person. It's a disgrace, I tell you."

Sir Edmund's brows drew together and he held Lady Hester's arm with obvious concern. "We should look into it, my dear. In fact *I'll* look into it. I can't have your tender heart burdened so."

Jenny smiled at him. His concern for her ladyship was a pleasing thing to hear. "Adam took Halibut," she told him. "I'd offered, too, who wouldn't? I've a feelin' everyone here will spoil Halibut and he willna want t'go home when the princess does return."

"*If* she does," Lady Hester said darkly. "But enough of that. Desirée has a good heart. We'll pray and our prayers will bring her back. Take these from me, please, Jenny. They grow heavy. Edmund, dear, where did you put the box?"

Jenny was forced to accept the slippery heap of fine fabrics.

Sir Edmund turned aside and passed between two urns carved in the shapes of tigers—with the most unpleasant red eyes—and into a book-lined room visible beyond. For a few moments he was out of sight, but he returned with a wooden box. "I put it in the library," he said.

"Good man. Carry it into Jenny's rooms, there's a lamb."

He smiled at Jenny, who juggled the dresses and got the door open.

"Put them in there," Lady Hester told Sir Edmund, indicating the bedroom. "The dresses can go on your bed, Jenny. Desirée brought them over for you. She's already left, y'know. If you don't want them—this is the message she insisted I give you—if you don't want them, they are to be cut up for cleaning rags, and knowing your pride—her words, not mine—knowing your pride, you'll offer to wield the scissors. On the other hand, and I'm still quoting, she suggested you might want to put empty pride aside, accept that we all know you haven't any money to speak of, and make us happy by enjoying her present. She also wanted me to tell you that to decline a gift from a friend is rude and hurtful.''

Jenny dropped the dresses on the bed and struggled to control her natural urge to ask for some scissors. Then she thought how childish the idea was and said, "Thank ye. Princess Desirée is a rare person. Perhaps when ye write t'her you'd gi' her my thanks, and tell her I will wear her beautiful dresses when I've a suitable time."

"Clever girl," Lady Hester said, and her smile turned her blue eyes even more blue. In a low-cut turquoise gown embroidered with tiny seed pearls, many strands of pearls at her neck, and a turquoise beret trimmed with more pearls, she was radiant. "I understand you're to have dinner at Finch's this evening. Certainly a most appropriate occasion for one of those dresses. Now we must be off. Sir Edmund is taking me to the theater. One of Mr. Shakespeare's plays. It was a favorite of Queen Elizabeth, I'm told. *A Midsummer Night's Dream*. Have a lovely evening."

"Thank ye."

Sir Edmund bowed smartly and the two off them descended the final flight to the foyer.

Jenny had little time to dither. She hurried to the bedroom and shed her work clothes. A jug of hot water had been placed on the commode and she washed quickly before setting about doing her hair.

When she was satisfied, she went to the bed and gingerly touched the very large pile of clothes. She didn't have time to decide what to choose from such a wealth of lovely things. And she wasn't suited to such finery. But she would wear one of the dresses to please Lady Hester—and Latimer.

Jenny closed her eyes, plunged a hand into the heap and began to ease out the first garment her fingers closed on.

* * *

Latimer paced slowly back and forth across the foyer. Throughout the day he'd recovered, little-by-little, from the accusations made by the woman in gray. Now he found he breathed normally and reason had taken over. Jenny had not been the one to make overtures to him. She had tried to keep their Bond Street meetings short. Not one thing had Jenny McBride asked of him, and she'd done her best to persuade him to forget her.

Whoever that woman had been, he'd lay odds that she was well acquainted with Morley Bucket. That vermin was desperate, thus the wild attempts to discredit Jenny to him—right down to suggesting Latimer should send her away from London. No doubt Bucket intended to kidnap her along the way.

She was the dearest of women, and she was to be his. He smiled, but when he heard soft footfalls on the stairs and turned around, he felt that smile dissolve.

Jenny came down toward him, her downcast eyes putting the lie to her straight shoulders and elevated chin. He had seen many beautiful and beautifully dressed women, but none had been given the power to move him until Jenny McBride. A gown of blue patent lace over white satin had been simply styled with a young woman in mind. Bands of white satin, obliquely placed, trimmed the short, puffed sleeves and she wore a shawl of blue crepe painted with white flowers—to match the white flowers tucked into the heavy coronet she'd made of her hair.

She drew closer and he found he couldn't speak.

On her feet she wore blue leather slippers over ribbed, white silk stockings.

"Am I late?" she said when she reached him. "I'm no' used to putting on complicated clothes, not that the effort wasn't fun. Princess Desirée left this for me—and a lot of other things. I took them from Lady Hester because I think I might ha' ruined her evenin' if I'd said no." She smiled up at him through her lashes. "And t'tell the truth, the temptation was too much."

"Gad," Latimer said when he found his voice. "You are glorious. Even more glorious. How like Desirée to sneak them in before she left. Jenny, you were made to wear beautiful things." It was true. She was stunning.

She poked out a shoe. "Look. They're so delicate and I love the little ribbons that cross. I've never owned a shoe to match a dress or anythin' else."

Her simplicity and lack of pretense delighted him. "From now on you shall have nothing but shoes that match your outfits. I had planned to take you shopping, but you've made me quake with your fierce determination to stop anyone from doing nice things for you. Will you let me take you now?"

She considered. "I don't think so, Latimer. Not until the time's appropriate. But I thank ye. I am going to use Desirée's things because they'll be out of style if she's away as long she said she would be, and they'll make sure ye're no' ashamed o' me."

He offered her his wrist, which she stared at.

"Put your hand on top," he told her, grinning. "I'll get my hat and we'll walk over. It's a beautiful night."

Jenny placed her hand on his wrist and said, "Well, that feels silly. It's no' comfortable."

"But it's the way things are done on occasion, so humor me. We're practicing. Come into 7A a moment."

Jenny did as he asked, thinking she'd walk on her hands for the man if that would make him happy. He was handsome in black, relieved only by his shirt. Like his waistcoat, his neckcloth was black and with his face bowed while he checked the simple knot, shadows painted flaring lines on his face and made him look…wicked. She gave a delighted little shudder at the thought and decided, not for the first time, that she had an unruly spirit.

Latimer looked up suddenly, his expression serious. "Close the door a moment, if you please."

She thought to demur but, held in thrall by those black eyes, did as he asked.

A few swift steps and he stood before her. "I've told you I love you, Jenny. The word is too weak. I adore you. I hoped that one day I'd meet a woman I'd want for my own, but doubted she'd ever become a reality. Now there's you, and you're more than I hoped for." He dropped to a knee in front of her and brought her left hand to his lips. "There is no going back for me. Night and day I dream of making you my wife. Of our having children and being a family. Jenny, dearest, will you marry me?"

"This only happens in fairy stories," she said, and her voice squeaked away to nothing.

Latimer smiled at her. "This isn't a fairy story. What's your answer, Jenny?"

"Did I no' a'ready gi' it?"

He rested his forehead on the back of her hand. "You wear a fellow down. In a manner of speaking, yes, you did. But I did things all wrong. I never did actually ask you, I just assumed. This is my official proposal."

Bending over him, she kissed his hair and pressed her cheek to his. Then she knelt also and said, "Yes. Thank ye very much for askin' and I'll be glad to accept your official proposal."

He laughed and jutted his chin toward her. "Women don't kneel when they're being proposed to."

"I dinna care what *women* do. I'm just one woman and I want to honor ye as much as ye honor me." Her lips parted, she let her eyes close and inclined her head.

Latimer held her and kissed her, until a small warning signal sounded from somewhere distant. The next kiss would be more ardent. Then he would be kissing her shoulders, and her breasts—and dinner would become something they'd forgotten.

Her eyes remained shut and she hugged him about the neck.

From his waistcoat pocket he took what had been his mother's betrothal ring. She had given it to him before she died and made him promise to give it to the girl he married.

He took her left arm from around his neck and slipped the ring onto her finger. "As a sign of my intentions," he said.

Jenny kept her face against his neck and used her thumb to feel the ring. She poked it as best she could. Then she extricated her other hand and turned his mother's large diamond encircled with dark, pear-shaped sapphires around and around.

"Look at it, little bird. It belonged to my mother. She gave it to me for just this purpose. You would have brought her such happiness."

Jenny gradually raised her head, and Latimer caught her about the waist, got up, and set her on her feet.

Her expression was startled. She looked at the ring and he noted that the skin on her hands was reddened from work and probably from not having any gloves. But her slim fingers were meant for beautiful rings and the diamond and sapphires sparkled there. Amazingly, the ring fit, but his mother had also been a delicately boned woman.

"I canna wear this," she whispered. "It wouldna be right. It should be Finch's."

"Finch has many beautiful rings. This one belonged to me, not to Finch. And now it belongs to you. We are betrothed, Jenny. We are to become man and wife." He felt strong and vital. If he thought she would allow it, he'd sweep her away and arrange a special license and marriage within the day—and night.

"Yes," she said, and lifted the layer of patent lace on her skirt to polish the ring on the satin beneath.

Latimer could think of nothing but hugging her to him. She was perfectly natural, and perfectly desirable.

However, Finch would be awaiting them and if they spoiled her meal, she would be a dragon to deal with. There was, however, one formality to be dealt with. "It would not be polite if I failed to speak to your father. And I'm sure you will want your family to share this joyous time."

He saw Jenny swallow. She said, "I dinna know where they are."

"You think they've moved since you came to London?"

Jenny turned her back on him and wandered the room, regarding his jade and ivory pieces one by one.

There were moments when patient silence, difficult as it might be, was the best course.

"I never knew my parents. I was abandoned."

He stung from the harshness of it. "But I thought—"

"I let ye think I had a family but that we were no' close. By not telling ye exactly how things were wi' me, I lied. Ye'd seen how I lived and I couldna' bear t'sound even more pathetic. I'm sorry."

"Where did you grow up? I mean, who cared for you?"

"I was lucky. Good women cared for me in an orphanage."

Latimer could only imagine what kind of childhood she must have had. "And when you left, you decided to come to London to make your fortune." He laughed. "What an idiotic thing to say. Forgive me, please."

"What are ye supposed t'say? There isna a right way to reply t'me. I'd made mysel' useful wi' the younger children. Mrs. Penny taught me things and I learned fast, so I could pass them on."

She learned fast. "Like reading and writing? Of course, you've been teaching Toby." And she had never made a secret of it.

"Aye. He's easy to teach." Jenny turned toward him. "At thirteen I had t'leave the orphanage because they've no means t'keep ye longer. I lived among the market stalls at the bottom of the castle walls for a while, but I was verra frightened. I went back to the home and they helped me as they could. Mrs. Penny knew a person with a position in a tradesman's house. They took me on and in return for doin' whatever was needed, I got my bed and meals. I was happy enough there."

"Why didn't you stay there?" How glad he was that she hadn't.

"I was sent away when I was fifteen." She sat on a chair and he could scarcely bear to see her face so tense. "The master's son was caught enterin' my room at night. They said I had enticed him and I was t'go."

"How old was this son?"

"Seven-and-twenty. The one good part of it all was that he was stopped on his way into my room and he hadna tried t'come there before. I was sorry t'lose my place, though—and t'have no references."

Latimer made fists and regretted that he was unlike to have an opportunity to place them where they belonged—giving a man of seven-and-twenty a beating for trying to ruin a fifteen-year-old.

"But I made my way. I'd learned t'sew by then and I had a feelin' for it, so I found work in a factory and stayed there until I came to London. So there ye have it. It's no' a prize ye've asked t'be your wife.''

He wanted to break something. He wanted to pay back all the people who had ever been cruel to his Jenny. His own passionate rage shook him. "Jenny, look at me."

She did so, but when he approached her he was appalled to see her flinch. "Do you think I would hit you?" he asked her, barely able to speak the words.

"No, o'course not."

"Perhaps not me, yet you flinched as if you thought you would be punished. Did you think that after hearing your story, I would shout at you, turn you aside?"

"I dinna know what I thought. I suppose I was ready for punishment—for bein' who I am. For bein' nothing. And it felt as if a blow was coming."

He held himself rigid. "Decent men do not hit women. *Ever.*" She needed gentleness, not displays of anger. "I will never harm you. You are my love and you will be my wife. No human being is *nothing,* and you are so much more than most. You are the greatest prize I could ever win. And think of it this way—" he offered her his hand and grinned "—I wish your parents no harm, but I'm rather grateful I need not present myself for approval."

She held his hand and eventually returned his smile. "I canna tell ye all that's in my heart. I dinna know the words t'explain, but I love a perfect man."

He drew her to her feet. "I'm not perfect, Jenny, but I do have perfect taste in women." And he'd rather she never discover just how far from perfect he'd been.

22

Just when he, Larch Lumpit, curate of St. Philomena's in Middle Wallop, had feared that all might be lost, he'd had a well-deserved piece of luck. He'd met a woman who recognized him—how he wasn't clear—and was aware of his plight with Jenny McBride. He was so excited, he twitched. He'd never seen this person before but she assured him that she would help him win Jenny, and her only demand in exchange was that he should help her.

Ah, yes, how the just were rewarded.

"Lady Kilrood," he said to his hostess, who had joined him in the drawing room at Number 8 Mayfair Square. "I am more than grateful to you for your hospitality."

The look she gave him wasn't kind. No doubt he could thank her brother and Jenny for that. Time to follow the instructions he'd been given by the woman in gray. "My Lady, this is presumptuous, but I should like to share a secret with you. I do this only because I have Jenny McBride's welfare at heart and, although I don't know him, I don't want any harm to come to Mr. More."

Lady Kilrood had been standing with her back to him, surveying woodland murals painted in recessed panels along walls covered with silk striped in two shades of pale yellow. He caught sight of her hands tightening behind her back. "Interesting remarks, Mr. Lumpit," she said, all nonchalance.

He rubbed his itching nose. "More than interesting, I think. But I shouldn't have brought this up. I debated about the wisdom of bothering you and thought I shouldn't at first. My initial instincts were good."

The lady faced him. He supposed she was striking enough to engage some men—as she evidently had Viscount Kilrood—but she didn't appeal to him.

"What is it you're trying to tell me?" she said.

Fiddle me. He had been so preoccupied, he'd forgotten his manners and remained seated in her presence. He worked his way to his feet and bowed—graciously, he thought. "When I came to London to see Jenny and discovered she was at Number 7 Mayfair Square, I did not tell the truth to the people who kindly entertained me there. I pretended Jenny and I had never met and that I was here because Ivy Willow begged me to come and save her friend from a difficult life. That wasn't true."

Lady Kilrood moved yellow roses about in a crystal bowl and finally said, "What is true?"

"I will not do anything to hurt Jenny. Do I have your word that anything I tell you will be between the two of us until I have found a means to save the day for all concerned, so to speak?"

She didn't answer him, so he didn't continue.

Lady Kilrood looked up suddenly. "Is this *secret* you want me to keep something that could hurt my brother?"

"I don't think it will—as long as I have time and opportunity to persuade Jenny to do what's right. At first I will have to convince her that I have accepted her change of heart where I'm concerned, but that I have another reason for remaining in Mayfair Square for a period. Then, if you agree that I should, I'll set about showing Mr. More that he has made a poor choice—and winning Jenny back myself. All that may take a day, two days, or a week or two. Being in the house next door to where she's staying will be a great help."

Lady Kilrood eyed him. "You'd better tell me your secret. Then I'll decide if your motive for wanting to stay here is to right a wrong, or if you are looking for free lodgings."

He slapped a hand to his breast and felt genuinely pained at her cruel suggestion. "Very well. I shall throw myself on your mercy and hope you will see that it could be disastrous if you spoke to your brother too soon because he is in the freshness of his passion for Jenny and likely to do something ruinous, like running off and marrying her before he can be stopped.

"Jenny and I already have an understanding. She is to marry me, my lady. We have known each other for half a year."

Lady Kilrood's hands dropped to her sides and her light golden eyes grew huge. "How could you have known her before? She lives in London and you don't."

"She came to Middle Wallop to visit Ivy Willow. They are old friends." He paused and put a hand over his eyes. That should appear most affecting. "My Lady, I still love her and I will take her back if she'll have me."

"You are telling me that Jenny is betrothed to you but pretending she doesn't know you?"

He sighed. "Yes. We saw each other on most Sundays. She would travel to Middle Wallop in time for Morning Song and we'd spend the day together, but she stopped coming some weeks ago. She wrote that she was dealing with a problem and would come when she could. I'm an understanding man so we continued to correspond, but I became worried and decided I should find her and do what I could to help.

"This is so difficult. It goes against my ethics to speak

of another's personal burdens, but I feel I must tell you all. I have learned all about Jenny's involvement with Mr. More." He had seen that gentleman watching her through the windows of the milliner's shop that morning and it had been shortly afterward that the woman dressed in gray had approached him and told him exactly what was what between More and Jenny McBride. "Their involvement will not be successful because Jenny is a lost soul who lies constantly. She seems hardly to know what the truth is. Eventually she would hurt Mr. More in some terrible manner."

"Oh, my goodness." The viscountess sat down. "Surely you don't expect me to agree to what you've asked."

"I do. If you don't, I shall be the one discredited— remember what an accomplished liar Jenny is—and there will be no stopping Mr. More from marrying her. She has obviously decided that your brother is both more glamorous and more wealthy than I am and so she wants to get rid of me."

"And this isn't a case of Mr. Lumpit wanting what another man has, and doing a little fibbing—the same sort of fibbing Jenny's been accused of?"

Larch Lumpit placed a hand over his heart again and said a silent prayer asking that allowances be made for the untruths he was forced to tell. "I don't blame you for questioning me, but what I have told you is true. Please have a calm mind, say your prayers as I shall, and we'll hope for the best. And now—because I want you to have faith in my honor—I'll leave your home at once."

Latimer kept Jenny's hand pressed firmly to his side and gave up his hat and gloves to Jennings, Ross's longtime valet, who preferred to stay in London and act as caretaker and butler while the family was in Scotland.

"Thanks, Jennings," Latimer said. "Just tell me where my sister is."

"Aye. She's upstairs in the drawing room wi' that person, Mr. Lumpit."

Jenny looked taken aback at the news that Lumpit was with Finch, but leaned forward and said, "Ye're from Scotland, too, Mr. Jennings?"

Jennings, wiry, bushy-browed and gray-haired, turned up his mouth at her. "That's right. And the both o' us from Edinburgh from what I hear. Best city in the world, but when ye get older and make friends elsewhere, ye like to bide near the friends."

"Aye," Jenny agreed.

"Up we go then," Latimer said and started for the stairs.

Before he took his second upward step, Finch called down, "Hello. You're late. Dinner's to be in the conservatory. Such a nice night it'll be warm enough to sit among the flowers and eat."

"How lovely," Jenny said, but then Lumpit appeared and she didn't say another word.

"Sorry to hold up dinner, Finnie," Latimer said, not as much as looking at Lumpit. "Nice intimate little gathering sounds first class. Just what we need. It's been too long since we talked."

"Tell Mrs. Hastings we're going in," Finch told Jennings.

"Gladly," he said. "She's fussin' over her soup gettin' too thick."

Finch led the way to the conservatory. Lovely in the deepening summer dusk, the scent of gardenias and the brilliant color of orchid blooms turned the copper and glass room into a magical place. Palms brushed the glass overhead and lush vines clung to their trunks. A round table had been placed beneath a green, cut glass chandelier in the center of the room and set with white linens, silver and crystal.

Lumpit had walked as far as the door to the conservatory and still stood there. He said, "Lady Kilrood. Just wanted to thank you again for allowing me to remain in your home. I'll go to my room now."

"Not a bit of it," Finch said, startling Latimer. "You'll join us for dinner. Now don't argue. I can't have you eating alone when we're to have a lovely meal and would enjoy your company. Wouldn't we, Latimer and Jenny?" She gave Latimer a beseeching look.

"Quite," was the best he could do to support her. Finnie's soft heart could be unfortunate sometimes.

"If you're sure," Lumpit said, coming into the conservatory. "You are all much too kind to me."

Finch approached the table and Lumpit hurried to hold her chair while she sat. Then he took the seat to her right, even though there were only three places set at the moment.

"Jenny, I know I'm breaking the seating rules, but I want you to sit by me," Finch said. "Latimer, there's a chair over there. Bring it to the table, would you? Jennings will make sure you have everything you need."

Holding back a chuckle, Latimer got the chair and seated himself with Lumpit at his left and Jenny at his right. She caught his eye and from the way she'd drawn her bottom lip between her teeth, he could tell she was struggling against laughter, too. Mr. Larch Lumpit's most amazing quality was his blissful ignorance of being a buffoon.

Jennings appeared with a young footman Latimer knew only by sight, and the meal commenced. Finch declared it an "ode to our Cornish roots" and promised modest fare. Latimer wasn't sure he recalled much turtle soup in the More household—their father being a lover of hefty meat pies and mountains of potatoes—but he found it delicious even if Lumpit's slurping consumption of three bowls put one off a bit.

Jenny hardly touched her soup and Finch didn't do much better.

Latimer and Lumpit drank Madeira, and champagne was poured for the ladies.

Jennings brought in the turbot in lobster sauce and served it himself.

"Plain Cornish fare?" Latimer said, raising an eyebrow at Finch. "Wasn't it fun to eat like this every night when we were growing up?"

Finch gave him an arch look and said, "Don't eat the turbot unless you really want to. I may surprise you yet."

"Very fond of turbot meself," Lumpit said. "If there's too much, I'll gladly help out. We wouldn't want to offend that nice Mrs. Hastings by having her think we disliked her cooking."

The man kept his face pointed at his food and barely took a breath between mouthfuls. This time Finch smiled as broadly as Latimer, but Jenny, who pushed food around her plate, looked unhappy.

"Jenny," Finch said. "You look lovely in that dress."

"Doesn't she?" Latimer said and found Jenny's hand beneath the table. He squeezed it, hoping she understood that he was asking her not to start talking about wearing Desirée's castoffs.

"Thank you," Jenny said. "Lady Hester and Sir Edmund brought lots of dresses down to me. Before she left for Mont Nuages, Princess Desirée decided she wouldn't need them again and left them for me. I shouldn't accept such gifts I know, but Lady Hester assured me they would go to waste if I didn't. In fact, Princess Desirée left instructions that the dresses be cut up for rags if I insisted upon being too proud, as she put it.''

By the end of her speech, Latimer had slumped against the back of his chair. She was forthright and there wasn't a thing he could, or should, want to do to change that.

He waited for Finch to notice their mother's ring on Jenny's hand, but since Jenny had declined the fish, she was able to keep her left hand in her lap and Latimer thought he knew why. She didn't want to have a personal discussion in front of Lumpit. After dinner, they must find a way to get rid of the man.

Salads followed, and pickled asparagus. Since using her fork in her right hand was acceptable, Jenny ate a little. Her table manners were excellent. Latimer considered how that would have come about. He still had a great deal to learn about her.

The footman staggered into the room under the weight of an enormous savory pie. Latimer could smell succulent meat and spices in the steam that wafted forth.

Jennings dispensed wedges of pie all around and added carrots and whole roasted potatoes, and small tender peas.

''*Voilà,*'' Finch said, raising her palms. ''A good, solid Cornish lamb pie. I told you this was to be a nostalgic meal.''

The Madeira glasses in front of Lumpit and Latimer were refilled—again. Finch and Jenny still had most of their champagne.

The ritual continued until they were served peach cream ices and once again Jenny ate and continued to keep her left hand in her lap.

''Now,'' Lumpit said, his face puce and his lips shiny. ''I have a request. Would the ladies please remain with the gentleman while I reveal something that is most awkward, but which must be said."

Jenny said, "I'm sure you'd prefer to—"

"I shall not stay without you, Jenny," Latimer told her.

"Quite so," Lumpit said. "And I want you, Jenny, and Lady Kilrood, to hear what I have to say. It will enlighten you as to why my behavior may have seemed odd on occasion. I have been through a most extraordinary series of events. A great deal has seemed like unbelievable coincidence, but I think not, I think a higher power is guiding me and circumstances are exactly as was intended."

Finch put her elbows on the table, laced her fingers beneath her chin and listened intently to every word Lumpit said. Latimer saw the man's fatuous pleasure in all the attention and wondered if a chair could be upended without exposing the villainous perpetrator of the crime.

"Please do not think ill of me," Lumpit said, "but my great-grandfather's brother's third wife was born out of wedlock."

Finch's face didn't move, but Jenny said, "A sad thing."

Latimer considered what to say to a man who thought such a revelation might reflect badly on him. A revelation about someone so far removed from him that Latimer was still working out the relationships involved.

"Ivy Willow was to have accompanied me to London but she looks after an elderly couple and the husband is too frail to be left at the moment. If she were with me, this would all have been much less trying. She would have helped me get things right, and Jenny would have been reassured by her presence. She may join us yet…"

Without warning, the chandelier with its elegant green glass candleholders and green crystal prisms rang out like a hoard of tiny bells, the prisms bouncing off each other while the whole thing swayed.

"Latimer?" Finch said loudly and jumped to her feet. "What is it? What's happening?"

Lumpit had beaten her to it and moved well back from the table. His lips moved in silent prayer.

The ringing stopped and the chandelier was still. "It's okay, Finnie," Latimer said and bent over Jenny. "It's all right, sweet. I think perhaps we had a small movement in the earth. Most unusual, in fact I've never experienced such a thing here. Of course, I have been in the Orient and such things happen regularly there. Bring coffee, please, Jennings, there's a good man. And reassure the staff. Things are bound to have been rattled a bit in the kitchens and so forth.

"Sit down everyone. We'll have coffee and some brandy to settle our nerves." He moved his chair closer to Jenny's. "If the earth didn't move, perhaps Mr. Lumpit was getting a message from his higher power." Latimer smiled around but fixed his attention on Lumpit, who had made no move to return to the table. The fellow stood where he was, his mouth still moving, his head shaking from time to time, and stared at the chandelier. "I was joking, Lumpit. Come and join the rest of us."

Lumpit said, "I'll try to remember everything," and wandered back to his seat as if in a trance.

"Here you go," Latimer said, "Take some of the Madeira. It'll fortify you."

Latimer's hand rested on his thigh and Jenny worked her hand beneath his palm. When he looked at her she smiled as if they were alone. How he wished they were. Finch was watching them. He felt her eyes on them but continued to look at Jenny. Lumpit spoke again and Jenny jumped.

"This woman who was born out of wedlock," he said, waving his glass about. "My great-grandfather's brother's third wife. Poor creature. Her mother disappeared. Probably sent away in disgrace. You know how those things are." He gave Latimer a knowing and obvious wink.

"As Jenny said," Latimer told the man. "Sad affair, very sad."

"Might have been anything but sad while it was going on," Lumpit said. "I understand the mother was a bit of a romp and really liked men."

Latimer clamped his teeth together. Nothing he said would take away the outrage of Lumpit having spoken so coarsely in front of ladies—one of whom was unmarried. Probably shouldn't have suggested more Madeira.

"The child's father was already married. But you will have guessed that. We all know how it is in these big houses." Lumpit rolled his eyes as if referring to Number 8. "Brilliant, sought-after, blissfully married couple, but the husband isn't welcome in his wife's bed often enough. He finds the dressing room doors locked on her side at night. Husband takes up with—" more Madeira made its way down Lumpit's throat and he wiped the back of a hand over his mouth "—husband takes up with luscious maid all too willing to give him a good roll for his money. Not that there would actually be any blunt involved, I'm sure. Once he'd had her, she'd have to be quiet or risk losing her place. Just as it should be when the lower classes are noticed by their betters. You agree with me More. I'm—"

Once more the chandelier tinkled but not so wildly this time. However, the table tipped, bringing one leg off the marble tiled floor, then tipped in another direction, cracking down the formerly elevated leg and raising another. It happened to each of the four legs but, miraculously, without tossing anything to the floor.

"Oh, my goodness," Finch said in a very small voice. With the exception of Lumpit, they'd all stood up. "I wish Ross were here."

"That's her husband," Jenny said to Lumpit. "O'course ye want him wi' ye, Finch. Verra frightening. Oh, it's verra frightening." She got up and threw her arms around Latimer's neck. "Hold me, please," she said.

A terrible chore, Latimer thought and wrapped her to him. "We'll be away from here shortly," he whispered. "You shall not be alone tonight."

She leaned away from him and shadows flitted in her eyes. Jenny was a vulnerable girl, and a temptress at the same time.

"I've got to recover myself," Lumpit said. "I'm trying to explain something very important. The girl was kept in the house, but not as the daughter of the master. Looked after by the servants she was, until she became one of them. She was a servant in her own home. That was before her father put her into service elsewhere. She was fortunate to meet my great-grandfather's brother after his second wife died.

"What exactly is the significance of this unhappy story—to us?" Latimer asked.

Jennings returned and poured coffee. He brought the brandy and glasses and set them on the table, then withdrew to stand to the left of the sideboard.

Finch drank coffee immediately and cradled the cup in her hands as if she were cold.

"I don't really know the significance of the story to you," Lumpit said, his big eyes doleful. "But you have been such good people to me and I thought you should know I am a blood relation of an illegitimate girl who was born at Number 7 Mayfair Square.''

Latimer and Finch looked at each other and seconds passed before Finch remembered to close her mouth. She leaned toward Lumpit and said, "You never said anything about—"

"About my shame?" He interrupted. "You know what they say about needing to walk a mile in someone else's shoes to know how they feel. You never have and never will be in my shoes, but they are dashed uncomfortable. I have need to reconcile my shame."

"That makes no sense, Mr. Lumpit," Jenny said. "Ye've even got it wrong, anyway. Ye're no a blood relative o' someone who married your great-grandfather's brother."

"Not really," Lumpit said, sniffing into his napkin. "But I bear the disgrace just the same. I couldn't believe it when I discovered the girl Ivy Willow and Phyllis Smart had spoken of was staying at Number 7 Mayfair Square. I barely remembered the infamous address, for it must have been told me a very long time ago."

Latimer's patience grew thin. "Put it behind you, why don't you? Best not to dwell on the past."

"When I found out Jenny was there, I knew it was an omen. I had to save her from the same fate as my great-grandfather's brother's third wife. And try to discover what I could about my great-grandfather's brother's wife, of course. Least I could do."

Jennings cleared his throat.

"Is the staff quieted down?" Finch asked him. "I hope there's been no damage."

"No damage a'tall, My Lady," Jennings said. "Nothin' happened in the kitchens, or anywhere else from what I gather."

Finch frowned and said, "*Nothing* happened elsewhere? What can you mean?"

"If the earth moved," Jennings said, "it only moved beneath the conservatory."

"Impossible," Latimer said.

"Nothing's impossible," Lumpit said. "Nothing at all. After all, could you have imagined that a man as upstanding as myself is related to so much *sin?*"

"But ye aren't," Jenny said. She sounded distressed. "Ye're no' related one wee bit."

"You are unschooled, Jenny," Lumpit told her. "But you will have heard of guilt by association. One cannot brush so close to depravity and not be touched by it. But...I have been sent an omen that will help me to heal myself by blotting out the family's black stains. I will prove that despite that man, we have grown strong."

"What man?" Latimer asked because he couldn't stop himself.

"The illegitimate woman's father, of course. He must be exposed, and any who have benefited from him in any way should be kept away from decent people."

Finch was the one who gathered her wits enough to ask, "And who, Mr. Lumpit, do you think the illegitimate father was?"

"The father wasna illegitimate," Jenny said. "The daughter was."

"The viscountess's tongue slipped," Lumpit said. "Happens often to women. The father's name was Spivey."

23

Spivey here.

In all my lives I have never, never, never been witness to such outrage! And you may wipe those smirks off your faces because I am not the only man named Spivey to live in this house.

Oh, bless me stars and garters.

Good grief…whatever made me say a common thing like that? Bucket. Been spending too much time trying to make sense of that one's shenanigans.

Bless me, did I actually start to defend myself against that incredible outpouring of twaddle from Lumpit there? Forget it if I did. Not a word he says against the great name of Spivey is true. There has never been an illegitimate… Well, the event that toad spoke of did not take place.

Spite. A foolish, empty-headed man thrashing around with an imaginary sword and hoping to wound his betters. Pathetic.

What? What did you say? Indeed? Well I don't think you're in a position to cast aspersions on my maturity. I think you have incredible impudence to as much as consider judging my actions. Anyway, how do you know the earth didn't move under the conservatory?

I shall not apologize for my advanced ghostly skills. If such things are ''pathetically stereotypical ghost stuff''

*then next time you may shake the chandelier—without
touching it. Took their attention off Lumpit's drivel, didn't
I? He told his story anyway, you say? You blithering... I
shall not sink to name-calling. Lumpit's babbling is the
real concern around here.*

*What? Ouija board techniques? That does it. After a
disgraceful insult like that, you and I shall never be
friends. And I had continued to nurture hopes—in the spirit
of my angelic efforts—that we should one day come to a
mutual respect. Throwing that table around was a fine
piece of technique.*

*No matter. I have no need to defend the pearls I throw
before you.*

*The point is, Lumpit is thinking for himself! Argh, he
was warned that he must never do that. The man is actually being ingenious. He's studied the foe and come to the
right conclusions. Gentility and kindness can be used
against those who insist upon being nice. He knows that
although they don't believe his story about another man
named Spivey, they will nevertheless never find the back-
bone to toss him out on his ear. He's one more lost lamb
and they excel in lost-lamb coddling around here. He'll be
allowed to stay at Number 8, interfering, getting in the
way, causing one to doubt the other, and creating trouble,
trouble...trouble.*

Hmm. Causing trouble...

*Well, why keep pretending when you've already guessed
the truth. Not a word that came from Lumpit's mouth was
his own. The whole idea was mine. I wasn't going to tell
you because I don't like to boast, but I know you will feel
more secure knowing that the one you admire most is,
indeed, brilliant.*

*All very nicely done, although I do say so myself. The
seeds of doubt need only minimal care and feeding to grow
strong. I intend to pile on the manure...*

24

The front door to Number 7 opened before Latimer could get his key into the lock. There stood Old Coot wavering dangerously on his toes, and even more dangerously each time he craned around to look behind him.

"Evening, Coot," Latimer said.

All Jenny could think about was that they were to spend the night together and that she was the happiest of women even if there were large obstacles in her way.

"Good evening, sir," Coot said. "You'd best come right on in, Jenny. Too cold for you out there."

"It's a bonnie evenin'," she told him. And it was. "But I'll come in gladly just the same."

They could hardly climb the stairs together in front of the butler. Jenny looked to Latimer for direction, but he was listening to Coot who whispered earnestly. Latimer shook his head several times, but Coot continued.

When Latimer straightened, Coot said, "She does say she knows you. Says you've talked recently and you'll want to hear what she's got to say."

Jenny remained at the foot of the stairs. She looked upward, then at the nearest newel post and tried to lose herself in studying the fine carvings there. She felt foolish, the one who didn't fit. "Excuse me, but I thank ye for taking me t'Number 8, Latimer. And for the interesting evening. I'd best away to my bed."

"Wait," Latimer said, and although it was an order, it was gentle enough. "Coot, Jenny and I are betrothed. I'm sure you will appreciate the opportunity to congratulate us."

Coot rotated to see Jenny, then turned back to Latimer. The brief glimpse she'd had of Coot's face left an impression of shock. He cleared his throat and said, "Yes, well, my congratulations, sir."

"Thank you," Latimer said. "Would you be good enough to see Jenny to her rooms? I like to know she's in safe hands. I'd best see this visitor."

He went into the guests' sitting room and his eyes met Jenny's the instant before he firmly shut the door. Latimer would come and talk to her later. She saw his promise in that look.

"Well, miss," Old Coot said. "Better get you upstairs. Don't worry about my aching joints. I'm a man who never neglects his duties."

Jenny happened to think the old man was asked to climb too many stairs, too often. "I'm absolutely safe t'go up on my own," she told him. "Away t'your rest, Mr. Coot. It's late and time we were all abed. I've t'be on my way to Bond Street early so I'd best be asleep soon."

"Well—" Coot's struggle with going against Latimer's request was evident. "If you're sure you'll be all right?"

"Absolutely," she told him and he gave her an unsteady bow before going in the direction of the kitchens with uncanny speed.

She'd started upward again when Adam entered the house, bringing the summer evening's warm, flower-scented air with him. He marched to the stairs and took several steps at a time, passing Jenny—without a word—on his second stride.

"Adam Chillworth," she said, surprising herself. "Is it

a new way wi' the gentility, t'ignore a body in such a way?''

He paused with his feet separated by three stairs. "Good night to you, Jenny McBride."

"I want t'catch up wi' ye, please." Jenny hurried to sit on a step just ahead of him. "If ye please, will ye talk wi' me?" Then she saw what he'd probably hoped to conceal from her. Inside a cloak too heavy for the weather, Halibut traveled with his head pushed out between a number of open buttons. "Halibut," she said, delighted. "There he is. I've missed him."

"No doubt," Adam said. "If you'll excuse me?"

"I willna," she told him. "Ye can stay right here. Ye're a worrisome creature—all frowns and grumpy noises, and hiding yoursel' away the way ye do. Sit down an' talk wi' me."

"Here on the stairs?" he said, making not the slightest move to join her.

She patted a space beside her.

Adam swung around with obvious annoyance and sat on the step immediately below her. Of late he'd given up wearing hats and each time she saw him, his hair was noticeably longer. And wonderful hair it was, too, thick and shiny, and so dark.

Jenny scratched Halibut's head. His long whiskers twitched and he nuzzled her hand. "How nice ye are t'take him for a walk."

"I didn't take him for a walk, I took... If you insist on probing into my business, he's been with me on an errand."

She felt sorry for the man. Then she felt ridiculous because he was a big, handsome, talented brute who probably gained pleasure from being surly to women—any women he didn't happen to love, which should account for all women, with the possible exception of one.

Adam stroked Halibut with the backs of his fingers. "Creatures are helpless, even if they do have tempers as bad as this fellow's. And when someone else charges you to make sure their animal is kept safe, it's a responsibility not to be taken lightly."

"Especially when the animal's owner happens to be Princess Desirée, I suppose."

Halibut purred and the sound was loud enough for Jenny to hope he didn't disturb anyone's sleep.

"I should feel the same responsibility toward any person for whom I'd promised to do a sensitive job."

"Ye're a good man. Bein' in love can be a painful thing."

"I wouldn't know about that," Adam snapped. "Never encountered the beast myself. I must be on my way."

"Why don't ye follow her? To this mountain country where her father lives?"

Adam got up and loomed over her like the shadow of a rangy tree. "Apparently you've lost your mind," he said. "Even if I cared about Desirée, and I don't—not beyond the limits of a pleasant friendship—even then I wouldn't consider making a nuisance of myself by following her around. Fortunately this isn't an issue."

Jenny scrambled to her feet and ran ahead of Adam. "When I finish work tomorrow, I'll gladly play wi' Halibut for ye—t'help lighten your burden."

"You will do no such thing," Adam said, frowning. "Definitely you shall not attempt to approach this cat if I am not there, and I most certainly won't be there when you arrive. Good night."

While he stormed toward the attic, Jenny stood outside

7B. Adam Chillworth was more than a wee bit too defensive on the subject of Princess Desirée.

Latimer resented having his plans interrupted by this woman who insisted on presenting herself swathed in gray as if it were a uniform of doom guaranteed to make her irresistibly mysterious.

So far she had said nothing of substance. She'd been sitting on a couch, hands in lap, back straight when he'd entered the room. Her "Good evening" had been as loquacious as she got. After a few moments of quiet, she'd risen and taken to wandering about the room, sighing loudly and keeping her fingers laced together in front of her.

Latimer's patience grew thin. He wanted to go to Jenny.

"When we met in Bond Street I was not quite honest with you."

"You mean you've changed your mind about Jenny? Perhaps she isn't a coiled snake ready to strike me after all? I didn't believe you, madam, but I appreciate your coming to tell the truth."

"It was true that I didn't come to you because *friends* sent me. But it was because of what I've heard some acquaintances talking about," she said. "How can you pretend that Mr. Morley Bucket has ceased to be a threat to your friend?"

He couldn't deny that the question caught him by surprise, but he would not let this woman know she'd touched a vulnerable spot. "I have no idea what you're talking about. It grows late. I prefer to be polite, but would you have your say, quickly, and leave, please?"

The woman planted her feet and turned her veil-swathed face toward him. "You, sir, are a rude man. The day will come, and soon, when you will thank me for my courage in coming to this house. At first I thought I was doing it because I considered you a real gentleman. You're not. But I'm persisting in the name of justice—and because someone else I know and care about more than any other will be hurt if the plot against you is carried out.''

On this occasion, her veil was stretched tightly beneath her chin and swept up like drapes of heavy cobwebs around the brim of her hat. A jet broach fastened the veil in place. She was a self-assured creature, and carried herself with a darkly determined air.

''You should have taken note of what I told you this morning and sent your friend far away. As it is, you're making certain people very unhappy with you. They'll have to move to protect their interests, and they'll do so—with help from your friend.

''Now don't misunderstand me. I have nothing against her personally, but I can't allow her to play innocent people like strings on a violin—even if there is a chance that she doesn't understand what she's about.''

Anger caused Latimer to make fists at his sides. ''So far all you've done is hint. You've attacked the character of the best woman I've ever known but you haven't told me what she's supposedly guilty of, or why. And you've shown me not one piece of evidence to support your accusations.''

''She's in debt.''

Latimer poured himself a glass of brandy and raised the decanter, offering a drink to this interloper. She shook her head.

''I'm well aware of Jenny's difficulties.'' He took a mouthful of brandy and swallowed. ''Why pretend we aren't talking about Jenny. At least be straightforward in that.''

The woman shrugged. ''Jenny, then.''

"And you are?"

"Mrs. Smith."

Latimer put a tongue in his cheek and said, "Of course."

"Jenny owes a goodly sum of money to Mr. Bucket who is a vindictive man. He has his ways of making people do what he wants."

Perhaps he was misjudging Mrs. Smith. She was wrong about Jenny, but she could have suffered at the hands of Bucket herself—and actually heard comments about Jenny. And she had confessed that Jenny might not know she was being used against him—if indeed she was being used at all.

"If I give you the sum owed by Jenny, could you take it to Morley Bucket and discharge the debt?"

She laughed for the first time. In other circumstances he might find the sound pretty. "You aren't the kind who wants his pound of flesh, are you, Mr. More? Bucket is such a man and he's made it clear that he wants revenge. He would refuse payment from anyone but Jenny and he knows she can't pay him. That is exactly what he wants. As long as she's in debt to him he has power over her."

"Revenge?" Latimer sputtered. "Revenge for what? Jenny couldn't pay him what she owes for that disgusting place where she lived but she told him she'd settle the account as soon as she could."

"Oh, saints preserve us. Do you refuse to take my meaning? Bucket wants Jenny's attention and to get that he'll threaten her because he doesn't understand women well enough to know she will never care for him. He has made threats to her already—that much is clear. He may have told her that unless she does his bidding, he'll make things hard on her family."

Latimer looked at her sharply. She obviously wasn't aware that Jenny didn't know who her family had been.

"Or that boy. Toby his name is. She's fond of him. Lord knows why." She hesitated and frowned. "Why didn't I work that out before? Of course, it's the boy. Bucket will have threatened to steal him away and do something awful to him."

"Who is this person you care for more than any other?" Latimer would think about the necessity to protect Toby—later. Presently the boy was safe in the midst of family, lodgers and staff.

Mrs. Smith bowed her head and said, "I can never reveal the name. Too dangerous."

"I'm tired," he said, even though he knew there would be no real peace until he sorted out Bucket and his hangers-on. And Lumpit had to go, too. "No doubt you've come to tell me to get rid of Jenny—again."

"I haven't come to *tell* you to do anything. I'm going to give you information that could cost me…my life. What you do with it is up to you. Mr. More, a theft is taking place and there are plans afoot to make sure you are accused of the crime."

He felt colder, but made sure he showed no particular emotion. "You'll have to speak plainer than that."

"Women should befriend other women," she said with a catch in her voice. "I didn't want to inform on Jenny, but she's decided she must sacrifice something—or someone—to save herself. If she believes Bucket would ever willingly set her free, then she's a fool, but not being a worldly one, she's still got her illusions. She is your Judas, Mr. More. Mark well what I say. Jenny McBride is a Judas and even though she won't want to, she'll point to you when the runners come. The stolen goods will be *found* and you will be arrested. Unless you dispatch her at once."

Latimer drank more brandy and bought time to think. "If, as you say, the plot against me is in motion, how will it help if Jenny isn't with me anymore?"

"Details, details." She took a man's fob watch from a tiny reticule that hung from her wrist, looked at the time and let out a sharp puff of air. "If Jenny isn't with you, it may not be considered necessary to have you arrested. They want to get her *away* from you."

"There's still something I'm unclear about," Latimer said. "What exactly would it benefit anyone if I were arrested for theft—particularly theft I didn't commit?"

"You really don't understand how some men are different from you, do you? You outwitted Bucket and made a fool of him in front of people who have envied him in the past. He wants retribution from you, and he wants Jenny. She's an innocent victim, really, and the kindest thing is to do as I have told you."

Latimer turned from Mrs. Smith and pushed his hands beneath his coattails. "I can't believe that she could be persuaded to plot against me."

Mrs. Smith laughed again. "You foiled Bucket by putting yourself between him and Jenny. There's no question but that she fell for you. Now he's wielding his power to make her follow his orders, and he expects her to run to him when you've been ruined. I can't tell you anymore and I've got to be on my way. This will all happen quickly now, but if you ignore me, I won't carry the guilt of not having tried to warn you."

A black mood descended on Latimer. "Surely you're going to tell me what I should do about all this." He waited for her to tell him again that he should turn away from Jenny. This woman must hate her and he'd pay a pretty penny to know why.

"I've told you. Send Jenny away. Then tell Bucket she's

not with you anymore and you don't know where she's gone. Give her money if it'll make you feel better. And if you care about her, send her far away. Out of the country. You must have friends abroad who would help her make a start. If you decide you want to go to her later—and I know men can be fools—then go. But always have someone watching your back if you do.

"And remember, for her own good she should never return to London."

An hour had passed since Latimer told Coot to see Jenny to her rooms. She'd seen every minute tick away. She supposed an hour wasn't so very long, but she wanted his company. And she couldn't bear to think of this night without his comforting presence in her bed. She'd already set out a heavy, white cotton nightrail and a robe from Desirée's amazing gift. To these she'd added a chemisette of fine wool, a pair of white cotton drawers, and sturdy wool stockings. If she was still cold outside the covers, she'd use the quilt from the bed in what had been Meg Smiles' room.

Fifteen minutes ago she'd heard the front door slam and, on looking out of the window, saw a woman hurrying away. No servant would leave at such a time of night. From what Coot had said, she thought Latimer's visitor had been a woman and felt certain the one who left had been she.

Latimer was probably getting his nightshirt and some slippers so that he could be comfortable.

Jenny went into the bedroom and undressed. She slipped on her layers of clothing for the night and carefully hung up the beautiful gown she'd worn. Then she went to sit on the edge of the bed and held her left hand under the candlelight. How was it possible that she was to marry Latimer and that she already wore this beautiful ring? She shivered with excitement. Madame Sophie would be very impressed, as she always was over expensive things, and she would twitter about it. She'd also be happy for Jenny because she'd found someone she loved and who loved her just as much.

Toby must see the ring, too. And she intended to tell him that he would be part of her wedding, an important part, although she didn't yet know what that might be. Latimer would help with those things, but Finch would probably be the one to guide them both through the formalities that would have to be attended to.

Ten more minutes had passed.

For two pins she'd go to him.

She wouldn't do any such thing. That would make her look weak and too clinging. Latimer didn't like weak women, if he did, he wouldn't have chosen her.

In the morning she must leave early for Bond Street because she wanted to make up for having given Madame less hours than she was due of late.

Jenny thought of the episode in the church with Bucket and shuddered.

She thought of being in the confessional with Latimer and flushed inside and out. A bad one she might be, but she hoped Latimer would soon decide to do some of those wonderful things again.

The remembered sound of candle glasses ringing together caused her to frown. There had been an unearthliness in Finch's conservatory. And the table just about spinning on its legs with Mr. Lumpit barely aware of it—frightening. Latimer and Finch hadn't mentioned it again, and Mr. Lumpit appeared a bit unearthly himself.

Latimer had taken the note she'd found in her bed, but Jenny hadn't forgotten it. Goose bumps rose on her arms and legs. It had been a threat against herself, but even more against Latimer, yet they continued on as if everything was normal. Not that there was anything else to do until something happened. *Until.* She had lived with deprivation and the constant struggle to survive, but those were things she knew, the threat of violence was new.

Jenny lay on the bed and turned on her side so that she could stare at the candle and at a little enamel clock. Another fifteen minutes gone by. She drew up her knees and folded her arms tightly. Why didn't he come?

25

Jenny would be waiting for him.

Latimer had already remained in his room too long.
What he'd been told was some sort of distortion. How
could that not be the case? But how could he be sure?
What was he really feeling—doubt? Did he doubt Jenny?

If he went to her, how should he behave?

His body stirred and he gritted his teeth. What hell was
this, to be a man completely in love with a woman who
wanted him, or insisted she did, but who had been accused
of plotting to destroy him? He could not believe it was
true, but he had no proof it wasn't.

Damn it all, he had to get fresh air—and space to think.
He snatched a cloak and took his ebony cane, the one with
an ivory-handle carved in the shape of a woman's beautiful
hand. The grateful Chinese customer who gave it to him
had insisted that every man should carry a sword. The
blade concealed inside ebony was narrow and deadly
sharp.

In the square he found an unexpectedly brisk breeze. He
walked along all four rows of fine houses, and repeated
the journey. Were it not for the note Jenny had found, he
could more easily brush aside Mrs. Smith as a mischief-
maker and find out if Jenny knew anything about her. But
there had been the note. For all he knew Mrs. Smith saw

Jenny as her rival in some manner and had been the one
to find her way into the house and leave the message.

Roses in the gardens smelled sweet, even at a distance.
Latimer crossed to enter the enclosed beds and pathways
by a gate in the black railings. Perhaps he would take
Jenny a rose and beg her forgiveness for taking so long to
come to her. He thought of orange silk petals that simply
appeared, and swaying chandeliers—and rocking tables.
He was a man beset by oddities, and not of the kind he
relished dealing in.

Jenny would be locked in her room as he'd instructed
her to be whenever she was there alone. And she would
be thinking about him.

Blood pumped hard in his veins and his arousal was
predictable.

"Difficulty sleeping, Latimer?"

Startled, the blade was halfway out of its hiding place
before he stopped reacting and saw Adam Chillworth sitting on a bench. "Damn you, man," he said, breathing
painfully, "I might have run you through. Never shock me
like that."

Silence met his announcement and Latimer went closer.
Adam also wore a cloak and his head was bare.

"What's the matter with you?" Latimer asked. "Sitting
in the dark waiting to frighten a man almost to his death?"

"You flatter yourself," Adam said. "I've watched you
march about the square and made no attempt to come near
you. I assure you I wasn't waiting for you and, if you
hadn't been about to stumble over me, you would never
have known I was here."

"Damned dramatics," Latimer muttered, thoroughly unnerved. "I repeat, what's the matter with you? You aren't
yourself and haven't been for days. Not that you aren't
always a bad-tempered villain, but this is beyond all."

"At least I don't carry a sword just in case I feel like cutting your throat," Adam said. "I'll bid you good night."

"The hell you will," Latimer said, too loudly. He dropped his voice and said, "If I wanted to do away with you, I shouldn't waste time on your throat—too slow. No, sir, it would be your heart I should remove and fry for my breakfast."

He brought his lips together but immediately started to laugh. Adam's baritone chuckles joined in and Latimer sat heavily beside him. He tapped the cane between his feet and shook his head.

"Posturing rattle," Adam said, and laughed again.

Latimer said, "An apt description of us both, friend. We are a sorry pair."

"Speak for yourself. A man should be able to take the air and choose to spend time in solitude among the flowers without having his life threatened."

"Adam among the flowers," Latimer said, turning toward the other man and hitching up a knee. "A lovely picture, I must say."

"You're in love with the little Scot, aren't you?" Adam said. "You've fallen for the big green eyes and red hair."

"I've fallen for a good deal more than that," Latimer said, and wished he hadn't. "Mind your own business."

"I am. You're a good friend to me and you're not yourself. That's my business—or I'm making it so."

Latimer removed his hat and ran fingers through his hair. "Fancy a drink?" he said.

"I'm not ready to go in."

"Neither am I. Been to The King's Fool lately?"

"Can't say I have. Come on then, it's close enough."

A left turn from the square and onto the High Street and they had only yards to cover before reaching a lane where the steamed-up windows of The King's Fool bulged over the pavement. Latimer pitied the inhabitants of the houses on either side of and across from the inn, for enough noise passed through those windows to keep even the devil awake.

Adam led the way and pushed into the smoky, ale-soaked air inside. When Latimer stood beside him, Adam leaned close and said, "Nice thing about all this noise is that you can be more alone than you were out there."

They found an empty corner table and slid to sit on two benches. A fire roared up a wide chimney and red faces ran with sweat. The late hour guaranteed the level of drunkenness and the openly lewd behavior of serving girls and patrons—to say nothing of a few ladies who had evidently come looking for customers with an itch in need of scratching.

"See what I mean?" Adam said, folding his arms on the table, "anonymous in a crowd."

"A crowd of well-acquainted people who don't know one another at all," Latimer added. He caught the eye of a blond girl who looked as if she should be at home on a farm and indicated that he wanted service. "What'll it be?" he asked Latimer, who watched him, amazed, while he parted his cloak just enough to allow Halibut to poke his head out.

"I'll have a pint of light ale," Adam said, and smoothed the fur between Halibut's ears.

"You're mad," Latimer whispered, then said, "Pint of light ale and a brandy, please," to the farm girl whose green blouse was more or less kept in place by her considerable breasts.

The girl looked into his eyes. Innocence hadn't been her companion for a long time. She smiled and said, "You can have anything you want, sir. You both can. There's plenty to go round.'' Then she saw the cat and left to get their order.

"Who brings a cat to an inn?" Latimer asked. "Who takes a cat walking?"

"I do."

Latimer considered his friend but didn't say what he was thinking, that Adam had Desirée on his mind and that he was a very lonely man.

"We're not here to talk about me," Adam said.

"Really? I didn't think we were here to talk about anything in particular."

Halibut blinked lazy eyes and seemed more than satisfied with his surroundings.

"So," Adam said, "we've established that you've fallen for a charming pauper—"

Latimer's hand twisted the neck of Adam's cloak, stopping him midsentence. "You'd do well to watch your tongue when you speak of Jenny," Latimer said. "She may have been through unpleasant times, but they're over now and she'll never be unhappy again."

"Because you'll make sure of that? A tall order."

"What are you going to do about Desirée?"

Adam groomed Halibut's whiskers while he watched a sailor lift the skirts of a passing prostitute. "I'm not doing anything about her. You're all imagining things. I don't think of her as anything but an entertaining little girl. I assure you I prefer experienced women who are responsible for themselves."

"Liar."

The sailor had bared the woman's bottom, and a very nice bottom it was. She bent forward to whisper in the man's ear.

"Blunt before bliss," Latimer said.

Silver changed hands. The sailor had the woman astride

his lap and performed to the shouts and jeers of his fellows.

The blonde returned with their drinks. She set them down and scratched Halibut. "I think you need something else to stroke," she told Adam, who ignored her. She winked at Latimer then and her expression became first serious, then excited. "I know who you are, don't I?"

Would he ever outrun his own foolish excesses? "I doubt it," he said. "I'd appreciate it if you'd keep your voice down."

She whispered, "The most daring—"

"That's enough," he said, cutting her off. "You mistake me for some other man."

Her face became cunning and she slid in beside him. "I saw you at one of them posh places. My boyfriend took me inside just to see. Women all around you and you wasn't above giving them a little of what they liked. Aren't I good enough?" She tugged the blouse down enough to give him an unobstructed view of her charms.

"You're delightful, but I'm here with my friend to have a quiet drink."

She raised her shoulders and giggled. "Well, you can't 'ave no quiet drink 'ere, can you?"

"Apparently not."

"I can see you don't want me 'angin' around. Show me 'ow you do one little thing and I'll be gone. They said you could…you know, while you was 'avin a drink and playin' cards."

"Could what?" Adam asked and Latimer itched to wipe the smile from the man's face.

The girl copied the way Adam's arms were crossed on the table, only it wasn't a cat she held on top of them. "They reckon 'e can give a girl just one pinch—in a certain way—and give 'er the best time she ever 'ad."

Adam drank ale and raised his eyebrows at Latimer.

"Do it for me, darlin'," the barmaid said, and gathered her skirts almost to her waist.

Firmly, Latimer pulled them down. He found several coins in his pocket and pressed them into her palm. "Get yourself out of this place," he told her. "Find a good man and go far away from here."

Her blush, and her downcast eyes moved him. She all but ran from him.

"Touching," Adam said. "But I've always known your soul was better than mine."

"Laugh if you want to," Latimer told him. "Watching a young girl ruin herself doesn't excite me."

"No, it wouldn't. Jenny McBride's the only woman who excites you now."

"You're right," Latimer said through his teeth. "Leave it alone. I've got trouble and it isn't pretty."

He had Adam's whole attention. "I knew it," he said. "The moment I saw you walking around the square I knew there was something wrong. Let me help you."

"I wish you could." Latimer was very serious. "This is one case where I have to figure things out for myself, then do what I decide is right."

"There's never any harm in saying what's on your mind to a good friend. Sometimes it all sounds better when you hear it. And sometimes the friend sees things you don't."

Latimer threw down half of his brandy and winced as it burned his throat.

"I won't pressure you, of course," Adam said. "But I'm here for you if you need me."

"I love her," Latimer muttered. "I want to marry her."

Adam was quiet for too long before he said, "From what I can tell, she's a good-hearted girl, and pretty to boot. But there is the matter of her lack of breeding. You move among the wealthy and you've got influential friends. In your business, don't you need a brilliant wife?''

''Jenny is brilliant. And she's got a natural polish.'' And given the opportunity, she would blossom. He hated the thoughts he entertained about her.

''But, as you said, you've got trouble? The two of you have trouble?''

Latimer nodded but he struggled against a feeling that he'd be betraying Jenny if he discussed what had happened. ''I've been told some things, that's all.''

''You mean someone's tried to put you off Jenny? Because she had humble beginnings? I've always thought the class thing was overdone myself.''

Latimer shaded his eyes and said, ''You just brought it up yourself. You talked about her lack of breeding.''

''I was testing you.''

''I'll let that pass. I don't know what to do and it's not what you think. It's more complicated.'' He saw a muscle contract beside Adam's mouth and decided to tell him all of it.

When Latimer had finished, Adam looked at him steadily. ''What proof do you have that she plans to harm you?''

''None.''

''You believe she loves you, too?''

''I know she does.''

Adam leaned against the whitewashed wall behind him. ''Then it's easy. Trust her. Ask her to marry you at once, as fast as you can get a license. Whether or not she does it will give you your answer. If she's guilty as charged, she'll run.''

26

Jenny had damped the candle and was trying to sleep when she heard a light tapping at the door. She sat up, gathering Meg's old quilt around her.

There had been plenty of sadness in her life, but none more wrenching than she'd suffered in recent hours.

The tapping sounded again and she got up. Trailing the quilt on the floor she went to unlock the door and peer out—at Latimer. He looked wild with his hair blown awry, a cloak hanging askew on his shoulders, and no neckcloth.

Without warning, he pushed his way in, bumping her as he strode past.

"Lock the door," he demanded, and she did as he asked. By the light of the fire he lit a candle and carried it into the bedroom.

Jenny's heart began a harsh, thud-thudding and she followed him timidly until she stood at the foot of the bed. Latimer relit the old candle from his new one and set them both on the table beside the bed.

He pointed to the bed and said, "Get in."

"It's your turn t'be inside," she said. "I've a quilt and I'll lie atop."

He pounded a fist against his brow. "Do what you like, but do it *now*. We have a good deal to accomplish this night."

Jenny could scarcely stand for the wobbling in her legs.

Her stomach flipped over. She made to crawl onto the bed, attempting to take the quilt with her, but Latimer snatched it away and said, "Lie down." When she did, he spread the quilt over her again. "I'm late," he announced. "I had unexpected things to attend to. Forgive me."

"O'course I will, but I missed ye."

He narrowed his eyes but didn't respond to her comment.

"Ye look so tired. Please get some rest."

"Rest?" he said and gave a cold laugh. "I doubt we'll rest tonight." He tossed the cloak aside and took off his coat.

"Ye look cold," she told him. "Ye were outside, I see. Is the weather changin'?"

"I neither know, nor care."

She sighed. "I see. Ye're not yoursel'."

"Get under the covers," he said shortly.

"I willna," she told him. "It's your turn and I'm perfectly happy where I am."

"Damn it all to hell," he said and fell to his knees beside her. "Why can't you be unappealing in my eyes. God knows what you've piled on your body. You look like a bundled child—braids and all. But you are the loveliest thing to me."

He kissed her so roughly, she couldn't catch her breath. Her arms flailed and he rose over her, pinned her to the bed with his weight, and held her head while he kissed her again and again, opening her mouth so wide her jaws hurt. But jumpy, pleasing little feelings darted about low in her tummy and she raised her hips without intending to.

She put her arms around his neck and he promptly released her and stumbled to his feet. He unbuttoned his waistcoat and removed it.

"Wouldn't ye like t'get a nightshirt?"

"No."

"Ye could wear one o' mine. Or one o' the princess's I should say."

He shook his head and she didn't care for his faint smile. "I fear I must decline your offer," he said.

Jenny refused to look away from Latimer's eyes, black and strange as they were. This behavior was to be expected from the male. She'd learned that very well now. Males were given to staring at women as if they wanted to be inside them and know every thought they had. Well, Mr. Latimer More wouldn't find a way to her secrets—unless she wanted him to.

Pretending not to notice all that breathless, unmoving silence—unmoving except for the way his eyes flickered over her, and the way he passed his tongue along his lower lip—she smiled at him and turned down the bedcovers on his side.

He groaned.

Her attention snapped back to him.

"You torture me," he said, his voice husky. "I can't think of anything but you, even though… Nothing matters but you. I must be guided to do the right thing."

Jenny kept on smiling but didn't understand much of what he said.

"I shall enjoy you first," he said. "The rest can come later."

He'd begun to frighten her badly and the fear brought a forbidden thrill.

He all but tore his clothes off and she could do nothing but watch him, fascinated, choked with emotion.

Naked, rather than get into the bed, he stretched out on top and put his hands behind his head.

"Ye'll freeze," she told him, studying his body, barely able to keep her hands off him. "Well, if ye insist on bein' hardheaded, share the quilt.'' And she spread it over him, wondering if its weight would discomfort his straining manhood.

"Thank you," he said. "What I have, you have. I will not tolerate all this sacrifice you feel you must endure."

To give him more of the quilt, she moved closer until their sides met. "If this is sacrifice, then I've been told lies because it's a fine thing."

Latimer made a strange sound and turned toward her. She rolled from her back to her side and their faces were separated only by inches. Driven by need, not boldness, she gradually closed the space between their lips and kissed him gently with her mouth closed.

He rested a large hand on the side of her face and head. She felt him restraining himself, holding back, and wondered how she could tell him she didn't want him to spare her anything. She'd learned enough to know that being with him like this could lead to a situation she should not share with a man who was not her husband.

"Were you sent to torment me?" he asked. "If you were, someone must be happy with his work."

"We were sent to each other because we're meant t'be together. Show me what will please ye." She would, Jenny thought, go wherever he chose to take her. Yes, her mind was made up.

"Be careful what you ask for." He nipped at her lower lip, then drew it between his teeth. His tongue entered her mouth, but only briefly before he licked her upper lip.

Jenny pressed herself to him and heard the keening sounds that came from her throat. His chest was rough, then smooth, the skin at his sides another texture again, and beneath the skin, muscles stood hard and shifted at her touch.

"No!"

His sudden cry alarmed her. "What have I done?"

"You have pleased me, that's what you've done. And you're taking me to a place where I may not be able to control my instincts. Don't you know what it does to a man to have a woman lie in his arms and kiss him, and run her hands over his body?"

Not exactly. "I suppose my hands may be too cold for ye. I'll rub them together."

"You *don't* understand and I'm glad of it. But I'm muddled, Jenny. I know what I want and that you would give it to me regardless of the cost to yourself, but it wouldn't be right. I cannot lie with you like this."

He must not leave her. "I'll not touch ye," she said. "Forgive me for bein' too bold. Anyway, I've an idea. Och, what a goose. Why did I no' think o' it before?"

She ducked her head beneath the quilt and managed an inelegant move like the childish dives she'd made when the children in the orphanage were taken swimming in the river. It was a flip, but a difficult one given the restriction of her clothes and the quilt's tendency to slide.

"Jenny," she heard Latimer say, but she was too preoccupied in getting where she was going to reply.

"There," she said when she'd finally put her head where her feet had been and hauled the quilt back into place. "Now it'll be easier for ye not t'be distracted." She stuck her face out and realized her bent legs were on the pillow and she was looking at Latimer's...at his thighs. By rights she needed to scoot farther down the bed but she was afraid to move a muscle in case she upset him and he went away.

"Jenny," he said again, and his voice sounded funny. "What do you think you've accomplished?"

"I've removed us from temptation," she said.

"Have you? It's odd how different two people's reactions can be." He planted a hand on her hip and peeled off her stockings as casually as you please. "You smell edible," he said, and rubbed a rough jaw on her shin.

Jenny didn't know what to do, so she said, "Thank ye. It's the soap they're kind enough t'gi' me."

"A woman has her own scent. Did you know that, Jenny?"

She blushed. He made everything so intimate. "I suppose I did. So do men. At least, so do you. I canna even describe it but it gives me strange and wonderful feelings."

"Tell me about the feelings."

"I canna." Impulsively she buried her face in his thighs. They were awful hard, and she liked that.

He slipped his fingers inside the drawers and she held her breath. "Your change of position was a brilliant idea. You've certainly saved me from temptation."

"Well, thank ye." His manhood moved, brushed her breasts, and she became rigid. She breathed with her mouth open. Latimer seemed content to rest quietly, except for rubbing her tummy and sliding his hand over her hip to caress her bottom. But he did it dreamily, so she thought he was probably relaxed. He might be stroking her in his sleep.

She supposed she should sleep, too. The movement against her breasts happened again. There would be no sleep as long as these things went on. Very hesitantly, trying to touch but not to have him know she had because she'd be mortified if he knew how curious she was, Jenny put the very tip of a finger on...well, she put it on the very tip of him. It was wet! And Latimer's hips moved. He pushed against her finger as if he liked the feel of it and wanted more.

Jenny stopped breathing and folded her fingers around

his shaft—and she wondered if all men carried such a proud burden about them.

The quilt was whisked away.

Latimer caught hold of her by the knees and turned on his back with Jenny on top of him. With her...oh, she could feel his breath down there, inside the divided drawers. And her face was...it was in his *lap*.

"Jenny, Jenny," he murmured. "If you tell me to, I'll try to stop. But I don't want to."

She rubbed her cheek back and forth over him and said, "I don't want to, either," in a silly, squeaky voice.

"You're killing me."

She held still. "How?"

"Figure of speech," he panted. "Don't stop what you're doing."

He pulled off the drawers...

And he kissed the insides of her thighs...

"Take off your robe and gown," he said. "I promise I'll keep you warm."

Easier said than done, she decided, working the garments upward when they were lodged between the two of them. At last she pulled them over her head and let them fall on the floor. "Is that better?" she asked.

He was busy with nipping kisses in her groin. She'd begun to ache and doubted she could bear for him to stop now.

"What's this?" With one hand, Latimer had smoothed her from hip to the middle of her back, passing beneath the woolen chemisette on the way. "A man might think you'd wrapped yourself up to keep him from finding you at all."

"No, no," she said, wriggling to drag off the offending garment. "It was just that I thought I'd best be warm for lying atop the bed."

He chuckled a little. "And how are you now? Hot or cold?"

"I'm verra hot," she told him. He'd pulled her higher and her breasts rested on his belly, which meant her face couldn't be anywhere but on top of his proud pinnacle. Oh, dear, she was harking back to the things she and the ladies in Sibyl's club had read. Silly things about women sacrificing themselves on pinnacles.

Latimer's mouth fastened over her most private place and she arched her back. He held her firmly in place with one arm while he pushed a hand between them to fondle her breasts.

He took the part that seemed to swell and grow hard between his teeth and sucked. He flipped his tongue back and forth and the aching throb became an irresistible pain.

This might not be right between unmarried people, but she would never stop him, didn't want to stop him.

"Don't do it if it repels you," he said, "but it would feel good if you took me into your mouth."

She understood what he meant and experienced a moment of panic. There was so much she didn't know.

Latimer set up a rhythmic play of his tongue and she couldn't keep her bottom still. She closed her eyes and slid his shaft into her mouth. The beauty of feeling herself joined with him brought tears. Careful not to hurt him, Jenny slid farther and farther over him. She slipped her moist lips away, almost far enough away to let him come out of her mouth altogether, but she timed her strokes well and matched his rhythm on her own body.

Faster and faster he moved his mouth and teeth on her, all the while squeezing her bottom, holding her thighs in hard, insistent hands, finding her breasts again and again and playing with her nipples until she was close to screaming.

The burning began and seared her, and she parted her legs wider to ride against his face. She raised and lowered her head, frenzied in her quest to please him. There were parts of him that were round and solid and she stroked them, cradled them.

Latimer's hands circled her waist and she realized what a big man he was in so many ways.

"Stop," he told her, but she shook her head and continued.

"I shall have to spank you for this," he said, and closed his lips over her. She heard him sucking, then felt a savage breaking loose that traveled from his mouth and throughout her body. She jerked, and burned, and drove down on him even harder. A crescendo came and she gave a thin scream. And, at the same time, Latimer's hips rose and fell like a smithy's mallet and all she could do was keep her mouth open to receive him.

"Move your face," he said in strangled tones. "Quickly. I can't hold on anymore."

Instead of doing as he asked, she fastened on him and met every thrust. His body streamed with sweat and her own hair stuck about her face.

One last, mighty jerk and Latimer threw wide his arms. He thrashed back and forth, and Jenny tasted the essence of him.

"Let it go," he said, gasping, and stroking her back. "Just let it go."

"I can't," she said, and felt heavy and warm—and safe.

He didn't persist with telling her what to do, but he did turn her around again and draw her up into his arms. They kissed for a long, long time and he held her so tightly, he hurt her ribs, but she didn't complain.

"You are my love," he said, when his heart no longer beat so hard against her breast. "A wonder. A gift I don't deserve. I have no excuse for doing what I just did, but I'm not sorry. We are well matched, I think. An amazing good fortune."

"I've an excuse for doing what I just did." Jenny kissed his neck and worked her way up to his mouth. "I wanted to do it, and I'll want to do it again. I love ye, Latimer More. And I'll do whatever ye tell me, always."

"The way you did what I told you to do a few moments ago?"

She rested heavily on him and smiled. "Just that way."

"I have something to ask you," Latimer said. "But I've worn you out, so sleep first, my darling. In the morning we'll talk."

She mumbled a deliberately sleepy, "Yes," and kept still, willing sleep to come.

Never had she been more wide-awake, or more aware of everything around her.

Latimer breathed deeply and slowly.

Did a man get angry if a woman was demanding…about sex?

The truth was that she didn't know but if she never tried it, she'd continue to be ignorant.

She propped an elbow and braced her head on a hand. The candles still flickered and she decided she could look at Latimer More forever. Although his features had smoothed out, there were lines at the corners of his eyes, and a straight line than ran vertically beneath each cheekbone. She'd seen how dimples formed there when he smiled.

Latimer had the kind of mouth a woman would be a fool not to watch whenever she could. The bottom lip was fuller than the top one and relaxed as he was, she could see the edges of his square, white teeth. The beard shadow on his face pleased her, and his tousled hair which had grown enough to curl at his neck. And his shoulders. She settled a flattened palm on his left one, curled her fingers around the muscle that gleamed there. The hair on his chest was still wet from his exertion. Jenny felt proud of her ability to tire him, and she also felt wicked for enjoying him so much.

When she looked at his face again, he looked back at her and her heart shifted. "I thought you were going to sleep," he said.

"Well, I'm younger than you. Mayhap I've more energy and I recover my strength quicker."

His evil grin sent tingling through every inch of her.

"You can always refuse," she told him, "but if it's all the same to you, I'd verra much like to do that over again—and see if we can find another adventurous way."

Latimer raised his chin and drove the back of his head into the pillow. "This is my fault. It was bound to happen. I've met my match and she's insatiable."

"Yes," she announced with glee and rose up to sit astride his hips. "I'm insatiable. I want you to teach me everything you know. What else can we do with this?" She lifted his partially erect shaft and stroked it carefully. She stroked until she felt it come alive, and swell, and turn rigid. When it was like that, even if she tried to press it down, it sprang up again.

"Your breasts," he said, "are the stuff of dreams. From now on I'll look at you in a certain way and you'll know I'm seeing you naked, and that in my mind I have your breasts in my hands and my tongue in your mouth, and I'll be inside you."

She held still. Latimer pinched her nipples and she jerked on his hips, but she considered what he had just said. "Inside me?"

"Slip of the tongue," he said, and laughed. "I didn't intend to say that."

"But that is what men and women do, isn't it? It's the way they have babies."

"Yes. But a baby isn't made every time a couple have intercourse."

"I see. It sounds lovely—I know I'd like it. But I suppose we'd best be careful. I've seen what happens to unwed women who have babies."

"You are not one of them," Latimer said. "Any child of yours will be my child and deeply loved by his parents. Or her parents if it's a girl, of course."

Jenny felt as if a swarm of butterflies had been let loose inside her. "Yes, but we must wait before we do it."

He turned his face away, but his thumb was flipping back and forth between her legs again. The instant flicker of response almost surprised her.

Jenny knelt and whipped the pillow from beneath Latimer's head. She placed his shaft against her and passed back and forth over him until he thrashed and made futile grabs at her.

Would all of that go inside her? she wondered. God wouldn't make men and women wrong for the things they needed to do. Not giving herself more time to think, she grasped him and pressed the head of his shaft in the entrance to her body. Gradually she lowered herself onto him, feeling him fill her. She started to cry without knowing why, but she couldn't stop.

Latimer let out a groan, caught hold of her hips and impaled her. The shock was great and she almost fell on top of him, but he held her there and began to move. "I can't believe we're doing this so soon," he said. "I thought you would be too frightened for more tonight."

"Frightened of what?"

She thought before saying, "I could do. Probably do. There's plenty about. Why?"

He sighed and said, "I just wondered. Jenny, will you marry me at once?"

"At once?" she said slowly. "What d'ye mean by at once?"

"Within a few days. A special license can be arranged and we'll marry in a small chapel I know. I don't want to wait."

Surely it wouldn't be easy to do what must be done for such an event, and do it within a few days.

"Jenny? What do you say?"

She pushed her fingers into his hair and tried to look at him seriously, to frown as if giving his request great consideration, but she ruined it all by laughing. "I say, yes. Yes, yes, please."

27

Spivey here:

Whatever you think, all is not lost.

And I must tell you that during the night you sank to new lows in my estimation. I understand the current, licentious appeal of such events to those who cannot rely on their own imaginations. I mean, those who need to be shown if they are to believe. I do not approve of treating private exhibitions like peep shows.

Yes, well, I will admit that what you saw was almost unbelievable...

I forget myself. What I want to tell you is that applause is a most unsuitable response on such occasions.

Justice will be done. Lumpit may yet win the day for me. By the way, far more has been accomplished than you give me credit for. Meg has left Number 7 and so has Finch. And Sibyl is married to Sir Hunter Lloyd.

Kindly avoid arguing with me. Of course I know Sibyl and Hunter still have rooms at the house, but I've already told you that since Hunter is a distant relative of mine, and there are no sons in direct line, I'm happy for him to remain. And at least 7B is empty. Was empty. Will be empty again.

There's no reasoning with you.

Hester has a soft heart—to my continual detriment—and when Lumpit approaches her with his sad story about needing to trace a certain member of his family, she will pity him, and help him. She will not want him at Number 8 discussing skeletons in closets. What an unfortunate remark—please forgive me.

Hester will take Lumpit in and give him More's rooms. After all, and as she'll point out, a married couple needs more appropriate accommodations—particularly since More is by way of being successful, if one can call being a merchant of any kind successful. And off they'll have to go once Hester shows they aren't welcome anymore.

Oh, no, no, you are wrong again…7B and 7A will not *be considered ample and suitable for them.*

Toby? What are you yammering about? Toby doesn't count as a Spivey loss. He's in servant quarters and anyway, Jenny and More will take him with them.

What's that? Why am I so sure when Lady Hester is so protective of him? I just am. Now, not another word on that topic.

And before you rub your hands together and remind me that all I will have done is swap More and Jenny for Lumpit, forget it. He'll never move in.

Oh, my goodness, look at that. Shakespeare hobnobbing with Mozart. Now there's a pair with something in common perhaps. Big questions about who wrote what there. But I shall be on my best behavior and not mention such things.

"Yes, and a good day to you, sirs. Comparing notes, are we? No, no, merely making a little joke. You know, writing notes and writing notes? Different sorts of notes?"

You see how they respect me for my kindly discourse? Not at all, the worms.

"I say, is that a wedding gown you have there? It is? Whatever for? Delivering it anonymously to a production of A Midsummer Night's Dream *because the one they have*

*is abysmal? Hmph. To be blunt, that is the most abysmal
tragedy I've ever witnessed and no wedding gown will
rescue it from being the laughable mess it is.*

"I shall not listen to you. We all know you lost control
of a tragedy and it became a comedy. Goodbye.

"Oh, if that don't beat all. Away with you both before
I report you to Sir Thomas—and Reverend Smiles."

*Imagine the unkindness. They said I could have the gown
in case I ever need it for Lumpit's wedding.*

*I repeat, I shall not have to worry about getting him out
of Number 7, because he'll never get in.*

28

"What happened to the notion that a wife should obey her husband?" Latimer asked, addressing Jenny while Mrs. Barstow bustled about the table where he'd taken his meals since coming to Number 7. She was setting three places for breakfast.

Jenny, dressed in her old green chintz dress, repeatedly tried to help Barstow, got in her way, and was waved off. "I'm no' your wife, sir, which means ye're no' my husband. I do have a sense of right and wrong and it's right that I return t'my work today. Madame Sophie has been kind t'me and I'll no' let her down."

"Do you have to wear—" Latimer closed his mouth and rethought what he ought to say. "Very well. I admire you for your fine principles and I shall take you to Bond Street myself. After breakfast. Finch will be here at any moment. We have a great deal to do."

Barstow had forgotten where she was in her task. She hummed lightly but with one ear cocked toward them.

"Mrs. Barstow," Latimer said. "You must wonder what all the fuss is about. There will be a great deal of coming and going at Number 7 for a few days and even then I doubt we shall settle down again very quickly. You see, Jenny and I are to be married."

Wearing her usual gray dress and with keys rattling at her waist, Barstow straightened. She smiled, her cheeks turning rosy. "Well, I did wonder from what was being said. I'm very happy for you, of course, very happy."

The door flew open and Finch stood there. Evans hovered behind. He appeared a little flustered. "You, Latimer More, are an exasperating man. You sat at my table last night, but you didn't bother to tell me you were actually making your marriage plans." She carried a bouquet of roses. "I had to hear the news from Evans when he arrived with your breakfast invitation."

"And you, Lady Kilrood, failed to notice the ring on my fiancée's finger last night."

Barstow left, closing off Evans's view of the proceedings.

Finch rushed to Jenny and raised her left hand. Tears sprang into her eyes, but she smiled and threw her arms around Jenny. "Our mother's ring," she said. "Mother was the daughter of a fisherman. My father adored her and was so proud that she was a natural lady. She loved beautiful things, and she would have loved you, Jenny. I wish she could be here. The ring looks perfect on you." She set down the roses and fumbled to undo a small gold pin at the neck of her blue dress. "My little gift to you for such a special day. This was our mother's, too."

"I canna take it," Jenny said. "I worry enough that ye'll no' like t'see the ring on me. And I'll gi' it t'ye if ye like, because—"

"Hush," Finch said. "I have my own rings. The one on your hand was given to Latimer for the woman he would marry."

"To say nothing of it being mine to give but not yours to give away, miss," Latimer said, although he loved the exchange between Jenny and Finch—and Finch's open acceptance of Jenny.

"Ye gave it t'me," Jenny said. "I thought ye meant for me to have it for my own."

"Children," Finch said loudly, and when they were both quiet and red-faced, she said, "That's better. Let me put this on you, Jenny."

The broach was their mother's favorite, a bluebird made of dark gold with sapphires studding its back. Finch pinned it to Jenny's poor dress as if she wore a ballgown, patted the shining thing, and said, "It's perfect for you, isn't it, Latimer."

It was. "Yes, perfect. I'm touched, Finnie. You're the best sister."

"I'm the only sister you have," she reminded him.

"Women," he said and turned up his palms. "What was my sin that I am surrounded by women who are too quick and clever for my peace of mind?"

Barstow came in again carrying a tray of food, and Foster followed with the coffee. Toby, holding a covered silver dish of something that smelled delicious, was the last to enter.

The troupe deposited their burdens and filed out, until Jenny said, "Please stay, Toby," before the boy could leave. "Have ye eaten your breakfast?"

"Yes. I always 'as it first thing now."

"Couldn't ye eat a wee bit more?"

Toby was a smart lad these days and Latimer thought he looked bigger already. He had certainly filled out a little.

"I s'pose I could manage somethin'."

Latimer pulled the table away from the wall and slid one of his green and gilt chairs in. "For you," he said to Toby. "Sit down and join in our celebration. After all, if it hadn't been for you, I might still be searching for Jenny."

Toby sat himself in the fine chair and looked very pleased with himself. "Nah. You'd 'ave kept goin' to the shop and talkin' to 'er."

"We haven't met, Toby," Finch said. "I'm Mr. More's sister."

"Yes, I know." Toby remembered himself and got to his feet quickly. "Mrs. Barstow told me. Your 'usband is a viscount and I'm t'call you Lady Kilrood."

They all sat and Finch poured coffee, including some for Toby in a fragile Chinese cup Latimer was particularly fond of.

The covered dish contained fluffy scrambled eggs. There were braised kidneys, kippers, fried tomatoes and bread. Latimer wished he had Toby's appetite, or even Finch's. He and Jenny showed their disinterest in food. He'd rather look at her, and have her look back at him in just the way she did now. From time to time she touched the bluebird broach or studied her ring. They were not lovely enough to compete with her.

Ignoring the rudeness of it, he leaned to whisper in her ear; she nodded and watched his mouth while she did so. He stirred yet again and grew hard. Beneath the table, she squeezed his thigh and he trapped her hand there.

"Toby," she said. "This is a celebration because Latimer and I are to be married."

"I know," he said. "Mrs. Barstow said."

Finch giggled, then struggled to find a serious expression.

"Well, Barstow shouldn't ruddy well—excuse me. Barstow should allow people to share their own news."

"You didna tell her she was no' t'say anythin'," Jenny pointed out.

Toby held his valuable cup in both hands and took a huge mouthful of coffee. He set the cup down again and added several teaspoonsful of sugar. This he stirred vigorously, clattering the spoon inside the thin china as he did so. "I'm very happy for you," he said, formally enough to cause Jenny to stare. "You're a lucky man, Mr. More. She's special, our Jenny is. I never met no one what cared so much for people of no account, nor no one who was so kind. She don't 'ave no one to speak up for 'er, so I'll be 'ere if she needs someone of 'er own."

Promptly Jenny burst into tears and covered her face. Toby hopped up and put his arms around her. With tears in her own eyes, Finch smiled upon the two of them and sighed.

"Finnie," Latimer said, trying to wring some of the emotion out of the moment. "Do you think the Archbishop would give his blessings?"

She sniffed and said, "Of course he will. He's a good friend. When shall the wedding be?"

"On Friday."

Her tears dried at once. "In *three* days? But—"

"In three days," he told her. "There's much you don't know but I shall be a great deal more comfortable when Jenny is legally under my protection. Do you approve, Toby?"

The boy swallowed and said, "Yes, I approve. You'll look after 'er."

"I'm going to ask Adam Chillworth from the attic to stand with me," he said, and added, "would you be good enough to be part of the groom's party also?" without having planned to say any such thing.

"Say yes," Jenny said softly. "The day wouldna be so special wi'out ye."

Toby pulled himself up tall and said, "A pleasure," with a most serious face.

"Three days," Finch muttered, her gaze still unfocused.

"My goodness. I must get a message to Ross at once. He should give Jenny away. If that's all right with you, Jenny."

Latimer's dear girl appeared bemused. She nodded her head but he doubted she had any idea what was going on—not the details.

"The chapel in St. John's Wood," Latimer said. "St. Stephen's. It's a pretty place and since we will be a small party, we shall fit it well."

"Invitations must go out at once to Sibyl and Hunter and Meg and Jean-Marc. How annoying that Desirée chose such a time to leave."

Latimer agreed with Finch. "The entire household of Number 7 and any friends who may seem appropriate."

"You have business acquaintances," Finnie pointed out. "And there's Father."

Latimer blinked and felt hushed inside.

"He must be invited," Finch said.

Jenny held his hand on the table and said, "O'course he must be."

"He won't come," Latimer said.

"I shall pray that he does," Jenny said quietly.

Finch added, "So shall I. He'll want to know his grandchildren."

Latimer glanced at Jenny but she'd lowered her lashes and turned pink. An insatiable lover she might be, but she was still shy in company.

The door opened again and this time it was Lady Hester, still wearing a nightcap, who appeared in a soft pink dressing gown and was obviously disturbed. "Did you think it fair to plan a wedding without as much as informing me of a betrothal? I am shocked. No, I am cast low by your treatment of me." A sigh raised her large bosom. Her face was shiny with some sort of potion that had been applied.

"Och, milady," Jenny said. "We wouldna do anythin' without your knowledge. I've t'go t'my work, but when I return I'll come t'ye—wi' Latimer although we've no' discussed it yet—and tell ye all about our plans. Not that I exactly know what they are except that we're t'be married on Friday."

"Friday? *Friday?*" Lady Hester produced a pink silk fan painted with red poppies and staggered to plop onto a chaise. "Married on Friday? Finch, how could you have allowed this to happen? We know Latimer is vague on occasion, but you—"

"She's only just discovered it hersel'" Jenny said. "And I'm sure if it doesna please ye, we can—"

"We will make sure that you are seated in the place of honor at St. Stephen's, Lady Hester," Latimer said before Jenny could finish what she'd wanted to say. "I think you'll approve. It's—"

"I know what St. Stephen's is like," she said through barely parted lips. "Toby dear, go to Barstow and have her start preparing invitations. She'll know what to write and be able to start without me. They must go at once— by rider to each invited guest." She inclined her cheek and Toby dropped a quick kiss on it as he passed. "The haste is unseemly, Latimer. One hopes it is your ardor, and not some other little inconvenience that causes the rush."

When had he lost control of his privacy, Latimer wondered. "Can't imagine what you're referring to," he told Lady Hester. "Jenny and I want to be together as quickly as we can."

"Will your father give you away, Jenny?" Lady Hester asked.

"No," Jenny said.

"Just as well. I shall ask Sir Edmund. He will do anything to please me and he is so distinguished."

Latimer cleared his throat and said, "Ross is to give her away, my lady, but I'm sure you will approve of that. How good of you to suggest Sir Edmund, though."

Lady Hester's fan moved briskly. "You're right. Appropriate for your brother-in-law to do it. Thought about a dress have we?"

No, he bloody well had not thought about a dress. Given his druthers, they be married in bed and naked. "Er, had we thought of a dress?" he asked, unashamed of his thoughts.

"Given the short notice, it had best be one of Princess Desirée's," Lady Hester announced. "We women shall examine them and have a modiste make any improvements necessary to the one we choose. Good heavens. Show me that ring at once."

Jenny hurried to do as she was told and Lady Hester produced a lorgnette to take a close look. "Worth a pretty penny," she said. "That bauble won't embarrass you, Latimer, my boy."

"It was my mother's," he said. "She gave it to me for this purpose and now it belongs to Jenny."

Lady Hester clapped her hands and her eyes took on a starry quality. "A wedding. I am moved at the thought. And I insist on giving the wedding breakfast here. We shall open the little ballroom for the occasion. And the wedding journey, Latimer. Surely you've thought of that. *Friday?* The license? Of course it must be a special license but even that must be hastily sought."

"Ross is a friend of the Archbishop," Finch said. "There will be no difficulty."

"Jenny," Lady Hester said. "We must go at once to see about your dress. And I—" she cleared her throat "—I take it you also have no mother available."

"No," Jenny said and Latimer wished he could take her

in his arms right then and there and show her she would never need anyone but him from now on.

Lady Hester coughed delicately and avoided looking in Latimer's direction. "Then I shall have a certain discussion with you that would normally be the obligation of a mother. I consider it my duty."

Latimer almost groaned, but Jenny said, "Thank ye kindly."

"Come with me now," Lady Hester said.

"Oh." Jenny chewed her lower lip. "I've t'be at work, my lady. Madame Sophie—"

Jenny didn't get to talk about Madame Sophie. Lady Hester became so irate that no one could be heard over her ringing tones. "Latimer is to be your husband. He needs a wife to be proud of and a wife who *sews* hats for a living will not fill the bill at all. I will send a messenger to Bond Street explaining your situation. If you think it appropriate, we could also have an invitation to the wedding delivered although I shall understand if you prefer that Madame Sophie not attend breakfast."

Silently Latimer cheered her ladyship on. He didn't want Jenny out of his sight and if she had to be, he'd prefer that she remain in this house and surrounded by protective friends.

Jenny got up. "I'd like Madame to be at breakfast, too." With shaking hands she pulled on her brown velvet pelisse and picked up her bonnet.

"You're going out in *that,*" Lady Hester said. "How can you shame your future husband by being seen in *that?*"

"I'm a milliner's assistant, my lady. What I wear is of little importance and it wouldna be appropriate for me to appear in finery."

When Latimer looked to Finch, she grimaced and shrugged.

"Look at Finch," Lady Hester said as if she'd noticed the exchange between brother and sister. "She is charmingly dressed. Her husband's heart swells with pride at the sight of her." It was true that in blue gros-de-Naples trimmed with a darker blue satin piping, Finch was lovely.

Jenny said, "Aye, she's lovely," and crammed on her bonnet.

"Oh," Finch said. "Something's wrong with the flower on that."

Latimer knew what he would see. The vision of only a few remaining orange rose petals didn't surprise him. He got up, went to his bedroom, and returned with the box containing his own two rosebuds. One of these he handed silently to Jenny, the other he threaded into his buttonhole. "Jenny made them," he said by way of explanation. "She's very good with her needle."

"So's Meg," Finch said. "Before she married, she earned her living sewing for people."

"*Before* she married," Lady Hester said. "Did you hear that, Jenny? Meg only sewed until she was married."

"When I'm married, I'll have to decide what t'do about my sewin'," Jenny said. She'd removed the bonnet, dislodged what was left of the old rose, and attached the new one with a pin she found in her reticule. "I'll sew it on properly when I've time," she said.

Latimer prepared to take Jenny to Bond Street. "I must take delivery of a large shipment to Whitechapel today. I'll use the opportunity to prepare my staff to keep things running smoothly for me while I attend to far more pleasant business." He smiled at Jenny. "On Friday you shall become my wife." But what he most needed his time for was to make sure they were not interfered with by Bucket or any of his fellows.

"I almost forgot," Finch exclaimed. "The roses. Mr. Lumpit sent them for you, Jenny. He says they are a token of his esteem. He did say some rather extraordinary things, you know, but… Oh, they're of no importance. I'm afraid the curate is quite lovelorn, and desperate enough to try anything to make you care for him."

"Poor man," Lady Hester said. "I met him the other day and he was most solicitous, although Sir Edmund didn't appear to care for him."

"Smart man," Latimer said and couldn't help sounding unpleasant. "The odious Lumpit is a nuisance."

Finch swayed in place and wouldn't meet his eyes. "Lady Hester, Mr. Lumpit would appreciate coming to see you later today. He has a personal matter he wishes to discuss."

Latimer opened his mouth to order Lady Hester to ignore Lumpit, but realized in time that he had no right to do so.

"I wish I could stay," Jenny said, "But Madame Sophie needs me."

They made to leave, but Old Coot came in with a box balanced on his rotund belly. His thin legs buckled slightly under the weight of what he carried.

"For Mr. More and Miss McBride," he intoned. "Delivered a short while ago."

"Delivered by whom?" Latimer said.

Coot put the box on the dining table and stood expectantly aside. He frowned and said, "Dash me, but I don't know. Left by the cloakroom it was. James took it in, he said, but he probably didn't. Never remembers anything anyway." He tapped the box.

"Oh, open it," Lady Hester said, standing up and positively bubbling with excitement. "It must be your first wedding gift. You can be sure one of the footmen has been out and about talking already, and the news is spreading among our friends and acquaintances."

Jenny said, "I don't know anyone, so it's really for you, Latimer. I'll find my own way to Bond Street. It's no' so far."

Latimer pulled her against his side and kissed her brow—and heard the other two ladies sigh. He sat Jenny in a chair by the table and used the small knife he carried to pry the lid off the box. Whatever was inside had been wrapped in many layers of white paper and had a yellow ribbon tied around it. He removed it gently, finding it heavier than he'd expected.

The ribbon he cut away with his knife. Then he unwound the paper and all three ladies gasped.

"It's beautiful," Lady Hester said. "A treasure, I should think."

"My goodness, Latimer," Finnie said.

He glanced at Jenny but she was staring, amazed, at what appeared, on cursory inspection, to be a gold, hexagonal tower clock. Latimer realized that it had been made in France in the 1500s and was worth a deal of money.

"There's a card," Finch said, and swept one up from the floor where it must have fallen. She gave it to Jenny and said, "Open it."

Latimer restrained himself from insisting upon reading it first.

"Such paper," Jenny said, opening the envelope and drawing out a card. "It's so thick and creamy. It says, *I'm glad for you. Best, A Friend.* Who might that be?"

Movement in the foyer caught Latimer's eye and he saw

Adam there, staring at him. The other man gave a salute and went up the stairs. "This good friend is a shy man," Latimer said. "He doesn't enjoy outward displays of emotion. I think I know him better than he knows himself."

The evening turban Jenny worked on was for Lady Lloyd. While she sewed gold braid on purple velvet, she felt light-headed at the thought of Sibyl and Sir Hunter being present for the wedding on Friday. Everything that was happening seemed a dream. All the fine people Latimer knew would be there and she shrank from the responsibility of it all.

Only she mustn't shrink from anything, certainly not from an event that would be the greatest joy of her life and one that meant so much to Latimer.

Latimer. For a little while she'd almost forgotten that the annoying rogue sat on an ancient, wobbly chair in the corner of her workroom, and observed every move she made while he pretended to doze.

He'd been there for more than an hour, since three, with his legs stretched out and his hat in his lap. His chin rested on his chest and if what little light there was didn't catch the glitter of his slitted eyes, she might think he really was asleep.

Latimer shifted, crossed his arms and raised his shoulders. A casual observer could believe he didn't know when his hat fell to the floor.

"Och," she said aloud. "I wonder if ticklin' feels different if ye're asleep."

He didn't as much as lift the corners of his mouth.

"A feather's a fine instrument of tickling torture, so I'm

told. This peacock feather should be just right—or perhaps that ostrich plume.''

The sound of Madame Sophie's rustling skirts approached and she stepped down into the cramped room. Latimer was instantly alert, on his feet, and smiling at her. ''There you are, Madame Sophie. I'd hoped you'd appear soon.''

The man was shameless, Jenny thought fondly.

''Did you receive your invitation to the wedding?''

''I did, thank you,'' Madame Sophie said. ''I shall look forward to the celebrations.''

Jenny looked from Latimer to Madame and had to remember to close her mouth. Madame Sophie hadn't said a word about getting an invitation.

''Good,'' Latimer said. He took a box from his pocket and gave it to Madame. ''Today I had a large delivery of special goods from the East. Mostly China. When I saw this, I thought of you. I'd like you to have it as a gift from Jenny and me. You have been more than kind to her.''

Madame took the white box tied with a silver ribbon, and Jenny had the sensation that she was a member of the audience at a play.

''Hasn't she, Jenny?''

She looked about her and said, ''Always very kind.''

Madame opened her gift swiftly and took out an exotically shaped flower carved from polished blue stone and outlined in gold. She pressed a hand to her cheek and gasped. ''I cannot take this. It is too beautiful.''

''It's an anemone and the stone is lapis lazuli. There is some question about its origins. I believe it is exceedingly old and probably carved in Egypt. And it is yours. From your shop, I know you favor blue and gold. Only you will appreciate it enough.''

She was marrying a man with a silver tongue. Jenny

accepted the flower from Madame and was surprised at its weight. "Ye've good taste, Latimer," she said, returning the piece to its new owner. "And ye know how t'choose the right gift for the right person."

Madame thanked him formally but held the lapis as if she would never let it go and smiled with delight.

Conversation faded.

There was a clearing of throats and Madame hummed a little.

Jenny put a few more stitches in the turban but couldn't concentrate.

"There's someone I want you to meet, Jenny," Madame said. She drew one of the drapes away from the entry to the shop and called, "Come, Elsie." To Jenny she said in a low voice, "A nice girl who sews well. Not as well as you, but she'll do."

Jenny's mouth became dry. She sought Latimer's eyes but he looked determinedly—and with a guilty air—at the floor.

Elsie couldn't be more than fifteen. Plump, dark-haired, with scrubbed, rosy cheeks and brown eyes, she came into what had been Jenny's domain these past years and glanced around with a big, soft smile. She went to Jenny's side and looked at the turban. "That's a wonder," she said. "Such fine stuff and you are clever with your needle. I'd like to be as clever as you one day."

"The girl doesn't do herself justice," Madame said. "She is already accomplished for one so young. With gowns rather than hats, but she will learn quickly. Aren't we fortunate to find her, Jenny—since you are to be married so soon and must spend every moment preparing for the event?"

"Verra fortunate," Jenny said when she could speak. Latimer's fine hand was so obvious behind this that she

began to plot revenge. Unfortunately he might not dislike most of the things that came to her mind.

"I hope you'll visit me when you have time," Madame Sophie said. "Perhaps you'll allow us to make hats for you."

Jenny got up slowly. She felt strange, unreal. "I'll come t'see ye," she said with a sense that she was expected to leave now. "This is a lovely place t'work, Elsie. Madame will teach ye to make beautiful hats and I'm happy for ye."

The girl slipped immediately into the chair Jenny vacated and picked up the turban. She looked closely at the stitching and examined the piece inside and out. Then the needle began to move and Jenny could see that Elsie would take her place so well that she wouldn't be missed for long.

After the goodbyes that went on too long, Latimer ushered Jenny to the street and handed her into his handsome, deep green carriage. A coachman folded the steps and closed the door, and soon the horses' hoofs clattered on cobbles, and leather creaked while the wheels ground along.

"It's a perfect day for new beginnings," Latimer said, sitting close beside her. "Warm. A bright blue day."

"It's a fine day," she said.

"There is so much to do so we mustn't be idle."

"I've never been idle a day in my life. Don't want t'be. Won't be."

Latimer's chest expanded. "I'm sure you won't."

"What d'ye have in mind t'fill my hours, then? Now that I dinna have a place anymore?"

"You'll have another place," he declared. "I have a great deal for you to do." He hit the roof with his stick and called to the coachman, "Whitechapel, Samuel." To Jenny he said, "We will take a little precious time for me to show you my warehouses. You will surely find plenty to do for me there.''

"Will ye need me t'sew bonnets there?''

"Don't be unreasonable," he snapped.

Jenny fell silent and watched through the window as the buildings of the center of London gave way to meaner streets and crowded houses.

The carriage rocked and she heard the coachman stopping the horses. Gradually the coach grew still and the horrid face of Morley Bucket appeared at Latimer's window. "Afternoon," he said, showing his yellowed teeth. "Forgive me for interrupting your pleasant drive but I've business with the lady here.''

"You have no business with Jenny. If you have something to say, say it to me." Latimer's anger made a mask of his face. "Hurry up, man. We have things to do.''

"I'm a busy man, too," Bucket said, looking at Jenny. "You and me 'ave unfinished business. Why not come along with me. You don't want to discuss yer private matters in front of the gent, 'ere. I'll bring you back to 'im quick enough.''

Before Jenny could answer, Latimer said, "You have no business with my fiancée that doesn't affect me. What do you want?''

Bucket's lip curled. He made a hissing sound at Jenny and she pressed her hands hard against her stomach. "It's *fiancée* is it? Bloody little nuthin' what wants to pretend she's somethin' better. Well, not without discharging your promises to me first. You owe me. I don't suppose you've got it all, but I want somethin' on account. Just to show you've got honorable intentions, like.''

She fiddled with her reticule, knowing she had no more than a few pennies inside.

Latimer put a hand on top of hers and held it still. Then

he slipped a money clip from an inside pocket in his jacket and said to Bucket, "What is the amount outstanding?"

"None of your infernal business. Like I said, my business is with the lady."

"Since the lady is my business now, you will deal with me," Latimer said, peeling notes from the clip and handing them to Jenny. "Give him these. They are yours because I give them to you. That should make the fellow happy."

Jenny leaned across Latimer and offered the money to Bucket. He took it and promptly threw it in her face. "I told yer we 'ad private business. If yer don't want all yer fancy plans spoiled, we'll 'ave that chat. Alone."

Latimer, tight-lipped with rage, hammered on the roof and the carriage swung away rapidly enough to land Mr. Bucket on his hands and knees in the street.

"Damn him," Latimer muttered. "I thought I knew his game, but now I'm not so sure. From his behavior, there's more riding on this than his pride or his personal interest in you. If he tries to get too close to you, I shall have to deal with him."

"Ye wouldna kill anyone?" Jenny said. If she told him Bucket had plans to discharge her debt by as good as selling her to another man, who knew what dreadful things might follow?

Latimer gathered the bank notes and gave them to her. "Put these in your reticule. I don't want you traveling with nothing to pay for whatever comes up."

"Ye mean ye're afraid I'll be waylaid when ye're no' wi' me." She thought that quite likely and was sickened at the prospect.

"Enough of that," Latimer said. "See where we are?"

Jenny looked outside again and wished she hadn't. "Aye, I know it well. Whitechapel's no friend o' mine."

"Yes, it is. I make my living here, and a respectable living it is."

In a street lined with pathetic houses on one side and warehouses on the other, the coachman stopped the horses and came to hand Jenny down.

"Take them around to the yard, Samuel," Latimer said. "I doubt we'll be here long."

When the carriage had rolled away, Latimer pointed to the houses, where most windows were covered with pieces of board and said, "Finch and Ross have an adopted son named Hayden. He was living there when they first met him."

"Another orphan," Jenny said. "Ye're kind people. Where is Hayden now?"

"He lives on the Scottish estate where Ross is teaching him to farm," Latimer told her with a hard edge to his tone. "We are not *kind* people, merely people with a gift for recognizing good things when we see them. I will not marry you out of charity, Jenny, but out of my deep love for you."

Shamed, she put a hand on his chest and said, "Your love for me canna be deeper than mine for you. Forgive me if I say silly things sometimes. I've had a lot to become familiar with."

"Quite." He didn't sound softened toward her. "In we go, then."

Inside a cavernous building where crates lined the walls and stood in clusters everywhere, Latimer introduced her to one man after another as they went quickly about their work. In some places stood statues, in others, furniture. Pottery and glass looked out of place displayed on shelves in such surroundings. She met Will Austin, who was Latimer's second-in-command, a pleasant, fair-haired man with a healthy build, who showed he was knowledgeable about the business.

"You've met everyone," Latimer said at last.

"Ye've good people workin' for ye," she told him. "They've everything under control and there's not a thing for me to do here—as you know."

He scowled at her. He'd removed his jacket and rolled up his shirtsleeves. He looked bursting with life and health. "Take a look at my office and we'll go. I think your wedding dress is the next order of business."

She went ahead of him into a big office in the center of the warehouse floor. Frosted windows enclosed it on all sides. More crates greeted her, and a big desk. A tray of tea things stood on top of a bookshelf. Jade buddhas, carved ivory, white marble figurines, boxes with jeweled lids and handfuls of polished stones littered every surface. "It's like a sorcerer's lair," she said. "I'd expect magic to happen among all these mysterious things."

"Would you indeed?" Latimer hung his coat on a peg and locked the door. "For security," he said.

"What's the stone on top o' this wee box?" she asked, showing him a gilt-edged container encrusted with gems but with a green and white jewel in its top, a jewel that flared red when she tilted the box.

He opened her hand, put the box on her palm, and folded her fingers around it. "A fire opal," he said. "It's yours, to keep the bluebird pin safe."

"I canna—"

Latimer, lifting Jenny to sit on his desk, silenced her. He propped a hand on either side of her and looked closely into her eyes. "Peacock feathers?" he said. "Ostrich plumes? Instruments of tickling torture you may be glad I don't possess here."

She nodded, but he used his fingertips to tickle her until

she writhed and tried to fight him off. "Ooh, stop, Latimer." She could scarcely catch her breath. "Your men will hear."

"If they do, they'll be justly jealous." He kissed her, then continued to torment her and behaved as if her hands were ladybirds to be swatted when she tried to stop him from tickling the sensitive places behind her knees.

He paused, breathless himself, and said, "One day I'll explain what I mean, but accept that I'm only living up to my reputation. I'm a daring man."

With that, he pulled her against him to undo the tapes on her dress, stripped her naked to the waist and flipped her backward onto the desk. And still he tickled her.

"Latimer," she wailed, but it must be hard for a man to listen to anything when he was intent on licking circles over his beloved's breasts and undoing his trousers at the same time. When she wriggled and spoke his name again, he pushed his head beneath her skirts and she forgot what she'd intended to say.

30

"Come here at once, Jenny," Sibyl said. "Finch, can you do anything with her? Latimer will be leaving for the chapel at any moment. If he looks up at the window, he'll see her. And it's bad luck." Sibyl was almost weeping when she finished.

"Jenny, dear," Finch said. "To please the one who is about to become your sister, will you come away from the windows?"

If Jenny didn't cough with nervousness each time she tried to open her mouth, she'd laugh at these two who had decided to be her mothers while Lady Hester sat on the blue-and-silver couch and looked serene in a heavenly shade of deep blue.

"Jenny," Sibyl cried.

"Do as you are told, girl," Lady Hester put in. "At once. You're behaving like an addlepated cuckoo—not an appealing combination."

Sighing, looking over her shoulder, Jenny turned from the lace draperies. "How would a man see through the curtains?" she said, longing for just a peep at her soon-to-be husband's broad shoulders as he left the house and passed beneath the windows. With Adam and Toby, he would enter the black barouche that waited there with its door open and a coachman in Lady Hester's livery standing to one side. Multi-colored ribbons had been tied to the door handles, to the back of the coach where two tigers—perhaps a little cramped in uniforms that hadn't been used in a long time and were small—stood dressed in purple and yellow, and to the shining rails on either side of the coachman's box. Each of four horses sported a matching rosette on its bridle.

"Stand here, and stand still," Sibyl ordered. "It really is the end that Meg and Jean-Marc have left for Ireland. Meg would be so much better suited to making the final tweaks to this dress."

There was a knock and Lady Hester said, "Come," admitting Evans with a bowl of summer flowers.

"From Mr. More," he said, putting them down. "And he wishes you to have these."

Jenny was presented with a round nosegay of wildflowers mixed with yellow and white roses and framed with lace. Ribbons the colors of those on the coach trailed from the enclosed stems.

"Most appropriate," Lady Hester said. "Evans? Where is Coot?"

"Not feeling well, milady. All the excitement is too much for him."

"Then he is to rest so that he may enjoy the breakfast," her ladyship said. "Please tell him not to come to the chapel unless he is completely recovered."

"Yes, milady. Mr. More did wish to remind Miss McBride that he is likely to expire if she keeps him waiting."

"Then I must go at once," Jenny said, picking up her skirts and preparing to run.

"And arrive *before* the groom?" Lady Hester said, but she smiled. "Impertinent fellow, but I'm proud of him. I have watched him make a triumph of his business and himself. Most gratifying to see one of my protégés do so

well. And you, too, Finch. And Sibyl and Meg. Most gratifying. Thank you, Evans. I should tell you that I am more
than grateful that Sir Edmund found you for me. Coot will
have his senior position in this household for the rest of
his life, but you will make a splendid second-in-
command.''

''Thank you, milady,'' Evans said and bowed from the
room.

''Put the flowers down,'' Finch said, darting from one
side of Jenny to the other and back again. ''Oh, Sibyl, is
the hem even? Put the flowers *down,* Jenny.''

''I willna,'' Jenny said and held them close. Latimer had
sent them to her. ''I want t'see him.''

Finch cast her eyes heavenward and said, ''You're behaving like a child. He hasn't left for the chapel yet. When
he does—regardless of his warnings—we'll wait a respectable interval, and go there ourselves. *Then,* and not a moment before, will you see your groom. And if he's expired,
you may be grateful you didn't marry the weakling.''
Finch laughed at her own little joke but Jenny's eyes filled
with tears—again.

''Look at her, Lady Hester,'' Sibyl said. ''Isn't she
beautiful?''

''They say even ugly gels are beautiful on their wedding
days. Don't ask me why when they're about to go through
the worst experience of their lives.''

Finch and Sibyl hushed her in unison.

Jenny didn't care what anyone had to say. She felt
pretty, she must *be* pretty, and this was the *happiest* day
of her life.

''Meg and Jean-Marc on that dreadful sea and crossing
to look at some Irish property they don't have time to
administer, beautiful as I'm sure it is.'' Sibyl complained.

"And Desirée in dreadful Mont Nuages where she's no doubt being ignored by her terrible father."

"Sibyl," Finch said, "I do believe you mixed a liberal dose of pessimism into your breakfast. It was ill fortune that caused the messenger to miss Meg, and Desirée had left some time previous. But not only were you still at Riverside, but Hunter was already on his way to accompany you to Cornwall. Now we have both of you. And thank goodness Ross got here in time. He most certainly would not have done so if he weren't already on his way because of his concern over what might be happening here. We are blessed, I tell you. And we shall celebrate again when everyone returns."

"Hmm," Sibyl said. "You are obviously an optimist, Finch, but I didn't have breakfast. I'm too nervous."

"I didna eat anythin'," Jenny said. "I couldna. Finch, may I say somethin' about your father?"

"What is there to say?" Finch's mouth made a straight, tight line.

"I'm verra sorry he didna send a response sayin' he'd come. Latimer told me it was the same for your own weddin'. You're both sad no doubt, but he's the sadder one. He's missin' so much."

"He's too proud," Finch said. "He said if we left Cornwall he'd turn his back on us and he has. But I'd lie if I said I didn't miss him—bad-tempered man that he is."

"Aye," Jenny said. A long mirror had been brought to her rooms and she rotated carefully to survey herself one more time. "Whatever may be wrong wi' me now, will stay wrong," she said. "D'ye think the roses in my hair will die before we get t'the chapel."

Lady Hester chuckled, then laughed, and wafted her blue silk fan before her pretty face. "You are all incorrigible. Tomorrow we shall laugh at all this nonsense. Jenny, the roses will not die and the dress is perfect. I've never seen a paler shade of mint green. Perfect with your coloring. Sibyl, go around the skirts and make sure the leaf ornaments are straight.'' Each satin leaf had a white satin daisy at its base and a lemon-colored butterfly sat on the petals. The dress was of tulle over the pale green gros-de-Naples. "Did I tell you Birdie's wearing a gown to match mine?"

She had, several times, but Jenny said, "I think she'll be lovely in it."

"You look as if you have dew on your skin," Finch said. "But I don't think you should wear the bluebird pin."

"I'm wearin' the pin," Jenny said and felt as stubborn as she sounded. "For ye, and for your mother—and because I like the way it looks."

"I like the pearls in your hair," Sibyl said. "Your hair is so very red and the pearls stand out."

"La," Jenny said, and caused an immediate gale of laughter. Since the first effort was so successful, she repeated, "*La*. I'm gorgeous and I thank ye for recognizing a gem in your midst. When can we leave?"

From below came the unmistakable sound of the front door closing sharply. Jenny made for the window but was detained by a pair of strong hands on each of her arms.

She gave up easily and stood with her head bowed, listening to voices in the street, then one voice rose above the rest, a manly voice laced with humor, "Don't be late, Jenny," Latimer cried. "I'll be waiting for you."

Adam had fallen silent and Toby was kneeling on his seat watching every detail from the windows. Latimer closed his eyes and used the rhythmic jounce of the carriage and the clatter and creak of the horses to help him focus his thoughts.

Concentration was a hard thing when your heart led you elsewhere. His wedding day. Only weeks ago this had been a vague dream he'd rashly promised himself would come true. He and Jenny were marrying without making all the decisions that would have been made if they'd had more time to prepare, but Adam had been right, her immediate acceptance of him gave the lie to any accusations that had been made against her—and anyway, he wanted her to be his wife at once.

He opened his eyes.

Lies had no place between a man and his wife. Lies, or failure to be honest. Jenny deserved to know that his hasty actions had been a test.

Not today. Today would not be spoiled by anything.

"I feel guilty," Adam said. "I pushed you into this."

"You did. Thank you."

Adam put his elbows on his knees. "It isn't too late to turn back. Jenny's a sensible girl. Tell her the two of you need more time to be ready for marriage."

Giving him a mighty slap on the back, Latimer laughed and sputtered, "It *is* too late and I've never been more glad of anything. We'll have growing to do and we'll do it together. Jenny is the best thing that ever happened to me."

Adam turned his serious gray eyes on Latimer, "You're sure?"

"Completely."

"You won't be banging on my door tonight and wanting to call me out for ruining your life?"

Latimer used the ivory handle of his cane to tip his hat back and he grinned at Adam. "I doubt if you'll see me tonight, old chap. If you get lonely, pop on over to Number

8 and keep Lumpit company." He was still looking for a way to thank Adam for the extravagant wedding gift.

"Wot d'you mean, Mr. Chillworth pushed you into marryin' our Jenny?"

"Toby," Latimer said, having forgotten the boy's presence. "You are a young man now and about to learn a great many things about what passes between men and women—when they're in love, that is. Keep your ears open and you'll be ready to deal with such matters when your own turn comes."

"But I asked—"

"Yes, yes." He might have known the boy would not be so easily silenced. "Just a joke between Adam and myself. We're old friends and have had our doubts that either of us would ever marry. Adam means he supported my decision to ask for Jenny's hand, nothing more."

"Ah," Toby said and went back to watching the buildings and gardens they passed.

Whereas Adam and Latimer wore black coats and dark gray trousers, Toby's coat was dark blue and his trousers buff. He was a handsome little devil with a sharp mind.

"I thought we was goin' to St. John's Wood," Toby said. His nose was pressed to the window now.

"We are," Adam said. "Probably a part you haven't seen."

Latimer checked his neckcloth, which Evans had volunteered to tie. The man had said the name of the knot, but Latimer didn't remember, or care. Surreptitiously he took his marmalade silk rose from inside his hat—the only place he'd been able to think of as a hiding place, and slipped it into his buttonhole.

"I ain't spent much time around 'ere where the nobs live," Toby said, "but I knows it enough. I thought St. Stephen's wasn't far from Regent's Park."

"It's not," Latimer said, alert to the scenery for the first time since leaving Mayfair Square. "Adam, the boy's right. We're nowhere near the Park, and St. John's Wood is behind us." He looked at his pocket watch. "Damn and blast, the idiot coachman. He'll have us late."

Adam was already hammering the roof inside the carriage. Latimer slid open the trap and called to the coachman, "Stop. You've taken a wrong turn. We must go back at once."

The coachman didn't turn around. Neither did the man who sat beside him. "Were there two drivers?" Latimer asked Adam over his shoulder.

"No," Adam said.

"There are now." He used his cane to poke the back of the nearest man and was ignored. Latimer closed the trap. "Something's gone wrong. Those men are nothing to do with Number 7 and they aren't stopping. In fact they're traveling faster."

Adam had moved to the front of his seat and was studying the view. "Hampstead," he said. "And unless I'm mistaken, the Heath. What foul business is this? If it's a robbery, they've gone to a great deal of trouble. But what else could it be?"

"Bucket," Latimer and Toby said together.

"Gad." Adam took off his coat and put it behind him. Latimer did the same. "We're going to have to fight, dammit."

"'Aven't you got a sword about yer?" Toby said. "We could kill 'em through that little 'ole without even getting out. Then I'll drive us back. We can't 'ave our Jenny waitin'."

The notion sickened Latimer, but Toby's idea, swashbuckling as it was, wouldn't work. Not exactly.

"Toby," he said. "I don't have time to explain everything that will happen. But you will remain in this coach. Understand? You will not get out of the coach and interfere or you may ruin our chances of escape.''

''Going a bit fast to get out anyway, aren't we?'' Adam said.

Latimer was in no mood for sarcasm. ''When the carriage slows, jump,'' he told Adam. ''We've got to stop the coach and deal with these men. Toby, you can be a help. Forget what I said about not getting out. Wait your moment. And you'll know what I mean when it happens. Then get up and keep a tight rein on the horses.''

Toby looked happy, as if he weren't in a carriage that had made a turn onto the Heath and was being driven madly between stands of trees toward rougher, more hilly ground.

''Ready?'' Latimer yelled to Adam. ''Here goes.''

He withdrew the slender blade from his walking stick, assessed the angle of the two bottoms seated atop the box, and took aim. He applied two short, but not too short, jabs to each rump and saw them rise. Blood seeped between splayed fingers and enraged yowls reached the passengers.

The carriage still hurtled on.

Latimer repeated his target practice, this time sending his blade deeper into the enemy's flanks.

Yowls turned to screams and the coach swayed, the horses complained loudly and the sounds were of the wheels screeching on hard, dry ground as they slowed.

Adam crouched with his hand on the door, ready to push it open and jump. Latimer prepared to leap from the same door, and Toby was in place on the opposite side.

''The tigers,'' Latimer said. ''They may be friend or foe. If they're foe they'll make this too uneven for comfort. Go for the quick stuff. Frightening 'em off would be to our good.''

The coach almost stopped and Adam jumped. He rushed at once for the back where the tigers would be clinging in their places.

Latimer waited one more moment, and, sword in hand, landed on the ground running. He threw himself at the horses, all the while praying the two ruffians in the driver's seat didn't have pistols.

Yells and sounds of begging came from the rear of the coach and Latimer hoped Adam's opponents were no match for him even if there were two of them. They needed miracles and Latimer wasn't above invoking them.

Keeping low, Latimer made it to the left lead horse and leaped onto its bare back. He lay on that back, knowing the horse behind him would act as a shield, and pulled back on the bridle. He talked to the horse, soothed him, and felt the animal break his stride. The others followed suit.

A pistol shot blasted Latimer's ears. *Dammit.*

He dismounted in time to see two burly men, wincing and cursing, getting gingerly down from their places while Toby climbed up from the opposite direction.

Latimer kept low and weighed the chances of running around to get up with Toby on the opposite side. The element of surprise could give time to pick up Adam and be away.

Bull-like bellows and the rapid, if limping, charge of a fellow wearing Lady Hester's colors, blew away Adam's hope of an easy escape. On horseback, he had held the delicate sword like a saber. Now he changed his grip and stood his ground.

"You'll pay for that one, you uppity bastard," the approaching man said, but he'd halted his advance.

"Where's the flamin' pistol?" his companion shouted. "Give it t'me."

The first man looked at his empty hands and his jaw slackened. He patted himself and said, "I ain't got it. Didn't 'e give it t'you?"

"The skinny whoremaster made you boss, remember," the second fellow said and added, "Said 'e only 'ad one and give it t'you. You knocked them others out with it. Oh, my gawd, you've lost it. Fix this one with the silly-lookin' sword then." He went in the other direction, toward the cries and sounds of scuffling from the rear of the coach.

But Latimer had heard a shot.

The kidnapper didn't take his eyes off the "silly looking sword." He said, "Throw that over there or I'll use it on you."

"Take it away from me, then," Latimer said, flicking the tip of the sword and taking his position. "Come on, man, take it from me. How else will you use it against me?"

"'Ow else?" Toby said in a loud, belligerent voice.

Latimer smiled a little.

The impostor coachman didn't. Unfortunately neither was he distracted by Toby.

Latimer made circles with his blade and feinted, but the other man seemed rooted to the ground. He put a hand to his rear again and glanced at the bloody fingers he withdrew. "Bastard," he muttered. "Attackin' a man from behind."

"Attackin' his behind from behind, yer mean," Toby called and chuckled at his own witticism.

Latimer didn't want to kill this piece of scum. Better that he suffer much longer. The chap was panting and sweat ran down his round, red face. He was, Latimer realized, scared. Scared of more than a blade. If that had been all, he'd have run away. "Morley Bucket's a hard master, is he?" he said. "Likely to take a whip to that sore arse of yours if you let us get away?"

"Shut yer mouth."

Latimer glanced at Toby and their eyes met. Then he looked back at the sweating man. He repeated the process, willing Toby to understand.

Another pistol shot sounded and he knew he had to get to Adam. "Jump on him, Toby," he cried, but Toby was already in flight from the carriage. Amid oaths and beefy arms that swung like windmill blades, the boy's weight, landing on the man's head and neck, knocked him to the ground and Latimer was upon him instantly, winding his arms behind his back until he screamed. "Something to bind him with," he told Toby, who was already scrambling onto the front of the carriage once more. He pulled gear from beneath the seat and cried out with triumph when he held a length of rein aloft. This he threw to Latimer who, with the aid of his sword, had little difficulty slicing off strips of leather and securing the man's wrists and ankles together before using another piece to haul his feet backward and up to his hands. He left the fellow writhing and yelling on the ground.

Crouched, going around the back of the carriage, Latimer all but tripped over the second man from the driver's seat. He appeared to be unconscious and blood trickled from a wound at his temple. His face bore multiple cuts and his closed eyes weren't going to open easily even when he wanted them to. One furrowed wound across the back of his neck could only have been made by a firearm.

"Adam," Latimer yelled. "For God's sake man, I didn't know you carried a pistol." Without waiting for a response, he launched himself into the writhing fray that turned over and over in a jumble of arms and legs, tattered black and purple silks, and Adam's flying hair.

The tigers were not boys, but small men who might well have been pugilists by the way they used their fists. Latimer took a punch to the corner of his eye that rendered him sightless on that side for moments. Rage overcame him. "That's it for you, you piece of filth." His fist rose and fell on the wiry fellow's head, with the odd blow to the belly, until Latimer watched consciousness slip away from his opponent.

Adam held the other "tiger" facedown on the dusty trail across the heath. And he ground that face into the dirt even when the man had stopped struggling.

"Adam," Latimer shouted, "Adam, you've knocked him out. Where's the pistol?"

"Over there," Adam said, tearing strips from the unconscious man's clothing and tying him up with them.

Latimer did the same thing with his man and both he and Adam ran to the fallen one by the rear of the carriage. "What happened back here?" Latimer said. "Hell's teeth, someone is going to suffer for this. My Jenny is waiting at that church by now. She may even have left again." He turned his eyes to Adam and felt a deep twisting in his belly. "Will she ever understand?"

"One look at you should be worth more than words, my friend," Adam said. "Quickly, finish with this one. I have been known to carry a pistol about me. Almost didn't today. Praise be I changed my mind. Put a shot in the air and sent those two over there running for their lives. Unfortunately this chap jumped me from behind and by the time I'd beaten him down and wounded him, the others had crept back and managed to get the pistol. You can fill in the rest. This one won't move until someone unties him."

31

An ensemble of strings and trumpet played the same piece of music for the second time. Jenny stood in the vestibule of St. Stephen's Chapel, clinging tightly to the arm of Ross, Viscount Kilrood, Finch's husband, whom she'd met for the first time shortly before he accompanied her from Number 7.

The viscount put his hand over hers on his arm and said, "Be calm, Jenny. Weddings are the very devil. One day soon Finch and I will tell you about ours. It very nearly didn't happen." His voice did calm Jenny a little. It was strong and deep and had a touch of her own Scottish brogue.

"Somethin's happened t'Latimer," she said in a shaky voice. "He left fifteen minutes before us and we've been here twenty. He's changed his mind. He's not comin'."

"If he values his life, he'll come." Sir Hunter Lloyd, who was married to Sibyl, marched back and forth with his hands clasped behind his back and a thunderous expression on his face. "The scoundrel will deal with me."

Jenny looked from Sir Hunter, with his light brown hair and eyes as green as her own, to Viscount Kilrood, whose eyes were the kind of blue that was difficult to look at, especially when the man's dark hair and brows were such a contrast. Two handsome, manly men. Jenny turned hot at the audacity of her own thoughts. But they were manly

and their wives—who were beautiful in their brocade and
sarcenet, with elegant coiffeurs and jewels sparkling on
necks, wrists and hands—were perfectly matched to their
husbands. She could never hope to be a suitable match for
Latimer. Of course he'd come to his senses and decided
not to go through with the marriage.

"Latimer's a good man," Finch said, aiming her comment and an annoyed frown at her husband. "Really,
Hunter, I think we should be more concerned for Latimer's
safety, than—"

"Shh," the other three told Finch in unison and Jenny
felt all eyes upon her.

Yes, what if he'd been hurt? What if he and Adam—
and Toby—were lying injured somewhere while she
blamed him and thought silly thoughts about his not loving
her. He did love her. And he wanted her.

"Where is he?" Jenny didn't care that her voice broke
or that tears welled in her eyes. "We should look for
him."

"If we leave this place, he'll arrive the moment we've
left," Finch said and Sibyl mumbled agreement.

The music was playing for the third time.

"Good job it's hard to know where the cannon starts
and ends," the viscount remarked. "They'll all think this
is part of the plan."

"Oh," Sibyl said, smacking her cream-gloved hands
against the skirts of a light blue brocade dress. "What
piffle, Ross. You and Hunter make a fine pair. You make
excuses for Latimer and Hunter threatens to kill him. And
not a soul in that chapel thinks this long introduction is
part of any plan. They all know something's wrong."

"That's right," Finch said, then tried to smile reassuringly at Jenny. The smile was a flop.

"I said nothing about killing Latimer," Sir Hunter said.

"Please stop," Jenny begged. "It's a bad time we're havin'. All o' us." But they didn't know the pain she felt, and that pain had nothing to do with the whispering people who had set up a rustle of shifting clothing in the chapel.

Treading remarkably lightly for such a big man, Larch Lumpit slipped from the chapel proper into the vestibule. He frowned and actually looked as if he might cry. "What's happening?" he asked. "Dear Lady Hester's all atwitter and so am I. The only calm one among us is Sir Edmund and he's already said that if Latimer More doesn't show up for his own wedding, then Jenny's better off without him."

Jenny bowed her head. She couldn't look at them anymore.

"Could I go and look for him, do you think?" Lumpit said, to Jenny's amazement. "I could you know, if someone would give me an idea where to start. A wheel could have come off the carriage. Or a horse gone lame. Don't look so sad, Jenny. He loves you, that's easy to see, so he's been unexpectedly delayed."

After that speech, Jenny kissed Lumpit's cheek and said, "Ye're a dear man, but I don't think ye'd be able t'find them when not one of us has an idea where they could be." She drew a difficult breath. "They would have come by the same route as we did. It's verra strange."

Lumpit folded his hands and nodded.

Three richly dressed elderly ladies came from the chapel. They looked at Jenny with pitying eyes and left the building. More people followed, in a trickle at first, and then steadily.

The viscount cleared his throat and Jenny looked up at him. He gave Finch a meaningful stare and she nodded. "Jenny," he said. "There will be an explanation for this, but I doubt there'll be a wedding today. We'd like to take you home and make you comfortable until we find out what's gone wrong.''

She took her hand from his arm.

"Good girl," Finch said. "You need a meal and perhaps something to calm you. Then a good sleep."

"And he needs to be horsewhipped," Sir Hunter muttered.

The congregation filed out in a rush, most avoiding even a glance in Jenny's direction.

"I insist we leave," Viscount Kilrood said.

Sibyl's sniffs had turned to tears and she went into her husband's arms where he held her and stroked her hair.

"You go," Jenny said, and felt like a tiny island in a large ocean. "Please go home and don't worry. Latimer will come, and when he does I must be here."

Finch's eyes grew glassy also, and her mouth trembled.

"I'll—" Sibyl's hand on Sir Hunter's mouth stopped his next threat against Latimer.

"Please leave me here," Jenny said. "I'd like to wait alone."

"Well, you bloody well can't wait alone," Sir Hunter said, and turned red. "Apologies for that. Not myself."

Both doors into the chapel stood open. In the front pews sat Lady Hester, Sir Edmund and the staffs from Number 7, Number 8, and Number 17, who had moved forward to help make a solid little group. Birdie and Lady Hester sat side by side in their matching blue dresses. Jenny also saw Madame Sophie.

Jenny walked away from those who gave such kind support and progressed slowly down the aisle. With each step she felt a little dying, until she reached what was left of the congregation. At the front of the church she turned to face them. "Latimer will be here," she said, "but I dinna know when."

Snuffles surged through the pews.

"He's no' a man who would cause someone such great unhappiness unless something happened that he couldna control."

She heard mutterings and knew most of those present thought Latimer a cad, and her a fool.

"Would ye please go home, now," she said. "I'll go to Mayfair Square when I find out about Latimer. Until then, I'll stay here."

Not a soul moved.

"Please," she said, fighting back tears, "I'd like t'be alone if ye please."

She went toward the sacristy where the door stood ajar and she could see a minister in rich robes sitting in a chair with his feet on a stool. He was reading.

Passing time until someone tells him he can go. Jenny straightened her back and checked the rosebuds in her hair. She felt speckles of moisture still clinging to the petals. Lady Hester had said they'd be fine for the wedding, and she was right.

A hollow silence fell upon the building. Jenny remained a few yards from the sacristy and leaned on the front of a pew. She would wait—forever if that's how long it took for him to get to her.

From the street outside she heard hoofbeats and men shouting, but then the sounds died away and all was quiet once more. Still those who remained were silent behind her.

They were little more than strangers, but they were good people who couldn't bear to allow her to suffer alone.

Boots clattered on stone.

Unintelligible voices rang out, bouncing from the walls.

Jenny saw the minister close his book and she thought he smiled.

The sacristy door was flung wide-open and Latimer strode toward her. She gasped at the sight of his injured face and dusty, torn clothes, but then he gathered her to him and squeezed her so hard she could scarcely take a breath.

"You didn't go away," he murmured against her ear. "You stayed."

"I waited for ye," Jenny told him. "I didn't know when ye'd come, but I knew ye would. My poor Latimer. What's happened t'ye? Who did this t'ye?"

"Not now," he told her. "This is our wedding day. I'll deal with those people, but not when I have my darling girl in my arms and about to become my wife."

"I love ye, Latimer."

"Jenny, I don't have the words to tell you how much I love you."

Latimer kissed her. He cradled her face and fondled her lips with his own until she felt she floated and the world went away. With the kiss they reaffirmed their commitment, and Jenny offered herself to Latimer, and he promised he would take her.

There was a masculine "Ahem."

Still they kissed. Still Jenny thrust her fingers into Latimer's hair.

"Hmm, hmm." The same voice intruded, then said, "Perhaps the wedding first, my children?"

"Let's do this," Latimer whispered. "It's what we want so much. The man who will marry us is the Archbishop."

Then Jenny saw Adam, and Toby, and the condition of their clothing, the scrapes on both of them and a wound over Adam's left eye. He also had dried blood on a cut near his mouth.

"Come, sweet," Latimer said and turned her to see Viscount Kilrood waiting in front of the Archbishop to give her away.

They were married.

32

Spivey here:

Most affecting, I must say. Ah, me. Yes, I think I recall how a heart beats at such times.

But this is not going at all as I'd planned. I am so tired. A rest in my post is what I need. I might even enjoy imagining the scent of all those flowers they've strewn over Number 7, but I can't. I can't cease my vigilance for an instant. Certainly not when my only usable pair of hands belong to the likes of Larch Lumpit. He offered to search for Latimer! What has happened? He thinks for himself and now he has defected to the other side—even if he doesn't have a notion in his noggin of what he's really about, or what he'll soon return to. Wait until he wanders into St. Philomena's in Middle Wallop, puzzling about what exactly he'd set off to do when he left (he won't remember how long ago he did leave) and is confronted by his infuriated vicar.

Hmm. Some satisfaction in that. But first things first. The game isn't over, friends (I call you friends because I choose to believe there is goodness in you after all) and, with Lumpit's unwitting assistance (the only kind of assistance he's capable of performing) we may yet see Latimer and Jenny depart Number 7. What am I saying? Of course

they'll leave the house. They'll have to have more suitable digs, his being a protégé *of whom Hester is so proud...*
   Piffle.
Have faith in Sir Septimus—and watch closely.

33

A single violinist played in the foyer at Number 7.

Flowers loaded the bannisters and stood in banks wherever one looked. Multicolored ribbon streamers gave a lighthearted impression.

Latimer used his handkerchief to blot raindrops from Jenny's smiling face, her neck and, very carefully, her hair. "How dare it rain on our wedding day," he told her. "Although a little moisture on those freckles is charming, Mrs. More."

"Mrs. More," she murmured and rose to her toes to smooth moisture from his cheek. "I like the sound of that. And I like rain on your hair, and in your eyelashes. I like everything about you, Mr. More." She leaned against him. The intimate gathering of family, a few staunch guests who had remained until Latimer arrived at St. Stephen's and the nuptials were performed, and such members of the staff who could pause from their duties, sighed.

"Come along," Lady Hester said. "Let's go up. Hunter, you and Finch were so right to open the old ballroom. Wait until you see it, Latimer—and you, Jenny—it's beautiful. A fairy-tale room for an extraordinary wedding."

Latimer restrained himself from telling Lady H that he had seen the ballroom before, during, and after its renovation.

"Mr. Latimer?"

He glanced around and saw Old Coot hovering outside 7A. "Ah, Coot. I heard you'd been unwell. Glad you can join us."

Coot rolled precariously from heel to toe, his eyes popping as he seemed to try to give Latimer a message without speaking.

"Go up," Latimer told everyone. "Be there to greet us as we enter."

"Exactly," Lady Hester said.

Birdie ran up the stairs with Toby a close second. Chattering together, smiling fondly at Latimer and Jenny, the rest of the company followed quickly. Ross's voice rose above the rest, "Don't suppose a few moments alone would be amiss, either." Laughter met his suggestion.

When he could, Latimer said, "What is it, Coot?"

"I'm told James went to warn you, but he must have missed you."

"Yes, yes," Latimer said. Jenny stood close beside him. "But what did you want to warn me about?"

Coot shook his head slowly. "Forgive me, sir. I should be in my bed. Poisoned by some food, that's what Mrs. Barstow says. And cook's in a tear about that, I can tell you. But I've got to do my duty, haven't I sir? I've got to see to the running of Number 7 like I always have."

"Yes, o'course ye do," Jenny said. "And it's away t'your bed ye go because ye've done your duty. James will be back soon enough."

"It's them in there," Coot said, cocking his head toward 7A. "Runners, if you can credit it. Here at Number 7. At least her ladyship doesn't know. Want to see you, they do sir. And they want me to say that they have men watching from outside in case you decide to go for a stroll. Their words, not mine." He bowed his head so low his face could not be seen.

Latimer patted his shoulder. "You've done all you can. I'll deal with this now. Jenny, dear, I'm sorry to ask this, but would you wait for me in the guests' sitting room." Someone should suffer for this.

"I'll remain wi' ye," Jenny said without any drama. She held his arm and guided him to his own door—their own door. "We'll soon deal with whatever the men want."

Latimer could not insist that she let him go in alone, so he opened the door. Once he and Jenny were inside and confronted by two burly fellows who faced them with serious expressions, he closed the door again and said, "Good afternoon."

"Afternoon," they said. "We're here to ask you some questions. The lady need not be present."

"The lady is his wife," Jenny announced sharply. "What ye've t'say t'Latimer, ye've t'say t'me."

The shorter and older of the two men pursed his mouth beneath a bushy gray mustache. "Very well then. Latimer More, is that who you are?"

"It is," Latimer said. "Who wants to know?"

"We don't have to tell you that. This is a matter for the law. We're here to arrest you for robbery."

Jenny gasped, but stepped forward with her hands on her hips. "Ye're daft. And this is our weddin' day so ye'd best be off."

Both men looked mildly abashed. The taller one, who was blond, blushed. "We're just doing our duty, lady," he said. "And we rarely see more audacious behavior from a criminal than we have from Mr. More here."

"*Criminal?*" Jenny said, and Latimer had to pull her back or she might have marched on the officers to let them know exactly what she thought of them. "How dare you call my husband a criminal."

"Well, here's the proof, large as life and out in the open

for all to see," the blond man said. "We had an anonymous tip. We don't take something like this lightly, so we followed up. Best come along quiet like, Mr. More. But would you like to explain why you've been in a fight first—a violent one from the looks of you?"

"My private business is none of your affair." Latimer said. "What proof are you talking about?"

"Right there," the one with the mustache said. "Right in the middle of the mantel as cheeky as you like."

It was the wedding gift he referred to, the clock. "Adam gave it to us," Jenny said. Her eyes were wide and she was very pale.

"And who might Adam be?"

"Adam Chillworth," Latimer told him. "An accomplished painter and a friend who also happens to live in this house. Are you saying you don't know who suggested the clock was stolen?"

"Not yet. But we were led to believe that we would as soon as you're in custody. So let's not make this difficult. You're caught red-handed." The taller man spoke in a disconcerting monotone and seemed not to have heard, or at least not to have understood, what Jenny had said about the clock being a gift.

A fierce knock on the door was Adam's announcement of his arrival. He entered the room and took in the scene, his eyebrows lowered ominously over his eyes.

"Adam," Jenny said, running to him. "These people are accusing Latimer of stealing the wedding gift ye gave us. They say they've an anonymous tip. We knew from the card that ye dinna want to be thanked, but we need your help."

Latimer watched his friend's face and although he covered it quickly, Adam wasn't quite quick enough to hide confusion from one who knew him well.

Could it be that what the woman in gray had warned him about was right there, above the fireplace? Latimer stared in disbelief at the piece he'd displayed without a moment of concern. She'd said Jenny was the "Judas," and it was true that she could have found an opportunity to put the box where it would be found by Coot. He found himself smiling and didn't care if strangers thought him mad. Jenny was true to him. She didn't have to be here at his side now and wouldn't have been if she'd had anything to do with a plot.

"Officers," Adam said. "I'm so shocked I don't know what to say. That's a good clock."

"Yes," said the man with the mustache. "Very good. What do you do for a living, sir?"

Adam gave a devilish smile, then assumed a modest air. "I'm a painter, my man. A very famous portrait painter. If you want proof, request to see my portraits of Princess Desirée of Mont Nuages. They're here in London. I can give you a long list of my credits. And since you infer that I can't afford to give my best friend and his lovely wife a valuable clock, I suggest you visit Carstairs and Pork near the Burlington Arcade. They're dealers in fine timepieces, mostly rare ones, and I purchased the piece from them. Now there's a tip that *isn't* anonymous, my good fellows. Why don't you go and ask questions there and allow us to enjoy a very fine wedding breakfast here?"

The two officers looked at each another. The blond man rolled the brim of his hat nervously. "All right," he said, jutting his chin. "We'll do that, but if you're lying, we'll track you down and take you in along with this one." He nodded pointedly at Latimer.

Even after the men from Bow Street had left and Adam had closed the door to 7A firmly, there was no conversation in the room.

At last Adam said in a low voice, "What the dickens, man? I didn't—"

"I can tell you didn't," Latimer told him. "So who did? Someone who wanted to do me harm, obviously." He was not about to spend time discussing the woman in gray when they should be considering what to do next.

"Morley Bucket," Jenny said. "He's no' giving up. He's got his buyer for me and…"

She stopped talking and now she stared at him, her green eyes dark with worry.

"The devil you say," Latimer said while his skin turned cold. "And you never said a word about it before?"

"I didna want t'make ye angry enough to go after him. I was afraid for ye. He's no' a fair man and he'd do what he had to t'get his way. Toby said something t'ye that first night when ye followed me. He told me he'd said Bucket wanted me t'do something I wouldna. That's what it was. A man wanted to pay him and take me as…take me. I dinna think Bucket's given up."

"Damnation," Latimer said. His head and heart pounded and he felt an urge that almost frightened him. He wanted to kill Morley Bucket. "We've got to find him and force him to tell the truth. And unmask his *client*. And we have to start now. Thank you for lying for me, by the way, Adam. Or should I say, thanks for trusting me over them, even if you have put yourself in a queer position."

Adam poured two measures of brandy, gave one to Latimer and held the rim of the other glass to Jenny's lips until she took a sip and puckered her face in comical fashion. Latimer smiled at Adam's surprisingly natural gesture. The rest of the brandy in his glass went down Adam's throat in a single swallow.

"Perhaps we should ask Sir Hunter for his help," Jenny said. "He's a barrister."

"Not now," Latimer told her. "Although your idea is sound. Hunter is part of the law and I can't put him on the spot. I say we go to Bucket's place, Adam."

"Latimer?" a small voice called from outside the door. "It's Birdie."

"Marvelous," Latimer said in low tones. "All I need." He strode to open the door and the little girl, still in her beautiful blue dress, trotted in. Latimer said, "I expect they sent you to find us. Will you be a very good girl and tell them we'll be along shortly."

"It's Jenny I came to see," Birdie said. "I knew she was here with you. Oh, Jenny, it's terrible. She tripped him up and tied something in his mouth. Now he's gone."

Ignoring her gown, Jenny knelt and took Birdie by the shoulders. "Hush," she said. "Who are ye talking about?"

"Toby," Birdie said, and began to cry quietly. "The lady did it. She's very strong and she put something over his face and he went all limp. She's dragged him away. I think someone helped her when she went round the corner by the library. I was to come straight to you, she said. 'Get Jenny alone,' she said." The child's eyes strayed to Latimer and Adam and she paled even more. "You won't say what I'm telling Jenny, will you? The lady told me Toby might get hurt if I wasn't careful."

"Birdie," Adam said. "You've always been a brave girl. Be brave now. A woman did something to Toby and dragged him away. What did she ask you to tell Jenny?"

"That she's to go to the High Street and follow it to the park at the end. The one that belongs to a big house. Tap or something. The lady will meet her in there. That's if Jenny wants Toby back."

There had been no stopping Latimer from following her at a distance. Jenny hurried but did not run because she feared drawing too much attention. Her husband knew what was at stake and he was no fool. He wouldn't risk Toby's safety.

It wasn't cold but the rain had grown heavier and Jenny was grateful for the voluminous cloak she wore over her wedding gown and the hood with which she covered her hair.

The weather had driven people from the streets, which meant she and Latimer would be more easily spotted. She glanced over her shoulder but didn't see him. There were a few folk about but not one who could possibly be mistaken for Latimer. She trembled with relief.

Adam had unwillingly remained at Number 7 with instructions to take Birdie back to the breakfast and make convincing remarks about the drugging effects of the honeymoon on the groom and his bride. They would arrive eventually, he was to tell everyone. Jenny cringed at the thought of the laughter that would follow.

She bumped into a man who walked down the center of the flagway and made no attempt to step aside. "Sorry," she said, spinning away from him. He went on his way, grumbling under his breath.

Harder and harder the rain fell. Jenny wore a pair of leather half-boots Adam had found in Sibyl's old closet, but nevertheless her feet were wet. In the distance thunder rolled but there had been no lightning so it must be far away.

Tapwell Park, that must be the place Birdie meant. Scarcely able to draw a breath, Jenny reached white railings that closed off the parklands around the house. In fact it was still a private house but since no one had lived there for years, people found ways into the grounds and ate picnics there.

A bear and a griffin stood on stone gateposts. The gate itself was chained shut but had been pushed askew so that the bottom leaned inward. Somehow Jenny managed to tame her voluminous skirts enough to scramble through.

She looked in every direction and repeatedly brushed away the water that ran from her hood and onto her face. At first she didn't see a soul, but then the slightest of movements attracted her attention. At a distance, an arm extended briefly from behind a large oak. A handkerchief fluttered and was then withdrawn.

Jenny hurried on, her boots squelching in mud. She must not look back or whoever awaited her would know someone followed and might bolt.

The arm didn't appear again and she feared the person who had been there might already have changed her mind and left.

Dragging wet air into her lungs, Jenny reached the tree, which was in fact several trees grown together into a massive trunk at the base. "I've come," she gasped. "Like you told me to." With fear lodged in her throat, she ran to the other side of the tree.

The woman had gone.

Jenny put both hands over her mouth and cast about. Ahead and close to a rise stood more trees. From a break between two great, domed sycamores, the handkerchief fluttered again.

Covering the ground grew harder as mud absorbed more water and turned to sludge that sucked at her feet. When she gained the sycamores, her legs were numb and she stumbled between the trunks with tears streaming down her cheeks.

Once more she didn't see the woman.

"Jenny." Latimer's voice came close to making her fall from shock He joined her and pulled her into his arms.

"Enough of this foolishness. I can't allow you to make yourself deathly sick. You're going home and I'll carry on without you. Send Adam to me. Tell him I'll be searching the area."

"I will not leave ye," she told him and pushed against his chest. "And I've got t'find Toby."

She freed an arm and scrubbed at her face with a sleeve.

The next sound Jenny heard was a grunt and she lowered her arm in time to confront Latimer, his eyes half-closed, falling forward. She screamed his name as he hit the sodden ground.

On her knees beside him, she tried to turn him onto his back but failed. She cradled his head and put her face close to his. He murmured and she kissed his cheek, said his name again and again. "Ye're sick," she told him. "We've got t'have help."

Latimer tried to push on his hands but slipped down again. He murmured something and she put her ear close to his mouth. He whispered, "I was just hit. They're there. Run."

"Out of the way, missus," a man said and she held Latimer with all her strength.

"We've got business with this one." She saw one ruffian clearly, a thick-bodied man with a round face. He held a short, heavy-looking stick in one hand. "Get out of the way unless you want us to 'it you, too."

"Hit me," Jenny cried. She threw herself over Latimer, covered as much of him as she could while a bright flash registered dimly as lightning very close by. Thunder roared and the rain became a torrent that soaked Jenny to her skin.

"You got to finish 'im, and take 'er," someone else shouted. "We won't get another chance, if you know what I means."

"Hit me, then," Jenny said again. "Leave him be. He'll do ye no harm and it's me ye came for."

"She's right."

Jenny couldn't differentiate between the voices.

"Come along, my girl. Don't cause no trouble and we won't trouble you. And we'll all be 'appy."

Rough hands tore her from Latimer's back and she was stuffed, flailing, into a big sack that scratched her skin.

The sack was swung until it landed hard against something. The something said, "Oof," and she knew she was being carried on a man's back. "Do 'im now," he said to the other one.

34

"Stop strugglin'."

Jenny ached all over and she didn't give a fiddle for whoever wanted her to lie quietly in his nasty sack just because it would make his life easier. She'd been thrown on a hard floor and heard a door slam. Now she discovered there was someone waiting to guard her.

She rolled over, not that her elbows or knees took kindly to another scrubbing against the burlaps. And she made noises. Unfortunately she'd started making noises as soon as she'd been captured and caused a quick stop along the way to jam a rag in her mouth and tie it behind her head.

"Hold still!"

Ooh, she'd do nothing this moldy oat cakes of a person asked of her. *Knees to nose and stretch out straight, knees to nose and stretch out straight.* The effort exhausted Jenny but she'd rather die making a nuisance of herself than like a scared mouse.

"Jenny McBride, can you hear me?"

She inclined an ear and was still for a moment.

"So you can hear after all. It's Toby 'ere and if you'll 'elp instead of throwin' yourself around, I'll get you out of the bag. We don't 'ave very long. I 'eard 'em say they'd bring you 'ere and come back for you when some Mr. Deep Pockets arrives."

Jenny felt Toby at work on untying the sack and didn't

move at all. She felt air—be it musty air—bathe her, but it was as dark outside the sack as inside.

"Come on," Toby said, his voice clear now. "I ain't never been so 'appy to see anyone. Not that I ain't always 'appy to see you."

He helped her climb from the sack, then pulled her to sit beside him on the floor.

"Where are we?" she whispered. "What kind o' place is this?"

"It's a big cupboard," he said. "I come to when they was bringing me up the stairs in this 'ouse, but I don't know where it is. That woman's a mean one. They tied me up and she slapped my face every chance she got."

"Ye said, 'they.' Who helped her?"

"Never saw. They 'ad me blindfolded. And I've already been told I won't leave this place on me two feet."

Jenny drew in a sharp breath. "We have to escape. Our lives aren't worth anythin' here and Latimer's lyin' in Tapwell Park—or he was. Two men set on us there and when I was taken away, they said they'd finish him."

Toby found Jenny's hand and held it tightly. "That's all of us in queer street, then. The door's locked tight. But we ain't giving up, Jenny. We'll see if there's a way to pick the lock."

She visualized Latimer lying dead, covered with mud and blood in some pit, or even thrown from a cliff in a place where he'd never be found.

"Don't cry," Toby said.

Jenny hadn't realized she was crying. "No," she said. "I mustna do that. But how would we pick a lock, Toby? We don't know how and we've nothin' t'do it with."

"Hairpins," Toby said promptly.

She was glad of the dark so that he couldn't see her face. "I heard a bolt."

Toby's fingers tightened in hers. "I didn't."

"They'd probably used stuff t'make ye sleep and ye just didn't notice. I heard one. They bolted the door on the outside. I doubt there's a keyhole at all and if there was it wouldn't do us any good."

"That woman said I oughta blame you," Toby said. "Right nasty piece of work, that one."

Jenny felt sick. Toby should blame her for being where he was. He'd only been taken to lure her away so they could capture her. "I'm sorry," she told him. "I've just got to pray and think, and hope there's a way to escape. Others will come looking, but not in time, not if Adam does what Latimer told him to do and pretends we'll arrive at the breakfast eventually."

A bolt on the door opened with the sharp force of a rifle shot. Jenny and Toby sat close together and shaded their eyes as light flooded in from a lantern. "Keep your voices down," a woman said. "Attract the wrong attention and we're all dead. I'm going to help you."

"Who are ye?" Jenny said.

"It doesn't matter."

"Nah, it don't matter," Toby echoed. "Thank you very much. Show us out and we're on our way."

The woman set the lantern aside and Jenny saw she was young and pretty, wearing a red dress and with her dark hair drawn into bunches of curls above each ear. "I've got a plan to take you out of here. We must go quickly. Follow me and don't make a sound."

Jenny had questions but since she had no options, she kept quiet and stood up in the low storage room with its sloping ceiling. She and Toby followed the woman as she'd instructed. And Jenny thumped against the other's back when she pulled up short and cried out.

The woman screamed, then turned her scream to laughter. "Mr. Bucket, you are always surprising me," she said. "I was just taking these two to deal with the necessary."

"Lying whore," Bucket yelled, his rasping voice unmistakable. "You were settin' 'em free. I 'eard every word you said. After all I've done for you, you were crossing me. You're in with someone else, aren't you?"

"*No,* Mr. Bucket. You know you're my only true love. I wanted them to think I was helping them so they wouldn't give me any trouble. I'm the practical one, remember. I take care of the little details. They'd have been back here soon enough."

Jenny listened, but she also sized up her surroundings as best as she could by the lantern light. Bucket hadn't brought so much as a candle. All she could make out was what looked like another, larger storeroom filled with crates. The only door she saw was closed fast, but she wasn't giving up. These two were involved enough in each other to give Jenny hope of grabbing a chance to get out.

She must get Toby out and find Latimer.

To her horror, Bucket landed an open-handed blow to the woman's head and knocked her over. While she crouched there, he took Toby by the neck, stuffed him, kicking all the way, back in the cupboard and bolted him in. "I'll be back to deal with you, me lad," he said. "On your feet, Persimmon. This time I know what I've got to do with you, my girl." He kicked her and she whimpered.

Jenny edged closer to the door.

"Mr. Bucket, I have given you my loyalty and my undying affection. I had hoped that since all this was about to be over—successfully—you and I might finally, well, you know."

Jenny took another careful step, and another.

"Silly, blubbering cow," Bucket said. "I can 'ave what I want from you for the price of a bauble. Why would I shackle myself to any bawd? Well, you can entertain me one more time—just to see if you can make me want to let you go free.''

"Oh, Morley," Persimmon whined. "I love you. How could you treat me like this? Leave her where she'll be found and let's go somewhere on our own. That beautiful pink room of yours. After all, you decorated it for me.''

Jenny stood immediately in front of the door and reached behind her for the handle. She grasped it firmly and turned.

Nothing happened.

Bucket had hauled Persimmon to her feet and was looking at Jenny with a gold-toothed smile. ''Oh, you wouldn't upset me by runnin' away from my 'ospitality, would you? I'm wounded.''

She turned around and pulled on the handle, rattled it, but to no avail. Bucket dragged her away and brought his mouth down on hers. His kiss was wet and disgusting, but Jenny didn't fight him. Every move she made could make the difference between getting to Latimer, and never seeing him again.

"Don't do that," Persimmon wailed. "The man who's paying you won't like it if you tamper with the goods. I did everything you asked, Morley. I got the boy, then sent the little girl with the message so Jenny would go after him. I did it for us.''

Bucket stared at Jenny. He undid her wet cloak and tossed it aside—and ran his tongue over his lips while he looked at the swell of her breasts above her sorry wedding gown. "All right," he said to Persimmon at last. "Wait for me 'ere.''

He picked Jenny up and slung her across his shoulder. "We've got some private business," he said, and produced a key to unlock the door. "Up we go. It's an honor to go where you're going, and don't forget it. Not many people ever go up these stairs. The man what wants you is very private.''

"Let me go," Jenny pleaded. "I can't promise you mercy, but it'll go better for you if you don't hurt me."

Bucket sniggered. "Oh, *I'm* not goin' to 'urt you. I'm doin' you a favor. You're goin' to be with a gent what's got real money to spend on you. This one's already got everything set up. A beautiful place where the two of you can be alone together. And 'e won't skimp on anything. He'll cover you with jewels." Bucket chuckled some more. "In fact I think I 'eard 'im say you wasn't going to wear anything but jewels and 'e can't wait to put 'em on you. Now keep your mouth shut." He was taking keys from his pocket again.

Jenny's heart thundered. She was trapped and she'd let Latimer down. She held still and felt a quietness steal into her. Quietness—but was there a distant voice, someone speaking to her? Jenny couldn't make out the words, but they soothed her. A petal from one of the roses in her hair fell against her cheek and stuck there—on tears, no doubt. Jenny picked it off. It hadn't come from the roses in her hair. The petal was of orange silk and she held it tightly in a palm. Latimer had worn the marmalade rose she'd made him to their wedding. She'd been surprised that despite the condition of his clothes, the flower remained unharmed. Latimer was near, she felt him, and he would deliver them both from this horror.

Bucket got to the top of a flight of stairs and carried Jenny through an open door. As they went, she saw that there was heavy padding, not only on the door, but along the outside walls.

"'Ere we are, then," Bucket said and set her on her

feet. "What d'you think of this then? A fortune there is in 'ere.''

Jenny backed away from him and glanced about her at a collection of clocks so excessive, she could not imagine the man who might cherish so many. They stood on shelves built from floor to ceiling on every wall. Tables were crowded together, every one weighted down by clocks of all sizes. Long case clocks stood against walls or hung on them. A glass-fronted cupboard displayed nothing but ormolu clocks in the most delicately colored enamels.

There were hundreds of clocks, including a huge, ancient-looking timepiece supported within an iron frame. The thing made enough noise to all but drown out the overwhelming ticking and whirring from around the room. Jenny watched a bronze man at the top of the contraption. He had four arms, eyes made from malachite, and wore a beaked helmet. With a pointed mallet, he struck a granite block in time to the minutes that clicked away. A gleaming pendulum swung and chain rotated over cogs. Little wonder there was padding outside so that the noise was deadened in the rest of the house.

"I can see you're taken with it all," Bucket said. "Which is a good thing since this is where you'll live—not in this room o'course. It's going to be a match made in heaven."

"I am already matched," she said, unable to hold her tongue any longer. "And my husband will be lookin' for me. He'll find this place and deal wi' ye."

"Will 'e?" Bucket's unconcerned leer tightened Jenny's throat. "I don't think I'm worried about that."

"Let me go, please," Jenny said. She didn't care how much she had to beg for her freedom.

"Let me go, please," he mimicked in a high voice.

"Can't do that. Someone's on 'is way to see you right now. Good thing we managed to make sure your so-called 'usband never 'ad 'is way with you. Your master wouldn't like soiled goods."

That Bucket had miscalculated her relationship with Latimer made little difference to Jenny. "Master? I have no master." *Please let someone come, someone who would help.*

Bucket pulled a chair forward and sat down. "Well then, the master you don't 'ave wants to take you for the first time in this room—since it means so much to 'im." He produced ropes of dark green jade beads from inside his coat. "You're to put these on. And there's bracelets for your wrists and ankles—and a girdle for your waist. Worth a fortune they are. Found special to match your eyes." Bucket rolled *his* eyes.

"I dinna want them," Jenny said. She still clutched the silk petal but she could no longer keep her breathing calm. "Give them back t'him."

"You can do that yourself if you want to. But you'll be wearing them when 'e comes through that door. Let's get those clothes off you for a start."

35

Latimer sat in the mud, his back against a tree, and marshaled his strength. He breathed heavily. Fury could drive a man with the strength of several, even if he had been knocked on the head. The blighter left with instructions to kill him lay sprawled on the ground a few feet away. If he came to at all, it wouldn't be for a long time.

The fight had been fierce only because Latimer was unarmed, while his opponent wielded a hefty cudgel. That cudgel was in Latimer's hand now.

The instant he'd replenished his wind, he'd be off and he knew just where he would go. Fear for Jenny caused him to sweat but his legs must be strong again before he tried to get to her.

He saw the approaching band of men before he heard them. They came quietly enough, but their boots sucked in the wet earth. Adam was the first to reach him.

"I told you to stay at Number 7 and make sure no one got anxious," Latimer said.

"And you," Adam said, pointing a long finger, "can stop giving orders and take a few."

Latimer struggled to his feet but still used the tree for support. "You're so interesting when you're angry, old man," he said. "But you'll have to excuse me while I find my wife."

Hunter, Ross and Sir Edmund Winthrop arrived, disheveled from the run and searching in every direction, obviously prepared for assailants.

"Damnation," Adam said, kicking the fallen man onto his back. "It's one of the fellows who hijacked your carriage, Latimer, the thinner one who came after me."

"Yes. And the other one took off with Jenny in a sack. I'd taken a blow to the head, but we've not time for that now. I'm off to a nuns' house, property of Morley Bucket. I think I'll find Jenny there."

"They would take a girl like Jenny to such a place?" Ross said. "What are we waiting for?"

"My breath to return," Latimer said. "And my heart to return to my chest. I'm going to kill someone for what they've done to Jenny. Now, we can't all rush into that house, and there's always a chance I'm mistaken and she won't be there. But we'll find her. I'll go to Bucket's alone. I want the rest of you to spread out and cover as much ground as possible. Hunter, could I prevail on you to check any places you think might be worth looking into." He met Hunter's eyes and knew they were both thinking of the establishments they'd frequented together when they were single men with too much time on their hands—and other parts of their anatomies.

"Yes," Hunter said and left immediately.

Latimer felt hesitant to order Ross, Viscount Kilrood, to do anything, but the man solved his problem by saying, "I know one or two low types who would probably be willing to give some useful information—for a price. What do you think?"

"Excellent," Latimer told him, and Ross broke into a run at once, heading for the narrow streets on the far side of Tapwell House.

"I'm coming with you," Adam said to Latimer. "You may need to be saved from yourself."

Latimer knew very well that Adam also thought Jenny had been taken to Bucket's place, and that he wanted to be there to take some of his own revenge on the man.

"Sir Edmund," Latimer said. "Perhaps you'd best return to Lady Hester and see if you can maintain calm at Number 7. I don't envy you the job of quieting the females, but they need a man there."

Winthrop frowned, as if considering whether to take instructions from a mere merchant. Then he said, "Right you are. On my way," and turned on his heel to retrace his steps.

"Come on." Latimer set off as rapidly as his still-recovering legs would take him. "We're for St. Paul's."

"I know where we're going," Adam said, and if Latimer hadn't been fearful for his wife and battered himself, he'd have laughed.

They left the park at High Street and set off, looking for a hackney. "Two fast horses for hire are what I'd like to see," Latimer said. "We can't take time to search some out." His belly felt flattened against his spine and he suffered dread such as he'd never experienced before.

"Why the devil didn't I think to bring horses myself?" Adam said. "Don't know if you were told, but Lady Hester's coachman and the tigers were pretty roughed up. She has them all in beds in the servants' quarters and they're being treated like kings."

"Good." Latimer only half listened. "Do you see what I see? *There.* Quickly, before he's out of sight."

Adam caught Latimer's arm and drove in his fingertips. "I'm damned," he said. "Winthrop going into the mews behind Mayfair Square. Well, I suppose that's one way to get there."

"It's not the way a man like Sir Edmund would choose to go. I doubt he's ever been back there in his life. Come on." Latimer broke into a headlong dash. "Keep up, man, there's something wrong there and we could lose him if we're not careful."

"And find him again in the ballroom at Number 7," Adam said, pounding along beside Latimer while they both dodged people on the shining wet pavements. "You don't know the man's habits. Probably always goes this way."

"And enters the homes of his neighbors—or even his own home—through the kitchens? I think not."

The drenched gray of the afternoon had waned into smoky murk. And still it rained. In the mews, the narrow cobbled way was slick and they had to slow down or risk either making too much noise, or falling.

"Hug the fences," Latimer said. "We'd be easier to spot by the stables." The distance between the gardens at the back of the houses and the stables that faced them was little enough, but the curve along the fences gave some cover.

Latimer hadn't time to warn Adam before throwing out an arm and shoving him into the overhanging branches of a tall lilac bush. "He's gone into a garden," Latimer whispered. "The next house down. Damned if I know the number but we're nowhere near Number 7."

The two of them crowded into the bush and held their hats while they peered over the fence. Winthrop walked rapidly along a brick pathway toward the back entrance to a house.

"It's his own house," Adam said, sighing. "He's making a stop on his way to looking after the ladies. We've wasted time."

"Stay," Latimer told him. "Perhaps we haven't wasted anything at all. What's Evans doing at Number 23 and letting Winthrop in through the back door as if they were old friends?"

"Evans was recommended to Lady Hester by Sir Edmund," Adam reminded him.

While they watched, Sir Edmund slapped Evans's back and allowed the blond-haired servant to take him by the elbow and steer him inside. They were both laughing. "The way I heard it," Latimer said, "Sir Edmund *found* Evans for Lady Hester. Supposedly they were not personally acquainted."

"It's strange," Adam said. "But it has nothing to do with our problem."

"Oh, my, God," Latimer said. "I knew it did. I felt myself guided here. Look at that. Over Evans's arm."

"What…" Adam leaned farther forward to see better. "A cloak perhaps?"

"Jenny's cloak if I'm not mistaken. The one she was wearing when she was taken away."

Spivey here:

Now don't detain me because I'm needed elsewhere. But when you have unkind thoughts about me, remember that I, too, know what is right and what is wrong, and I'm capable of putting my own good aside—even though it is more important—in order to fight on the side of justice.

I cannot glide by, pretend I haven't noticed a gentle young wife in the hands of despicable rogues, and not do what I can to help her.

Don't think for a moment that I am gone soft. First I had to do my duty and guide Latimer, but it will soon be time to deal with the frightful mess I have on my hands. I am a beleaguered fledgling angel.

Damn these humans.

The back door to Number 23 was unlocked. Latimer and Adam walked in and passed through gloomy, deserted kitchens that looked unused. They moved cautiously, expecting to encounter servants at any moment.

Nothing moved, or made a sound until they had climbed the steps from below stairs and arrived in a dark, wooden-paneled entrance hall where meager light cast dismal illumination. A woman in red stood flattened against a wall. Her face, although swollen from crying, was lovely. She saw Latimer before he could draw back and came toward him, keeping her palms on the paneling and moving them one over the other as if she was unsteady on her feet.

She reached them and rested her face on top of her hands.

"Who are you?" Latimer asked.

"Myrtle." She smiled as if amused. "Sir Edmund's late wife's niece."

Adam nudged Latimer and said, "Lady Hester's mentioned her. She looks in a bad way."

Latimer noted how full the woman's body was, how large her breasts for one so short in stature. He was also reminded of a voice he'd heard previously. "And you're the woman in gray," he told her. "The one who tried so hard to make me send Jenny away—as far away as possible."

"She was going to take my place," the woman said. "I didn't want that, not after all the hard work I've put in with Bucket and Sir Edmund. They owe me, not her."

"You're talking about my wife," Latimer said, swallowing his anger. "She isn't available to any man but her husband. Is she here in this house?"

"She is. And if you want your *wife* before someone else has her, you'd better hurry. If it isn't already too late. If it is, she'll never leave this house again because he'll hide her here."

Latimer grabbed her away from the wall. "Take me to her." He shook her. "Don't shilly-shally around."

The woman shed tears as if she were in pain, but wrenched away from Latimer and led the way upstairs. "I'm no danger to you," she said, breathing hard. "I tried to help her escape but Bucket caught me—and punished me. If I take you to her will you see to it that things don't go too hard for me?"

"This is no time for bargaining." They'd climbed two flights and started up a third. "Just hurry."

"There won't be another time for bargaining," the woman said. "Get me off. That nice Sir Hunter is a friend of yours. Ask him to fix it for me."

A padded wall and door confronted them at the top of the final flight. Latimer glanced back at Adam and saw apprehension that mirrored his own. "Are they in here?" he asked, and when Myrtle nodded he said, "Wait for us downstairs. We'll talk later."

With Adam close behind him, he entered a bizarre, noisy room crowded with clocks. But it was Jenny, not the clocks that he really saw. And she saw him but said nothing and shook her head as if warning him to go away.

Her gown had been ripped from neck to hem and she clutched it to her. Petticoats and other undergarments lay in a heap and a bare limb showed through the gap in her skirts. Heavy strands of carved jade beads, hanging from her neck, bemused Latimer and the sight of her hair loose about her shoulders drove him to near madness. He opened and closed his hands, assessing the rest of the scene.

Bucket lay facedown on the floor and Sir Edmund ground a boot into his back while he aimed a pistol at his head. The clocks made enough din to have masked Latimer and Adam's entry. There was no sign of Evans.

"Just give me the money and I'll be gone," Bucket cried. "You'll never see me again."

"Money?" Sir Edmund bellowed. "You've put your hands on her. I told you not to touch her. You won't get a penny out of me."

Latimer took a step into the room and signaled for Jenny to get out of the way. She opened her mouth but didn't move.

"I never touched 'er," Bucket shouted. "I never put a finger on 'er."

"So her gown tore itself and perhaps she took off her own petticoats? You were to bring her here and leave the rest to me."

"I was only tryin' to get 'er ready for you. You said you wanted 'er dressed in nothing but jewels and you showed me the jade."

"And you undressed her," Sir Edmund said in a strangled voice. "You took my pleasure. *Mine*." He raised his foot and brought it down again, hard enough to draw a scream from Bucket.

Latimer leaned to whisper in Adam's ear. "Give me your pistol."

"Where's your own?"

"This has been—believe it or not—my wedding day. Have you forgotten that pistols were not much on my mind. Give me yours."

Adam said, "I was at a wedding breakfast when I had to rush away. Not at all the thing, carrying a pistol at a wedding breakfast."

Latimer wasn't amused. He grasped Adam's lapel—and Sir Edmund saw them. The man aimed his pistol at Latimer's head.

"No!" Jenny screamed and barreled into Sir Edmund's back, and while he was off balance, Morley Bucket surged upward, grabbed the boot that had been on his back, and threw Winthrop to the floor.

Latimer made a dive for the pistol, but Bucket was already there. Sanity had left his eyes. If he saw at all, it must be through a white hot haze. With the weapon at Winthrop's throat, he hauled him to his feet and backed him across the room. Bucket snarled and bared his teeth, and hit Winthrop about the head with the pistol.

"Morley," Latimer said loudly. "Morley, we're here with you. We're going to help you." He dared not try to restrain the man for fear he'd shoot.

Jenny stumbled against him and he held her tightly in one arm. "My brave girl," he said. "Please go downstairs and get back to Number 7. There's a woman somewhere around. She's wearing red. Leave her be and she won't bother you. Now go." He released her and, shoulder to shoulder with Adam, advanced on Morley Bucket and Sir Edmund.

Bucket jabbered meaningless phrases. Sir Edmund whimpered, already bleeding profusely from head and facial cuts.

"Bucket!" Adam bellowed suddenly. "He's going to... Latimer we've got to stop him."

Too late.

With a mighty shove, Bucket thrust his victim into the workings of a huge clock. A Chinese clock, probably fourteenth century, and made for the purpose of signaling monks to meditation on the hour.

Sir Edmund's hair was immediately caught in rotating cogs and he shrieked. His eyes grew wide, then wider and he tried in vain to catch hold of the clock's metal frame.

Without discussion, Latimer and Adam separated and went at Bucket from two sides. His pistol, whipping back and forth between them and Winthrop, slowed their progress.

With his free hand, Bucket gave Winthrop another shove and the man's heels caught the lower frame of the clock, tipping him against a granite block. Bucket moved quickly to loop a piece of moving chain around Winthrop's neck and Latimer watched as the man, gurgling and turning purple, was drawn up high enough for a pointed mallet in the hands of a four-armed bronze figure to strike his left temple repeatedly. A deep, dark hole had opened in his head. His arms fell to his sides and he slumped in his noose of chain. The bronze man kept driving the point of the mallet into his blood-soaked skull.

Latimer launched himself at Bucket and brought him down. It was Jenny, still holding her gown around her, who grabbed the pistol.

"You were told to leave," Adam said to her, helping Latimer to restrain the writhing man on the floor.

"And I didna go, thank ye verra much," Jenny said, waving the pistol around and watching Winthrop helplessly. "I've a husband t'care for. Sir Edmund's no more, I'm afraid. He's strangled—among other things."

Latimer was otherwise engaged but he marveled at Jenny's courage and her matter-of-fact dealing with an outlandish death.

Finally Bucket was subdued.

"Mr. Bucket should die," Myrtle said, coming into the room and going directly to Adam's side. "See?" She pointed to a space in a showcase where a clean square amid dust suggested a clock had been removed. Next to the space stood the identical gallery clock to the one Jenny and Latimer had received as a "gift."

"I see it," Adam said. "The mate to that wretched clock is here, Latimer. They're a pair."

"Kill us both, please," Myrtle said. "That would be merciful."

"Och," Jenny said. "Ye're sick. Come away."

Calmly, the woman sat on the floor beside Bucket and waited. She didn't speak again.

"Ye're sure ye're not too tired for more gallivantin'?" Jenny asked.

"That gown is perfect for you," Latimer told her. "But I knew it would be"

"Dinna change the subject," Jenny said.

Latimer smiled and said, "I've never been less tired than I am now."

"Nor I," Jenny admitted. "D'ye think I'm a strange one not t'be more upset by what we saw happen?"

"I think you've been through a great deal in your short life. You've had to learn to harden yourself against some terrible things. If you hadn't, I doubt you would have survived—at least as the gentle, optimistic woman you are. I'm grateful you are not swooning away somewhere and that we may grasp some pleasure at such a time as our marriage."

They sat in the ballroom at Number 7, empty now since even the staff had been sent to their beds. Despite attempts to make them go to their rooms first, Jenny and Latimer had insisted they wished to stay up—alone—and watch the dawn come up on their first real day as man and wife.

The gown in question was made of dark green silk. The edges of deep horizontal pleating on the bodice were trimmed with gold lace, and gold lace ruffles decorated the hem. "How did ye know what size t'have it made?" Jenny asked. She wore gold slippers and a slender strand of solid gold pansies had been threaded through her rescued coiffeur. "And how did ye know I would have chosen just this?"

"I took the gown you wore to dinner at Finch's and gave it to a modiste. Then I told her to make this one exactly the same size. And this is how I knew what you would like." From a pocket, he took one of the little dolls she'd made while she was living in horrid Lardy Lane. "You gave this to me. It's wearing a ballgown of green silk with gold lace and I knew you'd designed something you would love to wear. Now you can."

"I thought ye were t'gi' the doll t'Birdie."

"I lied. I wanted it for myself."

They both laughed, but Jenny felt tension between them, the best possible tension.

"Lady Hester is a strong woman," Jenny said, knowing she was making conversation. "But she's had a bad shock over Sir Edmund and it'll take a wee while for her to recover."

"Yes," Latimer said. "But anger at what he did will help her. Persimmon—can you believe that name?—said Winthrop saw you coming and going from this house when you were part of Sibyl's group of ladies. He wanted you, and watched you ever since—all the time making plans to have you. His acquaintance with Lady Hester was formed because I'd been followed after I was seen meeting you, day after day, in Bond Street. Persimmon said he wanted to be sure he knew where I was at all times until Bucket could deliver you to him. He would not soil his hands by grabbing you himself. That would have spoiled the fantasy that you came to him on your own, and awaited him amid his beloved clocks. How shocked he must have been when I took you to Lady Hester that night."

Jenny looked at the rings on her finger and shook her head. "I'll never forget ye hittin' that nasty Evans as we came through the door here tonight. Imagine, he'd come back to behave as if his soul was white as snow when he'd spied on you and me, and helped Sir Edmund all the time."

"Evans is in the appropriate hands now," Latimer said. "We'll have more of that to deal with soon enough. For now we won't think about it. So, you will allow me to take you for a drive? What could be more romantic than a groom and his new bride riding through the darkness to chase the dawn? The perfect start to a honeymoon."

She shivered deliciously at the thought. "I'll allow ye t'take me," she told him. "I want ye to."

The early morning carried yesterday's chill and a heavy drizzle fell. Latimer had wrapped Jenny in the swansdown cape Finch had presented to her before leaving for Number 8 with Ross, and held an umbrella over her until they were inside Latimer's own carriage that waited at the curb.

"There is an armed guard at the back," Latimer said. "And the coachman is also armed. I arranged this so that you would feel safe."

"I always feel safe wi' ye," she said from her seat facing his.

"Even when you have to help me subdue criminals?" he said. "Then you are most unwise my dear."

The coach bowled away, the horses' hoofs ringing on the cobbles. Jenny looked from the windows but there was little to see as yet.

"I decided a short wedding journey was in order," Latimer said, his teeth showing white in faint light from the coach lamps. "An hour or two to be alone. We did everything in such a hurry there wasn't time to arrange a more splendid affair, but I will soon enough."

Jenny had never expected such happiness in her life. "I just want to be with you. Wherever ye are is a wonderful place."

"Wherever you are is where I *must* be. I had thought you a demure young thing, y'know. Shy and in need of my rescue."

"Then you were wrong." Jenny raised her chin. "I may ha' been shy. Still am in a way. Ye helped me a great deal. But I didna need rescuin' by any man."

"So I see," he said, and something in his voice sent a shiver up her spine, a lovely shiver. He continued, "I'd also thought it would take a long time to interest you in the, er, pleasures of the flesh, but—"

"Wrong again," she told him, boldly meeting his eyes. "I learned everythin' verra quickly. I do believe I was born for such things."

"Undoubtedly." His supposed cough into a fist didn't fool Jenny. He was laughing at her. "You were definitely born for love. But I must dispute your statement that you've learned *everything*. There is much more, dear Jenny, and I am the man to teach you the finer points."

"Are ye now?" She trembled inside, and trembled more so when Latimer lifted her feet onto his knees and removed her slippers. Surely he wouldn't do things in this coach that should be done in private.

"Am I unnerving you?" he asked, slowly rubbing her feet and ankles and gradually sweeping his hands higher and higher beneath her skirts with each sweep. "Trust me, Jenny. We shall enjoy our little jaunt."

She frowned at him. He was far too playful to be trusted at all. "We could ha' watched the dawn from Number 7," she told him. "From bed with the curtains open."

His nostrils flared and he said, "A charming thought. That shall be tomorrow night's plan. See what you are doing to me by just talking?'' He guided one of her feet against him. She jumped and she turned hot when she felt how his manhood had hardened.

''We're in a coach,'' she whispered. ''Wi' a man at either end and nothing but windows between us and anyone passing by outside.''

''But nobody will interrupt us,'' he responded, and covered the windows sharply. ''Sit on my lap.''

Jenny's scalp tightened and felt too small. Goose bumps blossomed all over her skin. She laced her fingers together and bowed her head.

Latimer moved her foot against him. His touch tickled and all those feelings he'd caused before happened again. ''Sit on my lap, Jenny,'' he whispered. ''Come on, come to me.''

''Where are we?'' she asked him.

''Does it matter?''

It didn't. She put her feet on the floor and sat forward on her seat. Latimer leaned across the confines of the carriage and she watched his thick, dark lashes lower as he brought his mouth to hers. Without touching her anywhere else, he courted her with his lips, nibbled sensitive skin and gently opened her mouth, rocked his face, and hers from side to side, flirted with the tip of her tongue and drew it into his own mouth.

Jenny trembled. She tingled. She wound her hands more tightly together lest she spoil the moment by reaching for him. And, oh, she wanted to hold him, to feel his bare skin, to smooth his chest and belly, and kiss everything she touched—everything.

His breath was warm and sweet. He deserted her swollen mouth and kissed her neck, the hollow at is base, and she arched closer to him. She opened her eyes to see the black arch of his brow, the sharp line of his cheekbone and jaw, his thick hair curling at his collar. And his head moved so slowly while he savored her.

He weakened her, yet made her urgent. Once more he returned to her lips, and his kisses became fierce. He drew back and opened his eyes—and he and Jenny looked at each other. She saw his heart in his eyes and knew he must see hers, but she also saw desire so fervent she felt stripped, opened to the tender tip of every nerve.

Latimer smiled faintly and caught her by the waist. He lifted her to sit on his lap and nuzzled beneath her chin, ran his tongue along the swelling flesh above the neck of her gown.

She shuddered and clung to him, wound an arm around his head and pressed him to her.

"Jenny," he murmured, "I'm going to hope you still love me when you learn what a bad man I am."

"Bad?" She raised his chin and found him grinning at her.

"Bad," he agreed. One hand moved upward from her waist and he slipped his fingers between two of the pleats on her bodice, smiling the broader when she gasped. "Oh, I am bad. Some might say I have practiced being so."

"Never," she said, and let out a very small cry when she felt air cross her breasts.

"No?" Latimer asked.

The gown was cleverly made. Between the two pleats that crossed the tips of her breasts, the silk parted and she understood the written instructions, supposedly from the modiste, that she should wear no chemise for fear of spoiling the fit of the gown.

"Latimer," she said, but could scarcely contain her excitement.

He widened his eyes as if he were a man maligned. "Yes, my sweet?"

Well, two could play games designed to drive another mad. "Nothing," she said, straightening the gown. Above her head was a single handle designed for gentlemen to hold themselves steady whilst readying themselves to alight from the carriage.

Jenny discovered that by standing on the tips of her bare toes, she could hang on to the handle and obtain exactly the result she desired. Her bodice parted and she felt her bare breasts freed so that her clever husband got a sight he would not have planned on. She twisted, showing herself from every angle. And Latimer drew his lips back from his teeth and bit hard enough on a knuckle for her to see the marks he made.

He made to get up.

"Stay, Latimer," she told him. "I've had an exhaustin' day and need to feel free. Perhaps I should undress entirely and stretch my body unfettered by such beautiful, but restricting clothes."

He fell against the back of his seat and she noted how his chest rose and fell. "Ye might take off your own clothes," she said, looking at the bulge in his trousers. "You look like a man in need o' freedom t'me."

"Baggage," he told her. "Take over my role, would you? You probably think teasing me is a punishment. Tease away, love. You only seal your own fate. You will not know the precise moment, but I shall take you as you can never have dreamed of being taken."

Her brazen confidence waned a little and she spoke in a low voice, "Well, in case ye're interested, I've not had much experience dreaming about bein'...*taken* as ye put it. But I'm an attentive student and ye'll not find me hard t'teach."

Latimer groaned. He moved suddenly, reached up and plucked at her nipples as if they were ripe berries on the vine. He took them between his knuckles and rubbed his thumbs across the hardened peaks. Only through willpower did she continue to grip the handle above her head.

"I knew I had designed this well," Latimer breathed, and eased her breasts fully free of the gown. "They deserve to be shown off and enjoyed by me." He suckled vigorously at each nipple, flicked his tongue there, then abandoned those aching places to press her flesh together and rub his cheek over her, to kiss her as the mood took him. Opening his mouth to draw as much of a breast inside as he could, he slipped his hands up the backs of her legs, parted her drawers and cupped the cheeks of her bottom.

"I canna do this longer," she told him, squirming. "I shall go mad."

"Beautifully mad," Latimer said, releasing her to loosen his own clothes. "But don't move please. I shall help you get comfortable soon."

He stripped to the waist and the skin over his strong shoulders and muscular chest shone. She wanted to feel the hair there against her breasts.

"Now," Jenny said. "Do something now. Please."

Showing the deep dimples beneath his cheekbones, he gave her a purely wicked smile. "You'd like that, would you?" he opened his trousers and Jenny all but fainted at the thrill of seeing his need—and anticipating how he would feel inside her.

"There's little room to lie down," she said. "Perhaps we should go back to Mayfair Square."

"You don't trust me to manage these things?" He stood up, passing his tongue over her nipples as he did so.

Jenny let go of the handle, but Latimer promptly returned her hands and said, "Take heed of what I tell you. You will need whatever help you can find if you are not to fall. Hold on, my love."

Latimer lifted her skirts and released the drawstring on her drawers. With one pull he sent them around her ankles then stepped on them while she pulled her feet free. He lifted her by the thighs and wrapped her legs around him. "Cross your ankles," he told her and she followed his instructions.

The coach made a violent rocking from side to side and Latimer steadied both of them. "Ready?" he asked and, without waiting for a response, arched upward and into her.

"Latimer," she squealed. "I canna hold mysel' here while ye... I canna."

"I'll help you."

"But dinna come out o' me," she told him.

He had passed the point of laughter. "Hold my shoulders," he said, replacing her hands on the handle with his own, "and let's see how strong you are."

With his feet on what had been her seat, Latimer raised himself beneath her and she saw him enter and retreat from her body. "It would be easier on ye... Oh, Latimer. Oh, oh..."

His hips set up a rhythm that pounded him into her and when she closed her eyes and concentrated on receiving him, she saw blackness streaked with bright light. She tightened around him and he panted, moaning deep in his throat, but he didn't stop moving. The aching ripple began and she felt the contractions inside her milk him. Latimer pumped harder and her pleasure broke over her in clenching waves, only to be followed by Latimer's warm rush into her body.

Everywhere she touched him he was slick. Jenny burned and would not think of the spectacle they would make if anyone saw them. "I want t'be naked wi' ye," she told him.

Latimer began to lower them both to a safer berth, but he slipped and landed them half on and half off a seat. Jenny giggled so hard, she almost feared the coachman would hear her, but he never could.

Depositing Jenny on her swansdown cape, Latimer quickly granted her wish by peeling off every stitch of her clothes. "Not cold, are you?" he said, grinning again. With the blinds pulled over the windows it was impossible to see the panes but she knew they would be steamed up with the heat the two of them had generated.

"You are so beautiful," Latimer said with awe in his voice. He had taken off his boots and trousers and she marveled at the figure he cut. His thighs, where he stood with them braced apart, bulged hard and he was ready to make love again.

"Won't they wonder what we're doing in here for so long?" Jenny asked, indicating the men riding outside.

Latimer cradled her breasts, touched the end of his manhood to first one, then the other, and repeated the process, and said, "I would be surprised if they didn't guess."

Jenny bit her lip. He was tumbling her thoughts again. She arched her back to force harder contact with his engorged rod. And Latimer let out a cry. He scooped her up and sat her astride his thighs with her back to him, then he pushed her to drape forward over his knees and took her again, with even more force than the first time, if that were possible. First he held her hips, then he anchored himself by holding her breasts, and brought her feet from the floor with each thrust. Her braids fell loose and soft hair started to unravel.

Too soon the spiraling sensations took over, then burned themselves out while Latimer's fierce penetrations gradually slowed.

Jenny stayed where she was with her head hanging forward, fighting to settle her breathing. And Latimer rested his face on her back.

A little while passed while Jenny slipped into a haze that felt as if she'd been drugged. Latimer rested against the back of the coach seat, but kept his hands on her bottom and stroked her softly, continuously.

The lethargy passed, but she didn't let him know until she was ready to twist away and go to her knees between his thighs. She marveled at the way he responded to her lips. Could it be that men could do this over and over again, all the time? Quite possibly, since it seemed she could do so herself.

With his fingers in her hair, he rocked his hips back and forth but allowed Jenny to take charge and bring him to an explosive climax. Finished, she kissed his belly and moved upward to bury her face in the hair on his chest.

"Things must always be even between us," Latimer said, his voice deep and warm. "This should do it."

Once more he stood her on her feet, only to sit her astride his lap and tip her smoothly upside down. She knew exactly what he intended and reveled in the anticipation. Exposed as she was, she felt right when he clamped her between his thighs. Some, she thought, might consider their behavior excessive, but she had no doubt she and Latimer would continue in much the same way on every possible occasion and intended to tell him she was more than ready to oblige him in this manner.

"Ah," she moaned. "Oh, Latimer. I don't ever want to stop."

There was the slightest pause in the ministrations of his tongue, but only the slightest before he sent her over the edge yet again and they scrambled to cling together, naked and hot, on one small seat. Latimer stroked her incessantly, and she stroked him.

The gold flower chain in her hair slipped free and he caught it. "Pretty thing," he said, holding it to catch the meager light. He dangled one end against her breasts and laughed when she writhed and tried, without success, to take it from him.

Pushing a hand quickly between her thighs and beneath her bottom, he passed the warm gold over tender flesh already distended by the sex they'd shared.

"Stop it, Latimer," she said, giggling and trying to take the chain from him. He was too strong, and too practiced in the art of evading any attempt to foil his plans. Slowly he twirled the little golden flowers, and Jenny couldn't keep her bottom on his knees. She bounced up and panted, and didn't try to stop him again. He twirled and twirled the flowers between the folds of her body and she crossed her legs to deepen the sensation, and bent forward, jerking at the pleasure he gave her. And when he accomplished his goal and sharp spasms shattered any shred of control, she fell backward over his arm and sagged, completely vulnerable to anything he might choose to do with her.

"I think you liked that," he whispered.

Jenny mumbled, "Yes," and rolled toward him, stroked his belly, but when she took hold of him in one hand and squeezed, he said, "I think we should consider dressing. The dawn is coming. I see light through the blinds."

"It can't be," she said, growing still and staring at a window. But it was.

The task of clothing themselves would have been easier if they'd had more space, and if they hadn't repeatedly interfered with each other's progress. When Jenny undid his trousers for the third time, Latimer restrained her by the wrists until he was buttoned in and proceeded to tickle her while she writhed and howled.

"Hair," he said, and bent over her, doing his best to

correct some of the damage that had been done. "Best to leave out the gold chain for now. We'll never get it back in before we arrive back home." He slipped it into a pocket. "I'm sure we'll find it useful again."

"You should see your own hair," she said, and tweaked him in sensitive places until he plunked her hands on her lap and pretended to sit on her. He raked his fingers through his hair, tied a passable neckcloth and straightened himself more than Jenny would have thought possible. Still he looked mussed and the middle of his lower lip was cracked. "I hope we aren't seen on the way to our rooms," Jenny said. "I do believe an experienced person will guess what you've been about."

With his hands on his hips, Latimer observed while Jenny put on her gold slippers and arranged her new cape around her shoulders. "And you, Mrs. More," he said, "have obviously had your husband between your legs—repeatedly."

She smacked his arm lightly, but all she got for her efforts was a devastating kiss.

Tentatively she raised a blind and let out a cry. "We've missed the dawn," she said. "The sun's up."

Latimer wrapped his arms around her and they looked at the new day together.

Jenny felt her husband's reluctance when he knocked the roof, signaling that they wished to return to Mayfair Square.

"With luck we can be in bed before anyone else gets up," Jenny said.

Latimer rested his head on her shoulder and said, "You'll be the death of me yet. You're insatiable."

Before she could think of a clever reply, they drew up in front of Number 7 and an expressionless coachman opened the door and put down the steps. He took Jenny's hand and helped her to the flagway. Latimer joined her and they mounted the front steps, walking rather slowly. For herself, Jenny felt the smallest amount sore and stiff and Latimer wasn't taking the steps with his customary two at a time vigor.

The front door, flying open to reveal Larch Lumpit, stopped them both where they were. "Good news, good news," Lumpit trilled. "So much good news. That fine little chap, Toby, is to be adopted by Lady Hester, just like Birdie, and they'll both be tutored together." He looked closely first at Latimer, then at Jenny. "I say, you two look as if sleep wouldn't go amiss. But I must finish. Your father has written, Latimer. What a lovely man. He will receive you in Cornwall and you may bring your wife with you. And to lessen the number of visits that can only disturb his busy life, Finch, that is the viscountess—and the viscount, of course—may take their children to see him at the same time. Most charming and straightforward."

Latimer was obviously speechless.

"Ye read Mr. More's post, then?" Jenny said, too weary to consider more unpleasantness.

"Had to," Lumpit said. "Might have been desperate news in it and since I'm a minister, and accustomed to keeping secrets, I felt it my duty to see what Mr. More Senior had written. Fortunately he seems quite well and even mentions how successful his china clay mines are. I told the staff and they are most impressed."

Latimer put an arm around Jenny's waist and ushered her into the house. He shook his head repeatedly and said in a dreamy voice, "One must make allowances, my dear, lots of allowances."

Jenny bobbed up to kiss his cheek and pushed her hand inside his shirt. Latimer made no attempt to remove that hand. "Good night then, Lumpit. Be kind enough to put my father's letter under our door and, should you have the opportunity, make sure we aren't disturbed for many hours.''

A minor cloud passed over Lumpit's sunny expression. "Yes, well...yes. I'll let you go, but I must tell you one last thing.''

Jenny sighed.

"As you can imagine, her ladyship is most upset. She confided in me that she had been lonely before Sir Edmund entered her life. And, once again, there are so few she can rely on to be present should she need to talk. But that won't matter anymore.''

Latimer and Jenny paused before 7A and Latimer said, "What does that mean?''

Lumpit chuckled comfortably. "I'd have thought you'd guess. I'm to move into 7B where I can be available to comfort Lady Hester at any hour of the day or night.

"Jenny, I am also appointing myself your spiritual advisor. No, no, I insist you don't thank me. Watching your soul unfold, white and pure, will be all the reward I need. Of course, you can always talk to me, too, Latimer.

"See you at breakfast." He glanced at Latimer's bared teeth and seemed taken aback. "Or lunch, or dinner or whatever. Get a good rest, won't you?''

_____ Epilogue-Part 1 ___

7 Mayfair Square
London
September, 1825

Fellow travelers—and sufferers:
Why would I take so long to recognize that you have taken
pleasure in my ire, and thrived on my struggles? Possibly
because my deep sense of honor does not allow me to see
mean-spiritedness in others. The latter is hard to believe
given the cruel treatment I have received at the hands of
that unscrupulous scribbler.

  At last I have seen the light and you are about to mourn
your stupidity!

  By the by, since I avoid avoiding the truth, I must say I
found all those hijinks in the carriage most stimulatin'.
After all, they are married, so why shouldn't I approve of
their passion?

  What? Dirty old ghost, you say? I shall not dignify that
with an answer other than the obvious: you don't under-
stand the importance of staying in one's place—particu-
larly when that place is as lowly as yours.

  Ah hah! I cannot keep it to myself an instant longer. All
this worry and fuss, and overtime, and for what? Nothing,

that's what. Think of it, if you can. You have two hands, start counting the fingers. Oh, the solution to my misery is so obvious and should always have been so had I not been wearing myself out dashing in the wrong direction.

Huh? I've bolloxed everything up? Is that what you said? Charming.

Listen up, well-meaning friends—and the rest of you. Just how many people can one house contain? Concentrate. The answer is, less than those upstarts are trying to stuff into Number 7.

All that time and effort spent, when the true remedy was to allow Hester and her motley collection of strays to do my work for me. The place is overflowing—I swear I can see the walls bulging. Very well, that was an exaggeration, but I think you get my point.

"Leave them alone, and they will come..." Dash it all, that's the wrong rhyme. "Leave them alone and they'll do themselves in, tra-la."

I'll be watching. Don't cry. In every life a little rain— no, no, not at all strong enough. No pain, no gain. Crow is fattening stuff that makes one's stomach ache. You're all going to grow very nicely, and you'll do so in pain.

A parting wish for you: May you be forced to watch that mangled tragedy, A Midsummer Night's Dream, *by our own Will, many times. Gad, here he comes again, and shaking a fist, no less.*

Spivey

_____ Epilogue-Part 2 __

Frog Crossing
Watersville
Out West

Dearest Friends:

Once more I am alone with my beloved animals, but, since this has been a most strange, and strangely unsettling time, I shall enjoy the opportunity to consider what has happened here, and what I have learned about human nature. Perhaps I should write "inhuman" nature, but Spivey hasn't been the only player to surprise me.

Spivey is an opportunist. Note how quick he is to turn his lemons into lemonade! Larch Lumpit (and who would have expected him to scratch out such a cozy niche for himself?) is obviously totally beyond Spivey's control. Lumpit becomes a self-starter and defies his puppeteer's string-pulling. The man thinks and acts for himself but Spivey, ever on the lookout for a chance to glorify himself, has the gall to pretend it was all his idea anyway...

Oh, rats, try as I may, I can't avoid admitting a certain growing fondness for the self-serving old reprobate. And, when he performed his most amazing act of kindness, he further amazed me with his modesty. I refer, of course, to his guiding Latimer to the church where Jenny was in such trouble. I do believe he felt uplifted by having made a difference, and being on the side of justice. And he mentioned justice again when he chose right over wrong on a second occasion.

He hints at not having given up his quest. Out of respect for the hard work he has obviously put in on self-improvement (A fledgling angel? Mercy me!) I am going to continue watching him with an open mind—more open than it has ever been. But I will be vigilant.

I can't leave you without writing that Latimer has also amazed me. A likable fellow, I always thought, and unarguably a handsome devil with a few secrets hovering around. But his versatility…well, yes, his versatility is invigorating, as is his capacity for unselfishness. And let us all hope that we and our daughters may be as courageous, as spirited, as Jenny.

Time to move on. I hear faint voices, growing louder, demanding my attention. More passion and trouble, no doubt. It really does become exhausting but what can I say, scribblers scribble and must be available to those who need our voices and our pens.

Just before I go for now, a word to the wise on Spivey. Watch him—he still has a long road to travel. I was disquieted by the tone of his parting words. He isn't giving up and one wonders exactly what he expects to happen just because Lady Hester has quite the houseful. I advocate trust, always have, but I have also been disappointed on occasion.

Alertness is key, now more than ever. Bravo Sir Septimus Spivey, you have shown more mercy than I would ever have thought possible. But don't slip, or my admiration will have been sadly wasted.

My friends, our job is not yet done. Hang out with me. Until next time, I am, as ever, your devoted and diligent scribbler,

Stella Cameron

USA Today Bestselling Author

NAN RYAN

The Scandalous Miss Howard

The boy who left to fight in the
Confederate army twenty years ago
had been a fool. He had trusted the
girl who promised to wait for him.
He had trusted the friend who
betrayed him. Now he has come home
to Alabama to avenge the loss of what they
stole from him—his heart, his soul, his world.

Laurette Howard, too, lost her innocence with the
news that the boy she loved had died in the war, and
with the loveless marriage that followed. Then
Sutton Vane arrived in Mobile, releasing the sensual
woman that had been locked away. She surrendered
to a passion so scandalous, it could only be destiny.
But was it a passion calculated to destroy her…
or to deliver the sweet promise of a love that
refused to die?

**"Nan Ryan knows how to
heat up the pages."
—Romantic Times**

MIRA®

Available
the first week
of April 2001
wherever
paperbacks are sold.

and legs. It had been a threat against herself, but even more against Latimer, yet they continued on as if everything was normal. Not that there was anything else to do until something happened. *Until.* She had lived with deprivation and the constant struggle to survive, but those were things she knew, the threat of violence was new.

Jenny lay on the bed and turned on her side so that she could stare at the candle and at a little enamel clock. Another fifteen minutes gone by. She drew up her knees and folded her arms tightly. Why didn't he come?

25

Jenny would be waiting for him.

Latimer had already remained in his room too long. What he'd been told was some sort of distortion. How could that not be the case? But how could he be sure? What was he really feeling—doubt? Did he doubt Jenny?

If he went to her, how should he behave?

His body stirred and he gritted his teeth. What hell was this, to be a man completely in love with a woman who wanted him, or insisted she did, but who had been accused of plotting to destroy him? He could not believe it was true, but he had no proof it wasn't.

Damn it all, he had to get fresh air—and space to think. He snatched a cloak and took his ebony cane, the one with an ivory-handle carved in the shape of a woman's beautiful hand. The grateful Chinese customer who gave it to him had insisted that every man should carry a sword. The blade concealed inside ebony was narrow and deadly sharp.

In the square he found an unexpectedly brisk breeze. He walked along all four rows of fine houses, and repeated the journey. Were it not for the note Jenny had found, he could more easily brush aside Mrs. Smith as a mischief-maker and find out if Jenny knew anything about her. But there had been the note. For all he knew Mrs. Smith saw

Jenny as her rival in some manner and had been the one to find her way into the house and leave the message.

Roses in the gardens smelled sweet, even at a distance. Latimer crossed to enter the enclosed beds and pathways by a gate in the black railings. Perhaps he would take Jenny a rose and beg her forgiveness for taking so long to come to her. He thought of orange silk petals that simply appeared, and swaying chandeliers—and rocking tables. He was a man beset by oddities, and not of the kind he relished dealing in.

Jenny would be locked in her room as he'd instructed her to be whenever she was there alone. And she would be thinking about him.

Blood pumped hard in his veins and his arousal was predictable.

"Difficulty sleeping, Latimer?"

Startled, the blade was halfway out of its hiding place before he stopped reacting and saw Adam Chillworth sitting on a bench. "Damn you, man," he said, breathing painfully, "I might have run you through. Never shock me like that."

Silence met his announcement and Latimer went closer. Adam also wore a cloak and his head was bare.

"What's the matter with you?" Latimer asked. "Sitting in the dark waiting to frighten a man almost to his death?"

"You flatter yourself," Adam said. "I've watched you march about the square and made no attempt to come near you. I assure you I wasn't waiting for you and, if you hadn't been about to stumble over me, you would never have known I was here."

"Damned dramatics," Latimer muttered, thoroughly unnerved. "I repeat, what's the matter with you? You aren't yourself and haven't been for days. Not that you aren't always a bad-tempered villain, but this is beyond all."

"At least I don't carry a sword just in case I feel like cutting your throat," Adam said. "I'll bid you good night."

"The hell you will," Latimer said, too loudly. He dropped his voice and said, "If I wanted to do away with you, I shouldn't waste time on your throat—too slow. No, sir, it would be your heart I should remove and fry for my breakfast."

He brought his lips together but immediately started to laugh. Adam's baritone chuckles joined in and Latimer sat heavily beside him. He tapped the cane between his feet and shook his head.

"Posturing rattle," Adam said, and laughed again.

Latimer said, "An apt description of us both, friend. We are a sorry pair."

"Speak for yourself. A man should be able to take the air and choose to spend time in solitude among the flowers without having his life threatened."

"Adam among the flowers," Latimer said, turning toward the other man and hitching up a knee. "A lovely picture, I must say."

"You're in love with the little Scot, aren't you?" Adam said. "You've fallen for the big green eyes and red hair."

"I've fallen for a good deal more than that," Latimer said, and wished he hadn't. "Mind your own business."

"I am. You're a good friend to me and you're not yourself. That's my business—or I'm making it so."

Latimer removed his hat and ran fingers through his hair. "Fancy a drink?" he said.

"I'm not ready to go in."

"Neither am I. Been to The King's Fool lately?"

"Can't say I have. Come on then, it's close enough."

A left turn from the square and onto the High Street and they had only yards to cover before reaching a lane where the steamed-up windows of The King's Fool bulged over the pavement. Latimer pitied the inhabitants of the houses on either side of and across from the inn, for enough noise passed through those windows to keep even the devil awake.

Adam led the way and pushed into the smoky, ale-soaked air inside. When Latimer stood beside him, Adam leaned close and said, "Nice thing about all this noise is that you can be more alone than you were out there."

They found an empty corner table and slid to sit on two benches. A fire roared up a wide chimney and red faces ran with sweat. The late hour guaranteed the level of drunkenness and the openly lewd behavior of serving girls and patrons—to say nothing of a few ladies who had evidently come looking for customers with an itch in need of scratching.

"See what I mean?" Adam said, folding his arms on the table, "anonymous in a crowd."

"A crowd of well-acquainted people who don't know one another at all," Latimer added. He caught the eye of a blond girl who looked as if she should be at home on a farm and indicated that he wanted service. "What'll it be?" he asked Latimer, who watched him, amazed, while he parted his cloak just enough to allow Halibut to poke his head out.

"I'll have a pint of light ale," Adam said, and smoothed the fur between Halibut's ears.

"You're mad," Latimer whispered, then said, "Pint of light ale and a brandy, please," to the farm girl whose green blouse was more or less kept in place by her considerable breasts.

The girl looked into his eyes. Innocence hadn't been her companion for a long time. She smiled and said, "You can have anything you want, sir. You both can. There's plenty to go round.'' Then she saw the cat and left to get their order.

"Who brings a cat to an inn?" Latimer asked. "Who takes a cat walking?"

"I do."

Latimer considered his friend but didn't say what he was thinking, that Adam had Desirée on his mind and that he was a very lonely man.

"We're not here to talk about me," Adam said.

"Really? I didn't think we were here to talk about anything in particular."

Halibut blinked lazy eyes and seemed more than satisfied with his surroundings.

"So," Adam said, "we've established that you've fallen for a charming pauper—"

Latimer's hand twisted the neck of Adam's cloak, stopping him midsentence. "You'd do well to watch your tongue when you speak of Jenny," Latimer said. "She may have been through unpleasant times, but they're over now and she'll never be unhappy again."

"Because you'll make sure of that? A tall order."

"What are you going to do about Desirée?"

Adam groomed Halibut's whiskers while he watched a sailor lift the skirts of a passing prostitute. "I'm not doing anything about her. You're all imagining things. I don't think of her as anything but an entertaining little girl. I assure you I prefer experienced women who are responsible for themselves."

"Liar."

The sailor had bared the woman's bottom, and a very nice bottom it was. She bent forward to whisper in the man's ear.

"Blunt before bliss," Latimer said.

Silver changed hands. The sailor had the woman astride

his lap and performed to the shouts and jeers of his fellows.

The blonde returned with their drinks. She set them down and scratched Halibut. "I think you need something else to stroke," she told Adam, who ignored her. She winked at Latimer then and her expression became first serious, then excited. "I know who you are, don't I?"

Would he ever outrun his own foolish excesses? "I doubt it," he said. "I'd appreciate it if you'd keep your voice down."

She whispered, "The most daring—"

"That's enough," he said, cutting her off. "You mistake me for some other man."

Her face became cunning and she slid in beside him. "I saw you at one of them posh places. My boyfriend took me inside just to see. Women all around you and you wasn't above giving them a little of what they liked. Aren't I good enough?" She tugged the blouse down enough to give him an unobstructed view of her charms.

"You're delightful, but I'm here with my friend to have a quiet drink."

She raised her shoulders and giggled. "Well, you can't 'ave no quiet drink 'ere, can you?"

"Apparently not."

"I can see you don't want me 'angin' around. Show me 'ow you do one little thing and I'll be gone. They said you could…you know, while you was 'avin a drink and playin' cards."

"Could what?" Adam asked and Latimer itched to wipe the smile from the man's face.

The girl copied the way Adam's arms were crossed on the table, only it wasn't a cat she held on top of them. "They reckon 'e can give a girl just one pinch—in a certain way—and give 'er the best time she ever 'ad."

Adam drank ale and raised his eyebrows at Latimer.

"Do it for me, darlin'," the barmaid said, and gathered her skirts almost to her waist.

Firmly, Latimer pulled them down. He found several coins in his pocket and pressed them into her palm. "Get yourself out of this place," he told her. "Find a good man and go far away from here."

Her blush, and her downcast eyes moved him. She all but ran from him.

"Touching," Adam said. "But I've always known your soul was better than mine."

"Laugh if you want to," Latimer told him. "Watching a young girl ruin herself doesn't excite me."

"No, it wouldn't. Jenny McBride's the only woman who excites you now."

"You're right," Latimer said through his teeth. "Leave it alone. I've got trouble and it isn't pretty."

He had Adam's whole attention. "I knew it," he said. "The moment I saw you walking around the square I knew there was something wrong. Let me help you."

"I wish you could." Latimer was very serious. "This is one case where I have to figure things out for myself, then do what I decide is right."

"There's never any harm in saying what's on your mind to a good friend. Sometimes it all sounds better when you hear it. And sometimes the friend sees things you don't."

Latimer threw down half of his brandy and winced as it burned his throat.

"I won't pressure you, of course," Adam said. "But I'm here for you if you need me."

"I love her," Latimer muttered. "I want to marry her."

Adam was quiet for too long before he said, "From what I can tell, she's a good-hearted girl, and pretty to boot. But there is the matter of her lack of breeding. You move among the wealthy and you've got influential friends. In your business, don't you need a brilliant wife?"

"Jenny is brilliant. And she's got a natural polish." And given the opportunity, she would blossom. He hated the thoughts he entertained about her.

"But, as you said, you've got trouble? The two of you have trouble?"

Latimer nodded but he struggled against a feeling that he'd be betraying Jenny if he discussed what had happened. "I've been told some things, that's all."

"You mean someone's tried to put you off Jenny? Because she had humble beginnings? I've always thought the class thing was overdone myself."

Latimer shaded his eyes and said, "You just brought it up yourself. You talked about her lack of breeding."

"I was testing you."

"I'll let that pass. I don't know what to do and it's not what you think. It's more complicated." He saw a muscle contract beside Adam's mouth and decided to tell him all of it.

When Latimer had finished, Adam looked at him steadily. "What proof do you have that she plans to harm you?"

"None."

"You believe she loves you, too?"

"I know she does."

Adam leaned against the whitewashed wall behind him. "Then it's easy. Trust her. Ask her to marry you at once, as fast as you can get a license. Whether or not she does it will give you your answer. If she's guilty as charged, she'll run."

26

Jenny had damped the candle and was trying to sleep when she heard a light tapping at the door. She sat up, gathering Meg's old quilt around her.

There had been plenty of sadness in her life, but none more wrenching than she'd suffered in recent hours.

The tapping sounded again and she got up. Trailing the quilt on the floor she went to unlock the door and peer out—at Latimer. He looked wild with his hair blown awry, a cloak hanging askew on his shoulders, and no neckcloth.

Without warning, he pushed his way in, bumping her as he strode past.

"Lock the door," he demanded, and she did as he asked. By the light of the fire he lit a candle and carried it into the bedroom.

Jenny's heart began a harsh, thud-thudding and she followed him timidly until she stood at the foot of the bed. Latimer relit the old candle from his new one and set them both on the table beside the bed.

He pointed to the bed and said, "Get in."

"It's your turn t'be inside," she said. "I've a quilt and I'll lie atop."

He pounded a fist against his brow. "Do what you like, but do it *now*. We have a good deal to accomplish this night."

Jenny could scarcely stand for the wobbling in her legs.

Her stomach flipped over. She made to crawl onto the bed, attempting to take the quilt with her, but Latimer snatched it away and said, "Lie down." When she did, he spread the quilt over her again. "I'm late," he announced. "I had unexpected things to attend to. Forgive me."

"O'course I will, but I missed ye."

He narrowed his eyes but didn't respond to her comment.

"Ye look so tired. Please get some rest."

"Rest?" he said and gave a cold laugh. "I doubt we'll rest tonight." He tossed the cloak aside and took off his coat.

"Ye look cold," she told him. "Ye were outside, I see. Is the weather changin'?"

"I neither know, nor care."

She sighed. "I see. Ye're not yoursel'."

"Get under the covers," he said shortly.

"I willna," she told him. "It's your turn and I'm perfectly happy where I am."

"Damn it all to hell," he said and fell to his knees beside her. "Why can't you be unappealing in my eyes. God knows what you've piled on your body. You look like a bundled child—braids and all. But you are the loveliest thing to me."

He kissed her so roughly, she couldn't catch her breath. Her arms flailed and he rose over her, pinned her to the bed with his weight, and held her head while he kissed her again and again, opening her mouth so wide her jaws hurt. But jumpy, pleasing little feelings darted about low in her tummy and she raised her hips without intending to.

She put her arms around his neck and he promptly released her and stumbled to his feet. He unbuttoned his waistcoat and removed it.

"Wouldn't ye like t'get a nightshirt?"

"No."

"Ye could wear one o' mine. Or one o' the princess's I should say."

He shook his head and she didn't care for his faint smile. "I fear I must decline your offer," he said.

Jenny refused to look away from Latimer's eyes, black and strange as they were. This behavior was to be expected from the male. She'd learned that very well now. Males were given to staring at women as if they wanted to be inside them and know every thought they had. Well, Mr. Latimer More wouldn't find a way to her secrets—unless she wanted him to.

Pretending not to notice all that breathless, unmoving silence—unmoving except for the way his eyes flickered over her, and the way he passed his tongue along his lower lip—she smiled at him and turned down the bedcovers on his side.

He groaned.

Her attention snapped back to him.

"You torture me," he said, his voice husky. "I can't think of anything but you, even though… Nothing matters but you. I must be guided to do the right thing."

Jenny kept on smiling but didn't understand much of what he said.

"I shall enjoy you first," he said. "The rest can come later."

He'd begun to frighten her badly and the fear brought a forbidden thrill.

He all but tore his clothes off and she could do nothing but watch him, fascinated, choked with emotion.

Naked, rather than get into the bed, he stretched out on top and put his hands behind his head.

"Ye'll freeze," she told him, studying his body, barely able to keep her hands off him. "Well, if ye insist on bein' hardheaded, share the quilt.'' And she spread it over him, wondering if its weight would discomfort his straining manhood.

"Thank you,'' he said. "What I have, you have. I will not tolerate all this sacrifice you feel you must endure.''

To give him more of the quilt, she moved closer until their sides met. "If this is sacrifice, then I've been told lies because it's a fine thing.''

Latimer made a strange sound and turned toward her. She rolled from her back to her side and their faces were separated only by inches. Driven by need, not boldness, she gradually closed the space between their lips and kissed him gently with her mouth closed.

He rested a large hand on the side of her face and head. She felt him restraining himself, holding back, and wondered how she could tell him she didn't want him to spare her anything. She'd learned enough to know that being with him like this could lead to a situation she should not share with a man who was not her husband.

"Were you sent to torment me?'' he asked. "If you were, someone must be happy with his work.''

"We were sent to each other because we're meant t'be together. Show me what will please ye.'' She would, Jenny thought, go wherever he chose to take her. Yes, her mind was made up.

"Be careful what you ask for.'' He nipped at her lower lip, then drew it between his teeth. His tongue entered her mouth, but only briefly before he licked her upper lip.

Jenny pressed herself to him and heard the keening sounds that came from her throat. His chest was rough, then smooth, the skin at his sides another texture again, and beneath the skin, muscles stood hard and shifted at her touch.

"No!''

His sudden cry alarmed her. "What have I done?"

"You have pleased me, that's what you've done. And you're taking me to a place where I may not be able to control my instincts. Don't you know what it does to a man to have a woman lie in his arms and kiss him, and run her hands over his body?"

Not exactly. "I suppose my hands may be too cold for ye. I'll rub them together."

"You *don't* understand and I'm glad of it. But I'm muddled, Jenny. I know what I want and that you would give it to me regardless of the cost to yourself, but it wouldn't be right. I cannot lie with you like this."

He must not leave her. "I'll not touch ye," she said. "Forgive me for bein' too bold. Anyway, I've an idea. Och, what a goose. Why did I no' think o' it before?"

She ducked her head beneath the quilt and managed an inelegant move like the childish dives she'd made when the children in the orphanage were taken swimming in the river. It was a flip, but a difficult one given the restriction of her clothes and the quilt's tendency to slide.

"Jenny," she heard Latimer say, but she was too preoccupied in getting where she was going to reply.

"There," she said when she'd finally put her head where her feet had been and hauled the quilt back into place. "Now it'll be easier for ye not t'be distracted." She stuck her face out and realized her bent legs were on the pillow and she was looking at Latimer's...at his thighs. By rights she needed to scoot farther down the bed but she was afraid to move a muscle in case she upset him and he went away.

"Jenny," he said again, and his voice sounded funny. "What do you think you've accomplished?"

"I've removed us from temptation," she said.

"Have you? It's odd how different two people's reactions can be." He planted a hand on her hip and peeled off her stockings as casually as you please. "You smell edible," he said, and rubbed a rough jaw on her shin.

Jenny didn't know what to do, so she said, "Thank ye. It's the soap they're kind enough t'gi' me."

"A woman has her own scent. Did you know that, Jenny?"

She blushed. He made everything so intimate. "I suppose I did. So do men. At least, so do you. I canna even describe it but it gives me strange and wonderful feelings."

"Tell me about the feelings."

"I canna." Impulsively she buried her face in his thighs. They were awful hard, and she liked that.

He slipped his fingers inside the drawers and she held her breath. "Your change of position was a brilliant idea. You've certainly saved me from temptation."

"Well, thank ye." His manhood moved, brushed her breasts, and she became rigid. She breathed with her mouth open. Latimer seemed content to rest quietly, except for rubbing her tummy and sliding his hand over her hip to caress her bottom. But he did it dreamily, so she thought he was probably relaxed. He might be stroking her in his sleep.

She supposed she should sleep, too. The movement against her breasts happened again. There would be no sleep as long as these things went on. Very hesitantly, trying to touch but not to have him know she had because she'd be mortified if he knew how curious she was, Jenny put the very tip of a finger on...well, she put it on the very tip of him. It was wet! And Latimer's hips moved. He pushed against her finger as if he liked the feel of it and wanted more.

Jenny stopped breathing and folded her fingers around

his shaft—and she wondered if all men carried such a proud burden about them.

The quilt was whisked away.

Latimer caught hold of her by the knees and turned on his back with Jenny on top of him. With her...oh, she could feel his breath down there, inside the divided drawers. And her face was...it was in his *lap*.

"Jenny, Jenny," he murmured. "If you tell me to, I'll try to stop. But I don't want to."

She rubbed her cheek back and forth over him and said, "I don't want to, either," in a silly, squeaky voice.

"You're killing me."

She held still. "How?"

"Figure of speech," he panted. "Don't stop what you're doing."

He pulled off the drawers...

And he kissed the insides of her thighs...

"Take off your robe and gown," he said. "I promise I'll keep you warm."

Easier said than done, she decided, working the garments upward when they were lodged between the two of them. At last she pulled them over her head and let them fall on the floor. "Is that better?" she asked.

He was busy with nipping kisses in her groin. She'd begun to ache and doubted she could bear for him to stop now.

"What's this?" With one hand, Latimer had smoothed her from hip to the middle of her back, passing beneath the woolen chemisette on the way. "A man might think you'd wrapped yourself up to keep him from finding you at all."

"No, no," she said, wriggling to drag off the offending garment. "It was just that I thought I'd best be warm for lying atop the bed."

He chuckled a little. "And how are you now? Hot or cold?"

"I'm verra hot," she told him. He'd pulled her higher and her breasts rested on his belly, which meant her face couldn't be anywhere but on top of his proud pinnacle. Oh, dear, she was harking back to the things she and the ladies in Sibyl's club had read. Silly things about women sacrificing themselves on pinnacles.

Latimer's mouth fastened over her most private place and she arched her back. He held her firmly in place with one arm while he pushed a hand between them to fondle her breasts.

He took the part that seemed to swell and grow hard between his teeth and sucked. He flipped his tongue back and forth and the aching throb became an irresistible pain.

This might not be right between unmarried people, but she would never stop him, didn't want to stop him.

"Don't do it if it repels you," he said, "but it would feel good if you took me into your mouth."

She understood what he meant and experienced a moment of panic. There was so much she didn't know.

Latimer set up a rhythmic play of his tongue and she couldn't keep her bottom still. She closed her eyes and slid his shaft into her mouth. The beauty of feeling herself joined with him brought tears. Careful not to hurt him, Jenny slid farther and farther over him. She slipped her moist lips away, almost far enough away to let him come out of her mouth altogether, but she timed her strokes well and matched his rhythm on her own body.

Faster and faster he moved his mouth and teeth on her, all the while squeezing her bottom, holding her thighs in hard, insistent hands, finding her breasts again and again and playing with her nipples until she was close to screaming.

The burning began and seared her, and she parted her legs wider to ride against his face. She raised and lowered her head, frenzied in her quest to please him. There were parts of him that were round and solid and she stroked them, cradled them.

Latimer's hands circled her waist and she realized what a big man he was in so many ways.

"Stop," he told her, but she shook her head and continued.

"I shall have to spank you for this," he said, and closed his lips over her. She heard him sucking, then felt a savage breaking loose that traveled from his mouth and throughout her body. She jerked, and burned, and drove down on him even harder. A crescendo came and she gave a thin scream. And, at the same time, Latimer's hips rose and fell like a smithy's mallet and all she could do was keep her mouth open to receive him.

"Move your face," he said in strangled tones. "Quickly. I can't hold on anymore."

Instead of doing as he asked, she fastened on him and met every thrust. His body streamed with sweat and her own hair stuck about her face.

One last, mighty jerk and Latimer threw wide his arms. He thrashed back and forth, and Jenny tasted the essence of him.

"Let it go," he said, gasping, and stroking her back. "Just let it go."

"I can't," she said, and felt heavy and warm—and safe.

He didn't persist with telling her what to do, but he did turn her around again and draw her up into his arms. They kissed for a long, long time and he held her so tightly, he hurt her ribs, but she didn't complain.

"You are my love," he said, when his heart no longer beat so hard against her breast. "A wonder. A gift I don't deserve. I have no excuse for doing what I just did, but I'm not sorry. We are well matched, I think. An amazing good fortune.''

"I've an excuse for doing what I just did.'' Jenny kissed his neck and worked her way up to his mouth. "I wanted to do it, and I'll want to do it again. I love ye, Latimer More. And I'll do whatever ye tell me, always.''

"The way you did what I told you to do a few moments ago?''

She rested heavily on him and smiled. "Just that way.''

"I have something to ask you,'' Latimer said. "But I've worn you out, so sleep first, my darling. In the morning we'll talk.''

She mumbled a deliberately sleepy, "Yes,'' and kept still, willing sleep to come.

Never had she been more wide-awake, or more aware of everything around her.

Latimer breathed deeply and slowly.

Did a man get angry if a woman was demanding…about sex?

The truth was that she didn't know but if she never tried it, she'd continue to be ignorant.

She propped an elbow and braced her head on a hand. The candles still flickered and she decided she could look at Latimer More forever. Although his features had smoothed out, there were lines at the corners of his eyes, and a straight line than ran vertically beneath each cheekbone. She'd seen how dimples formed there when he smiled.

Latimer had the kind of mouth a woman would be a fool not to watch whenever she could. The bottom lip was fuller than the top one and relaxed as he was, she could see the edges of his square, white teeth. The beard shadow on his face pleased her, and his tousled hair which had grown enough to curl at his neck. And his shoulders. She settled a flattened palm on his left one, curled her fingers around the muscle that gleamed there. The hair on his chest was still wet from his exertion. Jenny felt proud of her ability to tire him, and she also felt wicked for enjoying him so much.

When she looked at his face again, he looked back at her and her heart shifted. "I thought you were going to sleep," he said.

"Well, I'm younger than you. Mayhap I've more energy and I recover my strength quicker."

His evil grin sent tingling through every inch of her.

"You can always refuse," she told him, "but if it's all the same to you, I'd verra much like to do that over again—and see if we can find another adventurous way."

Latimer raised his chin and drove the back of his head into the pillow. "This is my fault. It was bound to happen. I've met my match and she's insatiable."

"Yes," she announced with glee and rose up to sit astride his hips. "I'm insatiable. I want you to teach me everything you know. What else can we do with this?" She lifted his partially erect shaft and stroked it carefully. She stroked until she felt it come alive, and swell, and turn rigid. When it was like that, even if she tried to press it down, it sprang up again.

"Your breasts," he said, "are the stuff of dreams. From now on I'll look at you in a certain way and you'll know I'm seeing you naked, and that in my mind I have your breasts in my hands and my tongue in your mouth, and I'll be inside you."

She held still. Latimer pinched her nipples and she jerked on his hips, but she considered what he had just said. "Inside me?"

"Slip of the tongue," he said, and laughed. "I didn't intend to say that."

"But that is what men and women do, isn't it? It's the way they have babies."

"Yes. But a baby isn't made every time a couple have intercourse."

"I see. It sounds lovely—I know I'd like it. But I suppose we'd best be careful. I've seen what happens to unwed women who have babies."

"You are not one of them," Latimer said. "Any child of yours will be my child and deeply loved by his parents. Or her parents if it's a girl, of course."

Jenny felt as if a swarm of butterflies had been let loose inside her. "Yes, but we must wait before we do it."

He turned his face away, but his thumb was flipping back and forth between her legs again. The instant flicker of response almost surprised her.

Jenny knelt and whipped the pillow from beneath Latimer's head. She placed his shaft against her and passed back and forth over him until he thrashed and made futile grabs at her.

Would all of that go inside her? she wondered. God wouldn't make men and women wrong for the things they needed to do. Not giving herself more time to think, she grasped him and pressed the head of his shaft in the entrance to her body. Gradually she lowered herself onto him, feeling him fill her. She started to cry without knowing why, but she couldn't stop.

Latimer let out a groan, caught hold of her hips and impaled her. The shock was great and she almost fell on top of him, but he held her there and began to move. "I can't believe we're doing this so soon," he said. "I thought you would be too frightened for more tonight."

"Frightened of what?"

"Minx," he said and got to his haunches without letting himself slip out of her. "Frightened of nothing, evidently. Depth is the thing, sweet woman. Let's see how far inside you I can get."

He pushed her to her back, raised her knees to her chest, and sank himself into her until she didn't think she could take anymore. And once again they moved together only this time it was different. The feelings mounted but he was within her. He paused to lean over and suck her breasts in turn. He swirled his tongue around and around her nipples and she did what she could to get even closer to him.

"Hold my hands," he said, and when she did he pulled them between her legs and thrust harder and faster, and then she felt his warm release flood her and she cried aloud.

"Jenny, dearest. Have I hurt you?"

"You haven't hurt me once. It's all so wondrous and I feel humble and so happy. And a little afraid of such joy."

He eased out of her and got them both beneath the covers. With her head in the hollow of his shoulder, he kissed her forehead and her hair and held her in arms that comforted but did not demand.

"Sweetheart, I want to ask you something," he said. He did not sound quite himself. "It's about our betrothal. Are you still happy we're to be married?"

"You tease," she said, and punched his chest lightly. "After what we've just shared, you ask me if I'm still happy t'marry ye. I can hardly wait, Latimer. And I promise I'll try my best t'make ye a good wife. I've learnin' t'do, but I manage new things quickly and I'll make ye proud o'me."

He smiled against her hair. "I'm already proud of you." He cleared his throat. "Do you know a Mrs. Smith?"

She thought before saying, "I could do. Probably do. There's plenty about. Why?"

He sighed and said, "I just wondered. Jenny, will you marry me at once?"

"At once?" she said slowly. "What d'ye mean by at once?"

"Within a few days. A special license can be arranged and we'll marry in a small chapel I know. I don't want to wait."

Surely it wouldn't be easy to do what must be done for such an event, and do it within a few days.

"Jenny? What do you say?"

She pushed her fingers into his hair and tried to look at him seriously, to frown as if giving his request great consideration, but she ruined it all by laughing. "I say, yes. Yes, yes, please."

*S*pivey here:

Whatever you think, all is not lost.

And I must tell you that during the night you sank to new lows in my estimation. I understand the current, licentious appeal of such events to those who cannot rely on their own imaginations. I mean, those who need to be shown if they are to believe. I do not approve of treating private exhibitions like peep shows.

Yes, well, I will admit that what you saw was almost unbelievable...

I forget myself. What I want to tell you is that applause is a most unsuitable response on such occasions.

Justice will be done. Lumpit may yet win the day for me. By the way, far more has been accomplished than you give me credit for. Meg has left Number 7 and so has Finch. And Sibyl is married to Sir Hunter Lloyd.

Kindly avoid arguing with me. Of course I know Sibyl and Hunter still have rooms at the house, but I've already told you that since Hunter is a distant relative of mine, and there are no sons in direct line, I'm happy for him to remain. And at least 7B is empty. Was empty. Will be empty again.

There's no reasoning with you.

Hester has a soft heart—to my continual detriment—and when Lumpit approaches her with his sad story about needing to trace a certain member of his family, she will pity him, and help him. She will not want him at Number 8 discussing skeletons in closets. What an unfortunate remark—please forgive me.

Hester will take Lumpit in and give him More's rooms. After all, and as she'll point out, a married couple needs more appropriate accommodations—particularly since More is by way of being successful, if one can call being a merchant of any kind successful. And off they'll have to go once Hester shows they aren't welcome anymore.

Oh, no, no, you are wrong again…7B and 7A will not *be considered ample and suitable for them.*

Toby? What are you yammering about? Toby doesn't count as a Spivey loss. He's in servant quarters and anyway, Jenny and More will take him with them.

What's that? Why am I so sure when Lady Hester is so protective of him? I just am. Now, not another word on that topic.

And before you rub your hands together and remind me that all I will have done is swap More and Jenny for Lumpit, forget it. He'll never move in.

Oh, my goodness, look at that. Shakespeare hobnobbing with Mozart. Now there's a pair with something in common perhaps. Big questions about who wrote what there. But I shall be on my best behavior and not mention such things.

"Yes, and a good day to you, sirs. Comparing notes, are we? No, no, merely making a little joke. You know, writing notes and writing notes? Different sorts of notes?"

You see how they respect me for my kindly discourse? Not at all, the worms.

"I say, is that a wedding gown you have there? It is? Whatever for? Delivering it anonymously to a production of A Midsummer Night's Dream *because the one they have*

*is abysmal? Hmph. To be blunt, that is the most abysmal
tragedy I've ever witnessed and no wedding gown will
rescue it from being the laughable mess it is.*

"*I shall not listen to you. We all know you lost control
of a tragedy and it became a comedy. Goodbye.*

"*Oh, if that don't beat all. Away with you both before
I report you to Sir Thomas—and Reverend Smiles.*"

*Imagine the unkindness. They said I could have the gown
in case I ever need it for Lumpit's wedding.*

*I repeat, I shall not have to worry about getting him out
of Number 7, because he'll never get in.*

28

"What happened to the notion that a wife should obey her husband?" Latimer asked, addressing Jenny while Mrs. Barstow bustled about the table where he'd taken his meals since coming to Number 7. She was setting three places for breakfast.

Jenny, dressed in her old green chintz dress, repeatedly tried to help Barstow, got in her way, and was waved off. "I'm no' your wife, sir, which means ye're no' my husband. I do have a sense of right and wrong and it's right that I return t'my work today. Madame Sophie has been kind t'me and I'll no' let her down."

"Do you have to wear—" Latimer closed his mouth and rethought what he ought to say. "Very well. I admire you for your fine principles and I shall take you to Bond Street myself. After breakfast. Finch will be here at any moment. We have a great deal to do."

Barstow had forgotten where she was in her task. She hummed lightly but with one ear cocked toward them.

"Mrs. Barstow," Latimer said. "You must wonder what all the fuss is about. There will be a great deal of coming and going at Number 7 for a few days and even then I doubt we shall settle down again very quickly. You see, Jenny and I are to be married."

Wearing her usual gray dress and with keys rattling at her waist, Barstow straightened. She smiled, her cheeks turning rosy. "Well, I did wonder from what was being said. I'm very happy for you, of course, very happy."

The door flew open and Finch stood there. Evans hovered behind. He appeared a little flustered. "You, Latimer More, are an exasperating man. You sat at my table last night, but you didn't bother to tell me you were actually making your marriage plans." She carried a bouquet of roses. "I had to hear the news from Evans when he arrived with your breakfast invitation."

"And you, Lady Kilrood, failed to notice the ring on my fiancée's finger last night."

Barstow left, closing off Evans's view of the proceedings.

Finch rushed to Jenny and raised her left hand. Tears sprang into her eyes, but she smiled and threw her arms around Jenny. "Our mother's ring," she said. "Mother was the daughter of a fisherman. My father adored her and was so proud that she was a natural lady. She loved beautiful things, and she would have loved you, Jenny. I wish she could be here. The ring looks perfect on you." She set down the roses and fumbled to undo a small gold pin at the neck of her blue dress. "My little gift to you for such a special day. This was our mother's, too."

"I canna take it," Jenny said. "I worry enough that ye'll no' like t'see the ring on me. And I'll gi' it t'ye if ye like, because—"

"Hush," Finch said. "I have my own rings. The one on your hand was given to Latimer for the woman he would marry."

"To say nothing of it being mine to give but not yours to give away, miss," Latimer said, although he loved the exchange between Jenny and Finch—and Finch's open acceptance of Jenny.

"Ye gave it t'me," Jenny said. "I thought ye meant for me to have it for my own."

"Children," Finch said loudly, and when they were both quiet and red-faced, she said, "That's better. Let me put this on you, Jenny."

The broach was their mother's favorite, a bluebird made of dark gold with sapphires studding its back. Finch pinned it to Jenny's poor dress as if she wore a ballgown, patted the shining thing, and said, "It's perfect for you, isn't it, Latimer."

It was. "Yes, perfect. I'm touched, Finnie. You're the best sister."

"I'm the only sister you have," she reminded him.

"*Women,*" he said and turned up his palms. "What was my sin that I am surrounded by women who are too quick and clever for my peace of mind?"

Barstow came in again carrying a tray of food, and Foster followed with the coffee. Toby, holding a covered silver dish of something that smelled delicious, was the last to enter.

The troupe deposited their burdens and filed out, until Jenny said, "Please stay, Toby," before the boy could leave. "Have ye eaten your breakfast?"

"Yes. I always 'as it first thing now."

"Couldn't ye eat a wee bit more?"

Toby was a smart lad these days and Latimer thought he looked bigger already. He had certainly filled out a little.

"I s'pose I could manage somethin'."

Latimer pulled the table away from the wall and slid one of his green and gilt chairs in. "For you," he said to Toby. "Sit down and join in our celebration. After all, if it hadn't been for you, I might still be searching for Jenny."

Toby sat himself in the fine chair and looked very pleased with himself. "Nah. You'd 'ave kept goin' to the shop and talkin' to 'er."

"We haven't met, Toby," Finch said. "I'm Mr. More's sister."

"Yes, I know." Toby remembered himself and got to his feet quickly. "Mrs. Barstow told me. Your 'usband is a viscount and I'm t'call you Lady Kilrood."

They all sat and Finch poured coffee, including some for Toby in a fragile Chinese cup Latimer was particularly fond of.

The covered dish contained fluffy scrambled eggs. There were braised kidneys, kippers, fried tomatoes and bread. Latimer wished he had Toby's appetite, or even Finch's. He and Jenny showed their disinterest in food. He'd rather look at her, and have her look back at him in just the way she did now. From time to time she touched the bluebird broach or studied her ring. They were not lovely enough to compete with her.

Ignoring the rudeness of it, he leaned to whisper in her ear; she nodded and watched his mouth while she did so. He stirred yet again and grew hard. Beneath the table, she squeezed his thigh and he trapped her hand there.

"Toby," she said. "This is a celebration because Latimer and I are to be married."

"I know," he said. "Mrs. Barstow said."

Finch giggled, then struggled to find a serious expression.

"Well, Barstow shouldn't ruddy well—excuse me. Barstow should allow people to share their own news."

"You didna tell her she was no' t'say anythin'," Jenny pointed out.

Toby held his valuable cup in both hands and took a huge mouthful of coffee. He set the cup down again and added several teaspoonsful of sugar. This he stirred vigorously, clattering the spoon inside the thin china as he did so. "I'm very happy for you," he said, formally enough to cause Jenny to stare. "You're a lucky man, Mr. More. She's special, our Jenny is. I never met no one what cared so much for people of no account, nor no one who was so kind. She don't 'ave no one to speak up for 'er, so I'll be 'ere if she needs someone of 'er own."

Promptly Jenny burst into tears and covered her face. Toby hopped up and put his arms around her. With tears in her own eyes, Finch smiled upon the two of them and sighed.

"Finnie," Latimer said, trying to wring some of the emotion out of the moment. "Do you think the Archbishop would give his blessings?"

She sniffed and said, "Of course he will. He's a good friend. When shall the wedding be?"

"On Friday."

Her tears dried at once. "In *three* days? But—"

"In three days," he told her. "There's much you don't know but I shall be a great deal more comfortable when Jenny is legally under my protection. Do you approve, Toby?"

The boy swallowed and said, "Yes, I approve. You'll look after 'er."

"I'm going to ask Adam Chillworth from the attic to stand with me," he said, and added, "would you be good enough to be part of the groom's party also?" without having planned to say any such thing.

"Say yes," Jenny said softly. "The day wouldna be so special wi'out ye."

Toby pulled himself up tall and said, "A pleasure," with a most serious face.

"Three days," Finch muttered, her gaze still unfocused.

"My goodness. I must get a message to Ross at once. He should give Jenny away. If that's all right with you, Jenny."

Latimer's dear girl appeared bemused. She nodded her head but he doubted she had any idea what was going on— not the details.

"The chapel in St. John's Wood," Latimer said. "St. Stephen's. It's a pretty place and since we will be a small party, we shall fit it well."

"Invitations must go out at once to Sibyl and Hunter and Meg and Jean-Marc. How annoying that Desirée chose such a time to leave."

Latimer agreed with Finch. "The entire household of Number 7 and any friends who may seem appropriate."

"You have business acquaintances," Finnie pointed out. "And there's Father."

Latimer blinked and felt hushed inside.

"He must be invited," Finch said.

Jenny held his hand on the table and said, "O'course he must be."

"He won't come," Latimer said.

"I shall pray that he does," Jenny said quietly.

Finch added, "So shall I. He'll want to know his grand-children."

Latimer glanced at Jenny but she'd lowered her lashes and turned pink. An insatiable lover she might be, but she was still shy in company.

The door opened again and this time it was Lady Hester, still wearing a nightcap, who appeared in a soft pink dressing gown and was obviously disturbed. "Did you think it fair to plan a wedding without as much as informing me of a betrothal? I am shocked. No, I am cast low by your treatment of me." A sigh raised her large bosom. Her face was shiny with some sort of potion that had been applied.

"Och, milady," Jenny said. "We wouldna do anythin' without your knowledge. I've t'go t'my work, but when I return I'll come t'ye—wi' Latimer although we've no' discussed it yet—and tell ye all about our plans. Not that I exactly know what they are except that we're t'be married on Friday."

"Friday? *Friday?*" Lady Hester produced a pink silk fan painted with red poppies and staggered to plop onto a chaise. "Married on Friday? Finch, how could you have allowed this to happen? We know Latimer is vague on occasion, but you—"

"She's only just discovered it hersel'" Jenny said. "And I'm sure if it doesna please ye, we can—"

"We will make sure that you are seated in the place of honor at St. Stephen's, Lady Hester," Latimer said before Jenny could finish what she'd wanted to say. "I think you'll approve. It's—"

"I know what St. Stephen's is like," she said through barely parted lips. "Toby dear, go to Barstow and have her start preparing invitations. She'll know what to write and be able to start without me. They must go at once— by rider to each invited guest." She inclined her cheek and Toby dropped a quick kiss on it as he passed. "The haste is unseemly, Latimer. One hopes it is your ardor, and not some other little inconvenience that causes the rush."

When had he lost control of his privacy, Latimer wondered. "Can't imagine what you're referring to," he told Lady Hester. "Jenny and I want to be together as quickly as we can."

"Will your father give you away, Jenny?" Lady Hester asked.

"No," Jenny said.

"Just as well. I shall ask Sir Edmund. He will do anything to please me and he is so distinguished."

Latimer cleared his throat and said, "Ross is to give her away, my lady, but I'm sure you will approve of that. How good of you to suggest Sir Edmund, though."

Lady Hester's fan moved briskly. "You're right. Appropriate for your brother-in-law to do it. Thought about a dress have we?"

No, he bloody well had not thought about a dress. Given his druthers, they be married in bed and naked. "Er, had we thought of a dress?" he asked, unashamed of his thoughts.

"Given the short notice, it had best be one of Princess Desirée's," Lady Hester announced. "We women shall examine them and have a modiste make any improvements necessary to the one we choose. Good heavens. Show me that ring at once."

Jenny hurried to do as she was told and Lady Hester produced a lorgnette to take a close look. "Worth a pretty penny," she said. "That bauble won't embarrass you, Latimer, my boy."

"It was my mother's," he said. "She gave it to me for this purpose and now it belongs to Jenny."

Lady Hester clapped her hands and her eyes took on a starry quality. "A wedding. I am moved at the thought. And I insist on giving the wedding breakfast here. We shall open the little ballroom for the occasion. And the wedding journey, Latimer. Surely you've thought of that. *Friday?* The license? Of course it must be a special license but even that must be hastily sought."

"Ross is a friend of the Archbishop," Finch said. "There will be no difficulty."

"Jenny," Lady Hester said. "We must go at once to see about your dress. And I—" she cleared her throat "—I take it you also have no mother available."

"No," Jenny said and Latimer wished he could take her

in his arms right then and there and show her she would never need anyone but him from now on.

Lady Hester coughed delicately and avoided looking in Latimer's direction. "Then I shall have a certain discussion with you that would normally be the obligation of a mother. I consider it my duty."

Latimer almost groaned, but Jenny said, "Thank ye kindly."

"Come with me now," Lady Hester said.

"Oh." Jenny chewed her lower lip. "I've t'be at work, my lady. Madame Sophie—"

Jenny didn't get to talk about Madame Sophie. Lady Hester became so irate that no one could be heard over her ringing tones. "Latimer is to be your husband. He needs a wife to be proud of and a wife who *sews* hats for a living will not fill the bill at all. I will send a messenger to Bond Street explaining your situation. If you think it appropriate, we could also have an invitation to the wedding delivered although I shall understand if you prefer that Madame Sophie not attend breakfast."

Silently Latimer cheered her ladyship on. He didn't want Jenny out of his sight and if she had to be, he'd prefer that she remain in this house and surrounded by protective friends.

Jenny got up. "I'd like Madame to be at breakfast, too." With shaking hands she pulled on her brown velvet pelisse and picked up her bonnet.

"You're going out in *that*," Lady Hester said. "How can you shame your future husband by being seen in *that?*"

"I'm a milliner's assistant, my lady. What I wear is of little importance and it wouldna be appropriate for me to appear in finery."

When Latimer looked to Finch, she grimaced and shrugged.

"Look at Finch," Lady Hester said as if she'd noticed the exchange between brother and sister. "She is charmingly dressed. Her husband's heart swells with pride at the sight of her." It was true that in blue gros-de-Naples trimmed with a darker blue satin piping, Finch was lovely.

Jenny said, "Aye, she's lovely," and crammed on her bonnet.

"Oh," Finch said. "Something's wrong with the flower on that."

Latimer knew what he would see. The vision of only a few remaining orange rose petals didn't surprise him. He got up, went to his bedroom, and returned with the box containing his own two rosebuds. One of these he handed silently to Jenny, the other he threaded into his buttonhole. "Jenny made them," he said by way of explanation. "She's very good with her needle."

"So's Meg," Finch said. "Before she married, she earned her living sewing for people."

"*Before* she married," Lady Hester said. "Did you hear that, Jenny? Meg only sewed until she was married."

"When I'm married, I'll have to decide what t'do about my sewin'," Jenny said. She'd removed the bonnet, dislodged what was left of the old rose, and attached the new one with a pin she found in her reticule. "I'll sew it on properly when I've time," she said.

Latimer prepared to take Jenny to Bond Street. "I must take delivery of a large shipment to Whitechapel today. I'll use the opportunity to prepare my staff to keep things running smoothly for me while I attend to far more pleasant business." He smiled at Jenny. "On Friday you shall become my wife." But what he most needed his time for was to make sure they were not interfered with by Bucket or any of his fellows.

"I almost forgot," Finch exclaimed. "The roses. Mr. Lumpit sent them for you, Jenny. He says they are a token of his esteem. He did say some rather extraordinary things, you know, but… Oh, they're of no importance. I'm afraid the curate is quite lovelorn, and desperate enough to try anything to make you care for him."

"Poor man," Lady Hester said. "I met him the other day and he was most solicitous, although Sir Edmund didn't appear to care for him."

"Smart man," Latimer said and couldn't help sounding unpleasant. "The odious Lumpit is a nuisance."

Finch swayed in place and wouldn't meet his eyes. "Lady Hester, Mr. Lumpit would appreciate coming to see you later today. He has a personal matter he wishes to discuss."

Latimer opened his mouth to order Lady Hester to ignore Lumpit, but realized in time that he had no right to do so.

"I wish I could stay," Jenny said, "But Madame Sophie needs me."

They made to leave, but Old Coot came in with a box balanced on his rotund belly. His thin legs buckled slightly under the weight of what he carried.

"For Mr. More and Miss McBride," he intoned. "Delivered a short while ago."

"Delivered by whom?" Latimer said.

Coot put the box on the dining table and stood expectantly aside. He frowned and said, "Dash me, but I don't know. Left by the cloakroom it was. James took it in, he said, but he probably didn't. Never remembers anything anyway." He tapped the box.

"Oh, open it," Lady Hester said, standing up and positively bubbling with excitement. "It must be your first wedding gift. You can be sure one of the footmen has been out and about talking already, and the news is spreading among our friends and acquaintances."

Jenny said, "I don't know anyone, so it's really for you, Latimer. I'll find my own way to Bond Street. It's no' so far."

Latimer pulled her against his side and kissed her brow—and heard the other two ladies sigh. He sat Jenny in a chair by the table and used the small knife he carried to pry the lid off the box. Whatever was inside had been wrapped in many layers of white paper and had a yellow ribbon tied around it. He removed it gently, finding it heavier than he'd expected.

The ribbon he cut away with his knife. Then he unwound the paper and all three ladies gasped.

"It's beautiful," Lady Hester said. "A treasure, I should think."

"My goodness, Latimer," Finnie said.

He glanced at Jenny but she was staring, amazed, at what appeared, on cursory inspection, to be a gold, hexagonal tower clock. Latimer realized that it had been made in France in the 1500s and was worth a deal of money.

"There's a card," Finch said, and swept one up from the floor where it must have fallen. She gave it to Jenny and said, "Open it."

Latimer restrained himself from insisting upon reading it first.

"Such paper," Jenny said, opening the envelope and drawing out a card. "It's so thick and creamy. It says, *I'm glad for you. Best, A Friend.* Who might that be?"

Movement in the foyer caught Latimer's eye and he saw

Adam there, staring at him. The other man gave a salute and went up the stairs. "This good friend is a shy man," Latimer said. "He doesn't enjoy outward displays of emotion. I think I know him better than he knows himself."

The evening turban Jenny worked on was for Lady Lloyd. While she sewed gold braid on purple velvet, she felt light-headed at the thought of Sibyl and Sir Hunter being present for the wedding on Friday. Everything that was happening seemed a dream. All the fine people Latimer knew would be there and she shrank from the responsibility of it all.

Only she mustn't shrink from anything, certainly not from an event that would be the greatest joy of her life and one that meant so much to Latimer.

Latimer. For a little while she'd almost forgotten that the annoying rogue sat on an ancient, wobbly chair in the corner of her workroom, and observed every move she made while he pretended to doze.

He'd been there for more than an hour, since three, with his legs stretched out and his hat in his lap. His chin rested on his chest and if what little light there was didn't catch the glitter of his slitted eyes, she might think he really was asleep.

Latimer shifted, crossed his arms and raised his shoulders. A casual observer could believe he didn't know when his hat fell to the floor.

"Och," she said aloud. "I wonder if ticklin' feels different if ye're asleep."

He didn't as much as lift the corners of his mouth.

"A feather's a fine instrument of tickling torture, so I'm

told. This peacock feather should be just right—or perhaps that ostrich plume.''

The sound of Madame Sophie's rustling skirts approached and she stepped down into the cramped room. Latimer was instantly alert, on his feet, and smiling at her. ''There you are, Madame Sophie. I'd hoped you'd appear soon.''

The man was shameless, Jenny thought fondly.

''Did you receive your invitation to the wedding?''

''I did, thank you,'' Madame Sophie said. ''I shall look forward to the celebrations.''

Jenny looked from Latimer to Madame and had to remember to close her mouth. Madame Sophie hadn't said a word about getting an invitation.

''Good,'' Latimer said. He took a box from his pocket and gave it to Madame. ''Today I had a large delivery of special goods from the East. Mostly China. When I saw this, I thought of you. I'd like you to have it as a gift from Jenny and me. You have been more than kind to her.''

Madame took the white box tied with a silver ribbon, and Jenny had the sensation that she was a member of the audience at a play.

''Hasn't she, Jenny?''

She looked about her and said, ''Always very kind.''

Madame opened her gift swiftly and took out an exotically shaped flower carved from polished blue stone and outlined in gold. She pressed a hand to her cheek and gasped. ''I cannot take this. It is too beautiful.''

''It's an anemone and the stone is lapis lazuli. There is some question about its origins. I believe it is exceedingly old and probably carved in Egypt. And it is yours. From your shop, I know you favor blue and gold. Only you will appreciate it enough.''

She was marrying a man with a silver tongue. Jenny

accepted the flower from Madame and was surprised at its weight. "Ye've good taste, Latimer," she said, returning the piece to its new owner. "And ye know how t'choose the right gift for the right person."

Madame thanked him formally but held the lapis as if she would never let it go and smiled with delight.

Conversation faded.

There was a clearing of throats and Madame hummed a little.

Jenny put a few more stitches in the turban but couldn't concentrate.

"There's someone I want you to meet, Jenny," Madame said. She drew one of the drapes away from the entry to the shop and called, "Come, Elsie." To Jenny she said in a low voice, "A nice girl who sews well. Not as well as you, but she'll do."

Jenny's mouth became dry. She sought Latimer's eyes but he looked determinedly—and with a guilty air—at the floor.

Elsie couldn't be more than fifteen. Plump, dark-haired, with scrubbed, rosy cheeks and brown eyes, she came into what had been Jenny's domain these past years and glanced around with a big, soft smile. She went to Jenny's side and looked at the turban. "That's a wonder," she said. "Such fine stuff and you are clever with your needle. I'd like to be as clever as you one day."

"The girl doesn't do herself justice," Madame said. "She is already accomplished for one so young. With gowns rather than hats, but she will learn quickly. Aren't we fortunate to find her, Jenny—since you are to be married so soon and must spend every moment preparing for the event?"

"Verra fortunate," Jenny said when she could speak. Latimer's fine hand was so obvious behind this that she began to plot revenge. Unfortunately he might not dislike most of the things that came to her mind.

"I hope you'll visit me when you have time," Madame Sophie said. "Perhaps you'll allow us to make hats for you."

Jenny got up slowly. She felt strange, unreal. "I'll come t'see ye," she said with a sense that she was expected to leave now. "This is a lovely place t'work, Elsie. Madame will teach ye to make beautiful hats and I'm happy for ye."

The girl slipped immediately into the chair Jenny vacated and picked up the turban. She looked closely at the stitching and examined the piece inside and out. Then the needle began to move and Jenny could see that Elsie would take her place so well that she wouldn't be missed for long.

After the goodbyes that went on too long, Latimer ushered Jenny to the street and handed her into his handsome, deep green carriage. A coachman folded the steps and closed the door, and soon the horses' hoofs clattered on cobbles, and leather creaked while the wheels ground along.

"It's a perfect day for new beginnings," Latimer said, sitting close beside her. "Warm. A bright blue day."

"It's a fine day," she said.

"There is so much to do so we mustn't be idle."

"I've never been idle a day in my life. Don't want t'be. Won't be."

Latimer's chest expanded. "I'm sure you won't."

"What d'ye have in mind t'fill my hours, then? Now that I dinna have a place anymore?"

"You'll have another place," he declared. "I have a great deal for you to do." He hit the roof with his stick and called to the coachman, "Whitechapel, Samuel." To Jenny he said, "We will take a little precious time for me

to show you my warehouses. You will surely find plenty
to do for me there.''

"Will ye need me t'sew bonnets there?''

"Don't be unreasonable,'' he snapped.

Jenny fell silent and watched through the window as the
buildings of the center of London gave way to meaner
streets and crowded houses.

The carriage rocked and she heard the coachman stopping the horses. Gradually the coach grew still and the
horrid face of Morley Bucket appeared at Latimer's window. "Afternoon,'' he said, showing his yellowed teeth.
"Forgive me for interrupting your pleasant drive but I've
business with the lady here.''

"You have no business with Jenny. If you have something to say, say it to me.'' Latimer's anger made a mask
of his face. "Hurry up, man. We have things to do.''

"I'm a busy man, too,'' Bucket said, looking at Jenny.
"You and me 'ave unfinished business. Why not come
along with me. You don't want to discuss yer private matters in front of the gent, 'ere. I'll bring you back to 'im
quick enough.''

Before Jenny could answer, Latimer said, "You have
no business with my fiancée that doesn't affect me. What
do you want?''

Bucket's lip curled. He made a hissing sound at Jenny
and she pressed her hands hard against her stomach. "It's
fiancée is it? Bloody little nuthin' what wants to pretend
she's somethin' better. Well, not without discharging your
promises to me first. You owe me. I don't suppose you've
got it all, but I want somethin' on account. Just to show
you've got honorable intentions, like.''

She fiddled with her reticule, knowing she had no more
than a few pennies inside.

Latimer put a hand on top of hers and held it still. Then

he slipped a money clip from an inside pocket in his jacket and said to Bucket, "What is the amount outstanding?"

"None of your infernal business. Like I said, my business is with the lady."

"Since the lady is my business now, you will deal with me," Latimer said, peeling notes from the clip and handing them to Jenny. "Give him these. They are yours because I give them to you. That should make the fellow happy."

Jenny leaned across Latimer and offered the money to Bucket. He took it and promptly threw it in her face. "I told yer we 'ad private business. If yer don't want all yer fancy plans spoiled, we'll 'ave that chat. Alone."

Latimer, tight-lipped with rage, hammered on the roof and the carriage swung away rapidly enough to land Mr. Bucket on his hands and knees in the street.

"Damn him," Latimer muttered. "I thought I knew his game, but now I'm not so sure. From his behavior, there's more riding on this than his pride or his personal interest in you. If he tries to get too close to you, I shall have to deal with him."

"Ye wouldna kill anyone?" Jenny said. If she told him Bucket had plans to discharge her debt by as good as selling her to another man, who knew what dreadful things might follow?

Latimer gathered the bank notes and gave them to her. "Put these in your reticule. I don't want you traveling with nothing to pay for whatever comes up."

"Ye mean ye're afraid I'll be waylaid when ye're no' wi' me." She thought that quite likely and was sickened at the prospect.

"Enough of that," Latimer said. "See where we are?"

Jenny looked outside again and wished she hadn't. "Aye, I know it well. Whitechapel's no friend o' mine."

"Yes, it is. I make my living here, and a respectable living it is."

In a street lined with pathetic houses on one side and warehouses on the other, the coachman stopped the horses and came to hand Jenny down.

"Take them around to the yard, Samuel," Latimer said. "I doubt we'll be here long."

When the carriage had rolled away, Latimer pointed to the houses, where most windows were covered with pieces of board and said, "Finch and Ross have an adopted son named Hayden. He was living there when they first met him."

"Another orphan," Jenny said. "Ye're kind people. Where is Hayden now?"

"He lives on the Scottish estate where Ross is teaching him to farm," Latimer told her with a hard edge to his tone. "We are not *kind* people, merely people with a gift for recognizing good things when we see them. I will not marry you out of charity, Jenny, but out of my deep love for you."

Shamed, she put a hand on his chest and said, "Your love for me canna be deeper than mine for you. Forgive me if I say silly things sometimes. I've had a lot to become familiar with."

"Quite." He didn't sound softened toward her. "In we go, then."

Inside a cavernous building where crates lined the walls and stood in clusters everywhere, Latimer introduced her to one man after another as they went quickly about their work. In some places stood statues, in others, furniture. Pottery and glass looked out of place displayed on shelves in such surroundings. She met Will Austin, who was Latimer's second-in-command, a pleasant, fair-haired man with a healthy build, who showed he was knowledgeable about the business.

"You've met everyone," Latimer said at last.

"Ye've good people workin' for ye," she told him. "They've everything under control and there's not a thing for me to do here—as you know."

He scowled at her. He'd removed his jacket and rolled up his shirtsleeves. He looked bursting with life and health. "Take a look at my office and we'll go. I think your wedding dress is the next order of business."

She went ahead of him into a big office in the center of the warehouse floor. Frosted windows enclosed it on all sides. More crates greeted her, and a big desk. A tray of tea things stood on top of a bookshelf. Jade buddhas, carved ivory, white marble figurines, boxes with jeweled lids and handfuls of polished stones littered every surface. "It's like a sorcerer's lair," she said. "I'd expect magic to happen among all these mysterious things."

"Would you indeed?" Latimer hung his coat on a peg and locked the door. "For security," he said.

"What's the stone on top o' this wee box?" she asked, showing him a gilt-edged container encrusted with gems but with a green and white jewel in its top, a jewel that flared red when she tilted the box.

He opened her hand, put the box on her palm, and folded her fingers around it. "A fire opal," he said. "It's yours, to keep the bluebird pin safe."

"I canna—"

Latimer, lifting Jenny to sit on his desk, silenced her. He propped a hand on either side of her and looked closely into her eyes. "Peacock feathers?" he said. "Ostrich plumes? Instruments of tickling torture you may be glad I don't possess here."

She nodded, but he used his fingertips to tickle her until

she writhed and tried to fight him off. "Ooh, stop, Latimer." She could scarcely catch her breath. "Your men will hear."

"If they do, they'll be justly jealous." He kissed her, then continued to torment her and behaved as if her hands were ladybirds to be swatted when she tried to stop him from tickling the sensitive places behind her knees.

He paused, breathless himself, and said, "One day I'll explain what I mean, but accept that I'm only living up to my reputation. I'm a daring man."

With that, he pulled her against him to undo the tapes on her dress, stripped her naked to the waist and flipped her backward onto the desk. And still he tickled her.

"Latimer," she wailed, but it must be hard for a man to listen to anything when he was intent on licking circles over his beloved's breasts and undoing his trousers at the same time. When she wriggled and spoke his name again, he pushed his head beneath her skirts and she forgot what she'd intended to say.

30

"Come here at once, Jenny," Sibyl said. "Finch, can you do anything with her? Latimer will be leaving for the chapel at any moment. If he looks up at the window, he'll see her. And it's bad luck." Sibyl was almost weeping when she finished.

"Jenny, dear," Finch said. "To please the one who is about to become your sister, will you come away from the windows?"

If Jenny didn't cough with nervousness each time she tried to open her mouth, she'd laugh at these two who had decided to be her mothers while Lady Hester sat on the blue-and-silver couch and looked serene in a heavenly shade of deep blue.

"*Jenny,*" Sibyl cried.

"Do as you are told, girl," Lady Hester put in. "At once. You're behaving like an addlepated cuckoo—not an appealing combination."

Sighing, looking over her shoulder, Jenny turned from the lace draperies. "How would a man see through the curtains?" she said, longing for just a peep at her soon-to-be husband's broad shoulders as he left the house and passed beneath the windows. With Adam and Toby, he would enter the black barouche that waited there with its door open and a coachman in Lady Hester's livery standing to one side. Multi-colored ribbons had been tied to the door handles, to the back of the coach where two tigers—perhaps a little cramped in uniforms that hadn't been used in a long time and were small—stood dressed in purple and yellow, and to the shining rails on either side of the coachman's box. Each of four horses sported a matching rosette on its bridle.

"Stand here, and stand still," Sibyl ordered. "It really is the end that Meg and Jean-Marc have left for Ireland. Meg would be so much better suited to making the final tweaks to this dress."

There was a knock and Lady Hester said, "Come," admitting Evans with a bowl of summer flowers.

"From Mr. More," he said, putting them down. "And he wishes you to have these."

Jenny was presented with a round nosegay of wildflowers mixed with yellow and white roses and framed with lace. Ribbons the colors of those on the coach trailed from the enclosed stems.

"Most appropriate," Lady Hester said. "Evans? Where is Coot?"

"Not feeling well, milady. All the excitement is too much for him."

"Then he is to rest so that he may enjoy the breakfast," her ladyship said. "Please tell him not to come to the chapel unless he is completely recovered."

"Yes, milady. Mr. More did wish to remind Miss McBride that he is likely to expire if she keeps him waiting."

"Then I must go at once," Jenny said, picking up her skirts and preparing to run.

"And arrive *before* the groom?" Lady Hester said, but she smiled. "Impertinent fellow, but I'm proud of him. I have watched him make a triumph of his business and himself. Most gratifying to see one of my protégés do so well. And you, too, Finch. And Sibyl and Meg. Most gratifying. Thank you, Evans. I should tell you that I am more than grateful that Sir Edmund found you for me. Coot will have his senior position in this household for the rest of his life, but you will make a splendid second-in-command.''

''Thank you, milady,'' Evans said and bowed from the room.

''Put the flowers down,'' Finch said, darting from one side of Jenny to the other and back again. ''Oh, Sibyl, is the hem even? Put the flowers *down,* Jenny.''

''I willna,'' Jenny said and held them close. Latimer had sent them to her. ''I want t'see him.''

Finch cast her eyes heavenward and said, ''You're behaving like a child. He hasn't left for the chapel yet. When he does—regardless of his warnings—we'll wait a respectable interval, and go there ourselves. *Then,* and not a moment before, will you see your groom. And if he's expired, you may be grateful you didn't marry the weakling.'' Finch laughed at her own little joke but Jenny's eyes filled with tears—again.

''Look at her, Lady Hester,'' Sibyl said. ''Isn't she beautiful?''

''They say even ugly gels are beautiful on their wedding days. Don't ask me why when they're about to go through the worst experience of their lives.''

Finch and Sibyl hushed her in unison.

Jenny didn't care what anyone had to say. She felt pretty, she must *be* pretty, and this was the *happiest* day of her life.

''Meg and Jean-Marc on that dreadful sea and crossing to look at some Irish property they don't have time to administer, beautiful as I'm sure it is.'' Sibyl complained.

"And Desirée in dreadful Mont Nuages where she's no doubt being ignored by her terrible father."

"Sibyl," Finch said, "I do believe you mixed a liberal dose of pessimism into your breakfast. It was ill fortune that caused the messenger to miss Meg, and Desirée had left some time previous. But not only were you still at Riverside, but Hunter was already on his way to accompany you to Cornwall. Now we have both of you. And thank goodness Ross got here in time. He most certainly would not have done so if he weren't already on his way because of his concern over what might be happening here. We are blessed, I tell you. And we shall celebrate again when everyone returns."

"Hmm," Sibyl said. "You are obviously an optimist, Finch, but I didn't have breakfast. I'm too nervous."

"I didna eat anythin'," Jenny said. "I couldna. Finch, may I say somethin' about your father?"

"What is there to say?" Finch's mouth made a straight, tight line.

"I'm verra sorry he didna send a response sayin' he'd come. Latimer told me it was the same for your own weddin'. You're both sad no doubt, but he's the sadder one. He's missin' so much."

"He's too proud," Finch said. "He said if we left Cornwall he'd turn his back on us and he has. But I'd lie if I said I didn't miss him—bad-tempered man that he is."

"Aye," Jenny said. A long mirror had been brought to her rooms and she rotated carefully to survey herself one more time. "Whatever may be wrong wi' me now, will stay wrong," she said. "D'ye think the roses in my hair will die before we get t'the chapel."

Lady Hester chuckled, then laughed, and wafted her blue silk fan before her pretty face. "You are all incorrigible. Tomorrow we shall laugh at all this nonsense. Jenny, the roses will not die and the dress is perfect. I've never seen a paler shade of mint green. Perfect with your coloring. Sibyl, go around the skirts and make sure the leaf ornaments are straight." Each satin leaf had a white satin daisy at its base and a lemon-colored butterfly sat on the petals. The dress was of tulle over the pale green gros-de-Naples. "Did I tell you Birdie's wearing a gown to match mine?"

She had, several times, but Jenny said, "I think she'll be lovely in it."

"You look as if you have dew on your skin," Finch said. "But I don't think you should wear the bluebird pin."

"I'm wearin' the pin," Jenny said and felt as stubborn as she sounded. "For ye, and for your mother—and because I like the way it looks."

"I like the pearls in your hair," Sibyl said. "Your hair is so very red and the pearls stand out."

"La," Jenny said, and caused an immediate gale of laughter. Since the first effort was so successful, she repeated, "*La.* I'm gorgeous and I thank ye for recognizing a gem in your midst. When can we leave?"

From below came the unmistakable sound of the front door closing sharply. Jenny made for the window but was detained by a pair of strong hands on each of her arms.

She gave up easily and stood with her head bowed, listening to voices in the street, then one voice rose above the rest, a manly voice laced with humor, "Don't be late, Jenny," Latimer cried. "I'll be waiting for you."

Adam had fallen silent and Toby was kneeling on his seat watching every detail from the windows. Latimer closed his eyes and used the rhythmic jounce of the carriage and the clatter and creak of the horses to help him focus his thoughts.

Concentration was a hard thing when your heart led you elsewhere. His wedding day. Only weeks ago this had been a vague dream he'd rashly promised himself would come true. He and Jenny were marrying without making all the decisions that would have been made if they'd had more time to prepare, but Adam had been right, her immediate acceptance of him gave the lie to any accusations that had been made against her—and anyway, he wanted her to be his wife at once.

He opened his eyes.

Lies had no place between a man and his wife. Lies, or failure to be honest. Jenny deserved to know that his hasty actions had been a test.

Not today. Today would not be spoiled by anything.

"I feel guilty," Adam said. "I pushed you into this."

"You did. Thank you."

Adam put his elbows on his knees. "It isn't too late to turn back. Jenny's a sensible girl. Tell her the two of you need more time to be ready for marriage."

Giving him a mighty slap on the back, Latimer laughed and sputtered, "It *is* too late and I've never been more glad of anything. We'll have growing to do and we'll do it together. Jenny is the best thing that ever happened to me."

Adam turned his serious gray eyes on Latimer, "You're sure?"

"Completely."

"You won't be banging on my door tonight and wanting to call me out for ruining your life?"

Latimer used the ivory handle of his cane to tip his hat back and he grinned at Adam. "I doubt if you'll see me tonight, old chap. If you get lonely, pop on over to Number

8 and keep Lumpit company.'' He was still looking for a way to thank Adam for the extravagant wedding gift.

"Wot d'you mean, Mr. Chillworth pushed you into marryin' our Jenny?"

"Toby," Latimer said, having forgotten the boy's presence. "You are a young man now and about to learn a great many things about what passes between men and women—when they're in love, that is. Keep your ears open and you'll be ready to deal with such matters when your own turn comes."

"But I asked—"

"Yes, yes." He might have known the boy would not be so easily silenced. "Just a joke between Adam and myself. We're old friends and have had our doubts that either of us would ever marry. Adam means he supported my decision to ask for Jenny's hand, nothing more."

"Ah," Toby said and went back to watching the buildings and gardens they passed.

Whereas Adam and Latimer wore black coats and dark gray trousers, Toby's coat was dark blue and his trousers buff. He was a handsome little devil with a sharp mind.

"I thought we was goin' to St. John's Wood," Toby said. His nose was pressed to the window now.

"We are," Adam said. "Probably a part you haven't seen."

Latimer checked his neckcloth, which Evans had volunteered to tie. The man had said the name of the knot, but Latimer didn't remember, or care. Surreptitiously he took his marmalade silk rose from inside his hat—the only place he'd been able to think of as a hiding place, and slipped it into his buttonhole.

"I ain't spent much time around 'ere where the nobs live," Toby said, "but I knows it enough. I thought St. Stephen's wasn't far from Regent's Park."

"It's not," Latimer said, alert to the scenery for the first time since leaving Mayfair Square. "Adam, the boy's right. We're nowhere near the Park, and St. John's Wood is behind us." He looked at his pocket watch. "Damn and blast, the idiot coachman. He'll have us late."

Adam was already hammering the roof inside the carriage. Latimer slid open the trap and called to the coachman, "Stop. You've taken a wrong turn. We must go back at once."

The coachman didn't turn around. Neither did the man who sat beside him. "Were there two drivers?" Latimer asked Adam over his shoulder.

"No," Adam said.

"There are now." He used his cane to poke the back of the nearest man and was ignored. Latimer closed the trap. "Something's gone wrong. Those men are nothing to do with Number 7 and they aren't stopping. In fact they're traveling faster."

Adam had moved to the front of his seat and was studying the view. "Hampstead," he said. "And unless I'm mistaken, the Heath. What foul business is this? If it's a robbery, they've gone to a great deal of trouble. But what else could it be?"

"Bucket," Latimer and Toby said together.

"Gad." Adam took off his coat and put it behind him. Latimer did the same. "We're going to have to fight, dammit."

"'Aven't you got a sword about yer?" Toby said. "We could kill 'em through that little 'ole without even getting out. Then I'll drive us back. We can't 'ave our Jenny waitin'."

The notion sickened Latimer, but Toby's idea, swashbuckling as it was, wouldn't work. Not exactly.

"Toby," he said. "I don't have time to explain everything that will happen. But you will remain in this coach. Understand? You will not get out of the coach and interfere or you may ruin our chances of escape.''

''Going a bit fast to get out anyway, aren't we?'' Adam said.

Latimer was in no mood for sarcasm. ''When the carriage slows, jump,'' he told Adam. ''We've got to stop the coach and deal with these men. Toby, you can be a help. Forget what I said about not getting out. Wait your moment. And you'll know what I mean when it happens. Then get up and keep a tight rein on the horses.''

Toby looked happy, as if he weren't in a carriage that had made a turn onto the Heath and was being driven madly between stands of trees toward rougher, more hilly ground.

''Ready?'' Latimer yelled to Adam. ''Here goes.''

He withdrew the slender blade from his walking stick, assessed the angle of the two bottoms seated atop the box, and took aim. He applied two short, but not too short, jabs to each rump and saw them rise. Blood seeped between splayed fingers and enraged yowls reached the passengers.

The carriage still hurtled on.

Latimer repeated his target practice, this time sending his blade deeper into the enemy's flanks.

Yowls turned to screams and the coach swayed, the horses complained loudly and the sounds were of the wheels screeching on hard, dry ground as they slowed.

Adam crouched with his hand on the door, ready to push it open and jump. Latimer prepared to leap from the same door, and Toby was in place on the opposite side.

''The tigers,'' Latimer said. ''They may be friend or foe. If they're foe they'll make this too uneven for comfort. Go for the quick stuff. Frightening 'em off would be to our good.''

The coach almost stopped and Adam jumped. He rushed at once for the back where the tigers would be clinging in their places.

Latimer waited one more moment, and, sword in hand, landed on the ground running. He threw himself at the horses, all the while praying the two ruffians in the driver's seat didn't have pistols.

Yells and sounds of begging came from the rear of the coach and Latimer hoped Adam's opponents were no match for him even if there were two of them. They needed miracles and Latimer wasn't above invoking them.

Keeping low, Latimer made it to the left lead horse and leaped onto its bare back. He lay on that back, knowing the horse behind him would act as a shield, and pulled back on the bridle. He talked to the horse, soothed him, and felt the animal break his stride. The others followed suit.

A pistol shot blasted Latimer's ears. *Dammit.*

He dismounted in time to see two burly men, wincing and cursing, getting gingerly down from their places while Toby climbed up from the opposite direction.

Latimer kept low and weighed the chances of running around to get up with Toby on the opposite side. The element of surprise could give time to pick up Adam and be away.

Bull-like bellows and the rapid, if limping, charge of a fellow wearing Lady Hester's colors, blew away Adam's hope of an easy escape. On horseback, he had held the delicate sword like a saber. Now he changed his grip and stood his ground.

"You'll pay for that one, you uppity bastard," the approaching man said, but he'd halted his advance.

"Where's the flamin' pistol?" his companion shouted. "Give it t'me."

The first man looked at his empty hands and his jaw slackened. He patted himself and said, "I ain't got it. Didn't 'e give it t'you?"

"The skinny whoremaster made you boss, remember," the second fellow said and added, "Said 'e only 'ad one and give it t'you. You knocked them others out with it. Oh, my gawd, you've lost it. Fix this one with the silly-lookin' sword then." He went in the other direction, toward the cries and sounds of scuffling from the rear of the coach.

But Latimer had heard a shot.

The kidnapper didn't take his eyes off the "silly looking sword." He said, "Throw that over there or I'll use it on you."

"Take it away from me, then," Latimer said, flicking the tip of the sword and taking his position. "Come on, man, take it from me. How else will you use it against me?"

"'Ow else?" Toby said in a loud, belligerent voice.

Latimer smiled a little.

The impostor coachman didn't. Unfortunately neither was he distracted by Toby.

Latimer made circles with his blade and feinted, but the other man seemed rooted to the ground. He put a hand to his rear again and glanced at the bloody fingers he withdrew. "Bastard," he muttered. "Attackin' a man from behind."

"Attackin' his behind from behind, yer mean," Toby called and chuckled at his own witticism.

Latimer didn't want to kill this piece of scum. Better that he suffer much longer. The chap was panting and sweat ran down his round, red face. He was, Latimer realized, scared. Scared of more than a blade. If that had been all, he'd have run away. "Morley Bucket's a hard master, is he?'' he said. "Likely to take a whip to that sore arse of yours if you let us get away?''

"Shut yer mouth.''

Latimer glanced at Toby and their eyes met. Then he looked back at the sweating man. He repeated the process, willing Toby to understand.

Another pistol shot sounded and he knew he had to get to Adam. "Jump on him, Toby,'' he cried, but Toby was already in flight from the carriage. Amid oaths and beefy arms that swung like windmill blades, the boy's weight, landing on the man's head and neck, knocked him to the ground and Latimer was upon him instantly, winding his arms behind his back until he screamed. "Something to bind him with,'' he told Toby, who was already scrambling onto the front of the carriage once more. He pulled gear from beneath the seat and cried out with triumph when he held a length of rein aloft. This he threw to Latimer who, with the aid of his sword, had little difficulty slicing off strips of leather and securing the man's wrists and ankles together before using another piece to haul his feet backward and up to his hands. He left the fellow writhing and yelling on the ground.

Crouched, going around the back of the carriage, Latimer all but tripped over the second man from the driver's seat. He appeared to be unconscious and blood trickled from a wound at his temple. His face bore multiple cuts and his closed eyes weren't going to open easily even when he wanted them to. One furrowed wound across the back of his neck could only have been made by a firearm.

"Adam,'' Latimer yelled. "For God's sake man, I didn't know you carried a pistol.'' Without waiting for a response, he launched himself into the writhing fray that turned over and over in a jumble of arms and legs, tattered black and purple silks, and Adam's flying hair.

The tigers were not boys, but small men who might well have been pugilists by the way they used their fists. Latimer took a punch to the corner of his eye that rendered him sightless on that side for moments. Rage overcame him. "That's it for you, you piece of filth." His fist rose and fell on the wiry fellow's head, with the odd blow to the belly, until Latimer watched consciousness slip away from his opponent.

Adam held the other "tiger" facedown on the dusty trail across the heath. And he ground that face into the dirt even when the man had stopped struggling.

"Adam," Latimer shouted, "Adam, you've knocked him out. Where's the pistol?"

"Over there," Adam said, tearing strips from the unconscious man's clothing and tying him up with them.

Latimer did the same thing with his man and both he and Adam ran to the fallen one by the rear of the carriage. "What happened back here?" Latimer said. "Hell's teeth, someone is going to suffer for this. My Jenny is waiting at that church by now. She may even have left again." He turned his eyes to Adam and felt a deep twisting in his belly. "Will she ever understand?"

"One look at you should be worth more than words, my friend," Adam said. "Quickly, finish with this one. I have been known to carry a pistol about me. Almost didn't today. Praise be I changed my mind. Put a shot in the air and sent those two over there running for their lives. Unfortunately this chap jumped me from behind and by the time I'd beaten him down and wounded him, the others had crept back and managed to get the pistol. You can fill in the rest. This one won't move until someone unties him."

31

An ensemble of strings and trumpet played the same piece of music for the second time. Jenny stood in the vestibule of St. Stephen's Chapel, clinging tightly to the arm of Ross, Viscount Kilrood, Finch's husband, whom she'd met for the first time shortly before he accompanied her from Number 7.

The viscount put his hand over hers on his arm and said, "Be calm, Jenny. Weddings are the very devil. One day soon Finch and I will tell you about ours. It very nearly didn't happen." His voice did calm Jenny a little. It was strong and deep and had a touch of her own Scottish brogue.

"Somethin's happened t'Latimer," she said in a shaky voice. "He left fifteen minutes before us and we've been here twenty. He's changed his mind. He's not comin'."

"If he values his life, he'll come." Sir Hunter Lloyd, who was married to Sibyl, marched back and forth with his hands clasped behind his back and a thunderous expression on his face. "The scoundrel will deal with me."

Jenny looked from Sir Hunter, with his light brown hair and eyes as green as her own, to Viscount Kilrood, whose eyes were the kind of blue that was difficult to look at, especially when the man's dark hair and brows were such a contrast. Two handsome, manly men. Jenny turned hot at the audacity of her own thoughts. But they were manly and their wives—who were beautiful in their brocade and sarcenet, with elegant coiffeurs and jewels sparkling on necks, wrists and hands—were perfectly matched to their husbands. She could never hope to be a suitable match for Latimer. Of course he'd come to his senses and decided not to go through with the marriage.

"Latimer's a good man," Finch said, aiming her comment and an annoyed frown at her husband. "Really, Hunter, I think we should be more concerned for Latimer's safety, than—"

"Shh," the other three told Finch in unison and Jenny felt all eyes upon her.

Yes, what if he'd been hurt? What if he and Adam—and Toby—were lying injured somewhere while she blamed him and thought silly thoughts about his not loving her. He did love her. And he wanted her.

"Where is he?" Jenny didn't care that her voice broke or that tears welled in her eyes. "We should look for him."

"If we leave this place, he'll arrive the moment we've left," Finch said and Sibyl mumbled agreement.

The music was playing for the third time.

"Good job it's hard to know where the cannon starts and ends," the viscount remarked. "They'll all think this is part of the plan."

"Oh," Sibyl said, smacking her cream-gloved hands against the skirts of a light blue brocade dress. "What piffle, Ross. You and Hunter make a fine pair. You make excuses for Latimer and Hunter threatens to kill him. And not a soul in that chapel thinks this long introduction is part of any plan. They all know something's wrong."

"That's right," Finch said, then tried to smile reassuringly at Jenny. The smile was a flop.

"I said nothing about killing Latimer," Sir Hunter said.

"Please stop," Jenny begged. "It's a bad time we're havin'. All o' us." But they didn't know the pain she felt, and that pain had nothing to do with the whispering people who had set up a rustle of shifting clothing in the chapel.

Treading remarkably lightly for such a big man, Larch Lumpit slipped from the chapel proper into the vestibule. He frowned and actually looked as if he might cry. "What's happening?" he asked. "Dear Lady Hester's all atwitter and so am I. The only calm one among us is Sir Edmund and he's already said that if Latimer More doesn't show up for his own wedding, then Jenny's better off without him."

Jenny bowed her head. She couldn't look at them anymore.

"Could I go and look for him, do you think?" Lumpit said, to Jenny's amazement. "I could you know, if someone would give me an idea where to start. A wheel could have come off the carriage. Or a horse gone lame. Don't look so sad, Jenny. He loves you, that's easy to see, so he's been unexpectedly delayed."

After that speech, Jenny kissed Lumpit's cheek and said, "Ye're a dear man, but I don't think ye'd be able t'find them when not one of us has an idea where they could be." She drew a difficult breath. "They would have come by the same route as we did. It's verra strange."

Lumpit folded his hands and nodded.

Three richly dressed elderly ladies came from the chapel. They looked at Jenny with pitying eyes and left the building. More people followed, in a trickle at first, and then steadily.

The viscount cleared his throat and Jenny looked up at him. He gave Finch a meaningful stare and she nodded. "Jenny," he said. "There will be an explanation for this, but I doubt there'll be a wedding today. We'd like to take you home and make you comfortable until we find out what's gone wrong.''

She took her hand from his arm.

"Good girl," Finch said. "You need a meal and perhaps something to calm you. Then a good sleep."

"And he needs to be horsewhipped," Sir Hunter muttered.

The congregation filed out in a rush, most avoiding even a glance in Jenny's direction.

"I insist we leave," Viscount Kilrood said.

Sibyl's sniffs had turned to tears and she went into her husband's arms where he held her and stroked her hair.

"You go," Jenny said, and felt like a tiny island in a large ocean. "Please go home and don't worry. Latimer will come, and when he does I must be here."

Finch's eyes grew glassy also, and her mouth trembled.

"I'll—" Sibyl's hand on Sir Hunter's mouth stopped his next threat against Latimer.

"Please leave me here," Jenny said. "I'd like to wait alone."

"Well, you bloody well can't wait alone," Sir Hunter said, and turned red. "Apologies for that. Not myself."

Both doors into the chapel stood open. In the front pews sat Lady Hester, Sir Edmund and the staffs from Number 7, Number 8, and Number 17, who had moved forward to help make a solid little group. Birdie and Lady Hester sat side by side in their matching blue dresses. Jenny also saw Madame Sophie.

Jenny walked away from those who gave such kind support and progressed slowly down the aisle. With each step she felt a little dying, until she reached what was left of the congregation. At the front of the church she turned to face them. "Latimer will be here," she said, "but I dinna know when."

Snuffles surged through the pews.

"He's no' a man who would cause someone such great unhappiness unless something happened that he couldna control."

She heard mutterings and knew most of those present thought Latimer a cad, and her a fool.

"Would ye please go home, now," she said. "I'll go to Mayfair Square when I find out about Latimer. Until then, I'll stay here."

Not a soul moved.

"Please," she said, fighting back tears, "I'd like t'be alone if ye please."

She went toward the sacristy where the door stood ajar and she could see a minister in rich robes sitting in a chair with his feet on a stool. He was reading.

Passing time until someone tells him he can go. Jenny straightened her back and checked the rosebuds in her hair. She felt speckles of moisture still clinging to the petals. Lady Hester had said they'd be fine for the wedding, and she was right.

A hollow silence fell upon the building. Jenny remained a few yards from the sacristy and leaned on the front of a pew. She would wait—forever if that's how long it took for him to get to her.

From the street outside she heard hoofbeats and men shouting, but then the sounds died away and all was quiet once more. Still those who remained were silent behind her.

They were little more than strangers, but they were good people who couldn't bear to allow her to suffer alone.

Boots clattered on stone.

Unintelligible voices rang out, bouncing from the walls.

Jenny saw the minister close his book and she thought he smiled.

The sacristy door was flung wide-open and Latimer strode toward her. She gasped at the sight of his injured face and dusty, torn clothes, but then he gathered her to him and squeezed her so hard she could scarcely take a breath.

"You didn't go away," he murmured against her ear. "You stayed."

"I waited for ye," Jenny told him. "I didn't know when ye'd come, but I knew ye would. My poor Latimer. What's happened t'ye? Who did this t'ye?"

"Not now," he told her. "This is our wedding day. I'll deal with those people, but not when I have my darling girl in my arms and about to become my wife."

"I love ye, Latimer."

"Jenny, I don't have the words to tell you how much I love you."

Latimer kissed her. He cradled her face and fondled her lips with his own until she felt she floated and the world went away. With the kiss they reaffirmed their commitment, and Jenny offered herself to Latimer, and he promised he would take her.

There was a masculine "Ahem."

Still they kissed. Still Jenny thrust her fingers into Latimer's hair.

"Hmm, hmm." The same voice intruded, then said, "Perhaps the wedding first, my children?"

"Let's do this," Latimer whispered. "It's what we want so much. The man who will marry us is the Archbishop."

Then Jenny saw Adam, and Toby, and the condition of their clothing, the scrapes on both of them and a wound over Adam's left eye. He also had dried blood on a cut near his mouth.

"Come, sweet," Latimer said and turned her to see Viscount Kilrood waiting in front of the Archbishop to give her away.

They were married.

32

Spivey here:

Most affecting, I must say. Ah, me. Yes, I think I recall how a heart beats at such times.

But this is not going at all as I'd planned. I am so tired. A rest in my post is what I need. I might even enjoy imagining the scent of all those flowers they've strewn over Number 7, but I can't. I can't cease my vigilance for an instant. Certainly not when my only usable pair of hands belong to the likes of Larch Lumpit. He offered to search for Latimer! What has happened? He thinks for himself and now he has defected to the other side—even if he doesn't have a notion in his noggin of what he's really about, or what he'll soon return to. Wait until he wanders into St. Philomena's in Middle Wallop, puzzling about what exactly he'd set off to do when he left (he won't remember how long ago he did leave) and is confronted by his infuriated vicar.

Hmm. Some satisfaction in that. But first things first. The game isn't over, friends (I call you friends because I choose to believe there is goodness in you after all) and, with Lumpit's unwitting assistance (the only kind of assistance he's capable of performing) we may yet see Latimer and Jenny depart Number 7. What am I saying? Of course

they'll leave the house. They'll have to have more suitable
digs, his being a protégé *of whom Hester is so proud...*
  Piffle.
Have faith in Sir Septimus—and watch closely.

33

A single violinist played in the foyer at Number 7.

Flowers loaded the bannisters and stood in banks wherever one looked. Multicolored ribbon streamers gave a lighthearted impression.

Latimer used his handkerchief to blot raindrops from Jenny's smiling face, her neck and, very carefully, her hair. "How dare it rain on our wedding day," he told her. "Although a little moisture on those freckles is charming, Mrs. More."

"Mrs. More," she murmured and rose to her toes to smooth moisture from his cheek. "I like the sound of that. And I like rain on your hair, and in your eyelashes. I like everything about you, Mr. More." She leaned against him. The intimate gathering of family, a few staunch guests who had remained until Latimer arrived at St. Stephen's and the nuptials were performed, and such members of the staff who could pause from their duties, sighed.

"Come along," Lady Hester said. "Let's go up. Hunter, you and Finch were so right to open the old ballroom. Wait until you see it, Latimer—and you, Jenny—it's beautiful. A fairy-tale room for an extraordinary wedding."

Latimer restrained himself from telling Lady H that he had seen the ballroom before, during, and after its renovation.

"Mr. Latimer?"

He glanced around and saw Old Coot hovering outside 7A. "Ah, Coot. I heard you'd been unwell. Glad you can join us."

Coot rolled precariously from heel to toe, his eyes popping as he seemed to try to give Latimer a message without speaking.

"Go up," Latimer told everyone. "Be there to greet us as we enter."

"Exactly," Lady Hester said.

Birdie ran up the stairs with Toby a close second. Chattering together, smiling fondly at Latimer and Jenny, the rest of the company followed quickly. Ross's voice rose above the rest, "Don't suppose a few moments alone would be amiss, either." Laughter met his suggestion.

When he could, Latimer said, "What is it, Coot?"

"I'm told James went to warn you, but he must have missed you."

"Yes, yes," Latimer said. Jenny stood close beside him. "But what did you want to warn me about?"

Coot shook his head slowly. "Forgive me, sir. I should be in my bed. Poisoned by some food, that's what Mrs. Barstow says. And cook's in a tear about that, I can tell you. But I've got to do my duty, haven't I sir? I've got to see to the running of Number 7 like I always have."

"Yes, o'course ye do," Jenny said. "And it's away t'your bed ye go because ye've done your duty. James will be back soon enough."

"It's them in there," Coot said, cocking his head toward 7A. "Runners, if you can credit it. Here at Number 7. At least her ladyship doesn't know. Want to see you, they do sir. And they want me to say that they have men watching from outside in case you decide to go for a stroll. Their words, not mine." He bowed his head so low his face could not be seen.

Latimer patted his shoulder. "You've done all you can. I'll deal with this now. Jenny, dear, I'm sorry to ask this, but would you wait for me in the guests' sitting room." Someone should suffer for this.

"I'll remain wi' ye," Jenny said without any drama. She held his arm and guided him to his own door—their own door. "We'll soon deal with whatever the men want."

Latimer could not insist that she let him go in alone, so he opened the door. Once he and Jenny were inside and confronted by two burly fellows who faced them with serious expressions, he closed the door again and said, "Good afternoon."

"Afternoon," they said. "We're here to ask you some questions. The lady need not be present."

"The lady is his wife," Jenny announced sharply. "What ye've t'say t'Latimer, ye've t'say t'me."

The shorter and older of the two men pursed his mouth beneath a bushy gray mustache. "Very well then. Latimer More, is that who you are?"

"It is," Latimer said. "Who wants to know?"

"We don't have to tell you that. This is a matter for the law. We're here to arrest you for robbery."

Jenny gasped, but stepped forward with her hands on her hips. "Ye're daft. And this is our weddin' day so ye'd best be off."

Both men looked mildly abashed. The taller one, who was blond, blushed. "We're just doing our duty, lady," he said. "And we rarely see more audacious behavior from a criminal than we have from Mr. More here."

"Criminal?" Jenny said, and Latimer had to pull her back or she might have marched on the officers to let them know exactly what she thought of them. "How dare you call my husband a criminal."

"Well, here's the proof, large as life and out in the open

for all to see," the blond man said. "We had an anonymous tip. We don't take something like this lightly, so we followed up. Best come along quiet like, Mr. More. But would you like to explain why you've been in a fight first—a violent one from the looks of you?"

"My private business is none of your affair." Latimer said. "What proof are you talking about?"

"Right there," the one with the mustache said. "Right in the middle of the mantel as cheeky as you like."

It was the wedding gift he referred to, the clock. "Adam gave it to us," Jenny said. Her eyes were wide and she was very pale.

"And who might Adam be?"

"Adam Chillworth," Latimer told him. "An accomplished painter and a friend who also happens to live in this house. Are you saying you don't know who suggested the clock was stolen?"

"Not yet. But we were led to believe that we would as soon as you're in custody. So let's not make this difficult. You're caught red-handed." The taller man spoke in a disconcerting monotone and seemed not to have heard, or at least not to have understood, what Jenny had said about the clock being a gift.

A fierce knock on the door was Adam's announcement of his arrival. He entered the room and took in the scene, his eyebrows lowered ominously over his eyes.

"Adam," Jenny said, running to him. "These people are accusing Latimer of stealing the wedding gift ye gave us. They say they've an anonymous tip. We knew from the card that ye dinna want to be thanked, but we need your help."

Latimer watched his friend's face and although he covered it quickly, Adam wasn't quite quick enough to hide confusion from one who knew him well.

Could it be that what the woman in gray had warned him about was right there, above the fireplace? Latimer stared in disbelief at the piece he'd displayed without a moment of concern. She'd said Jenny was the "Judas," and it was true that she could have found an opportunity to put the box where it would be found by Coot. He found himself smiling and didn't care if strangers thought him mad. Jenny was true to him. She didn't have to be here at his side now and wouldn't have been if she'd had anything to do with a plot.

"Officers," Adam said. "I'm so shocked I don't know what to say. That's a good clock."

"Yes," said the man with the mustache. "Very good. What do you do for a living, sir?"

Adam gave a devilish smile, then assumed a modest air. "I'm a painter, my man. A very famous portrait painter. If you want proof, request to see my portraits of Princess Desirée of Mont Nuages. They're here in London. I can give you a long list of my credits. And since you infer that I can't afford to give my best friend and his lovely wife a valuable clock, I suggest you visit Carstairs and Pork near the Burlington Arcade. They're dealers in fine timepieces, mostly rare ones, and I purchased the piece from them. Now there's a tip that *isn't* anonymous, my good fellows. Why don't you go and ask questions there and allow us to enjoy a very fine wedding breakfast here?"

The two officers looked at each another. The blond man rolled the brim of his hat nervously. "All right," he said, jutting his chin. "We'll do that, but if you're lying, we'll track you down and take you in along with this one." He nodded pointedly at Latimer.

Even after the men from Bow Street had left and Adam had closed the door to 7A firmly, there was no conversation in the room.

At last Adam said in a low voice, "What the dickens, man? I didn't—"

"I can tell you didn't," Latimer told him. "So who did? Someone who wanted to do me harm, obviously." He was not about to spend time discussing the woman in gray when they should be considering what to do next.

"Morley Bucket," Jenny said. "He's no' giving up. He's got his buyer for me and…"

She stopped talking and now she stared at him, her green eyes dark with worry.

"The devil you say," Latimer said while his skin turned cold. "And you never said a word about it before?"

"I didna want t'make ye angry enough to go after him. I was afraid for ye. He's no' a fair man and he'd do what he had to t'get his way. Toby said something t'ye that first night when ye followed me. He told me he'd said Bucket wanted me t'do something I wouldna. That's what it was. A man wanted to pay him and take me as…take me. I dinna think Bucket's given up."

"Damnation," Latimer said. His head and heart pounded and he felt an urge that almost frightened him. He wanted to kill Morley Bucket. "We've got to find him and force him to tell the truth. And unmask his *client*. And we have to start now. Thank you for lying for me, by the way, Adam. Or should I say, thanks for trusting me over them, even if you have put yourself in a queer position."

Adam poured two measures of brandy, gave one to Latimer and held the rim of the other glass to Jenny's lips until she took a sip and puckered her face in comical fashion. Latimer smiled at Adam's surprisingly natural gesture. The rest of the brandy in his glass went down Adam's throat in a single swallow.

"Perhaps we should ask Sir Hunter for his help," Jenny said. "He's a barrister."

"Not now," Latimer told her. "Although your idea is sound. Hunter is part of the law and I can't put him on the spot. I say we go to Bucket's place, Adam."

"Latimer?" a small voice called from outside the door. "It's Birdie."

"Marvelous," Latimer said in low tones. "All I need." He strode to open the door and the little girl, still in her beautiful blue dress, trotted in. Latimer said, "I expect they sent you to find us. Will you be a very good girl and tell them we'll be along shortly."

"It's Jenny I came to see," Birdie said. "I knew she was here with you. Oh, Jenny, it's terrible. She tripped him up and tied something in his mouth. Now he's gone."

Ignoring her gown, Jenny knelt and took Birdie by the shoulders. "Hush," she said. "Who are ye talking about?"

"Toby," Birdie said, and began to cry quietly. "The lady did it. She's very strong and she put something over his face and he went all limp. She's dragged him away. I think someone helped her when she went round the corner by the library. I was to come straight to you, she said. 'Get Jenny alone,' she said." The child's eyes strayed to Latimer and Adam and she paled even more. "You won't say what I'm telling Jenny, will you? The lady told me Toby might get hurt if I wasn't careful."

"Birdie," Adam said. "You've always been a brave girl. Be brave now. A woman did something to Toby and dragged him away. What did she ask you to tell Jenny?"

"That she's to go to the High Street and follow it to the park at the end. The one that belongs to a big house. Tap or something. The lady will meet her in there. That's if Jenny wants Toby back."

There had been no stopping Latimer from following her at a distance. Jenny hurried but did not run because she feared drawing too much attention. Her husband knew what was at stake and he was no fool. He wouldn't risk Toby's safety.

It wasn't cold but the rain had grown heavier and Jenny was grateful for the voluminous cloak she wore over her wedding gown and the hood with which she covered her hair.

The weather had driven people from the streets, which meant she and Latimer would be more easily spotted. She glanced over her shoulder but didn't see him. There were a few folk about but not one who could possibly be mistaken for Latimer. She trembled with relief.

Adam had unwillingly remained at Number 7 with instructions to take Birdie back to the breakfast and make convincing remarks about the drugging effects of the honeymoon on the groom and his bride. They would arrive eventually, he was to tell everyone. Jenny cringed at the thought of the laughter that would follow.

She bumped into a man who walked down the center of the flagway and made no attempt to step aside. ''Sorry,'' she said, spinning away from him. He went on his way, grumbling under his breath.

Harder and harder the rain fell. Jenny wore a pair of leather half-boots Adam had found in Sibyl's old closet, but nevertheless her feet were wet. In the distance thunder rolled but there had been no lightning so it must be far away.

Tapwell Park, that must be the place Birdie meant. Scarcely able to draw a breath, Jenny reached white railings that closed off the parklands around the house. In fact it was still a private house but since no one had lived there for years, people found ways into the grounds and ate picnics there.

A bear and a griffin stood on stone gateposts. The gate itself was chained shut but had been pushed askew so that the bottom leaned inward. Somehow Jenny managed to tame her voluminous skirts enough to scramble through.

She looked in every direction and repeatedly brushed away the water that ran from her hood and onto her face. At first she didn't see a soul, but then the slightest of movements attracted her attention. At a distance, an arm extended briefly from behind a large oak. A handkerchief fluttered and was then withdrawn.

Jenny hurried on, her boots squelching in mud. She must not look back or whoever awaited her would know someone followed and might bolt.

The arm didn't appear again and she feared the person who had been there might already have changed her mind and left.

Dragging wet air into her lungs, Jenny reached the tree, which was in fact several trees grown together into a massive trunk at the base. "I've come," she gasped. "Like you told me to." With fear lodged in her throat, she ran to the other side of the tree.

The woman had gone.

Jenny put both hands over her mouth and cast about. Ahead and close to a rise stood more trees. From a break between two great, domed sycamores, the handkerchief fluttered again.

Covering the ground grew harder as mud absorbed more water and turned to sludge that sucked at her feet. When she gained the sycamores, her legs were numb and she stumbled between the trunks with tears streaming down her cheeks.

Once more she didn't see the woman.

"Jenny." Latimer's voice came close to making her fall from shock He joined her and pulled her into his arms.

"Enough of this foolishness. I can't allow you to make yourself deathly sick. You're going home and I'll carry on without you. Send Adam to me. Tell him I'll be searching the area."

"I will not leave ye," she told him and pushed against his chest. "And I've got t'find Toby."

She freed an arm and scrubbed at her face with a sleeve.

The next sound Jenny heard was a grunt and she lowered her arm in time to confront Latimer, his eyes half-closed, falling forward. She screamed his name as he hit the sodden ground.

On her knees beside him, she tried to turn him onto his back but failed. She cradled his head and put her face close to his. He murmured and she kissed his cheek, said his name again and again. "Ye're sick," she told him. "We've got t'have help."

Latimer tried to push on his hands but slipped down again. He murmured something and she put her ear close to his mouth. He whispered, "I was just hit. They're there. Run."

"Out of the way, missus," a man said and she held Latimer with all her strength.

"We've got business with this one." She saw one ruffian clearly, a thick-bodied man with a round face. He held a short, heavy-looking stick in one hand. "Get out of the way unless you want us to 'it you, too."

"Hit me," Jenny cried. She threw herself over Latimer, covered as much of him as she could while a bright flash registered dimly as lightning very close by. Thunder roared and the rain became a torrent that soaked Jenny to her skin.

"You got to finish 'im, and take 'er," someone else shouted. "We won't get another chance, if you know what I means."

''Hit me, then,'' Jenny said again. ''Leave him be. He'll do ye no harm and it's me ye came for.''

''She's right.''

Jenny couldn't differentiate between the voices.

''Come along, my girl. Don't cause no trouble and we won't trouble you. And we'll all be 'appy.''

Rough hands tore her from Latimer's back and she was stuffed, flailing, into a big sack that scratched her skin.

The sack was swung until it landed hard against something. The something said, ''Oof,'' and she knew she was being carried on a man's back. ''Do 'im now,'' he said to the other one.

34

"Stop strugglin'."

Jenny ached all over and she didn't give a fiddle for whoever wanted her to lie quietly in his nasty sack just because it would make his life easier. She'd been thrown on a hard floor and heard a door slam. Now she discovered there was someone waiting to guard her.

She rolled over, not that her elbows or knees took kindly to another scrubbing against the burlaps. And she made noises. Unfortunately she'd started making noises as soon as she'd been captured and caused a quick stop along the way to jam a rag in her mouth and tie it behind her head.

"Hold still!"

Ooh, she'd do nothing this moldy oat cakes of a person asked of her. *Knees to nose and stretch out straight, knees to nose and stretch out straight.* The effort exhausted Jenny but she'd rather die making a nuisance of herself than like a scared mouse.

"Jenny McBride, can you hear me?"

She inclined an ear and was still for a moment.

"So you can hear after all. It's Toby 'ere and if you'll 'elp instead of throwin' yourself around, I'll get you out of the bag. We don't 'ave very long. I 'eard 'em say they'd bring you 'ere and come back for you when some Mr. Deep Pockets arrives."

Jenny felt Toby at work on untying the sack and didn't

move at all. She felt air—be it musty air—bathe her, but it was as dark outside the sack as inside.

"Come on," Toby said, his voice clear now. "I ain't never been so 'appy to see anyone. Not that I ain't always 'appy to see you."

He helped her climb from the sack, then pulled her to sit beside him on the floor.

"Where are we?" she whispered. "What kind o' place is this?"

"It's a big cupboard," he said. "I come to when they was bringing me up the stairs in this 'ouse, but I don't know where it is. That woman's a mean one. They tied me up and she slapped my face every chance she got."

"Ye said, 'they.' Who helped her?"

"Never saw. They 'ad me blindfolded. And I've already been told I won't leave this place on me two feet."

Jenny drew in a sharp breath. "We have to escape. Our lives aren't worth anythin' here and Latimer's lyin' in Tapwell Park—or he was. Two men set on us there and when I was taken away, they said they'd finish him."

Toby found Jenny's hand and held it tightly. "That's all of us in queer street, then. The door's locked tight. But we ain't giving up, Jenny. We'll see if there's a way to pick the lock."

She visualized Latimer lying dead, covered with mud and blood in some pit, or even thrown from a cliff in a place where he'd never be found.

"Don't cry," Toby said.

Jenny hadn't realized she was crying. "No," she said. "I mustna do that. But how would we pick a lock, Toby? We don't know how and we've nothin' t'do it with."

"Hairpins," Toby said promptly.

She was glad of the dark so that he couldn't see her face. "I heard a bolt."

Toby's fingers tightened in hers. "I didn't."

"They'd probably used stuff t'make ye sleep and ye just didn't notice. I heard one. They bolted the door on the outside. I doubt there's a keyhole at all and if there was it wouldn't do us any good."

"That woman said I oughta blame you," Toby said. "Right nasty piece of work, that one."

Jenny felt sick. Toby should blame her for being where he was. He'd only been taken to lure her away so they could capture her. "I'm sorry," she told him. "I've just got to pray and think, and hope there's a way to escape. Others will come looking, but not in time, not if Adam does what Latimer told him to do and pretends we'll arrive at the breakfast eventually."

A bolt on the door opened with the sharp force of a rifle shot. Jenny and Toby sat close together and shaded their eyes as light flooded in from a lantern. "Keep your voices down," a woman said. "Attract the wrong attention and we're all dead. I'm going to help you."

"Who are ye?" Jenny said.

"It doesn't matter."

"Nah, it don't matter," Toby echoed. "Thank you very much. Show us out and we're on our way."

The woman set the lantern aside and Jenny saw she was young and pretty, wearing a red dress and with her dark hair drawn into bunches of curls above each ear. "I've got a plan to take you out of here. We must go quickly. Follow me and don't make a sound."

Jenny had questions but since she had no options, she kept quiet and stood up in the low storage room with its sloping ceiling. She and Toby followed the woman as she'd instructed. And Jenny thumped against the other's back when she pulled up short and cried out.

The woman screamed, then turned her scream to laugh-

ter. "Mr. Bucket, you are always surprising me," she said.
"I was just taking these two to deal with the necessary."

"Lying whore," Bucket yelled, his rasping voice unmistakable. "You were settin' 'em free. I 'eard every word
you said. After all I've done for you, you were crossing
me. You're in with someone else, aren't you?"

"*No*, Mr. Bucket. You know you're my only true love.
I wanted them to think I was helping them so they
wouldn't give me any trouble. I'm the practical one, remember. I take care of the little details. They'd have been
back here soon enough."

Jenny listened, but she also sized up her surroundings
as best as she could by the lantern light. Bucket hadn't
brought so much as a candle. All she could make out was
what looked like another, larger storeroom filled with
crates. The only door she saw was closed fast, but she
wasn't giving up. These two were involved enough in each
other to give Jenny hope of grabbing a chance to get out.

She must get Toby out and find Latimer.

To her horror, Bucket landed an open-handed blow to
the woman's head and knocked her over. While she
crouched there, he took Toby by the neck, stuffed him,
kicking all the way, back in the cupboard and bolted him
in. "I'll be back to deal with you, me lad," he said. "On
your feet, Persimmon. This time I know what I've got to
do with you, my girl." He kicked her and she whimpered.

Jenny edged closer to the door.

"Mr. Bucket, I have given you my loyalty and my undying affection. I had hoped that since all this was about
to be over—successfully—you and I might finally, well,
you know."

Jenny took another careful step, and another.

"Silly, blubbering cow," Bucket said. "I can 'ave what
I want from you for the price of a bauble. Why would I

shackle myself to any bawd? Well, you can entertain me one more time—just to see if you can make me want to let you go free."

"Oh, Morley," Persimmon whined. "I love you. How could you treat me like this? Leave her where she'll be found and let's go somewhere on our own. That beautiful pink room of yours. After all, you decorated it for me."

Jenny stood immediately in front of the door and reached behind her for the handle. She grasped it firmly and turned.

Nothing happened.

Bucket had hauled Persimmon to her feet and was looking at Jenny with a gold-toothed smile. "Oh, you wouldn't upset me by runnin' away from my 'ospitality, would you? I'm wounded."

She turned around and pulled on the handle, rattled it, but to no avail. Bucket dragged her away and brought his mouth down on hers. His kiss was wet and disgusting, but Jenny didn't fight him. Every move she made could make the difference between getting to Latimer, and never seeing him again.

"Don't do that," Persimmon wailed. "The man who's paying you won't like it if you tamper with the goods. I did everything you asked, Morley. I got the boy, then sent the little girl with the message so Jenny would go after him. I did it for us."

Bucket stared at Jenny. He undid her wet cloak and tossed it aside—and ran his tongue over his lips while he looked at the swell of her breasts above her sorry wedding gown. "All right," he said to Persimmon at last. "Wait for me 'ere."

He picked Jenny up and slung her across his shoulder. "We've got some private business," he said, and produced a key to unlock the door. "Up we go. It's an honor to go where you're going, and don't forget it. Not many people ever go up these stairs. The man what wants you is very private."

"Let me go," Jenny pleaded. "I can't promise you mercy, but it'll go better for you if you don't hurt me."

Bucket sniggered. "Oh, *I'm* not goin' to 'urt you. I'm doin' you a favor. You're goin' to be with a gent what's got real money to spend on you. This one's already got everything set up. A beautiful place where the two of you can be alone together. And 'e won't skimp on anything. He'll cover you with jewels." Bucket chuckled some more. "In fact I think I 'eard 'im say you wasn't going to wear anything but jewels and 'e can't wait to put 'em on you. Now keep your mouth shut." He was taking keys from his pocket again.

Jenny's heart thundered. She was trapped and she'd let Latimer down. She held still and felt a quietness steal into her. Quietness—but was there a distant voice, someone speaking to her? Jenny couldn't make out the words, but they soothed her. A petal from one of the roses in her hair fell against her cheek and stuck there—on tears, no doubt. Jenny picked it off. It hadn't come from the roses in her hair. The petal was of orange silk and she held it tightly in a palm. Latimer had worn the marmalade rose she'd made him to their wedding. She'd been surprised that despite the condition of his clothes, the flower remained unharmed. Latimer was near, she felt him, and he would deliver them both from this horror.

Bucket got to the top of a flight of stairs and carried Jenny through an open door. As they went, she saw that there was heavy padding, not only on the door, but along the outside walls.

"'Ere we are, then," Bucket said and set her on her

feet. "What d'you think of this then? A fortune there is in 'ere."

Jenny backed away from him and glanced about her at a collection of clocks so excessive, she could not imagine the man who might cherish so many. They stood on shelves built from floor to ceiling on every wall. Tables were crowded together, every one weighted down by clocks of all sizes. Long case clocks stood against walls or hung on them. A glass-fronted cupboard displayed nothing but ormolu clocks in the most delicately colored enamels.

There were hundreds of clocks, including a huge, ancient-looking timepiece supported within an iron frame. The thing made enough noise to all but drown out the overwhelming ticking and whirring from around the room. Jenny watched a bronze man at the top of the contraption. He had four arms, eyes made from malachite, and wore a beaked helmet. With a pointed mallet, he struck a granite block in time to the minutes that clicked away. A gleaming pendulum swung and chain rotated over cogs. Little wonder there was padding outside so that the noise was deadened in the rest of the house.

"I can see you're taken with it all," Bucket said. "Which is a good thing since this is where you'll live—not in this room o'course. It's going to be a match made in heaven."

"I am already matched," she said, unable to hold her tongue any longer. "And my husband will be lookin' for me. He'll find this place and deal wi' ye."

"Will 'e?" Bucket's unconcerned leer tightened Jenny's throat. "I don't think I'm worried about that."

"Let me go, please," Jenny said. She didn't care how much she had to beg for her freedom.

"Let me go, please," he mimicked in a high voice.

"Can't do that. Someone's on 'is way to see you right now. Good thing we managed to make sure your so-called 'usband never 'ad 'is way with you. Your master wouldn't like soiled goods."

That Bucket had miscalculated her relationship with Latimer made little difference to Jenny. "Master? I have no master." *Please let someone come, someone who would help.*

Bucket pulled a chair forward and sat down. "Well then, the master you don't 'ave wants to take you for the first time in this room—since it means so much to 'im." He produced ropes of dark green jade beads from inside his coat. "You're to put these on. And there's bracelets for your wrists and ankles—and a girdle for your waist. Worth a fortune they are. Found special to match your eyes." Bucket rolled *his* eyes.

"I dinna want them," Jenny said. She still clutched the silk petal but she could no longer keep her breathing calm. "Give them back t'him."

"You can do that yourself if you want to. But you'll be wearing them when 'e comes through that door. Let's get those clothes off you for a start."

35

Latimer sat in the mud, his back against a tree, and marshaled his strength. He breathed heavily. Fury could drive a man with the strength of several, even if he had been knocked on the head. The blighter left with instructions to kill him lay sprawled on the ground a few feet away. If he came to at all, it wouldn't be for a long time.

The fight had been fierce only because Latimer was unarmed, while his opponent wielded a hefty cudgel. That cudgel was in Latimer's hand now.

The instant he'd replenished his wind, he'd be off and he knew just where he would go. Fear for Jenny caused him to sweat but his legs must be strong again before he tried to get to her.

He saw the approaching band of men before he heard them. They came quietly enough, but their boots sucked in the wet earth. Adam was the first to reach him.

"I told you to stay at Number 7 and make sure no one got anxious," Latimer said.

"And you," Adam said, pointing a long finger, "can stop giving orders and take a few."

Latimer struggled to his feet but still used the tree for support. "You're so interesting when you're angry, old man," he said. "But you'll have to excuse me while I find my wife."

Hunter, Ross and Sir Edmund Winthrop arrived, disheveled from the run and searching in every direction, obviously prepared for assailants.

"Damnation," Adam said, kicking the fallen man onto his back. "It's one of the fellows who hijacked your carriage, Latimer, the thinner one who came after me."

"Yes. And the other one took off with Jenny in a sack. I'd taken a blow to the head, but we've not time for that now. I'm off to a nuns' house, property of Morley Bucket. I think I'll find Jenny there."

"They would take a girl like Jenny to such a place?" Ross said. "What are we waiting for?"

"My breath to return," Latimer said. "And my heart to return to my chest. I'm going to kill someone for what they've done to Jenny. Now, we can't all rush into that house, and there's always a chance I'm mistaken and she won't be there. But we'll find her. I'll go to Bucket's alone. I want the rest of you to spread out and cover as much ground as possible. Hunter, could I prevail on you to check any places you think might be worth looking into." He met Hunter's eyes and knew they were both thinking of the establishments they'd frequented together when they were single men with too much time on their hands—and other parts of their anatomies.

"Yes," Hunter said and left immediately.

Latimer felt hesitant to order Ross, Viscount Kilrood, to do anything, but the man solved his problem by saying, "I know one or two low types who would probably be willing to give some useful information—for a price. What do you think?"

"Excellent," Latimer told him, and Ross broke into a run at once, heading for the narrow streets on the far side of Tapwell House.

"I'm coming with you," Adam said to Latimer. "You may need to be saved from yourself."

Latimer knew very well that Adam also thought Jenny had been taken to Bucket's place, and that he wanted to be there to take some of his own revenge on the man.

"Sir Edmund," Latimer said. "Perhaps you'd best return to Lady Hester and see if you can maintain calm at Number 7. I don't envy you the job of quieting the females, but they need a man there."

Winthrop frowned, as if considering whether to take instructions from a mere merchant. Then he said, "Right you are. On my way," and turned on his heel to retrace his steps.

"Come on." Latimer set off as rapidly as his still-recovering legs would take him. "We're for St. Paul's."

"I know where we're going," Adam said, and if Latimer hadn't been fearful for his wife and battered himself, he'd have laughed.

They left the park at High Street and set off, looking for a hackney. "Two fast horses for hire are what I'd like to see," Latimer said. "We can't take time to search some out." His belly felt flattened against his spine and he suffered dread such as he'd never experienced before.

"Why the devil didn't I think to bring horses myself?" Adam said. "Don't know if you were told, but Lady Hester's coachman and the tigers were pretty roughed up. She has them all in beds in the servants' quarters and they're being treated like kings."

"Good." Latimer only half listened. "Do you see what I see? *There.* Quickly, before he's out of sight."

Adam caught Latimer's arm and drove in his fingertips. "I'm damned," he said. "Winthrop going into the mews behind Mayfair Square. Well, I suppose that's one way to get there."

"It's not the way a man like Sir Edmund would choose to go. I doubt he's ever been back there in his life. Come on." Latimer broke into a headlong dash. "Keep up, man, there's something wrong there and we could lose him if we're not careful."

"And find him again in the ballroom at Number 7," Adam said, pounding along beside Latimer while they both dodged people on the shining wet pavements. "You don't know the man's habits. Probably always goes this way."

"And enters the homes of his neighbors—or even his own home—through the kitchens? I think not."

The drenched gray of the afternoon had waned into smoky murk. And still it rained. In the mews, the narrow cobbled way was slick and they had to slow down or risk either making too much noise, or falling.

"Hug the fences," Latimer said. "We'd be easier to spot by the stables." The distance between the gardens at the back of the houses and the stables that faced them was little enough, but the curve along the fences gave some cover.

Latimer hadn't time to warn Adam before throwing out an arm and shoving him into the overhanging branches of a tall lilac bush. "He's gone into a garden," Latimer whispered. "The next house down. Damned if I know the number but we're nowhere near Number 7."

The two of them crowded into the bush and held their hats while they peered over the fence. Winthrop walked rapidly along a brick pathway toward the back entrance to a house.

"It's his own house," Adam said, sighing. "He's making a stop on his way to looking after the ladies. We've wasted time."

"Stay," Latimer told him. "Perhaps we haven't wasted anything at all. What's Evans doing at Number 23 and letting Winthrop in through the back door as if they were old friends?"

"Evans was recommended to Lady Hester by Sir Edmund," Adam reminded him.

While they watched, Sir Edmund slapped Evans's back and allowed the blond-haired servant to take him by the elbow and steer him inside. They were both laughing. "The way I heard it," Latimer said, "Sir Edmund *found* Evans for Lady Hester. Supposedly they were not personally acquainted."

"It's strange," Adam said. "But it has nothing to do with our problem."

"Oh, my, God," Latimer said. "I knew it did. I felt myself guided here. Look at that. Over Evans's arm."

"What…" Adam leaned farther forward to see better. "A cloak perhaps?"

"Jenny's cloak if I'm not mistaken. The one she was wearing when she was taken away."

Spivey here:
Now don't detain me because I'm needed elsewhere. But when you have unkind thoughts about me, remember that I, too, know what is right and what is wrong, and I'm capable of putting my own good aside—even though it is more important—in order to fight on the side of justice.

I cannot glide by, pretend I haven't noticed a gentle young wife in the hands of despicable rogues, and not do what I can to help her.

Don't think for a moment that I am gone soft. First I had to do my duty and guide Latimer, but it will soon be time to deal with the frightful mess I have on my hands. I am a beleaguered fledgling angel.

Damn these humans.

The back door to Number 23 was unlocked. Latimer and Adam walked in and passed through gloomy, deserted kitchens that looked unused. They moved cautiously, expecting to encounter servants at any moment.

Nothing moved, or made a sound until they had climbed the steps from below stairs and arrived in a dark, wooden-paneled entrance hall where meager light cast dismal illumination. A woman in red stood flattened against a wall. Her face, although swollen from crying, was lovely. She saw Latimer before he could draw back and came toward him, keeping her palms on the paneling and moving them one over the other as if she was unsteady on her feet.

She reached them and rested her face on top of her hands.

"Who are you?" Latimer asked.

"Myrtle." She smiled as if amused. "Sir Edmund's late wife's niece."

Adam nudged Latimer and said, "Lady Hester's mentioned her. She looks in a bad way."

Latimer noted how full the woman's body was, how large her breasts for one so short in stature. He was also reminded of a voice he'd heard previously. "And you're the woman in gray," he told her. "The one who tried so hard to make me send Jenny away—as far away as possible."

"She was going to take my place," the woman said. "I didn't want that, not after all the hard work I've put in with Bucket and Sir Edmund. They owe me, not her."

"You're talking about my wife," Latimer said, swallowing his anger. "She isn't available to any man but her husband. Is she here in this house?"

"She is. And if you want your *wife* before someone else has her, you'd better hurry. If it isn't already too late. If it is, she'll never leave this house again because he'll hide her here."

Latimer grabbed her away from the wall. "Take me to her." He shook her. "Don't shilly-shally around."

The woman shed tears as if she were in pain, but wrenched away from Latimer and led the way upstairs. "I'm no danger to you," she said, breathing hard. "I tried to help her escape but Bucket caught me—and punished me. If I take you to her will you see to it that things don't go too hard for me?"

"This is no time for bargaining." They'd climbed two flights and started up a third. "Just hurry."

"There won't be another time for bargaining," the woman said. "Get me off. That nice Sir Hunter is a friend of yours. Ask him to fix it for me."

A padded wall and door confronted them at the top of the final flight. Latimer glanced back at Adam and saw apprehension that mirrored his own. "Are they in here?" he asked, and when Myrtle nodded he said, "Wait for us downstairs. We'll talk later."

With Adam close behind him, he entered a bizarre, noisy room crowded with clocks. But it was Jenny, not the clocks that he really saw. And she saw him but said nothing and shook her head as if warning him to go away.

Her gown had been ripped from neck to hem and she clutched it to her. Petticoats and other undergarments lay in a heap and a bare limb showed through the gap in her skirts. Heavy strands of carved jade beads, hanging from her neck, bemused Latimer and the sight of her hair loose about her shoulders drove him to near madness. He opened and closed his hands, assessing the rest of the scene.

Bucket lay facedown on the floor and Sir Edmund ground a boot into his back while he aimed a pistol at his head. The clocks made enough din to have masked Latimer and Adam's entry. There was no sign of Evans.

"Just give me the money and I'll be gone," Bucket cried. "You'll never see me again."

"Money?" Sir Edmund bellowed. "You've put your hands on her. I told you not to touch her. You won't get a penny out of me."

Latimer took a step into the room and signaled for Jenny to get out of the way. She opened her mouth but didn't move.

"I never touched 'er," Bucket shouted. "I never put a finger on 'er."

"So her gown tore itself and perhaps she took off her own petticoats? You were to bring her here and leave the rest to me."

"I was only tryin' to get 'er ready for you. You said you wanted 'er dressed in nothing but jewels and you showed me the jade."

"And you undressed her," Sir Edmund said in a strangled voice. "You took my pleasure. *Mine*." He raised his foot and brought it down again, hard enough to draw a scream from Bucket.

Latimer leaned to whisper in Adam's ear. "Give me your pistol."

"Where's your own?"

"This has been—believe it or not—my wedding day. Have you forgotten that pistols were not much on my mind. Give me yours."

Adam said, "I was at a wedding breakfast when I had to rush away. Not at all the thing, carrying a pistol at a wedding breakfast."

Latimer wasn't amused. He grasped Adam's lapel—and Sir Edmund saw them. The man aimed his pistol at Latimer's head.

"No!" Jenny screamed and barreled into Sir Edmund's back, and while he was off balance, Morley Bucket surged upward, grabbed the boot that had been on his back, and threw Winthrop to the floor.

Latimer made a dive for the pistol, but Bucket was already there. Sanity had left his eyes. If he saw at all, it must be through a white hot haze. With the weapon at Winthrop's throat, he hauled him to his feet and backed him across the room. Bucket snarled and bared his teeth, and hit Winthrop about the head with the pistol.

"Morley," Latimer said loudly. "Morley, we're here with you. We're going to help you." He dared not try to restrain the man for fear he'd shoot.

Jenny stumbled against him and he held her tightly in one arm. "My brave girl," he said. "Please go downstairs and get back to Number 7. There's a woman somewhere around. She's wearing red. Leave her be and she won't bother you. Now go." He released her and, shoulder to shoulder with Adam, advanced on Morley Bucket and Sir Edmund.

Bucket jabbered meaningless phrases. Sir Edmund whimpered, already bleeding profusely from head and facial cuts.

"Bucket!" Adam bellowed suddenly. "He's going to... Latimer we've got to stop him."

Too late.

With a mighty shove, Bucket thrust his victim into the workings of a huge clock. A Chinese clock, probably fourteenth century, and made for the purpose of signaling monks to meditation on the hour.

Sir Edmund's hair was immediately caught in rotating cogs and he shrieked. His eyes grew wide, then wider and he tried in vain to catch hold of the clock's metal frame.

Without discussion, Latimer and Adam separated and went at Bucket from two sides. His pistol, whipping back and forth between them and Winthrop, slowed their progress.

With his free hand, Bucket gave Winthrop another shove and the man's heels caught the lower frame of the clock, tipping him against a granite block. Bucket moved quickly to loop a piece of moving chain around Winthrop's neck and Latimer watched as the man, gurgling and turning purple, was drawn up high enough for a pointed mallet in the hands of a four-armed bronze figure to strike his left temple repeatedly. A deep, dark hole had opened in his head. His arms fell to his sides and he slumped in his noose of chain. The bronze man kept driving the point of the mallet into his blood-soaked skull.

Latimer launched himself at Bucket and brought him down. It was Jenny, still holding her gown around her, who grabbed the pistol.

"You were told to leave," Adam said to her, helping Latimer to restrain the writhing man on the floor.

"And I didna go, thank ye verra much," Jenny said, waving the pistol around and watching Winthrop helplessly. "I've a husband t'care for. Sir Edmund's no more, I'm afraid. He's strangled—among other things."

Latimer was otherwise engaged but he marveled at Jenny's courage and her matter-of-fact dealing with an outlandish death.

Finally Bucket was subdued.

"Mr. Bucket should die," Myrtle said, coming into the room and going directly to Adam's side. "See?" She pointed to a space in a showcase where a clean square amid dust suggested a clock had been removed. Next to the space stood the identical gallery clock to the one Jenny and Latimer had received as a "gift."

"I see it," Adam said. "The mate to that wretched clock is here, Latimer. They're a pair."

"Kill us both, please," Myrtle said. "That would be merciful."

"Och," Jenny said. "Ye're sick. Come away."

Calmly, the woman sat on the floor beside Bucket and waited. She didn't speak again.

"Ye're sure ye're not too tired for more gallivantin'?" Jenny asked.

"That gown is perfect for you," Latimer told her. "But I knew it would be"

"Dinna change the subject," Jenny said.

Latimer smiled and said, "I've never been less tired than I am now."

"Nor I," Jenny admitted. "D'ye think I'm a strange one not t'be more upset by what we saw happen?"

"I think you've been through a great deal in your short life. You've had to learn to harden yourself against some terrible things. If you hadn't, I doubt you would have survived—at least as the gentle, optimistic woman you are. I'm grateful you are not swooning away somewhere and that we may grasp some pleasure at such a time as our marriage."

They sat in the ballroom at Number 7, empty now since even the staff had been sent to their beds. Despite attempts to make them go to their rooms first, Jenny and Latimer had insisted they wished to stay up—alone—and watch the dawn come up on their first real day as man and wife.

The gown in question was made of dark green silk. The edges of deep horizontal pleating on the bodice were trimmed with gold lace, and gold lace ruffles decorated the hem. "How did ye know what size t'have it made?" Jenny asked. She wore gold slippers and a slender strand of solid gold pansies had been threaded through her rescued coiffeur. "And how did ye know I would have chosen just this?"

"I took the gown you wore to dinner at Finch's and gave it to a modiste. Then I told her to make this one exactly the same size. And this is how I knew what you would like." From a pocket, he took one of the little dolls she'd made while she was living in horrid Lardy Lane. "You gave this to me. It's wearing a ballgown of green silk with gold lace and I knew you'd designed something you would love to wear. Now you can."

"I thought ye were t'gi' the doll t'Birdie."

"I lied. I wanted it for myself."

They both laughed, but Jenny felt tension between them, the best possible tension.

"Lady Hester is a strong woman," Jenny said, knowing she was making conversation. "But she's had a bad shock over Sir Edmund and it'll take a wee while for her to recover."

"Yes," Latimer said. "But anger at what he did will help her. Persimmon—can you believe that name?—said Winthrop saw you coming and going from this house when you were part of Sibyl's group of ladies. He wanted you, and watched you ever since—all the time making plans to have you. His acquaintance with Lady Hester was formed because I'd been followed after I was seen meeting you, day after day, in Bond Street. Persimmon said he wanted to be sure he knew where I was at all times until Bucket could deliver you to him. He would not soil his hands by grabbing you himself. That would have spoiled the fantasy that you came to him on your own, and awaited him amid his beloved clocks. How shocked he must have been when I took you to Lady Hester that night."

Jenny looked at the rings on her finger and shook her head. "I'll never forget ye hittin' that nasty Evans as we came through the door here tonight. Imagine, he'd come back to behave as if his soul was white as snow when he'd spied on you and me, and helped Sir Edmund all the time."

"Evans is in the appropriate hands now," Latimer said. "We'll have more of that to deal with soon enough. For now we won't think about it. So, you will allow me to take you for a drive? What could be more romantic than a groom and his new bride riding through the darkness to chase the dawn? The perfect start to a honeymoon."

She shivered deliciously at the thought. "I'll allow ye t'take me," she told him. "I want ye to."

The early morning carried yesterday's chill and a heavy drizzle fell. Latimer had wrapped Jenny in the swansdown cape Finch had presented to her before leaving for Number 8 with Ross, and held an umbrella over her until they were inside Latimer's own carriage that waited at the curb.

"There is an armed guard at the back," Latimer said. "And the coachman is also armed. I arranged this so that you would feel safe."

"I always feel safe wi' ye," she said from her seat facing his.

"Even when you have to help me subdue criminals?" he said. "Then you are most unwise my dear."

The coach bowled away, the horses' hoofs ringing on the cobbles. Jenny looked from the windows but there was little to see as yet.

"I decided a short wedding journey was in order," Latimer said, his teeth showing white in faint light from the coach lamps. "An hour or two to be alone. We did everything in such a hurry there wasn't time to arrange a more splendid affair, but I will soon enough."

Jenny had never expected such happiness in her life. "I just want to be with you. Wherever ye are is a wonderful place."

"Wherever you are is where I *must* be. I had thought you a demure young thing, y'know. Shy and in need of my rescue."

"Then you were wrong." Jenny raised her chin. "I may ha' been shy. Still am in a way. Ye helped me a great deal. But I didna need rescuin' by any man."

"So I see," he said, and something in his voice sent a shiver up her spine, a lovely shiver. He continued, "I'd also thought it would take a long time to interest you in the, er, pleasures of the flesh, but—"

"Wrong again," she told him, boldly meeting his eyes. "I learned everythin' verra quickly. I do believe I was born for such things."

"Undoubtedly." His supposed cough into a fist didn't fool Jenny. He was laughing at her. "You were definitely born for love. But I must dispute your statement that you've learned *everything*. There is much more, dear Jenny, and I am the man to teach you the finer points."

"Are ye now?" She trembled inside, and trembled more so when Latimer lifted her feet onto his knees and removed her slippers. Surely he wouldn't do things in this coach that should be done in private.

"Am I unnerving you?" he asked, slowly rubbing her feet and ankles and gradually sweeping his hands higher and higher beneath her skirts with each sweep. "Trust me, Jenny. We shall enjoy our little jaunt."

She frowned at him. He was far too playful to be trusted at all. "We could ha' watched the dawn from Number 7," she told him. "From bed with the curtains open."

His nostrils flared and he said, "A charming thought. That shall be tomorrow night's plan. See what you are doing to me by just talking?'' He guided one of her feet against him. She jumped and she turned hot when she felt how his manhood had hardened.

"We're in a coach," she whispered. "Wi' a man at either end and nothing but windows between us and anyone passing by outside."

"But nobody will interrupt us," he responded, and covered the windows sharply. "Sit on my lap."

Jenny's scalp tightened and felt too small. Goose bumps blossomed all over her skin. She laced her fingers together and bowed her head.

Latimer moved her foot against him. His touch tickled and all those feelings he'd caused before happened again. "Sit on my lap, Jenny," he whispered. "Come on, come to me."

"Where are we?" she asked him.

"Does it matter?"

It didn't. She put her feet on the floor and sat forward on her seat. Latimer leaned across the confines of the carriage and she watched his thick, dark lashes lower as he brought his mouth to hers. Without touching her anywhere else, he courted her with his lips, nibbled sensitive skin and gently opened her mouth, rocked his face, and hers from side to side, flirted with the tip of her tongue and drew it into his own mouth.

Jenny trembled. She tingled. She wound her hands more tightly together lest she spoil the moment by reaching for him. And, oh, she wanted to hold him, to feel his bare skin, to smooth his chest and belly, and kiss everything she touched—everything.

His breath was warm and sweet. He deserted her swollen mouth and kissed her neck, the hollow at is base, and she arched closer to him. She opened her eyes to see the black arch of his brow, the sharp line of his cheekbone and jaw, his thick hair curling at his collar. And his head moved so slowly while he savored her.

He weakened her, yet made her urgent. Once more he returned to her lips, and his kisses became fierce. He drew back and opened his eyes—and he and Jenny looked at each other. She saw his heart in his eyes and knew he must see hers, but she also saw desire so fervent she felt stripped, opened to the tender tip of every nerve.

Latimer smiled faintly and caught her by the waist. He lifted her to sit on his lap and nuzzled beneath her chin, ran his tongue along the swelling flesh above the neck of her gown.

She shuddered and clung to him, wound an arm around his head and pressed him to her.

"Jenny," he murmured, "I'm going to hope you still love me when you learn what a bad man I am."

"Bad?" She raised his chin and found him grinning at her.

"Bad," he agreed. One hand moved upward from her waist and he slipped his fingers between two of the pleats on her bodice, smiling the broader when she gasped. "Oh, I am bad. Some might say I have practiced being so."

"Never," she said, and let out a very small cry when she felt air cross her breasts.

"No?" Latimer asked.

The gown was cleverly made. Between the two pleats that crossed the tips of her breasts, the silk parted and she understood the written instructions, supposedly from the modiste, that she should wear no chemise for fear of spoiling the fit of the gown.

"*Latimer,*" she said, but could scarcely contain her excitement.

He widened his eyes as if he were a man maligned. "Yes, my sweet?"

Well, two could play games designed to drive another mad. "Nothing," she said, straightening the gown. Above her head was a single handle designed for gentlemen to hold themselves steady whilst readying themselves to alight from the carriage.

Jenny discovered that by standing on the tips of her bare toes, she could hang on to the handle and obtain exactly the result she desired. Her bodice parted and she felt her bare breasts freed so that her clever husband got a sight he would not have planned on. She twisted, showing herself from every angle. And Latimer drew his lips back from his teeth and bit hard enough on a knuckle for her to see the marks he made.

He made to get up.

"Stay, Latimer," she told him. "I've had an exhaustin' day and need to feel free. Perhaps I should undress entirely and stretch my body unfettered by such beautiful, but restricting clothes."

He fell against the back of his seat and she noted how his chest rose and fell. "Ye might take off your own clothes," she said, looking at the bulge in his trousers. "You look like a man in need o' freedom t'me."

"Baggage," he told her. "Take over my role, would you? You probably think teasing me is a punishment. Tease away, love. You only seal your own fate. You will not know the precise moment, but I shall take you as you can never have dreamed of being taken."

Her brazen confidence waned a little and she spoke in a low voice, "Well, in case ye're interested, I've not had much experience dreaming about bein'…*taken* as ye put it. But I'm an attentive student and ye'll not find me hard t'teach."

Latimer groaned. He moved suddenly, reached up and plucked at her nipples as if they were ripe berries on the vine. He took them between his knuckles and rubbed his thumbs across the hardened peaks. Only through willpower did she continue to grip the handle above her head.

"I knew I had designed this well," Latimer breathed, and eased her breasts fully free of the gown. "They deserve to be shown off and enjoyed by me." He suckled vigorously at each nipple, flicked his tongue there, then abandoned those aching places to press her flesh together and rub his cheek over her, to kiss her as the mood took him. Opening his mouth to draw as much of a breast inside as he could, he slipped his hands up the backs of her legs, parted her drawers and cupped the cheeks of her bottom.

"I canna do this longer," she told him, squirming. "I shall go mad."

"Beautifully mad," Latimer said, releasing her to loosen his own clothes. "But don't move please. I shall help you get comfortable soon."

He stripped to the waist and the skin over his strong shoulders and muscular chest shone. She wanted to feel the hair there against her breasts.

"Now," Jenny said. "Do something now. Please."

Showing the deep dimples beneath his cheekbones, he gave her a purely wicked smile. "You'd like that, would you?" he opened his trousers and Jenny all but fainted at the thrill of seeing his need—and anticipating how he would feel inside her.

"There's little room to lie down," she said. "Perhaps we should go back to Mayfair Square."

"You don't trust me to manage these things?" He stood up, passing his tongue over her nipples as he did so.

Jenny let go of the handle, but Latimer promptly returned her hands and said, "Take heed of what I tell you. You will need whatever help you can find if you are not to fall. Hold on, my love."

Latimer lifted her skirts and released the drawstring on her drawers. With one pull he sent them around her ankles then stepped on them while she pulled her feet free. He lifted her by the thighs and wrapped her legs around him. "Cross your ankles," he told her and she followed his instructions.

The coach made a violent rocking from side to side and Latimer steadied both of them. "Ready?" he asked and, without waiting for a response, arched upward and into her.

"Latimer," she squealed. "I canna hold mysel' here while ye… I canna."

"I'll help you."

"But dinna come out o' me," she told him.

He had passed the point of laughter. "Hold my shoulders," he said, replacing her hands on the handle with his own, "and let's see how strong you are."

With his feet on what had been her seat, Latimer raised himself beneath her and she saw him enter and retreat from her body. "It would be easier on ye… Oh, Latimer. Oh, oh…"

His hips set up a rhythm that pounded him into her and when she closed her eyes and concentrated on receiving him, she saw blackness streaked with bright light. She tightened around him and he panted, moaning deep in his throat, but he didn't stop moving. The aching ripple began and she felt the contractions inside her milk him. Latimer pumped harder and her pleasure broke over her in clenching waves, only to be followed by Latimer's warm rush into her body.

Everywhere she touched him he was slick. Jenny burned and would not think of the spectacle they would make if anyone saw them. "I want t'be naked wi' ye," she told him.

Latimer began to lower them both to a safer berth, but he slipped and landed them half on and half off a seat. Jenny giggled so hard, she almost feared the coachman would hear her, but he never could.

Depositing Jenny on her swansdown cape, Latimer quickly granted her wish by peeling off every stitch of her clothes. "Not cold, are you?" he said, grinning again. With the blinds pulled over the windows it was impossible to see the panes but she knew they would be steamed up with the heat the two of them had generated.

"You are so beautiful," Latimer said with awe in his voice. He had taken off his boots and trousers and she marveled at the figure he cut. His thighs, where he stood with them braced apart, bulged hard and he was ready to make love again.

"Won't they wonder what we're doing in here for so long?" Jenny asked, indicating the men riding outside.

Latimer cradled her breasts, touched the end of his manhood to first one, then the other, and repeated the process, and said, "I would be surprised if they didn't guess."

Jenny bit her lip. He was tumbling her thoughts again. She arched her back to force harder contact with his engorged rod. And Latimer let out a cry. He scooped her up and sat her astride his thighs with her back to him, then he pushed her to drape forward over his knees and took her again, with even more force than the first time, if that were possible. First he held her hips, then he anchored himself by holding her breasts, and brought her feet from the floor with each thrust. Her braids fell loose and soft hair started to unravel.

Too soon the spiraling sensations took over, then burned themselves out while Latimer's fierce penetrations gradually slowed.

Jenny stayed where she was with her head hanging forward, fighting to settle her breathing. And Latimer rested his face on her back.

A little while passed while Jenny slipped into a haze that felt as if she'd been drugged. Latimer rested against the back of the coach seat, but kept his hands on her bottom and stroked her softly, continuously.

The lethargy passed, but she didn't let him know until she was ready to twist away and go to her knees between his thighs. She marveled at the way he responded to her lips. Could it be that men could do this over and over again, all the time? Quite possibly, since it seemed she could do so herself.

With his fingers in her hair, he rocked his hips back and forth but allowed Jenny to take charge and bring him to an explosive climax. Finished, she kissed his belly and moved upward to bury her face in the hair on his chest.

"Things must always be even between us," Latimer said, his voice deep and warm. "This should do it."

Once more he stood her on her feet, only to sit her astride his lap and tip her smoothly upside down. She knew exactly what he intended and reveled in the anticipation. Exposed as she was, she felt right when he clamped her between his thighs. Some, she thought, might consider their behavior excessive, but she had no doubt she and Latimer would continue in much the same way on every possible occasion and intended to tell him she was more than ready to oblige him in this manner.

"Ah," she moaned. "Oh, Latimer. I don't ever want to stop."

There was the slightest pause in the ministrations of his tongue, but only the slightest before he sent her over the edge yet again and they scrambled to cling together, naked and hot, on one small seat. Latimer stroked her incessantly, and she stroked him.

The gold flower chain in her hair slipped free and he caught it. "Pretty thing," he said, holding it to catch the meager light. He dangled one end against her breasts and laughed when she writhed and tried, without success, to take it from him.

Pushing a hand quickly between her thighs and beneath her bottom, he passed the warm gold over tender flesh already distended by the sex they'd shared.

"Stop it, Latimer," she said, giggling and trying to take the chain from him. He was too strong, and too practiced in the art of evading any attempt to foil his plans. Slowly he twirled the little golden flowers, and Jenny couldn't keep her bottom on his knees. She bounced up and panted, and didn't try to stop him again. He twirled and twirled the flowers between the folds of her body and she crossed her legs to deepen the sensation, and bent forward, jerking at the pleasure he gave her. And when he accomplished his goal and sharp spasms shattered any shred of control, she fell backward over his arm and sagged, completely vulnerable to anything he might choose to do with her.

"I think you liked that," he whispered.

Jenny mumbled, "Yes," and rolled toward him, stroked his belly, but when she took hold of him in one hand and squeezed, he said, "I think we should consider dressing. The dawn is coming. I see light through the blinds."

"It can't be," she said, growing still and staring at a window. But it was.

The task of clothing themselves would have been easier if they'd had more space, and if they hadn't repeatedly interfered with each other's progress. When Jenny undid his trousers for the third time, Latimer restrained her by the wrists until he was buttoned in and proceeded to tickle her while she writhed and howled.

"Hair," he said, and bent over her, doing his best to

correct some of the damage that had been done. "Best to leave out the gold chain for now. We'll never get it back in before we arrive back home." He slipped it into a pocket. "I'm sure we'll find it useful again."

"You should see your own hair," she said, and tweaked him in sensitive places until he plunked her hands on her lap and pretended to sit on her. He raked his fingers through his hair, tied a passable neckcloth and straightened himself more than Jenny would have thought possible. Still he looked mussed and the middle of his lower lip was cracked. "I hope we aren't seen on the way to our rooms," Jenny said. "I do believe an experienced person will guess what you've been about."

With his hands on his hips, Latimer observed while Jenny put on her gold slippers and arranged her new cape around her shoulders. "And you, Mrs. More," he said, "have obviously had your husband between your legs—repeatedly."

She smacked his arm lightly, but all she got for her efforts was a devastating kiss.

Tentatively she raised a blind and let out a cry. "We've missed the dawn," she said. "The sun's up."

Latimer wrapped his arms around her and they looked at the new day together.

Jenny felt her husband's reluctance when he knocked the roof, signaling that they wished to return to Mayfair Square.

"With luck we can be in bed before anyone else gets up," Jenny said.

Latimer rested his head on her shoulder and said, "You'll be the death of me yet. You're insatiable."

Before she could think of a clever reply, they drew up in front of Number 7 and an expressionless coachman opened the door and put down the steps. He took Jenny's hand and helped her to the flagway. Latimer joined her and they mounted the front steps, walking rather slowly. For herself, Jenny felt the smallest amount sore and stiff and Latimer wasn't taking the steps with his customary two at a time vigor.

The front door, flying open to reveal Larch Lumpit, stopped them both where they were. "Good news, good news," Lumpit trilled. "So much good news. That fine little chap, Toby, is to be adopted by Lady Hester, just like Birdie, and they'll both be tutored together." He looked closely first at Latimer, then at Jenny. "I say, you two look as if sleep wouldn't go amiss. But I must finish. Your father has written, Latimer. What a lovely man. He will receive you in Cornwall and you may bring your wife with you. And to lessen the number of visits that can only disturb his busy life, Finch, that is the viscountess—and the viscount, of course—may take their children to see him at the same time. Most charming and straightforward."

Latimer was obviously speechless.

"Ye read Mr. More's post, then?" Jenny said, too weary to consider more unpleasantness.

"Had to," Lumpit said. "Might have been desperate news in it and since I'm a minister, and accustomed to keeping secrets, I felt it my duty to see what Mr. More Senior had written. Fortunately he seems quite well and even mentions how successful his china clay mines are. I told the staff and they are most impressed."

Latimer put an arm around Jenny's waist and ushered her into the house. He shook his head repeatedly and said in a dreamy voice, "One must make allowances, my dear, lots of allowances."

Jenny bobbed up to kiss his cheek and pushed her hand inside his shirt. Latimer made no attempt to remove that hand. "Good night then, Lumpit. Be kind enough to put my father's letter under our door and, should you have the opportunity, make sure we aren't disturbed for many hours.''

A minor cloud passed over Lumpit's sunny expression. "Yes, well...yes. I'll let you go, but I must tell you one last thing.''

Jenny sighed.

"As you can imagine, her ladyship is most upset. She confided in me that she had been lonely before Sir Edmund entered her life. And, once again, there are so few she can rely on to be present should she need to talk. But that won't matter anymore.''

Latimer and Jenny paused before 7A and Latimer said, "What does that mean?''

Lumpit chuckled comfortably. "I'd have thought you'd guess. I'm to move into 7B where I can be available to comfort Lady Hester at any hour of the day or night.

"Jenny, I am also appointing myself your spiritual advisor. No, no, I insist you don't thank me. Watching your soul unfold, white and pure, will be all the reward I need. Of course, you can always talk to me, too, Latimer.

"See you at breakfast.'' He glanced at Latimer's bared teeth and seemed taken aback. "Or lunch, or dinner or whatever. Get a good rest, won't you?''

_____ Epilogue-Part 1 __

7 *Mayfair Square*
London
September, 1825

*F*ellow travelers—and sufferers:
Why would I take so long to recognize that you have taken
pleasure in my ire, and thrived on my struggles? Possibly
because my deep sense of honor does not allow me to see
mean-spiritedness in others. The latter is hard to believe
given the cruel treatment I have received at the hands of
that unscrupulous scribbler.

At last I have seen the light and you are about to mourn
your stupidity!

By the by, since I avoid avoiding the truth, I must say I
found all those hijinks in the carriage most stimulatin'.
After all, they are married, so why shouldn't I approve of
their passion?

What? Dirty old ghost, you say? I shall not dignify that
with an answer other than the obvious: you don't under-
stand the importance of staying in one's place—particu-
larly when that place is as lowly as yours.

Ah hah! I cannot keep it to myself an instant longer. All
this worry and fuss, and overtime, *and for what? Nothing,*

that's what. Think of it, if you can. You have two hands, start counting the fingers. Oh, the solution to my misery is so obvious and should always have been so had I not been wearing myself out dashing in the wrong direction.

Huh? I've bolloxed everything up? Is that what you said? Charming.

Listen up, well-meaning friends—and the rest of you. Just how many people can one house contain? Concentrate. The answer is, less than those upstarts are trying to stuff into Number 7.

All that time and effort spent, when the true remedy was to allow Hester and her motley collection of strays to do my work for me. The place is overflowing—I swear I can see the walls bulging. Very well, that was an exaggeration, but I think you get my point.

"Leave them alone, and they will come..." Dash it all, that's the wrong rhyme. "Leave them alone and they'll do themselves in, tra-la."

I'll be watching. Don't cry. In every life a little rain— no, no, not at all strong enough. No pain, no gain. Crow is fattening stuff that makes one's stomach ache. You're all going to grow very nicely, and you'll do so in pain.

A parting wish for you: May you be forced to watch that mangled tragedy, A Midsummer Night's Dream, *by our own Will, many times. Gad, here he comes again, and shaking a fist, no less.*

Spivey

_____ Epilogue-Part 2 __

Frog Crossing
Watersville
Out West

Dearest Friends:

Once more I am alone with my beloved animals, but, since this has been a most strange, and strangely unsettling time, I shall enjoy the opportunity to consider what has happened here, and what I have learned about human nature. Perhaps I should write "inhuman" nature, but Spivey hasn't been the only player to surprise me.

Spivey is an opportunist. Note how quick he is to turn his lemons into lemonade! Larch Lumpit (and who would have expected him to scratch out such a cozy niche for himself?) is obviously totally beyond Spivey's control. Lumpit becomes a self-starter and defies his puppeteer's string-pulling. The man thinks and acts for himself but Spivey, ever on the lookout for a chance to glorify himself, has the gall to pretend it was all his idea anyway...

Oh, rats, try as I may, I can't avoid admitting a certain growing fondness for the self-serving old reprobate. And, when he performed his most amazing act of kindness, he further amazed me with his modesty. I refer, of course, to his guiding Latimer to the church where Jenny was in such trouble. I do believe he felt uplifted by having made a difference, and being on the side of justice. And he mentioned justice again when he chose right over wrong on a second occasion.

He hints at not having given up his quest. Out of respect for the hard work he has obviously put in on self-improvement (A fledgling angel? Mercy me!) I am going to continue watching him with an open mind—more open than it has ever been. But I will be vigilant.

I can't leave you without writing that Latimer has also amazed me. A likable fellow, I always thought, and unarguably a handsome devil with a few secrets hovering around. But his versatility…well, yes, his versatility is invigorating, as is his capacity for unselfishness. And let us all hope that we and our daughters may be as courageous, as spirited, as Jenny.

Time to move on. I hear faint voices, growing louder, demanding my attention. More passion and trouble, no doubt. It really does become exhausting but what can I say, scribblers scribble and must be available to those who need our voices and our pens.

Just before I go for now, a word to the wise on Spivey. Watch him—he still has a long road to travel. I was disquieted by the tone of his parting words. He isn't giving up and one wonders exactly what he expects to happen just because Lady Hester has quite the houseful. I advocate trust, always have, but I have also been disappointed on occasion.

Alertness is key, now more than ever. Bravo Sir Septimus Spivey, you have shown more mercy than I would ever have thought possible. But don't slip, or my admiration will have been sadly wasted.

My friends, our job is not yet done. Hang out with me. Until next time, I am, as ever, your devoted and diligent scribbler,

Stella Cameron